W.K. PHOENIX

Peculiar Cases Of Something Devine

Something That My Head Had Said

FOR MY MUSES & LIFELINES:
A.B.
A.C.
A.D.C.
A.R.B.
E.C.
G.A.
J.B.
J.P.
K.C.
N.C.
S.R.B.
S.S.
W.B.SR.
V.B.
V.R.

Contents

Acknowledgement

I just want to give a heartfelt thank you to all of those who believed in me and continue to believe in me every day.

Also, for all of you with dreams that may seem so far or hard to accomplish, don't let that stop you from making a move today. Even the smallest of moves counts.

Thank you readers for supporting this dream-come-true for me. A series that's been in the works for so many years now has finally come to life.

For my family. For my friends. For the world.

“We Live Because We Die”

Chapter One

A second corpse landed with a thud after being dragged across the kitchen floor. The previous night's rainstorm, the first one in months, flooded the passageway to the basement again. To get the corpse where it needed to be, of course, it had to go through the chute in the kitchen, shooting straight down into the morgue's preparation room.

Amy Devine didn't have to see the bodies to know the process. Her eyes shot open. She failed to fall back asleep until it was over and was now burdened with multiple obnoxious *thumps* against her bedroom door, adding to her morning dread.

"For shit's sake," Amy groaned. "This is just getting ridiculous."

Thump. The unseen aggressor knocked quicker by the second.

Amy sat upright in her bed and wrestled with her long, bushy hair. She jumped off the bed and moved for the door.

"Feebs, I swear—" She swung the door open, but there was no one there.

"Will you move it away from the table?" Rezna Devine's voice carried from downstairs, giving someone absolute Hell. Her deliberate and precise tone was always a pleasure to wake up to, especially when it wasn't Amy herself being chastised. "There is a reason I moved it over there. My granddaughter has to have her breakfast there, you imbecile!"

Amy stepped back into her room and kept the door an inch ajar, slumping down next to it. She hugged her long legs with her caramel lanky arms, burying her head between her knees. Another breakfast ruined. The grunts of men from downstairs followed by large clunks, and then the sound of what Amy knew was the body falling through the kitchen chute and into the basement.

Amy stepped over her drenched jacket and opened the blinds on her window. The streets below were busier than usual, as a small crowd had gathered. Amy met the gaze of an old woman, who scowled at her. Amy rolled her eyes and closed the blinds.

The commotion downstairs went on for another half hour as Amy got ready before making her way downstairs once she felt the coast was clear. Amy crunched carefully into her toast, trying to lock out the memory of what had been laying on the floor beneath her about a half-hour ago. Her eyes fell on the small door just below one of the counters—the chute door leading into that special room in the basement. A tall glass dropped right in front of her, waking her from her trance, filled to the brim with a strawberry smoothie. Amy gave a weak smile as she looked up at Rezna.

"Thanks, Gma."

"Of course darling," Rezna replied as she sat next to Amy. The wrinkles on her face made her piercing blue eyes stand out. "I'm sorry about this morning, the flooding, dreadful shit. I'm nearly saved up to have the remodeling done for downstairs."

"It's okay," Amy said. "It's quite a tragedy, isn't it? That poor family…"

"Indeed. Mother and father dead, a girl left lingering. First murder case in decades. Disaster surely wipes its ass with us and expects us to smile. Anyway, you came in late last night. Care to explain?"

"I wanted to get some training done, but that awful storm caught up with me. Speaking of awful, you *need* to do something about Feebs.

She's driving me up the wall with her constant pestering."

"You two need to get along. Feebs is my oldest and dearest friend, and she's welcome to stay for as long as she needs to figure things out. The afterlife isn't child's play."

"You don't have any friends."

"Do not—" Rezna said, throwing her a look, "—be late for training tonight. By the way—"

Amy's smile grew as the kitchen walls illuminated with white circles connected by white lines.

"The new box is here!" Amy snatched up her smoothie, jumped up, and ran out of the kitchen.

The living room walls were decorated with mirrors alongside each other and glued between them and all over the rest of the wall sat beige stones of similar shape and size, leaving no trace of the actual wall color. A large entertainment center sat on one side of the room, looking as though it was stuck between two eras. Housed in its middle compartment sat an electronic box that was glowing white. The front of the box had the word ZiccoLynx embossed in bright white.

"About time." Amy ran in and stooped down in front of the ZiccoLynx box, unable to contain her excitement. She sipped her smoothie. "One thousand ziccolights. I can't even imagine."

"And you won't even witness them if you don't get home in time for training," Rezna called from the kitchen.

"I will, Gma, I will. You wanted this thing as much as me."

"You're just lucky I didn't have to shell out a dime. Your townsfolk are raving about their free new sets. Test dummies."

"Bout time some luck stroked this depressing town," Amy said. She ran back to the kitchen, threw back the last drop of her smoothie, then placed the cup into the sink. The faucet turned on automatically, half of the stream water, the other half thick soap. A small compartment opened on the right side of the sink's base and a tiny mechanical arm with a bronze brush came out of it. The arm split in two—one half picked up the cup and placed it under the stream—the other half brushed the inside and outside of the cup.

"I'm running late anyway," Amy said. She kissed Rezna's forehead.

"Brush your hair, girl." Rezna placed a hand on one of Amy's. "And update your training diary. It could be useful for tonight. Don't be late."

Training. Great. Amy had a love/hate relationship with training. On the one hand, it always felt like it brought her and Gma closer. On the other, it was all just preparation for the worst. But Amy couldn't worry about that right now.

Amy raised the collars on her jacket past her ears as she darted down the front steps and pushed through the big black creaking gates, and after a few seconds, they closed right behind her. She dug her head deeper into her jacket. She passed her mailbox of 267 Bleecker Lane and smiled at a small, white, red-eyed bat that sat on top of the box.

"Morning Archie." Amy made a kissing sound, still hiding in her jacket, pacing down the block. Archie 'cooed' before flying off behind her, both of them leaving behind the cemetery they shared a home with.

The air in the small-but-actually-medium-sized town of Jadesfeld was always cold and unnerving, cooler than most of London, but this morning more so.

Amy eased her jacket's collars back down as she and Archie moved down the empty blocks, walking right in the middle of the street. To her left, a chrome-colored Irish terrier barked at a group of laughing children, balanced on top of one another creating a ladder to the top of a house, where the girl on top grabbed a ball from the roof. The robotic terrier ran in circles around them.

"Get the hell down from there"! A grumpy man came from inside the home, pointing his finger at the children.

The girl on top of the child ladder cocked her hand back, aiming the ball at the grumpy man. She turned to Amy and froze. The kids jumped down from their spots and ran away with the robotic dog following them.

A few blocks down, Amy passed by a noisy crowd gathered outside a two-story attractive country home-styled residence now burdened with the metallic lime torsos of Policebots. Their silver mechanical arms raised to either side of them, with their hands joined to form a barrier in front of the house. Human detectives moved in and out of the house and all around the property.

"Please keep back. An investigation is ongoing. Please keep back. An investigation is ongoing." The Policebots sang in unison.

A couple of people watched Amy walk past, but Amy kept her eyes ahead.

"Here she comes."

"Such a weird one."

"I bet she had something to do with this one too."

"After all these years."

Archie chirped as he followed close behind Amy.

"Pay them no mind, Arch," she said.

Archie turned to her and made a small "coo".

I don't even know why I'm here, dealing with these people. Any bit of drama excites their disturbingly boring lives.

Sometime later, Amy made her way up the concrete steps of Highbridge Intermissionary School. She tapped a sleek sheet of glass on her thick black wristband. Small white lights rose from it and formed the letters GCID in mid-air. The lights reformed into 09:45 AM.

Late again. Oh well.

Amy walked inside the school's wide hall and went right through the large Human Class Detector scanner. A screen above the HCD chimed and read CLASS STATUS APPROVED.

Amy turned to Archie, who flew in circles behind the HCD.

"You know the rules. Not inside," Amy said. "Thank you for walking me to school." She curtseyed.

Archie landed at her feet and bowed his head and his left wing. He shot back into the air and flew outside. Amy smiled as she watched him go.

Amy moved past the flesh-colored walls, not caring to make eye contact. She'd give anything to skip this day. Hell, she could be training right now. At least that had its benefits.

Wow, you sound just like Gma.

She waved her GCID in front of her locker and opened it. She pulled out two books and rolled her eyes as she slammed her locker shut, now facing Madeline Watts. Her two henchwomen stood on either side of her. Together they formed the self-proclaimed 'Lockheart Girls'. Always together, never apart. Amy had only one class with them, and of course, it was her favorite class.

"Looney Devine," Madeline started, as always. "I just knew I'd find you off nob-dicking. Graveyard ghouls keeping you up at night?" She poked her long, scrawny index finger straight into Amy's chest, towering over her.

Her second in command, Kassandra Owens, a seductress in her movements, brought her dark eyes up to Amy for the first time, smirking. Third rank Tilly Thompson giggled hysterically as though watching a comedy show.

"You know, if I were to smash your nose in right now it would be self-defense," Amy said.

Madeline stepped back. Tilly shut up. Kassandra twirled a lock of her hair, popping gum.

"Relax Devine," Madeline said. "I'm just concerned about your everlasting health. Can't be too good being locked up in a home for the dead all your life. Callisto's Honor." She placed a hand over her heart. "By the way, you wouldn't have had anything to do with what happened at the Murder House last night, would you? Sorrowful things seem to happen around you after all."

"Last warning, Watts," Amy threatened. "Or I will finish what Demora started."

"Doubt it, normie," Madeline retorted as she moved past Amy. Tilly snickered as she followed, with Kassandra right behind, leaving Amy with a look of scorn.

Amy smirked. The hallway was clear, except for them. Perfect. She brushed a hand along the wall and the hallway walls flashed white. Amy closed her eyes and moved her other hand down.

Rip! Madeline's jaw dropped as she whipped around. She looked from her torn skirt to Amy, then to her two minions.

"What the bloody Hell?" she exclaimed.

"Size too small there, Maddie?" Amy said, trying to hold back her laughter.

Madeline gave her last glare before the Lockheart Girls scampered away.

Probably shouldn't have done that. A bit risky out in the open.

But she had grown tired of living sheltered. Madeline's words hit certain chords within Amy that have remained unsung for all these years. At least the dead could keep their secrets for eternity. Amy held her secrets deep down and time couldn't be crueler. It had only been seventeen years of living so far.

Halfway through the day, that thought still hadn't left her mind, even as she sat in her favorite class, frowning at the empty seat beside her. Wednesdays were usually a lot more tolerable sitting in her election class, Animalia Criminology, or 'Walking With Watson', as she called it.

"Desolation. I reside inside a farce. These shallow forms of comfort and stability consume me," Professor Watson recited as he moved around the room, a thick book in his hands. "These were the words written by Daniel E. Caudsworth in *Memoirs of the Forgotten*, regarding his awakening after his first werewolf transformation. Can anyone tell me what was unique about Caudsworth's wereform versus the usual?"

Amy's hand shot up into the air. "His fangs were curled inwards. Also, there were distinct wing-like pieces of flesh under his arms. Some say the time he spent underwater during his venture in the late 2040s caused some mutations in his DNA."

"That's quite right, Ms. Devine, very good," Mr. Watson said. "Now—"

Amy checked her GCID as it flashed. A raspberry sound came from a few seats behind, but Amy didn't even bother turning around to look at Madeline.

"Distracting, much?" Madeline's voice whispered. "The only freak who wears her GCID on the outside. Why is that Devine?"

Amy stuck a middle finger up without looking back, putting it down just before Watson turned back in her direction.

Watson swept his hands through the air as though conducting an orchestra. "There were many profound breakthroughs during the crusades of the 2050s to 70s that can be attributed to Caudsworth's dissection of what it is to be part of the Animalia kingdom. What it is to be human. And perhaps, the one distinction that separates us from them."

"Murder," said a white-haired girl named Gina, from one corner of the room. Her eyes bore into Watson, then moved to Amy. "The members of the Animalia Kingdom don't murder, at least not like before. Prey is still prey, a predator is a predator, but the animals are more considerate in their killings. They take—"

"What's necessary for survival," Watson finished, smiling. "Yes, precisely, Ms. Gallagher. Caudsworth made some powerful arguments for what he sees through the eyes of the wolf. He sees power in the wolf's way that he never found during normal human life. It was a power that drove him mad, right after publishing *Memoirs of the Forgotten.*"

Watson took his glasses off, placed them on the desk, and wiped his eyes. "In this class, we sometimes go over some very gruesome details. To be a prominent journalist and investigator, you must unlock truths you may want nothing to do with."

Amy sets her eyes down on her hands. She caressed them before holding either side of her arms.

"To be a brilliant detective," Watson continued, "the key to finding the truth… is to consider all possibilities."

Watson put his glasses back on. "The intelligence of not only our kind but those beings within the Animalia Kingdom has also grown exponentially. Not to mention those that live outside those… categories. We find ourselves at a sort of crossroads in history. Are we still Dominus Maximus or is our time on the edge of extinction?"

Not a single breath escaped the classroom. Amy met Gina's eyes again. Gina smiled and turned away.

Dismissed, Amy waited for a few minutes after the Lockheart Girls exited before making her way to the door.

"Ms. Devine," Mr. Watson called. "If you have a moment?"

"What's up, Professor Watson?" Amy walked up to the desk as the last student left the room.

"I got the chance to look at your secondary schooling election classes, and your essays on the Animalia Kingdom were quite impressive. Seems you also have a keen eye for the paranormal."

"I just have a sense for digging up bullshit, I suppose," Amy said, cringing at how truthful she did not mean to be. "Sorry."

"Well, aye-aye, Ms. Devine. You aren't wrong. A world without conflict is the worst of all. Creates a false sense of security. When one battle dies, another is sure to take its place. It's inevitable. I teach what I teach because I want to prepare my students for anything."

"I know a little too much about preparation."

"Plan on taking up the morgue business one day, then?"

"Not on Callisto's grave," Amy scoffed.

"Detective work?"

"I… It's an option. But then I have no interest in Class cases."

"There's some work to be done in the Peculiar section, I hear."

"Oh, yeah?" Amy's face shot up, but avoided his eyes.

"There's a special unit. Very undeveloped, but perhaps with promise. We collaborate when they need the eyes of a scholar. They specialize in all that's beyond our current understanding. After all, what's normal today certainly wasn't normal in the 2020's. Your thesis on how we haven't yet transcended the supernatural was quite engaging. We should talk more about it sometime."

"Professor Watson!" The Headmistress' assistant Mrs. Rechert came running towards them. "Professor Waston, the Headmistress would like to see you immediately!"

"Well Mrs. Rechert," Professor Watson said, "you're going to lose your footing running like that. What's that thing you always tell our students?"

Mrs. Rechert leaned up to his ear and whispered something. Professor Watson's eyes went wide.

"Stay safe, Ms. Devine," Professor Watson said, before running ahead of Mrs. Rechert.

"Thanks, Professor," Amy called, but they had already gone around the corner.

Wonder what that was about?

The rest of the day's classes went on, more boring than each that preceded, until Amy gleefully dashed down the school steps and jogged away. She had a good head start, as she knew the Lockheart Girls would try to corner her again.

Amy made her way down several streets, almost certain the steps of the Lockheart Girls were growing louder, the pace picking up. But they could never outpace her.

Amy dipped through a hole in a fence leading to a bushy field, and moments later the footsteps of the Lockheart Girls came dashing after.

Amy climbed up and over a small hill, disappearing from view. She hid behind a large tree as the Lockheart girls wandered about the surrounding high bushes, looking for her. Amy put her arm down into the bushes underneath her and waved her hand. A gust of wind blew East through the bushes, like a mouse scurrying from its prey. The Lockheart Girls spotted the movement and chased after it. Amy made her way in the opposite direction.

Amy coughed, kicking up dust as she worked her way through some thorns. She fought her way through tall green stalks until finally reaching a clearing. She smiled down at a large patch of dirt in the shape of a circle in the middle of the green maze. Amy threw her arms up to the sky, a glimmer of the sun peeking through the towering trees.

"Alright!" Amy called to the sky. "How's it gonna be this time, Demora?"

Silence. A strong breeze ran through the thick strands of her hair. She pulled back her red headband and twisted its elastic body to tie the end of her hair into a high ponytail. She put her hand on her hip as she raised an eyebrow, carefully scanning the trees above her.

Something awakened inside her. Her chest got hot. Her eyes went wide.

Amy reached around, catching the arm of her best friend Demora Corbyn-McDonald, a young woman with short-cut bobbed blonde hair and wild green eyes.

"C'mon then! Show me what you've learned!" Demora laughed as she twisted Amy's arm behind her back, and shook her shoulder-length hair out of her face.

Amy reached her arm out. An orange surge of light, Amy's aura, energized around her hand, mimicking its shape. Her aura grabbed the arm Demora had around her, picked her up, and tossed Demora into a nearby tree.

"Now we're talking!" Demora cackled, dusting herself off. She aimed her palm towards the ground. Her aura, a vibrant pink, swept up dirt and tossed it right into Amy's face. "That's your blind spot!"

"You dirty cheat!" Amy clutched her eyes shut. She threw both of her arms forward, her aura's energy charging out of them like two nimbus clouds.

Demora shot her arms forward, her aura shooting out to meet Amy's.

Sometime later, the two girls sat in the middle of a small crater they've created in the ground. The girls' faces wore specks of dirt mixed with sweat, some twigs in their hair.

"How come you didn't show last night, wench?" Demora said, chewing on a piece of twig.

"I got super high and got caught out in the storm, I reckon. Least that's what I told Gma." Amy chuckled. "Found my coat drenched and ripped. Must've done some intense training."

"You still blacking out then? Don't you think you should let her know?"

"Only happens when I really get into it. She's been up my ass with extra training as well." Amy nudged Demora. "You ready to return to school? You've left me all alone with Madeline and her terrible twins."

"Ugh. School's the proper bore. I'm already planning on my next vacation."

"You are *not* getting suspended again, Demo. Bloody hell, I'm already up in arms. Surely your parents won't-"

"I don't want to talk about them." Demora stood fast, her face scrunched up.

Amy knew she hit a nerve. She mouthed 'sorry' and followed her.

"It's whatever." Demora raised her eyebrows. "I'm just tired of being the fuckup. I'm sixteen and ready to get these credits and far from Jadesfeld."

"Well, just make sure you don't leave me too far behind."

"Wouldn't dream of it," Demora smiled. "Oh! Let me show you how far I've gotten!"

Demora pulled Amy up by the arms and ran towards a tree. She pulled a small branch off of it, to which Amy gave her a look, raising her arms.

"Yes yes, I know. The tree has life and all of that," Demora said as she poked the branch into the ground and dug deeper and deeper with a screwing motion.

"What are you doing?"

"Shh shh shh. I'm just waiting for one… I read in this book how Peculiars used to trap things in their aura by separating it."

"Well, that doesn't sound too appealing. Why would you want to break apart your aura?"

"Here we are!" Demora lifted the branch out of the ground, as a long, brown tail hung on tight. It uncoiled itself bit by bit as more of its torso came out of the ground. A hairy head was the last bit to uncoil, and hairier legs unraveled from either side of it, four on each. The taracede made a small screeching sound.

Demora's aura grew around her and the branch, her aura suspending the taracede inside of it. The taracede jumped up and the aura ball broke apart, retreating into Demora's hand.

As it fell to the ground, the taracede's legs uncurled from underneath it before scurrying away.

"Bollocks." Demora's expression sunk.

"You'll get it." Amy patted her friend on the back. "Come on, let's practice together."

Hours later, as the moon invaded the sky, Amy hauled ass down her block.

"Shit, shit shit shit." Amy held her jacket collars high above her head and dashed up the front steps. She waved her GCID at the front door, cursing under her breath as Archie fluttered beside her. They hurried inside as the front door swung open.

Amy slammed the door shut, took a deep breath, then exhaled, closing her eyes. She hung her jacket up on the rack and rushed to grab a bag of BAT TRIX off the table nearby. She poured some of the food into a small bowl and Archie attacked it. Amy returned the bag and headed towards a door down the end of the hall.

Amy made her way down a dark, creaky staircase. The lights flickered on, one by one, as she made each step. Upon reaching the bottom, she entered the dimly lit basement, took another deep breath, and closed her eyes.

"Late. Again." Rezna's outline called out from a darker corner of the room. Amy could barely make out Rezna's face, but the folded arms and crooked mouth sold the story.

Rezna's icy blue eyes stepped into the light. Her expression could sever the thickest block of ice.

Amy was not ready.

Chapter Two

"Sorry, I—" Amy started.

Rezna waved a hand of silence. She pointed to a corner of the room. The change in their dynamic had taken over. That loving woman who brought strawberry smoothies was now a cold and calculating instructor. She watched a defeated Amy step over some books on her way to the corner she was being sent to, stopping in front of it.

"One," Amy said. She dragged herself towards the adjacent corner, side-stepping cabinets full of junk.

"Two." She made her way towards the third corner, coughing as dust rolled into her face.

"Three." Eyes still shut, Amy rolled a trunk to the side, nearly tripping over a rod. She stopped in front of the last corner of the room.

"Four." She whirled around at the sound of a lightbulb smashing. Rezna was nowhere in sight.

Amy crept towards the center of the room. All the junk she had just moved past now sat right in the center of the room, balanced on top of one another, creating a leaning tower held up all on its own.

"It is never enough to just be with aura," Rezna's voice echoed from various points throughout the room. "It is an extension of you. If you are not confident in yourself, your aura will act as your guide. When you are under duress, your aura becomes your self-defense. As you would sneak and quiet your footsteps into the night, your aura will move as undetected as you will it. But you must first trust it to be one with you."

Another lightbulb smashed behind Amy. She stepped over it and moved about the room. She tried to feel something, anything. But that warm feeling she usually got in her chest when near another's aura was now missing.

"Where am I, Amy?" Rezna's voice said.

"Is this the new technique?" Amy's legs flew into the air as her butt smacked the cold cellar floor. She groaned as she rubbed her lower back and sat up.

"Mind your matter, girl. Heart. Mind. Body. Aura. These are the four components that bond you. Lose one and the rest will follow. The first three create strength for the fourth. And that fourth one- the aura- can carry you long after the rest have failed. Now—Get. Up."

"Is this necessary to learn the new technique?" Amy stood. She studied the junk piled on top of each other in the center of the room. She walked up to it and tried to pull the items off one another, but they felt as though they were all glued together somehow. "Maybe just tell me what it is you're trying to—"

One chair in the pile budged. The entire pile fell on top of Amy.

"Distractions will get you killed. When your other senses are unsure, your aura will bring you clarity."

"I can't even feel you. How are you doing that?" Amy groaned as she hurled the junk off of her and got to her feet.

"Your enemies won't reveal their secrets to you. So why should I?"

"Well, it'd be helpful to learn, would it not?"

"Everything is a joke to you it seems." Rezna came from out of nowhere and dashed up to Amy, nostrils flaring. "How do you expect to learn a new technique if you don't apply yourself? You show zero discipline and can barely get home on time. You want answers but won't put in the work to gain the knowledge you seek. What's the point of training you if you are only going to limit yourself?"

"What's the point of training if I don't know what I'm supposed to be learning?"

"Enough!" Rezna waved her hand and Amy fell silent. "Three thousand words, aura over hand, on the Classes and why they matter to you. Tomorrow." Rezna spun around, whipping her shawl as she made her way up the stairs.

Amy sat on the floor, crossed-legged, staring up at the ceiling. Her eyes closed at the sound of a door upstairs slamming shut. Amy reached into the overturned desk and picked out a pen and paper. She laid the pen on top of the paper and steadied her breaths. Her entire body illuminated with her orange aura, and a part of it mocked her hand and picked up the pen. The aura-hand shook as it tried steadying the pen, forming words on the paper.

Archie came flying down the stairs and landed on one of Amy's knees. He nestled down under the orange glow and 'cooed', closing his eyes. Amy smiled at him.

"Just make sure I don't fall asleep down here, Arch."

Amy woke up in her bedroom to the same blaring siren she woke to last week.

Another swarm alert? That thing must be broken...

"BEE SWARM ALERT! BEE SWARM ALERT! BEE SWARM ALERT!" The message came from outside.

Amy jumped out of bed as the corners of the walls illuminated white. She ran out of her room and down the stairs, cutting the corner and into the living room. Amy could hear the booming, robotic voice that played out over the town.

"ALL RESIDENTS MUST GET INSIDE A STRUCTURE!"

The ZiccoLynx box glowed white as several thousand tiny white lights rose from it and formed into a screen. On-screen, a reporter sat behind the desk.

"Be advised residents," the reporter began, "the alarm you are hearing is not a test nor a mechanical issue. We have received reports that a second swarm is heading towards the southern region of London this morning—"

Amy ran out of the living room and back up the stairs. She ran into her room as a metal sheet slid down her window, blocking out the sunlight.

Amy sat at her computer desk and an actugraphic computer screen formed on the wall in front of her. She stabbed into the actugraphic keyboard that materialized on her desk. On the computer screen, a camera feed came up. It was a bird's-eye view from the top of her home. Amy waited, not taking her eyes off the screen.

A humming, then buzzing sound grew. Moments later, on-screen, several specks flew from left to right, out of Amy's view. The swarm kept rolling past the screen, some specks coming into view. Bees the size of a toddler's hand passed right by the camera.

One bee smacked right into the camera, causing Amy to jump back. She turned as something fell near her window, on the other side of the metal covering.

Several minutes later, a single beeping sound came from outside, lasting for ten seconds. The corner of the walls lost their white glow. Amy sat in her towel on the bed, her hair wrapped up in another towel. She turned to the window as the metal covering rose and hid inside the panel it came from.

Amy got up and walked over to the open window. A large bee laid on its stomach in between the window's groove. The bee rolled over onto its back.

The walls inside the classroom seemed to reverberate the depressed sighs of the students. *ECONOMICS 3* was written across the chalkboard as a homely older woman, Mrs. Colt, preached to the class.

Amy sat in the far left corner of the room, staring out the window. She surveyed the streets below, searching for some inspiration. Her eyes stopped on a woman with a small, crying boy. The child stopped walking and pulled away from the woman.

The woman shouted at the boy and walked past him. She lifted a parked car they had passed and reached underneath it for a couple of seconds, until pulling out a small red ball. The woman charged towards the boy, her muffled yells filling the air. She slammed the ball into the boy's hand and jerked his free arm forward, dragging him away.

What an awful woman.

Amy winced as the screaming chalk dug into the board. She shook it off and smiled at the insides of her notebook. She moved her head from side to side to go along with her low hums and wrote:

Contraband was my heart.... Scrutinize is my art...

Scrutiny is my art.... Contraband was my heart...

Contraband was my heart.... Scrutinize is my art...

No. Maybe. It's as if the words didn't want to cooperate.

Amy groaned, sinking into her chair. She sat upright, a surge of fire building within her chest, rolling down her arms and up to her fingertips. She looked outside the cracked door. In the hallway, a piece of paper glided by.

Amy... Amy... Amy...

Amy stood, staring out the door as the voice called out to her. Mrs. Colt stopped speaking and watched her. Amy walked to the door, ignoring the teacher's calls.

Amy walked out into the hallway as the paper glided down the hall as though carried by a powerful wind. Amy followed close behind. The voice that called her before lowered into a whisper, then soon became incoherent. Amy knew there were many eyes on her, but that wouldn't stop her from finding out where she needed to be led. It was so clear that she needed to go there. Wherever there was.

Amy turned a corner, but the piece of paper was nowhere to be found. A faint indistinguishable whisper came from behind her.

"Amy," the voice whispered louder.

A tear rolled down Amy's face.

"You're dead." Mrs. Colt stood right behind Amy. Her head cocked to the side, watching Amy's teary eyes.

Amy's head jumped off of her desk at the sound of a slamming textbook, held by Mrs. Colt, who stood right in front of her.

"Thank you for rejoining us, Ms. Devine," she said, making her way back to the front of the classroom.

Amy readjusted herself, wiping the drool off the side of her mouth, and averted the gaze of the snickering students around her.

Mrs. Colt pointed her textbook towards Amy.

"You know, Ms. Devine, if you want others to invest in you, you have to first invest in yourself. I teach economics so that I can invest in the futures I see sitting in each one of these seats. What are you going to invest in?"

As she sat in Animalia Criminology, Amy had spent until now thinking about just that. At least she wouldn't be bored in this class. However, five minutes passed and no sign of Professor Watson. He was never late.

What did Mrs. Rechert want yesterday...

The classroom door burst open. A short, red-haired man entered hastily, stepped in front of the class, cleared his throat, and flashed a smile. His eyes dug into and across the room. "Apologies for my tardiness, class! I'm Mr. Perry. I recognize some faces from the Summer program over in Hemlith Academy, the next town over. Professor Watson will be out for some time, so I'll be taking over for your Animalia Criminology class until further notice." He picked up the copy of Memoirs of the Forgotten and looked it over. "Let's see here..."

"What's happened with Professor Watson?" Amy asked.

"Just some family business to attend to, but don't you worry that lovely head of yours. Mr. Perry is here for all of your needs."

Amy watched Mr. Perry turn some pages, looking confused as he walked behind the desk. So much for an escape from her current reality. From what she heard of Mr. Perry, he could bore a snail into submission. Today would not feature a look inside a remarkable case solved within our history, but it would feature a look inside of a book. A book she would never read if ever assigned to her, anyway.

"Ah, well, congratulations are in order," Mr. Perry said. "Seems Professor Watson was able to grab a hold of copies of this book for each one of you!" He picked up books from behind the desk and placed them on the table.

Well, so much for that. A hardcover at that.

It was worse than she could imagine. Her town was one of the last few towns not fully adapted to ZiccoLynx technology. Almost every other school had the luxury of digital notes, assignments, and the material all synced within the cloud. Not Jadesfeld. Oh no, her town stood proudly, flaunting their claim of having the best education reliant on traditional learning.

Amy raised an eyebrow as a copy of Memoirs of the Forgotten was passed back to her.

"Now put those aside," Mr. Perry said. "I'll give you that assignment near the end of class. Let's try a novel approach. I find we gain a lot of solid knowledge through conversation."

Maybe he's not such a bore after all.

"Who can tell me what a Peculiar is?" Mr. Perry asked.

The small chatter from moments before was now absent as the class fell silent. All eyes were on Mr. Perry. One student raised their hand.

"They're a dangerous bunch," the student said. "They blow things up."

"They don't just blow things up," a girl said next to him. "They're like—energy suckers. Then they expel that energy and murder people."

"Yeah, but they don't exist anymore. Do they?" another student chimed in. "Lot of us weren't even born close to the time they were active. No offense Mr. Perry."

Some laughter came from the class. Mr. Perry crossed his arms.

"Yes, well, those of us who were around when they were most active remember them quite well," Mr. Perry snapped back. "Years full of terror is what it was. The most devastating times since the end of the second evohuman war."

Amy nervously tapped her finger on her desk, but stopped after realizing how loud it sounded. Her eyes scanned the room before landing back on Mr. Perry, who wiped his lenses with his suit lapel and sat on Professor Watson's desk.

"Human evolution has been a blessing, but with every blessing comes a curse," Mr. Perry said. "They were ten of these cursed individuals that were extraordinarily powerful, and they left behind an insurmountable amount of destruction that we're still recovering from to this day. All but one were, uh, put down, for lack of a better term. The last one is locked far away, deep within the depths of a prison somewhere. Only a select number of individuals know of its whereabouts."

Amy could feel the sweat dripping down the back of her neck. She couldn't shake the dirty feeling she got being surrounded in this room of people who would cast her out, or worse if they knew what she really was. The dread of it all dripped from her eye sockets like fresh dew off of a dandelion.

"Are you alright there, Ms… what's your name dear?" Mr. Perry pointed at Amy.

"Yes," Amy said, straightening up. "Amy Devine." She wiped the treacherous puddle from underneath her eyelids. "This is Animalia Criminology, why are we talking about Peculiars?"

"Well, Ms. Devine, I'd say it's important for your lot to be well informed of any potential future dangers."

"Are you saying Peculiars are around again?" A girl in the back called out.

"No, no, no, that's not what I'm saying. In this class, you learn about various crimes amongst the Animalia Kingdom, yet you learn nothing about Peculiar activities of the past. Over at Hemlith Academy, we have courses dissecting the history of the Peculiars, but here you have not one. Travesty, really. Therefore, from this moment on we will analyze Peculiar activity on Tuesdays and Thursdays as it's important for you all to be aware and be prepared. Peculiars may be gone but there's always something creeping about."

"I don't see how this is necessary for our curriculum," Amy spat out. She cleared her throat. "Mr. Perry."

"Well, my dear," Mr. Perry said. He walked over to Amy's desk and leaned into it. "Frankly, this isn't about what you believe is necessary. It's about what's best for you." He walked back to the front. "A little spunk in this lot! I like that."

What does he know about anything, anyway?

Amy sat back in her chair. It was time for her second escape. She turned a page in her notebook and put pen to paper:

Contraband was my heart…

Did that even make sense? She almost caught herself humming too loud, but the quiet melody of her classmates chattering drowned out any sound she had made. A little bird fluttered off the windowsill, adding more to the symphony within the room. It was all random but created a sort of beautiful blueprint for Amy to follow. Catchy, but messy. Messy, but then some of the most riveting experiences in life are. She smirked at how silly she sounded. Poetic, maybe, but silly. The lyrics she needed seemed to glue themselves together inside her head. She even vaguely traced the cadence of Mr. Perry's voice as he lectured, and it added something to her orchestra.

Can't wait till Professor Watson returns. Listening to this buffoon...

Amy's head jerked forward. She reached back, fumbling with her hair, and pulling apart a piece of gum sticking to her hair. She heard Tilly snickering somewhere behind her. Amy rose and whipped around.

Madeline smiled back at her, doing a flicking motion with her fingers.

"I've just about had it with you, you ol' pair of tits with no brain," Amy's voice raised at a steady pace but she lowered it, as though she practiced this. A passive-aggressive shouting whisper, as her eyes dug into Madeline's soul. Amy massaged her own throat.

"Aw, the normie can speak up a bit after all," Madeline said. "Go on then, show us what you've got—if you can."

Amy could feel her aura surging at her fingertips. She felt it pricking around her now enclosed fist, begging to escape. It waited for her command. She only had to make her mark.

"What's the fit, girls?" Mr. Perry grabbed Amy's shoulders as he moved between the girls.

"She chucked gum in my hair," Amy growled, shrugging Mr. Perry's embrace off.

"Prove it," Madeline said.

"Alright, that's enough," Mr. Perry broke in. "Off to the Head-mistress, both of you."

Moments later, Amy and Madeline walked side by side behind the Headmistress's assistant, Mrs. Rechert. Madeline grilled Amy.

"Why are you such a freak? What's eating you, Devine?"

"A pesky blood-ant named Madeline," Amy assured her.

"One way or another—" Madeline came close to Amy's face. "I'm going to expose you for the freak you are, Devine. Something's always fucking up around you, and I'm going to find out why. Your little savior isn't here to get you out the shitter."

The three ascended the tight gray staircase. As they passed a side door to the third floor, Amy stopped in her tracks. A strange sensation rose within her as confusion grew onto her face.

Something was here. It saw me. It's watching.

Amy crept towards the slightly ajar door leading onto the third floor.

Was that? It couldn't have been. An aura.

She peeked into the opening, into the third-floor hall. A few lights buzzed in and out of power, but nothing noteworthy was in sight.

"Ms. Devine, we haven't got all day," Mrs. Rechert beckoned.

Amy looked up at her impatient face, to Madeline's puzzled one, back to the opening on the third floor.

Amy's mind had still been on her staircase encounter as she walked into the Headmistress's office. Those thoughts soon flew out of her head as she sat down in front of the Headmistress, Ms. Graves. She was an imposing woman of 28 years of age. Her movements seemed so unphased by her surroundings. She tipped her glasses onto her nose as she remained focused on a document in front of her.

"Good Day, Ms. Graves," Amy said.

"Ms. Devine," Ms. Graves said, not taking her eyes off of her document. "So I've heard Ms. Watt's side of things. What's your story, Ms. Devine?"

"I've spent the last ten minutes picking pieces of gum out of my hair.

I'd hardly say she got the better end of things. She—"

A cool rush explored the length of Amy's arms. It was almost like two separate entities were battling each other. Like a married couple bickering. Amy grasped the arms of her seat, digging into them. Ms. Graves' face came back into focus.

"Ms. Devine? She what?" Ms. Graves asked.

Amy just stared at her, dumbfounded. Oh right, she was in the middle of a conversation, before being a looney.

"She… I don't know. Nothing. It's nothing," she answered.

"You're a smart girl, Ms. Devine," Ms. Graves exhaled, taking off her glasses. She folded her hands together, her big brown eyes on Amy's soft black eyes. "Clever, driven—"

"A lot like yourself when you were my age, right? Sorry…" Amy blurted out and immediately regretted it.

What is wrong with you?

She's heard that so many times from Gma and other adults that the words irritated her. It was just something older people said to the young without considering how different things had become. Still, she wasn't sure why she just came out like that. She dug herself into her chair, averting Ms. Graves' stare.

"I have the patience of an alligator," Ms. Graves said, returning her eyes to her paperwork. "They wait for long periods before sneaking up on their prey. When the right moment comes—they snap."

Ms. Graves tapped her fingertips together with every syllable. Turned some pages in front of her, shaking her head at each.

"The last thing their prey sees is a seventeen-inch silhouette beaming straight towards them. Meanwhile, the twenty-five-inch spartagator comes from the depths and uses its nearly impenetrable spikey body as a weapon to pulverize and then feast on the base alligator. It isn't its natural prey, but it does it for fun. For the love of dominating the bigger game."

Ms. Graves holds two pens apart from each other, one bigger than the other.

"Alligator. Spartagator." The question, Ms. Devine: Are you going to continue going after scraps or are you ready to attack the bigger game?"

Amy and Demora sat on a fallen tree trunk, staring across the watering hole of their secret spot. The ears of a gang of eagorts flew them over the pond, their small trunks dipping into and drinking the water.

"Lost at sea?" Amy asked.

"Completely," Demora responded. "My parents are off their mark. I swear, sometimes they've lost their minds. They can't accept who I am. Imagine if they knew about my aura…"

"It'll all figure itself out." Amy placed a hand on Demora's and squeezed. "We are what we are."

"Yeah, well, my dad's always one step closer to shipping me off to a correctional facility." Demora rose and walked off, and Amy followed right behind her.

"Don't say that, Demo. It'll never happen. As harsh as they are, they wouldn't."

"Full of bollocks, the lot of them." Demora kicked some rocks into the pond as she stomped down the pasture. She waved her hand, and her aura swept a couple of pebbles across the pond. She faced Amy and folded her arms. "Absolute rubbish. One day I'm going to head the World Committee and I'll abolish all these stupid rules. Teach the world how wrong they are about Peculiars." Demora shook her head and wiped a tear away. She smiled down at her feet. "Come here, you little bastard." Demora picked up a taracede and showed Amy. "Ames, let me show you. I can feel it. I've got this."

Demora's pink aura grew around her entire body. She extended her arm forward, with the hand holding the taracede.

The taracede bit down into Demora's palm, causing her to drop it. It scurried away.

"Demo, are you okay?"

"I'm fine!" Demora jerked away from Amy, holding her palm. "That one had no bands, it's nonvenomous. There it is!"

Demora pointed her hand towards a nearby tree, and her aura shot out towards the ground. Her aura-hand dragged the taracede towards her.

The taracede's head and torso flattened against the ground. Its legs flailed on either side.

"Alright, be gentle now, Demo," Amy said. "It only flattens its body like that when under stress."

Demora curled her hand inward and her aura-hand mimicked her, then formed a ball of aura around the taracede. The aura ball levitated off the ground as the taracede body jerked around inside it.

"Yes, yes, yes, c'mon now," Demora said, her eyes not leaving the trapped taracede. "Now for the finish." She curled her hand into a fist. The taracede continued to wriggle.

"Hey Demora, that's enough now," Amy said, stepping forward.

"So close. Come. On." Demora ignored her and kept opening, then curling her hand back into a fist as the taracede's wild body spasms bumped around inside the aura ball.

"I said that's enough." Amy grabbed Demora's arm. Demora's aura died out. The taracede scurried off as the girls watched it disappear into some bushes.

"What is your problem, Devine? You said you'd help me figure this thing out!"

"That was before I saw how—painful it looked."

"Oh, there was no pain, don't be such a pansy."

"I'm not being a pansy, I'm being humane. What was that?"

"I read Peculiars can separate your aura at will. I want to learn more. It could be useful if you need to contain something horrible. Or someone."

"It sounds dangerous, and why would you ever want to separate from your aura? It goes against the natural selection of things."

"Oh, rubbish," Demora said, storming off.

"Are you going to follow everything that you read, no matter the source? Sounds like you were reading something not meant to be read. Where is this book?"

"Don't you dare!" Demora spun on her heel, walking backward while pointing at Amy. "Don't you dare lecture me, Devine! Get off your high horse! If it wasn't for my sparring with you, who's to say whatever the hell you and ol' Rezna get up to is even half—"

Demora fell on her butt as she tripped, her leg ripping away the unkept parchment that camouflaged the body amongst the Fall leaves. She scampered back along the ground.

Amy scanned the long log that Demora tripped over. Except it wasn't a log. A black mass of hair sat at the end of it and Amy's heart sank way below the Earth's surface and the world seemed to freeze around her. She couldn't take her eyes off the dead grey ones staring straight up into the sky, as though gazing upon the Sun, soaking in the heat that was quickly deteriorating the body that sat hidden underneath piles of bush and leaves. The cool Jadesfeld's air suddenly felt like bubbling lava sinking into every pore on Amy's body. Her arms, legs, and torso lost their motor functions as her mouth hung open.

Demora found her footing and waved her hand as her aura brushed more leaves onto the body, covering some of it.

"Hey, hey, it's alright, Ames. Just—it's okay. Don't even look. We'll just call the police and—"

The wind blew the leaves off the disturbed body, and its full state was now on full display. Deep slashes decorated the flesh, with meaty bits hanging off like paper flaps. The mouth hung agape, also slashed, giving it the look of a gaping old tree stump. Before Demora could say anything else, a rustle crept alive a few feet away from them.

A teenage boy groggily got to his feet, gripping something on his way up. He held his head, staring at the two girls before him. The horror awoke on his face as he looked over at the dead body.

"Dad?!" he yelled. His breaths grew as he stammered, tears rolling down his face. He raised his hand, with a sharp crimson-tipped jagged blade tight in his grasp. He brought his murderous eyes to Amy and Demora.

"What did you do?" he growled, as his fist enveloped with a red aura.

Amy was still in her trance. Muffled out screaming all around her, her peripherals picking up the young boy charging at Demora. A flash of light and a powerful gust of wind accompanied the loss of sound as leaves and dirt rained all around her.

"Amy!" Demora shook Amy by the shoulders as Amy found her way back to reality.

Amy's mouth closed, her eyes finding Demora's. Behind Demora, the teenage boy was unconscious, with a log by his bleeding head and the bloody blade a few feet away.

Chapter Three

A blue light shined on Amy's face as her eyes bore into the steel table in front of her. With Demora at her side, they sat across from two detectives; one was chubby with a bushy mustache, and the other lanky with a cone-shaped beard hanging off his chin.

A blue-colored hologram creating a perfect replica of the crime scene took up the table's real estate. The chubby detective traced a metallic pointer around small holographic figures of Amy, Demora, the teenage boy, and his dead father. The images cut off, then on again.

"Goddamn old tech. This town's an old-school charmer, eh?" the chubby detective said. "You've been quiet, Ms. Devine. Can you tell me what you did after the suspect ran towards you? In your own words," he added while tossing a zip-it motion at Demora.

"I froze," Amy said. "When I was younger—" she trailed off, speaking without actually hearing her own words as a warm feeling entered the middle of her chest. Her body rose in heat as it longed to find the source of energy that was somewhere nearby. Her gaze landed on the one-way mirror, where she only saw her own reflection.

"Well, we just needed to grab your statements. Being on the scene of such a crime isn't exactly an easy ordeal," the chubby detective said.

"The boy. What's going to happen to him?" Amy asked, not sure why she thought of that at this moment, but she had to ask.

"Oh well, his fingerprints alone seal the deal. You two are very lucky to be alive. Very few have come face to face with a Peculiar without a scratch."

He nodded his head as he looked over at his partner. The lanky detective sat forward, his eyes rolling over from his partner to land on the two girls. His thin mouth separated, showing his teeth grinding together.

"Let me explain something to you, girls. This is a very serious situation that has become an unusually annoying and dangerous pest to our small and humble community. It is best that there is not a single worth of information being withheld that could hold back our investigations."

"We have told you exactly everything that happened, detective, and I want to know why we're still here," Demora said.

"Ladies, take no offense," the chubby detective said, as he flashed his big smile once again. He opened his arms as though waiting for an embrace. "It's been a troubling start to all of our weeks. Three precious families have been torn apart, and it's all just very unfortunate. We'd like to sort this out and find the culprit responsible before more damage can occur."

"Three?" Amy asked.

"Two." The chubby detective cleared his throat and took a glance at his partner.

"So you believe a murderer is still out there?" Amy asked.

"Well." The chubby detective frowned at the glance his partner gave him. He cleared his throat again and smiled. "We're just considering all possibilities, Ms. Devine. Investigations are still ongoing."

"What are your names?" Demora asked, crossing her arms and tipping her nose towards the detectives. "I want to file a report against you both for being asshats."

"Oh, I'm Detective Burt," the chubby detective chuckled. "and this here's Detective Skitinsky. Please, feel free, Ms. Corbyn-McDonald. Please, take care now. We'll be in touch if we have any more questions."

Detective Skitinsky narrowed his eyes on the two girls as they got up and left the room.

Amy and Demora walked down the hall, which was swarming with Detectives and policebots.

Must be the busiest day of their career since the Murder House fiasco.

A flicker of heat grazed across Amy's chest and she glimpsed squeaky brown shoes moving into another room behind her.

What was that?

Amy tripped over her own feet and grabbed Demora's hand.

"Come off it," Demora said as she pulled her hand away and walked ahead of her.

The car ride home was a silent one except for the joyful dancehall tune that played over the radio. Its built-in driver moved his robotic head from side to side as it watched the road ahead, with the back of its seat labeled REMSEN.

In the back seats, Amy stole several glances at Demora, but her hopes of catching her best friend's eye got demolished each time. Demora kept her gaze out the window at the extraordinary nothingness of their town's streets.

I'm a bloody coward and she knows it. We almost got killed, and I just stood there. Stupid coward.

After what seemed like the longest winter ever, the car stopped in front of Demora's short, stubby-looking house. The robotic Remsen looked into the shabby windows, then faced the girls.

"I am told that your parents are away, Ms. Corbyn-McDonald. Once again, Ms. Devine said if you want to spend the—"

"No thanks," Demora answered, opening the door mid-sentence and shutting it. She threw Amy a quick glance and wave before jogging up to her front door.

Remsen waited until she went inside before driving off. He cleared his shrill robotic throat.

"You should know, Ms. Devine would like you to meet her in the cellar."

Amy nodded. She already knew what was coming. It was a perfect opportunity. This awful day would cause an endless night.

As she descended the basement stairs, Amy only saw Rezna's legs sitting in her chair, the rest of her sunken in the depths of shadows. This throne where she sat was where Amy saw her grandmother most unnerved, and after fighting so many battles in her time, she had surely earned the seat.

Amy took a deep breath before reaching the bottom step, then walking over to her, head down and arms crossed. She closed her eyes as well.

"Your mind, body, and spirit must be one," Rezna said, not moving an inch, her eyes still closed. "Your aura makes up your very soul. The energy from it guides you, and you guide it. Now. Tell me exactly what happened today."

"I… I froze. I just froze up."

The basement scene disappeared from Amy's mind. When she opened her eyes, nothing surrounded her but never-ending blackness.

Several white shapes swooped down in front of Amy and swirled around until they pieced together a ghostly form of Rezna's body.

Amy winced as bone, then flesh came over the ghostly form, all coloring itself right before Amy's eyes.

"Embrace your aura's spirit form, girl. Hit me," Rezna said, looking down on Amy.

"What?"

"Hit me. Not with your fists, but with your aura."

Amy turned her hands over, again and again, wondering how it could be missing.

"That's... How do you even... I can't feel anything."

Rezna's spirit body grew taller and her green aura engulfed her entirely, its blinding light scattering throughout the dense darkness. The green aura shot balls of energy straight towards Amy.

Amy ducked and the impressive balls of light crashed on either side of her, rebounded, then reabsorbed back into Rezna's spirit body.

"You're not fighting," Rezna said. "You're running."

Amy's eyes found their orange glare. She threw her arms forward and her aura shot out at Rezna.

Rezna raised a hand, and Amy's aura subsided.

"How?"

"So we now know for a fact you're incapable of hitting anything with your aura. How about you try to hit me with your actual fists? You're supposed to make your way towards me and lift your hand. Then you make each of your little fingers close—"

"I know how to make a fist!" Amy shouted.

"Ah, using your big girl voice to shout in this realm because you can't use it out in the real world?"

Amy had enough. She charged at Rezna, fists blazing orange. Although she was running as fast as she could, to the point of being a blur, she could not reach Rezna. It was as though she were on an endless treadmill.

"This world operates differently than the physical world, dear. You'll need to use your aura to propel you. The rest of you is literally nothing within this realm without your aura."

"What is this place?" Amy stopped, huffing and puffing.

"This. This is the Realm of Lucidity. It is where an auraist can travel for solitude, secret conversation with another, or even infidelity. While we are here, our bodies remain paralyzed, waiting for us to return to them."

Rezna's legs disappeared from underneath, replaced by a stream of her green aura. She raced around Amy, throwing her arms out, and her aura shot out in different directions. The aura shots created various structures, animals, and even people around Amy before disappearing seconds after they formed.

"This is also where we can gain an immense advantage against our enemies. Against any threat that may come our way."

Several faceless bodies formed from Rezna's aura, growing taller every second behind Rezna. They all moved towards Amy, looking down at her.

"But you will never reach this level without accomplishing an important step in your training." Rezna shook her head at Amy.

Amy opened her eyes, back in the real world. Rezna had her hands on Amy's face, to what Amy had to second guess, whether it was sadness or disappointment.

"You need to fight back, girl! You cannot hesitate, you can never hesitate! It will help unlock your potential. This world isn't gentle with our kind. It never has been."

"Then just teach me whatever you want me to learn." Amy jerked from her grip, pacing as she clenched her fists. "Give me some kind of hint. I'm ready for the new technique. Instead, you give me these lessons on basic shit I already know. I need something new, something that'll help me when I'm really in a tight spot. If I was better equipped—"

"You would have still frozen." Rezna circled Amy, her nose flaring. "And mind your tone with me. Quite the temperamental one lately, aren't you? Questioning, questioning constantly. Expecting results with so little effort."

Little effort?

Amy's nails cut into her palms as scarlet drips hit the cold cellar floor.

"Do not come to me with hunger when you've barely finished your plate," Rezna said.

Amy's hands lost the aura that had formed around them a second ago. She took a deep breath as her eyes left Rezna's and found their home at her feet.

Rezna gestured towards the throne. Amy hesitated but took a seat. She had only sat here two other times in her life. Each time had been after an event of grave misfortune.

"Your assignment," Rezna said as she crossed her arms. "Where is it?"

Shit.

Amy hoped to see the sheet of paper she left down here last night lingering about, but she hardly remembered even getting upstairs and into bed. She clenched the armrests of the throne and stuck her chest straight out.

"The Classes." Amy took a deep breath. "The Classes are important because they define who we are in society and who we can perceive as—"

"Stop. You are literally—" Rezna shook her hand before it coiled into a fist. "What defines you has little but shit to do with what society labels you. Perception can deceive, and manipulation surrounds you daily. YOU are your definition of importance."

"Will you let me finish?!" Amy grabbed her throat, her eyes going wide before returning to normal once more. "I don't need a lecture. I want to become stronger, but I don't need you to babysit my training."

"You are better than this, Amy. So much better than this and you have no idea. Be better."

Amy's eyes twitched at the corners as Rezna leaned against a table, taking her eyes off Amy. A treacherous stream pushed behind her eyes, but Amy would not allow it freedom.

"If you take nothing from any of this, understand this much: You must always stay on guard. The general public is squeamish enough, but there are others out there who will kill you on sight. They will hunt you. They are hunting you. No explanation except you being what you are. Different. The Classes should matter to you because they remind you what your society has in mind for you. What your society wants to do to you. Your world considers you a threat. They call us Peculiars because they do not understand our nature. The world does not understand that we as Auraists can control and harbor this energy at will; using it to fight against those who want to burn this world to the ground. Light vs shadow. That's all there is to it. The sooner you can grasp this concept, the better you will fare. If you're unable to do what it takes, I'm afraid you'll meet the same fate that your parents did."

Rezna rose and made her way upstairs. Amy's hands shook on top of her knees as her back arched forward, accepting the depths of the throne's welcoming mouth.

Chapter Four

T he biggest funeral of 2170 had been one for the ages. The most popular, and richest man in town, Mr. Conrad Bakers, fell asleep in his bathtub and, unable to pull himself up, he drowned. He had Crowman's disease, an affliction that left its poor victim with a back hooked forward, the spine bulging out of its skin like the beak of a crow.

But the name actually came after a man in the 2080s went mad trying to merge his DNA with that of an actual crow. It was the start of a new pinnacle of technology known as Animaging. Man could not get enough of enhanced strength and agility and had to take things one step further, combining their flesh with animal parts. All in the name of scientific exploration.

But even seven-year-old Amy knew that was crow's shit.

She wasn't sure why, but she lacked empathy for the man. Maybe it was the time he scolded her for trudging up dirt on his front porch. She and Gma came to deliver some items he left behind after his mother's funeral. The unmarried man opened his front door and immediately dug into Amy, causing Gma to raise her voice at him.

Or it could have been the time Amy bumped into him outside the old town's library. She, a young boy named Felix, and Demora were racing inside to see what they could dig up on the Desert Scavengers they heard some of the older kids and adults speak of. Alien beings that supposedly roamed the deserts. Amy, being front and center, ran face-first into Mr. Baker's long legs and he chastised her for being so careless.

The adults in this town had always been… testy. None more so than Mr. Conrad Bakers.

On the day of Mr. Bakers' funeral, Amy had been playing with Felix, who, other than Demora, was her one and only genuine friend in town. Every Summer, Demora's parents sent her away to a boarding academy for troubled youths. This left Amy lonely, except for last year when she met Felix. The other children may want nothing to do with her, but at least he did. Felix did so enthusiastically.

They had just started a new game of Find and Tag when Felix's mother came calling. Amy hugged her knees, hiding underneath a cupboard in an oversized bathroom area, groaning as the woman called over and over for her son. Amy pushed open the cupboard's door, slamming into something outside of it that squealed out loud.

Amy stepped out of the cupboard onto the marble-tiled floor and looked up at Mrs. Temeltry. The woman dusted off her long midnight skirt and scowled at Amy.

"Just what are you doing sneaking about my parlor?" she asked.

"Very sorry, Mrs. Temeltry. You were as quiet as a mouse. I had not figured you were that close."

"You dreadful, dreadful girl," Mrs. Temeltry said through bared teeth. "I suppose you haven't any idea where my son Felix is, do you?" She raised a stubby finger and her eyes narrowed. "If he crinkles a single thread on his suit, I'll have words with your grandmother."

"Well no, ma'am. That is the point of the game, for him to find me and tag. But now you've left me exposed, so I've got to hide elsewhere."

"There will be no more games. The service is starting soon. Run along and find your nan. Dreadful, dreadful girl." Mrs. Temeltry stomped out of the room.

Amy stuck her tongue out behind her and closed the cupboard door.

Amy stepped into the main room, searching for Felix. Standing room was scarce, as only a few people took seats at the moment. A beautiful sea-green mahogany closed-casket sat on the main stage, fit for the rich man that now lived inside. A ziccolight sign illuminated the holographic caution ribbon surrounding a good portion of the area around the casket. The sign read: Do Not Stand Too Close!

"Felix! Felix, where are you? The games over now, come out," Amy called out.

Amy jumped as a shuffle came behind her. Her eyes traced the gold outline of the beautiful casket's edges and waited.

Nope.

"Amy, what are you up to?" Rezna placed a hand on Amy, smiling around the room. "The Temeltry boy is missing, and his mother is causing a ruckus. You haven't seen him, have you?"

"No Gma, I was just looking for him but I'm not sure where he went off to."

"Keep your eyes peeled, girl. Hopefully, he turns up soon. Or else I'll have to snap that old witch's mouth shut. This would've never happened if she just had the service at my parlor instead of *Endfield*. Between her and her dead brother, I don't know who's worse." Rezna walked away, greeting the guests with smiles and nods.

Amy frowned. She knew Rezna was a bit more worried than usual. That calm demeanor was diminishing. She'll do what she can to help her Gma out. Always. She'll search harder for Felix and—

Amy spun around quick enough to see the casket shift to the side, sliding a bit off the edge of the counter it was on. Her eyes went wide. The shallow breaths escaping her mouth matched the rhythm of her heaving chest.

"Amy!" a voice whispered.

A young boy around the corner waved at her.

"Felix," Amy said, rushing up to him. "Where have you been? Your mum's looking for you."

"Noah is *in* there. Help me get him out!" Felix pointed at the casket.

"You dirty liar, Noah is not—"

The casket on the stage shook.

Amy and Felix gazed at each other with their mouths half-open.

"I can't explain right now, but you've got to help me get him out, Amy. They're gonna—"

"Felix! Boy, where are you?!" Mrs. Temeltry's voice rang out.

"Shit," Felix said before running off.

Amy stared at the casket. She balled her fists and moved towards it with caution in every step.

A muffled voice came from inside the casket. Or was it two? She felt warmth as she passed the caution ribbon and felt warmer as she neared the casket. The muffled voices grew clearer, unmistakable now.

I should call Gma.

Amy swung around on her heel.

The casket top swung open and a blue-skinned boy—Noah—poured out of it, arms flailing, screaming bloody murder as a discolored hand grabbed him by the collar. He jumped out, bringing the casket tumbling off the counter, right into Amy's back. An edge of the casket cracked Noah in the head, and the casket pinned both him and Amy to the ground.

Amy picked herself up off her stomach and pushed Noah's unconscious body off of her, as screams filled the entire room.

Discolored fingers tickled the back of her head, and the hand grabbed Amy by the neck.

Amy turned and met the decomposing face of Mr. Conrad Bakers.

His eyes rolled in their sockets until their grayness fell upon Amy. He pulled himself on top of her as the wetness from his tongue dripped down her earlobe.

"You ruined everything, you little bitch!"

That was only the first time Death taunted Amy.

Amy grew tired of waking up to that horrible memory. She sat at the desk in her room.

"PC, logon."

The corners of her room lit up white and a beam of light shot from the center of the wall in front of her and materialized a holographic screen on her desk, and a holographic keyboard on the desktop.

She spent the rest of the morning digging up what she could find on the boy, Lucor, who had killed his father. The boy who triggered thoughts of her own encounters with the dead who came back, or Lifesnatchers as they're known. On the bright side, this time the deceased did not return to his flesh.

It felt horrible to be so angry, so selfish when a man had just lost his life. At the hands of his own son. But it wasn't fair that her entire life seemed to revolve around the dead.

Her thoughts shifted as Amy stumbled on an article detailing intimate details of the family's life, and she couldn't help that disgusting feeling in the pit of her stomach when hearing the media dissociate so much from who they were. The article read like a list of events from a history book and here she was feeding into it like everyone else. Unable to turn away, but growing more furious as the words scrolled on.

Amy's eyes closed as her skin crawled from her fingertips up to the small hairs on her long arms, then to the top of her shoulders. It only took a few more seconds before a burning sensation on her chest took over. There was more than a reader's remorse going on. Her head spun around her room, clutching her chest.

Amy flung her window open and peered outside. The streets were empty. Her eyes narrowed on the browning leaves on the trees on either side of her neighbors' houses.

A quick burning sensation scorched the right side of her chest. Her attention cut to the side of her building and the green pastures of the cemetery residing in the backyard of her home.

Amy walked down the stairs to the main entrance hall, grabbed her coat, and moved past the living room, towards the back end of the hall. She went through the dimly lit dining room, passing the flickering candles along the walls.

Entering another smaller hall past the dining room, Amy put her coat on and turned her collars up to cover either side of her face. She opened a gigantic bolt on the door in front of her and pushed the door open.

Amy stepped out onto the damp grass, keeping her eyes straight ahead. She walked up beside the first headstone in a row of them, stopping to close her eyes and catch her breath. One foot forward, then another, as she took long, deliberate steps between rows of headstones. As she moved, her body shivered, jumping a bit when she got too close to the marked graves.

Every step seemed to raise her temperature tenfold. Her breath got caught inside her throat. She paused at two headstones by her right foot and felt her heart drop. Although she didn't recognize the names written, she had this horrible, sinking feeling that she could not shake. One thing was certain and bought her some relief: the energy she felt was no longer coming from the graves below her feet.

"Do I know you?" A shrill voice called from behind.

Amy faced a boney-faced woman with mahogany hair tied up in an elaborate bun. A small girl with the same hair color and silver eyes stood at her side.

Amy stared at them, opening her mouth, but nothing came out.

"Well? Did you know my sister and her husband?" the woman asked.

"No. No, I… I'm…"

"Good morning, Norma," Rezna said as she approached the questioning woman.

"Please, it is Ms. Jones in front of the children."

"I see, Mrs. Jones—"

"*Ms*. Jones. I am separated."

"My apologies—"

"Unnecessary. This girl, here, seems to be gawking at my relatives. I'm quite tired of the folk in this town fantasizing over my family's tragedy."

"I wasn't fantasizing," Amy said.

"I'm terribly sorry," Rezna said. "This is my granddaughter, and as it is her home, she explores it freely. I assure you, she meant no disrespect."

"Tends to wander, eh? Perhaps she could tend to some chores. Or surely there's homework to be done, no?"

"Not at the moment," Amy said. It was true, but she felt the need to stick it to the shrill woman.

"Amy," Rezna said. "If you'd please go back inside."

"But Gma, I—"

"Amy."

Rezna had a way of making her voice boom without yelling and Amy took her cue. Although annoyed she didn't figure out what drew her out there, she wasn't about to push Rezna's buttons. She needed to get out of the house, anyway.

Amy walked back through the house instead of taking the shortcut through the front of the graveyard. When she got to and opened her front door, her expression shifted to confusion seeing Madeline Watts at her door.

"On our way out?" Madeline questioned, stepping straight into the main hall.

"What are you doing here?"

"Charming one, aren't you? I'm here to do you some good."

"No good deal goes easily through you."

Madeline handed her a small vial.

"Beeswax." Amy and Madeline said together. Madeline cleared her throat.

"Swarms have made it easy to grab ahold of some and Mr. Perry thought it a good idea for us to study its composition over the weekend. You'll see the rest of the assignment details in your email."

"And this couldn't be sent via the trolley?" Amy asked, getting more annoyed with this intrusion with every passing second.

"Well, I wanted to be sure it didn't just go missing. You know, with how crazy things have been going in our quaint little town as of late. Especially after your most recent encounter. Thought you may need—"

"A friend?" Amy scoffed at the idea.

"Word has it you ran into a Peculiar. Is it true?"

"That's not public knowledge."

Madeline shrugged. "My dad is friends with the Chief."

"Course he is."

"Well? Is it true?"

"I can't talk about it, Madeline."

"Yes, you can. I already know, and you're the only one in town who's ever faced a Peculiar. I was just curious—"

"And you thought you'd come over here, I'd put on a spot of tea, and we'd chat like old friends by the fireplace? One sec, I'll get the kettle going."

"Don't be a bitch."

"Now I know why they call you Mad Maddy."

Madeline's eyes narrowed as she put a hand on her hip and leaned forward.

"They say misfortune follows you like a crow on a corpse's tail end and you reek of death." Madeline smirked. "I found it even more delightful hearing how you seemed to lose your wit at the crime scene. Sounds just like a normie to me."

Amy leaned in close to Madeline's face. "You know, Madeline, there's going to come a day when you find out if the rumors you've heard about me are true. And misfortune may find its way right to you."

Madeline's nose flared. She lifted her chin and stepped backward outside the house.

"I'm watching you, Devine." She turned on her heel and power-walked away.

Amy slammed the door shut. There wasn't any way she could head out now with that little witch on her tail.

Training.

Surely this would bring her mind at ease.

Minutes later, Amy found herself in the basement in her grey tank top and shorts with a magnificent pool of sweat soaking her chest. She stood in the middle of four metallic pillars only a few inches taller than herself. The digitized screen above them read SPEED LVL III - TIME LASTED: 05:00. Amy tapped into the screen and stepped back, fists raised, ready to fight.

Four blue light beams emitted from each of the pillars to form an existographic featureless human figure before Amy. A stream of white light traced along the edges of the existogram as it raised its fists. The countdown on the digital screen above them reached zero and then read BEGIN.

The existogram threw lefts and rights at Amy, aiming for her body when she covered her head.

Amy dodged successfully before landing a couple of her own blows to the figure.

Why couldn't you have done this yesterday? Coward.

Amy dodged a sharp right hook. The speed of the machine jumped from three to four then back to three.

Stupid device. I need to get it fixed soon. But that shop on Marroway Street-

Amy dodged a sharp uppercut and tripped backward.

What stopped you from junking that boy, Ames? He could have killed your friend!

Amy caught her balance.

The existogram fighter threw a series of head shots followed by body shots, catching Amy off balance again.

Amy threw a couple of unaimed jabs to maintain some distance.

Only a matter of time before you fail them all.

"Shut up." Amy missed a left hook and fell straight into a right hook to the face. She fell onto her hands.

The existogram stepped back and disintegrated as the lights of the machine went off.

Amy blew her hair from her face and slammed her hands into the ground. She crawled over to and leaned against the boxing simulator. As she threw her head back, her eyes fell onto a door that she knew led to the morgue's preparation room.

Two for two Ames?

Amy, with a nose pincher on, opened the door to the prep room.

This room was different from the rest of the house, completely metallic white. Its clean finish gave it a shine that made it almost dreamlike in appearance. The irony made Amy chuckle as this room was anything but a dream to her. She had only wandered in here once when she was younger and never returned.

Amy took her time exploring the edges of the room, her eyes going over every inch as though completing a health inspection. She rubbed her shivering arms. Her eyes averted the seven metal examination tables in the middle of the room, each with a nice rounded glass cover on top of them and a soft blue light humming inside. Only one of the tables had a white sheet over it, meaning it was occupied.

Don't be chickenshit now, you've come this far.

Amy opened a drawer under the room's large sink and pulled out a pair of thick medical gloves. She slipped them on as she approached the occupied metal table.

A screeching sound made her jump. She shook her head, realizing her hip had bumped one of the tables and its wheels carried it a few inches from its perfect alignment with the others.

Amy made her way to what she figured to be the head of the unfortunate. She held onto the white sheet.

Deep breath.

Amy inhaled and shut her mouth tight, not wanting to take in any scent of what would probably soon fill the room.

She tugged at the white sheet but pulled back. No. She'd use her non-dominant left hand in case she had to strike. Her left hand shook violently as it crept closer to the sheet. She stopped just inches from touching it with her fingertips.

Her shoulders tensed and her arms jerked side to side as she ground her teeth. She wanted to scream. Her hands found her throat, and she massaged it while taking several steps back. She quivered, throwing her hands away, hating that she touched herself.

This is stupid.

Amy snapped off the gloves and washed her hands in the sink with a vigor that rivaled a bird taking a bath. She moved over to the far corner of the room, grabbing a towel off the rack and wiping her hands dry.

Her eyes fell onto a door that she had noticed before, but wasn't too keen on exploring. The indistinguishable red circular mark on its top half always made her wonder what it could mean, only realizing now that she never asked about it.

I've got to get one sort of win today.

Amy placed the towel neatly back onto the rack and went for the backdoor. As she pulled it open, a cloud of dust kissed her face. Coughing, she pulled the string for an old school light switch that was inside this large walk-in closet.

The inside was wooden, seemingly from a different era than from the room it was in. There were ornaments and trinkets that Amy had heard or seen in books and online. One item, in particular, caught her eye.

It was a wooden trunk that met her knees with a gold brim around where it should open.

Something's inside.

Amy felt a pair of eyes on her, but no one was there. She went back to the trunk and tugged on its lock. Her eyes grew orange and her aura outlined her.

Amy squeezed and the lock broke into many little pieces. She lifted the latch and took her time opening the trunk.

A strong glimmer peeked out and intensified as she further opened the trunk. She peered inside, a bit confused about what she was looking at.

"Amy, I hope you've started your assignments! We'll need time for training!" Rezna called from somewhere upstairs.

Amy's aura diminished, and she slammed the trunk shut, cut the light off, and ran out the closet. She closed the door to the morgue prep room behind her and jumped as Archie flew onto her shoulder.

"A *normie* wouldn't have been able to hear that call from down here. Stupid Watts." Amy pet Archie's head and made her way up the stairs.

Laying on her bed, Amy tapped her GCID, and a beam of white

light formed a holographic keyboard. She typed on the keyboard and waited. After a few moments without a response from Demora, she rolled her eyes and turned over on her back, letting out a huge puff of air.

Sometime later, Amy walked over a pile of clothes, steadied a cup of tea onto her desk, and worked diligently on her computer. Archie laid across the bed frame with a sock over his face. A little snore escaped him.

Amy raised her arm towards the dresser across from her small work desk, and her aura escaped her palm and mocked the outline of her hand. Her aura-hand shot into the open dresser and picked out her copy of *Memoirs of the Forgotten*. The aura-hand flipped through pages until settling on one and brought the book close to Amy's face.

"We never really know what it is we're looking for until we find it. It's not uncommon… For us to hide… It's not uncommon for us to hide… It's not uncommon for us to hide plain truths in familiar places."

Amy shook her head. Her eyes widencd at a single word that replaced every other word on her entire document on her computer screen.

Death

Amy's breath snatched back into her throat as more words appear on the screen:

Kill. Unworthy. Unsavable. They must all die. You will save yourself.

Amy's arm slipped off the desk as she snapped awake and rubbed her eyes. The document she had been typing was all normal.

"Driving me mad."

She got up, grabbed her cup, and exited the room.

Amy yawned as she walked downstairs. She reached the bottom and dropped her teacup.

With only the lower portion of her body visible, Rezna laid out on the floor, the rest of her hidden under the kitchen table.

Amy ran to her side.

"Gma! Gma are you—" Amy froze, not expecting to gaze into Rezna's open, still eyes.

Amy walked backward until she bumped into the sink. Her eyes swelled up, but the tears were trapped inside. Her body shook against her will as she hyperventilated. Her hands found their way around her neck, pressing into her throat.

Amy jumped at the sound of a footstep in the hallway. A small scream woke her legs as she rushed back into the hallway and froze once more.

The boy who killed his father, Lucor, held Demora from behind with his hand over her mouth. He held a bloody hand with an even bloodier knife up to Demora's throat.

Amy's hand shook as she raised it towards him.

Lucor smiled. That smile turned into a groan as he cried out and shook his hand.

"Argh! Bitch bit me!"

"Amy, save me!" Demora cried out, right as Lucor sliced the knife across her throat.

"No!" Amy cried out.

Demora's eyes went wide as she slipped from his grasp and dropped to the floor, clutching her slit throat. She landed face first, her dead eyes staring at Amy's feet.

Amy dropped to her knees, tears falling onto the wooden floor beneath her. Her eyes stayed on Demora's as Lucor charged towards her.

"Amy! Amy! AMY!" He said.

Amy jumped up from her desk, knocking her chair aside. She gasped as Rezna grabbed both of her shoulders and shook her.

"Amy, what's happening? Answer me, girl!"

Amy hugged her, crying into her chest.

Amy twirled her finger around in her half-full teacup. Her eyes met Rezna's, who sat across from her at the kitchen table. Amy had seen that look before on her Gma, that look that is studying every inch of Amy's insides and extracting her information that she'll soon begin to interrogate her with.

"I don't think I should leave you in this state," Rezna said.

"It's fine, Gma. Really. I just had a terrible nightmare. It happens."

"Lately, more frequently." Rezna sipped from her mug and shook her head. "I'm getting seriously worried about you, Amy."

"I…" Amy stirred in her seat, pulling her finger out of her cup. "I just want to know… I don't want to get stuck. Again."

Rezna nodded. She peered into her mug and took a deep breath.

"There are things around and away, my dear. Things you'll never reach in time. Things you'll never even know about. It is a fact though, that you can't save everyone, Amy."

Amy sank in her seat, taking a hold of Rezna's reaching hands and bringing them into her own. She found a look of sorrow for the first time in a long time in Rezna's eyes. Amy couldn't remember the last time she saw her Gma like this.

"A long time ago," Rezna started, "I was a part of a secret coven. We had encountered a being so powerful that there weren't any known weaknesses we could exploit. At that time, the mysteries of our world were still adolescent, therefore answers were barren."

"What type of beast was it?" Amy asked, but Rezna waved a hand and shook her head.

"I had studied everything and even anything unrelated, trying to learn about this monster. It wiped out half of my coven. Many others ran into hiding. All except for myself and a select few. I put all of my time and energy into knowing this beast. I traveled the world, learning of its origins, and eventually cast away my doubts as I thought I had stumbled on a solution."

Rezna took her hands away from Amy's and stared at them.

"One day, I came face to face with the beast. I survived. But it took someone who was of great importance to me. I vowed to never let it happen again as I learned from my mistakes, regrouped, and solidified the solution I had discovered."

Rezna took a sip from her mug. Her eyes returned on Amy's face.

Amy wiped a bit of sweat from her forehead. She could feel the aura burning within Rezna, which was unusual since it was normally undetectable.

"The point is, dear, you cannot save everything that you love without consequence. What you can do is prepare. That said, no amount of preparation will ever make you invincible, but that is why we train. We can overcome anything because of what's inside of us. Aura and soul are one."

Amy nodded.

I need to get better.

Rezna rose from her seat and placed her mug into the sink.

"I've got to run into the next town for some business, also supplies and such. I'll be gone for a day or two, at the request of the Mayor. Think you'll be alright? I can tell him to fuck off, my granddaughters had a bit of a ruckus."

Amy laughed. She got up and hugged Rezna.

"I'll be alright, Gma. Thank you."

Rezna nodded and made her way into the hall.

"Gma, wait."

Rezna turned back to face her.

"What happened to the beast?" Amy asked.

Rezna rubbed her chin and stood silent for a few seconds before making eye contact with Amy again.

"We silenced the beast."

55

Chapter Five

There was no turning back. Amy marched down every street with a revitalized spirit. What lay ahead of her may be unpleasant, but someone may still be out there torturing her quiet little town with their murderous spree. As much as she hated to admit it, this was her home, at least for the time being. One day, she'd venture outside its walls and explore the vast world and beyond. But right now, she has some detective work to do.

The cool air struck Amy like a butcher's knife on this busy October day. She had gotten a few stares as she moved through the town, but stayed out of sight once she left the main roads.

Reaching her and Demora's secret spot in the forest, Amy missed the warm feeling she usually got from Demora's aura when arriving here. Memories of their last training session came to mind. Then memories came of their last conversation. Their last argument. And then, of course, their unfortunate encounter.

Amy retraced their steps from their spot, down along the path by the water that brought them to that unpleasant moment in time. She wasn't sure exactly what she was looking for or what she'd end up finding, but she thought this was as good of a place to start as any other.

Ok, Professor Watson says that the first step in any investigation is to retrace your steps or the steps of the accused. Where are you now, Professor?

Amy stood in the spot she was when it all transpired. A chill went down her spine as she stared down at where she first saw that poor man's corpse. She wondered what she would've done if the man's aura had returned to its body.

That thought left her mind as she felt a tingle in her chest. That small tingle turned into a huge, burning pit and then some, as it seemed to jump around within her. It felt almost familiar, but she did not know why. What she knew was that this vast amount of energy was dangerous in its approach and Amy would not be caught frozen in time again.

Amy whipped around with her aura burning over her entire body, aiming her hands at whatever was on its way.

A detective approached with his E-Mak handgun drawn on her, his wide auburn eyes matching his curly hair. He took one hand off his weapon and held its palm up towards her.

"Whoa now, just slow it down there, Ms. Devine. I don't want to hurt you," he said.

Amy's chest heaved in and out. She had already messed up big time. But now wasn't the time to back down.

"I could say the same for you, Detective."

"Jimmy. Call me Jimmy. H-how are you doing that?" He pointed at her hands, his words coming out breathless.

Amy looked around, trying to understand what he meant before realizing no one besides Rezna and Demora had seen her aura.

"I'm surprised you haven't shot me yet."

Why the fuck would you say that, Amy?

"I just want to understand," detective Jimmy said. "I've never seen anyone control it before. Any Peculiars—"

"I am not a Peculiar. That's a derogatory term from people who don't understand what aura is and how it can be controlled."

The two stood silently. The cool air cut across Amy's sweaty throat as she swallowed a pint of her nerves. What would Gma say, no, what would Gma *do,* if she ended up in prison for such a foolish mistake? She'd rather be dead.

"Aura? I apologize," Jimmy said. "Listen, I happen to be a bit more… open-minded, you could say."

Amy's narrowed eyes tracked him.

"You're squeaky brown shoes."

"I beg your pardon?"

"Inside you. You're with aura as well. At the station the other day, that was you I felt."

"How—" Jimmy's mouth fell open. "How could you tell? That's—that's amazing! Incredible! Do you just…" He made a strange motion, waving his free hand in the air as though it was a drunk dragon flying over a castle.

"What are you doing?" Amy said.

"You know." He made some more crazy motions before Amy had enough.

"Look, I can just sense it. It takes a considerable amount of concentration, but I can feel the aura residing within you. It's like a sugar rushed child jumping around a tiny room."

Jimmy chuckled and mouthed 'incredible'. He raised his E-Mak in the air and slowly placed it in his holster.

"Against the better judgment of my superiors, I'm going to attempt to have a calm conversation with you, Ms. Devine."

"And how do you know you can just trust me?"

"Oh, I don't. Last time I did this, I got shot." Jimmy pointed to his left shoulder. "I can show you the wound if you're skeptical. I heal slow."

Attack him now? Or try another approach?

"Alright," Amy said, dropping her arms, and her aura disappeared. "Alright, Jim-my. You better not try anything. I can bring it back in a nanosecond."

"Let's slow down here." Jimmy walked around her and leaned against a tree. "First, I'd like for you to tell me exactly what you are doing here, Ms. Devine. This is still technically a crime scene."

"I was curious."

"Curious?"

"Curious." Amy crossed her arms as Jimmy placed his hands in his pockets.

"You're gonna have to give me more than that if you expect me to trust you."

"Who said I wanted your trust?"

"I just want to understand," Jimmy sighed.

"Well," Amy unfolded her arms. "I was trying to find out what really happened. Ever since that family was murdered, I've been feeling… off. I feel like my aura's been off." Admitting it out loud for the first time left Amy feeling cold, despite still feeling both her own and Jimmy's bustling energy still at heightened levels.

"What do you mean by off?"

"It's difficult to explain," Amy said. She could feel her thoughts trailing off but was not about to give this strange man any more info.

"I see," Jimmy nodded. "You've got an amazing talent, Ms. Devine, and it's going to be hard for me to watch that rotting in a cell."

Amy's aura burst to life, and she threw her arms forward. The aura around her hands mimicked them and closed into fists.

"Whoa, whoa, whoa! Bad joke, bad joke!" Jimmy waved his hands, tripping backward. "Let's bring it back to two. I think I have a way for us to help each other out. I'd like for you to help me do some tracking at the other crime scene."

"You mean the—"

"Yes. As the kids distastefully have been calling it—the Murder House. The Bates home. You help me there and your secret is safe with me. For now, at least. Let's be honest, I still have no idea what you're capable of. I won't hurt you unless push comes to shove."

Amy's aura subsided. She rolled her eyes.

"You couldn't hurt me."

"Do we have a deal?"

Amy studied him up and down, from his brown shoes up to his checkered brown jacket, to the brown pocket square in his breast pocket, then finally resting her eyes on his face.

"As long as we're clear, this little adventure stays between us two," Any said. "Besides, I know something *Peculiar* about you too. "

Jimmy walked up to her and held out his hand. Amy looked at it, confused, before nodding. Her aura illuminated her left hand while she shook his hand with her right.

"Got a lot of trust to work on, don't we?" Jimmy said.

"You wear a hell of a lot of brown."

"Goes well with the hair, don't you think?" Jimmy pointed at his hair.

"Not really." Amy walked off. "And don't try something funny. Remember—in a nanosecond."

Jimmy smiled and followed her.

After some time carefully moving through many high and sharp bushes, Amy and Jimmy walked along the edges of the town. It was a bit of work making sure someone didn't see them together, as the questions raised would be too great.

"My department was designed to investigate cases involving Peculiars," Jimmy said. "They've had me on house duty for the past couple of days. Keeping me out of the way, honestly. Let's just say I don't have the best reputation with my colleagues."

"Wouldn't picture you as a bad boy, Jimmy," Amy said.

"Ha. Well, I, uh, took some personal stake in the matters. I began feeling… differently, lately. Around the time the Bates couple was murdered," Jimmy said.

"It's called aura manipulation," Amy said, not wanting to say too much so soon, but sensing the aura inside him dwindling down a bit. She was also excited about teaching someone about her world. "Controlling your aura is sort of like lowering yourself until you're slightly outside your own consciousness. With the recent events in town, it feels like I slip past the state of comfort and lose track of where my aura ends and another begins. It's maddening."

"Sounds like it. How do you stop it then?"

"It's impossible to contain the energy inside, so you can only guide it. Those who can't control it are what you all call Peculiars. I admit, their power can frighten, as their energy seems to subdue their BP way below what you'd consider normal standards."

"BP?"

"Brainpower. It's what my Gma says is a part of the entire calculation." Amy bit her tongue, hating herself for mentioning Rezna. It was bad enough she exposed herself, but there was no need to bring her only family down with her.

"Ah, your grandmother can manipulate her—what you call it—aura, as well? You all seem to handle it well to not have been caught after all this time."

"Brainpower balanced with energy level equals control over your aura level," Amy said, ignoring his question.

"I see. So, if the aura grows too strong, it reduces your brainpower? How are you faring so well?"

"I've been training myself my whole life. My grandmother doesn't know," Amy lied. "My grandmother has a PhD in psychology, so she has her theories. But she doesn't know what I can do."

Jimmy looked her over. He nodded.

"The human body can only withstand so much energy," Amy continued. "Keeping up your physical body allows for you to handle more energy. Expanding your knowledge allows you to stay mentally capable. The combination strengthens your aura. Or else I would've gone mad years ago, I reckon."

"This is… a lot," Jimmy nodded. "I'd say groundbreaking! The way you're able to just manipulate all of that energy. Aura. Imagine when the world takes all that in!"

"That's what G—I hope for. You've seen what happens to those who try to bring understanding to Peculiars. They go missing."

"And your grandmother knows nothing about this?"

Amy hesitated. She had said too much but gotten away with being excited about sharing things she only ever discussed with Gma or Demora. But Demora always preferred the physical aspects, not being really interested in the whys and hows, while Gma was insistent on mental training and education.

"No."

As they reached the top of a small hill, Jimmy pushed Amy backward, motioning for her to duck, and they crouched within the bushes.

"What's happening?" Amy asked.

"What's Burt doing here?" Jimmy pointed towards the front of the Murder House, where Detective Burt from her interrogation the other day stood.

"Dammit. Listen, meet me back here at, say, 9 pm," Jimmy said. "Think you can do that?"

Amy hesitated, watching Jimmy's face.

"I promise, your secret is safe with me. I promise."

"Yeah," Amy said, slowly nodding. "Sure."

"I'll see you then." Jimmy stood and ran up the hill. He called out to and met Burt in front of the house, and they shook hands. Barely making out what was being said, Amy made her way back down the hill.

When she got home, Amy fed Archie before resuming her lost-in-thought trance. A lot had processed through her mind about the day's events. She sat on the couch in the living room, twirling her hair. A smile crept on her face at the thought of investigating her first crime scene, but it left, knowing a horrible crime had to take place in order for her to get this opportunity. In less than a week, two families perished.

That poor little girl. Parents gone, staying with their only relative. I know the story too well.

Amy looked over her shoulder, out the window.

Have I told him too much? Police will probably show up any second now... What would Gma say? What would she have to do?

"AND NOW!"

Amy whipped around as a screen made of ziccolights materialized out of the ZiccoLynx box. A small dot grew quickly on the black screen, shortly becoming a string of white words that spun rapidly forward.

"Do-dee-lee, do-dee-lee, do-dee-lee-doooo! Do-dee-lee, do-dee-lee, do-dee-lee-doooo! Le-Do-de-lee, do-de-lee, do-de-lee-doooo! Do-de-lee, do-de-lee, do-de-lee-doooo!"

A handsome, clean-cut man with an infectious, wide, wooden smile stared straight at Amy.

"Hey there De-veen Household! Welcome to The Basic Survival of Tomorrow's World... show! Glad you can join us as we venture to discover the best ways to navigate in our world today," the man on the screen said. He kept rambling on.

"ZiccoLynx, turn off personalization mode and power down TV, please," Amy said.

The screen flickered before going dark.

Amy sighed and slumped back on the couch, staring at her reflection in the many mirrors around the room. One day she'd have to talk to

Gma about her obsession with mirrors. Windows to the soul, she'd tell Amy. And it was so boring how these old antique mirrors were without ziccotech. No way of seeing how different outfits would look on her beforehand with that wonderful StyleTrial feature Demora loved raving about.

Amy stirred awake as she wiped her eyes clean. This gave her a clear look at her wrist device, and 08:55 PM flashed on her GCID.

Shit.

Moments later, Amy ran down the empty streets. As she gained speed, a familiar sensation built up in her legs. She steadied herself as though lifting the heaviest of weights.

A siren sounded off in the distance. Amy stopped and sighed, eying the traffic cam at the nearest corner.

They fixed it. Shit. Shit. Shit.

"STOP!" rang several robotic voices as a ring of policebots rolled in from all directions and surrounded her. One of the bots rolled up to Amy.

Amy stared at her reflection in the policebot's green, diamond-shaped lens. An emerald light beamed out of it and ran over her face, scanning down to her feet.

"Please present your identification," it asked.

Amy rolled her eyes. She stretched out her arm and touched her GCID's screen. The policebot brought its lens down over it.

"Do you realize how fast you were walking, ma'am?"

"No, but I reckon you've got a notch for that somewhere inside that chrome cranium."

"Please refrain from making the funnys, ma'am."

"Snarky little G1 model, eh?" Amy nodded at the green and white patch on its chest. "Haven't seen one of you—"

"Amy Devine, 17 years of age, Class Two-A," the G1 policebot said as random lines of data scrolled up in its lens. "You were running at

50 miles per hour. We will have to do an energy screen. Hold still, please."

"It's the wind, I swear," Amy said, rolling her eyes.

Another policebot rubbed an alcohol wipe on her forearm. A different bot's fingertip opened up, revealing a needle, and stuck it into Amy's arm for a few seconds before pulling it out.

"Energy levels at twenty-seven percent, Chief," it said. "Class Two-A, type A. No performance-enhancing drugs were detected."

"Confirmed," the Chief G1 policebot said. "I have detected no illegal items on you. You are free to go tonight, however, the reason for your accelerated speed is unknown. Be aware that you are scheduled for a full examination on the 17th of October 2180. I have sent a ticket for the amount of fifty UDs to your email on file. For your record, this is Strike Three. Have a splendid night Ms. Devine. And remember—"

The G1 Chief bot stood at attention as the other policebots lined up behind it and each raised a finger.

"If you have time to do the crime, then you have time to pay the fine," the policebots said in unison as Amy mocked each word. She made a gun-hand and fired at her head, rolling her eyes. The policebots rolled away as quickly as they came.

Amy exhaled a vast amount of air and checked her GCID: 09:00 PM. She broke into a jog, getting faster with each step. She stopped.

The U.C.

She dipped around a corner and into an alleyway.

Amy knocked a brick wall halfway down the alley. Someone pulled out a brick in the wall from the other side.

"Spanner in the works after Creaevix shit hit the fan, then took the piss after a bloody bender," Amy said into the hole.

The brick wall pushed out and then slid off to the side.

A shadowed figure beckoned Amy inside.

Inside the hole in the wall, the shadowed figure pushed the secret wall shut again. The figure walked into the darkness and a torch came to life.

Half his face lit by the torch, the old Under City dweller nodded at Amy. His dirty face forced a second-long smile before reverting to its scowl.

"Ah, the Devy girl," he said. "Been a while. Welcome back to the Under City. How's the moon shining these days?" He grunted and motioned for her to follow him.

"Clear but cloudy, Mr. J. You're a little grumpy today. Have you lost your weekly stipend again?"

"Argh, no no no," Mr. J said, waving his hands around. "It's these damn flickering lights. They expect me to splash out for what?!"

Amy followed him through the brick passageway. Torches on either side of the walls gave momentary glimpses of their faces while the darkness ate the rest. Mr. J doused his torch's fire and tossed it aside.

"I called one of 'em newbies to get it done, but you know how it goes. Moaning and whining, bitching, and nothing ever gets done. I've got my accolades, but ain't much a swot these days. Ain't got time to mess with such insignificance, I tell 'em."

"Ah, there've been more newcomers coming around then?"

"Yeah, yeah, the freeloadin' bastards," Mr. J said. "Got some gypsies speaking of dark energies looming. I haven't sensed a thing. Takin' the mickey o' me. Liars. Where ya headed?"

"Gotta get as close to Leveelady Lane as possible."

Mr. J led Amy around a corner, where several homeless people rested along the walls. Mr. J waved his hands at them as though swapping dozens of flies, and opened another door.

"You can get just about everything you need down here. Yet all these freeloaders seem to need is trouble. Trouble this, trouble that, trouble me. Nonsense."

They made their way down steps made of grass, wood, and metal parts. Reaching the bottom, Mr. J grabbed a torch off the wall, using it to light the dark passage ahead.

"And another thing. This part ain't got no light whatsoever! What's the point o' having extra hands around if no one lifts a finger! Bunch of scaredy cats…"

Mr. J unlocked and pushed through a huge metal door that led into the moonlight.

Amy stepped out, stopping in front of a stone staircase. She touched her GCID's screen a few times.

"A little something to help you get things going around here," Amy said.

"Ah." Mr. J pulled out a bulkier GCID and touched the screen. "Thanks, Devy. Always appreciated, this'll be going straight to the savings. Gotta finish the big project."

"See you later, Mr. J."

Mr. J closed the metal door, its exterior matching the bushy hill it was a part of.

Amy walked down the darkness of Leveelady Lane, where all the streetlights were out. Checked her GCID: 09:10 PM. She stopped in front of what is now known around town as the Murder House. She hugged her arms and looked up and down the quiet street. Only three other houses sat on either side, with plenty of space in between them.

"Hey!" Jimmy came from around the side of the house, flashlight in hand. "I was just checking the perimeter."

"Sorry, I got stopped."

"Oh yeah, I know. Saw the report come in. Remember, if you have time to do—"

"Please stop."

"And uh," Jimmy chuckled, "try to keep it down. I've already had to shoo away some wandering neighbors just 'taking out the trash'

Called in a little favor to get the lights cut, discreetly. As far as the neighbors know, maintenance will be ongoing for a few hours. Let's get this show on the road."

Jimmy unlocked the front door and led Amy inside.

As she walked in, Amy couldn't help but stare at the timely decor. The bright, mustard-colored walls were off-putting compared to the dark exterior of the house. Amy stepped into the living room, greeted with a grand fireplace that seemed to take over the room. Many photos sat on top of it on an ovular shelf facing the center of the room, where a cream-colored sofa and two wooden chairs with soft turquoise cushions lay. Amy ran her hand over the top of one chair and gazed over at the soft white light humming from a corner lamp.

"It's upstairs," Jimmy said. His finger pointed up, and Amy's eyes followed it. The bright yellow ceiling was surely opposite the dark horrors that had taken place on the upper level.

As they crept up the stairs, Amy's shallow breaths were more a force of concentration than of fatigue. She took her hand off the banister and rubbed her fingertips together, wiping away the dust. It was such a crime that a lovely home has been falling under such stress.

They entered the hall on the second floor, and Jimmy cut off his flashlight and turned to Amy.

"Alright, so how does this work?" Jimmy asked. "I cut this bad boy out so it wouldn't interfere with your light show." He waved the flashlight around.

"No sweat. Your little flashlight won't affect my aura."

"Do you… feel anything?"

"Give me a sec." Amy closed her eyes and took a deep breath. After a few minutes, she reopened her eyes and shook her head.

Jimmy leaned against the banister, throwing his flashlight up and catching it before turning to face her. "Nothing?"

"No. I haven't got a great handle on it yet. It seems to creep up on me when I'm least expecting it or when I'm being threatened, apparently."

"Take that," Jimmy said, swinging his flashlight as though hitting her on the head.

"What are you doing?" Amy asked.

"Sorry, nervous joke. Dark places give me the creeps. I'll uh, turn this back on," he said as he cut his flashlight back on. "Lemme show you where it happened."

Amy followed him to the end of the hall. Jimmy opened a door at the end of it and Amy watched him disappear inside. She stopped just short of the door and looked back at the door she just passed. She turned around and opened it.

The inside of this room looked as though a rainbow exploded, as its walls were coated with many colors splattered against them. The slick white furniture inside seemed out of place, along with the spotless white-tiled floor, with several toys, markers, and some clothing littering the countertops of everything else in the room.

Amy ran her fingers across the dresser to her left, surprised to find not a lick of dust coating it.

"What's up?" Jimmy said, popping his head in the room. "You got something?"

"I'm just admiring the little artist."

"Come check out the main room." Jimmy walked away, pushing the door more open.

A piece of paper behind the door waved from the door push. Amy closed the door a bit and pulled the paper off the door.

It was a drawing done with a combination of crayon and marker. There were so many colors on it, it was almost impossible to make out what was up and could easily be mistaken as random colors diced onto the page.

Amy narrowed her eyes and made out a house that looked very much like the outside of the one she was in. Amy folded the paper and slipped it into her pocket before exiting the room.

When she entered the master bedroom, Amy turned to look back down the hall, feeling like a pair of eyes was on her. Nothing. She closed the door.

The master bedroom was a lot like the exterior of the house. Dark and elegant. The beautiful craftsmanship of the furniture accented the minimalist look of the room within.

Amy thought she felt a tingle in her chest, but she chucked it down to be her usual nerves when exploring the insides of a new building.

"We found the wife here," Jimmy said as he shined his light on the bare mattress and frame. "She was a sound sleeper, so it's likely she never woke up. The sheets we took had no traces of any DNA besides the two parents. Their daughter apparently never entered the room, said it scared her. The little girl was fast asleep, never woke up through the night."

Amy moved around the room, wiping her finger against the many surfaces throughout. She got down on her knees and looked under the bed.

"No security footage?"

"None. Their ZLynx box record was clear. Nothing but a family picnic several weeks beforehand."

Amy got back up on her feet, meeting Jimmy's raised eyebrow.

"What are you looking for?" Jimmy asked. "We've already swept this room a hundred times."

"Well, the thing is, we never really know what it is we're looking for until we find it." She could axe herself for that cheesy line. "It's a bit weird that this house has been catching a ton of dust buildup. All except for that other room."

"You mean their daughter's room?"

Amy nodded. The face Jimmy made as she had just told him something he was unaware of silently pleased her. Until this point,

Amy felt like a ride-along, but now she was truly living out a childhood fantasy of being a detective.

A thump against the wall made them both turn to face the closet in the room.

Jimmy drew his gun before moving towards it.

Amy brought her hands up, ready to attack.

Jimmy opened the closet. He waved some clothes around inside as Amy peeked over his shoulder. A few shuffles later, a sock came tumbling out of the closet, landing feet away from Amy. A screeching sound came from within the bundle.

"Wait, don't—" Jimmy said as Amy reached down and yanked the sock upwards.

"What are you doing here, Arch?" Amy sighed and shook her head down at Archie. Archie's eyes looked from Amy to Jimmy. He let out a couple of small 'coos'.

"Looks like there's a small hole down here," Jimmy said, still shuffling inside the closet. "Might lead straight outside."

"Come here." Amy picked up Archie and put him on her shoulder.

Archie opened his feet and a piece of metal dropped onto Amy's arm. She picked it up and studied it. She scanned the room as Jimmy continued shuffling about.

Amy walked over to the window across from the head of the bed. She held the metal piece up to the window frame, but the markings did not match. A glimmer caught her eye, and she peered down into the darkness in front of the home, into the tall swaying flowers of the front lawn.

Archie flew on top of Amy's head and bore a hole into the room door. He backed up, whimpering, and flew onto her shoulder, taking a strand of her hair with him.

"Ah! Arch, what the—" Amy grabbed her chest, faced the room door, and stumbled to the side, grabbing a hold of the bed frame.

"Are you alright?" Jimmy said, moving to her side.

"No…" Amy looked at Archie, then nodded towards the door. "Someone's out there."

Jimmy aimed his E-Mak at the door as he moved towards it.

"This is Detective Wimblestyn of the JFPD! Put your hands behind your head and step six feet back!"

There were three slow, precise knocks at the door. Amy stepped back while Jimmy pressed forward. Archie flew into the sleeve of Amy's jacket, quaking under it.

A white light came from underneath the door. A stream of black light crept on top of it.

"Jimmy, watch out!" Amy's eyes grew orange. Her aura spun around her body into a giant ball of energy that spiraled around them. The rotating energy ball grew to the ceiling at a much quicker rate than Amy had intended until it touched every corner of the bedroom.

The door threw itself open. The black and white light from the other side flushed into the room, the blinding energy shoving Amy's protective aura sphere further and further back.

Amy braced her feet, creating craters on the old floor beneath her. But it wasn't enough.

The black and white aura blew Amy's aura sphere straight through the side of the house. Amy's aura dropped as she and Jimmy landed flat on their backs.

Amy's eyes opened just a hair. In the house's opening, a figure stood in the darkness. The figure stepped back, disappearing inside.

Amy's eyes closed as Jimmy's faint cries filled the night.

Chapter Six

Amy's eyelids slid up, revealing the whites of her eyeballs before her irises rolled back to front and center. The blades of the ceiling fan kept a steady rhythm that she counted off in her head as she sat up, trying to ignore the ringing, sharp pain right above either earlobe.

Jimmy snored, sitting in a chair at her bedside, with a string of drool falling out of his open mouth.

"Jimmy. Jimmy." Her soft, hoarse voice called, but Jimmy only stirred in his chair. "Jimmy. Jim-my!"

"Wai-what-what?" Jimmy stomped, jerking forward in his chair. His head shot from side to side before falling on Amy. He wiped his mouth and rubbed his eyes.

"You're up, you're alright. You scared the crap of me. I-I-I was driving to the hospital, but then I didn't know how to explain. Your aura kept flickering in and out, I just brought you here, and then you said you were cold and I made you tea, but then you were burning up actually so I cut the fan on and kept putting the ice packs on you but they kept melting! And then I tossed you in the tub—not actually tossed—and I threw a bunch of ice and had to run to the store and got about a dozen bags and tossed them over you. And it seemed to work and then I made more tea—for myself this time and eventually you cooled down and I brought you here and had this thing hooked up to your arm and I just—"

"Jimmy, shut up. Thank you. Really, you made the right call." Amy pulled the temperature band off her forearm and shifted her legs onto the floor. She cleared her throat and checked her wrist device. "I used a considerable amount of energy last night. I can barely feel it. Using that much in such a short time can cause some irregular effects that are a lot more dramatic in appearance than they actually are."

Amy massaged her throat. Her hand hit her pocket, and she felt the outline of something. She reached in and pulled out the metal piece that Archie had found.

"Almost forgot, Archie, found this somewhere in the house."

"Hm." Jimmy took the metal piece from her and studied it. "I'll run it through the lab. Guess I'll have to run it through Burt first. He's been calling me. News traveled fast of the enormous crater in the side of the Murder House."

"You're working with Detective Burt now?"

"Oh crap, right—His superior, Detective Skitinsky, was found dead in his home late last night. Heart attack."

"Skitinsky's dead?"

"Yeah, it's crazy. Just saw him yesterday morning. Are you alright there?" Jimmy pointed at Amy's hand, which still massaged her throat.

"Last night, what happened after I blacked out?"

"Oh, you, uh, got this nasty shake. You started yelling and just thrashing around at one point. Probably from the fever."

"What?" Amy's eyes went wide and she jumped up, ran over to her desk, and pulled a mirror out of the drawer. She opened her mouth wide, checking the insides at all angles, trying to see down her throat.

"Are you alright there?" Jimmy said.

Amy kept her back to him as she held the mirror down, her own reflection's sad eyes staring right back at her.

In the kitchen, Amy carried two steaming cups from the sink to the table, giving one to Jimmy. He nodded as Amy sat down across from him.

"I had throat cancer when I was a baby. Doctors had to keep me sedated most of the time since you can't really tell a baby not to scream or cry. When I got older, they cured it, but it left my throat in shambles." Amy pointed at her throat. "They installed a device that keeps it in shape, but I can't yell or even speak above a certain level. The tea helps but not always."

Amy drank from her cup and looked away from Jimmy. "Years ago, Gma and I got into a bit of a row. I had stolen a portable karaoke machine because I wanted to pursue singing. Music was always so beautiful to me. The sounds that instruments and voices create. Gma wouldn't listen and seemed more upset about that than the theft. It was a nasty bit, the both of us going at it. The last I remember was my head jerking back. I woke up in the hospital. My throat was scorching. That's when she told me everything and they installed the device."

Amy petted Archie's head as he nestled into the inner groove of her arm. "The first thing I saw when I woke up was her face. I had never seen her look so scared before in my life and I immediately promised her I would never bring up the topic again. Kept that promise, yet something kept pulling me into this dream. Lyrics would form in my head, and everything around me was a symphony. So I did some research and trained my voice, trying to create a style that wouldn't be so much of a strain. I thought I was onto something. One day I went to a club in another town. Was able to whip up a fake ID and a silly disguise. When I first got on stage, I thought everything was going great. Until the boos came pouring in."

Amy's smile grew smaller. "My voice gave out on me and my throat cracked. After that night, I gave up on that dream. But, I still write. I just write lyrics." Amy sipped from her mug. "Are you American? Had to ask. That accent is a bit off."

"Yeah." Jimmy laughed, then sipped from his own cup. "You know I come from a line of glassmakers," Jimmy said. "No one had much use for the craft once technology took over. The era of ziccotech took over, and it replaced everything with that technology. But something was missing. Something that could not only handle the energy that tech needed but was also durable enough while still providing a clear experience." He walked over to the window and knocked on it. "Now we have these nearly impenetrable windows in almost every home around the world. All because my family didn't quit. Even your, ahem, Glass Communication International Device."

Jimmy's smile stretched across his face as he pointed at Amy's GCID while wagging his other finger in the air.

Amy rolled her eyes.

"They couldn't pre-install mine because of the risk of interference," Amy said. She raised her GCID close to her throat. "Funny how that works."

"I, uh, didn't want to ask, but that makes sense," Jimmy said. He waved his hand around the room. "But anyway, I always wanted to help people by solving crimes. I mean, there's so much in our world left unknown, and given everything that's happened, we need to prevent horrible events from taking place again. There hasn't been a war throughout the world in over seventy years, but there's still so much to do. But of course, they expected me to follow the family blueprint."

Jimmy put his cup in the sink. "Then my uncle Rogers went missing. Now, he's a free soul that goes off now and then working on something new, but this was different. So I went against my family's wishes and made my way into the police academy. The rest of my family wasn't all that concerned about my uncle's disappearance, but I wasn't giving up on my theory."

"Theory?"

"I feel he's in some kind of trouble. He never left without saying goodbye to me. Until that one night, he did. I've got to find him… I owe it to him. For everything."

Jimmy pulled a small bottle out of his inside jacket pocket.

"I've got a secret, too. Approaching my twentieth birthday, I started getting sick. Doctors couldn't explain a thing. But my uncle knew… something. I could tell he didn't want to say too much, but he started giving me this medication to take for it.

"Once I started taking it, things got better. I take it twice a day. It keeps my nerves in check. I've… I've always been afraid of becoming like the ones you see on TV. I grew up knowing those like you as Peculiars, and now I had the same symptoms you get right before you lose it. Right before you lose all control. So I've taken my medication ever since. Uncle Rogers knew something more about this whole thing. It's the reason I didn't drag you away in cuffs. I knew there was something going on inside that I couldn't explain. Seeing you have a handle on it gave me hope."

"Your aura awakens when it reaches its prime, at twenty," Amy said. "There's no stopping it, no resisting it. But with training, you can guide it to great use."

Jimmy nodded. "I know that now."

"Can I show you something?"

In the morgue prep room, Amy opened the door to the wooden storage closest and led Jimmy inside.

"Wow, a 2031 BoxIt Simulator!" Jimmy said, pointing back to where they came from. "Z-light speed on that baby must be ancient."

"Keeps up well half the time. Had a friend help overclock it. Here it is."

She stooped down to the wooden trunk and clicked it open. Jimmy's eyes went wide.

"This is… incredible!" Jimmy put his hand inside and pulled out a shimmering piece of broken glass. Various colors of light danced across the glass surface.

"Don't touch it! I don't know what it is," Amy said.

"It's just glass. Well, it's a bit more advanced, actually. This is like a project my uncle was working on. A sort of protective glass that uses energy to reflect damage. I know my family planned to lease it out to a few companies… but uncle Rogers was against the idea. How'd your grandmother get a hold of it?"

"Gma keeps a bunch of things she encounters on her travels here. She doesn't say much about what's in here. She always says 'One day you'll know all.'"

"Remarkable." Jimmy twirled the glass close to his face.

"Can you fix it?" Amy asked.

"I could take a crack at it. Get it? Crack?"

"You're a riot."

"What?" Jimmy chuckled as he stood up. "I don't know if we should tamper with your Gma's things. Maybe ask her first?"

"C'mon, I'd like to surprise her. And I see that cheeky, little look. You're dying to get your hands on it."

Jimmy laughed. "I'd be lying if I said I wasn't intrigued."

"What would uncle Rogers do?"

"Fine, I'll take a stab at it," Jimmy said, taking one of the glass shards and stabbing the air with it.

Amy shook her head and walked out of the room, leaving Jimmy mouthing 'What?'

Upstairs, Amy threw her hands towards Archie's bag of Bat Trix that had spilled on the floor.

"Archie…" Amy stared at her open hand, but nothing happened. "Shit."

"What is it?"

"I spent so much energy last night, I think my aura is depleted."

"It's WHAT?!" Jimmy's eyes and mouth went wide. "Holy Callisto, what the hell—"

"Jimmy. Chill. This can happen, it's completely normal. My aura is just taking a little break, that's all. Although I hope I can get it back before Gma returns. Or she'll have questions."

Amy opened the front door. Jimmy carried a plastic container in his arms out the door.

"Let me know when you can get the glass reformed or whatever," Amy said, pointing at the container.

"Will do. You sure you'll be alright?"

"I'm chill, I swear. We need to get you some loofy to relax you."

"Oh no, I've never smoked the ol' reefer!" Jimmy's nose twitched. "Is that raspberry I smell?"

"Take it." Amy holds out a small ZenDrop in a purple wrapper.

"That's a rare one," Jimmy said, taking the candy.

"Yeah, I got a guy in the UnderCity. It's still so hard to get the lemon-flavored ones. They always run out first. They're my faves, you know."

"I'll uh, hold on to this one for safekeeping." Jimmy wrestled the container under one arm while pocketing the purple ZenDrop.

"Oh, wait!" Amy pulled out and unfolded the drawing she had taken from the Murder House. "I found this in that little girl's room. I don't know why but it could be important."

"You stole evidence?" Jimmy put his free hand on his hip.

"Hardly seemed important since your lot left it behind. The building in the drawing, it's just like the Murder House itself. And there were some markings on it that I couldn't make out."

"Hm." Jimmy took the drawing from Amy. "Suppose I could take a trip up there next."

"Right now? I'll come with!"

"Well not right, right now, been a long night and all. And absolutely not! You held up your end of the bargain helping me out at the house, your secrets—emphasis on the s—are safe with me."

"Jimmy, think about it. What you and I saw at that house no one else did. I can help in ways your force can't. If you give up this lead, they'll put someone else on it and keep you out."

"Amy, no—"

"Remember what you told me. Remember why you joined the force in the first place."

"I know, but I—"

"What would uncle Rogers do?"

Jimmy exited the driver's seat and slammed his door. He moved right past a beaming Amy.

"Quaint little car by the way." Amy took a second to study the exterior of Jimmy's 2033 brown Maserati. "Come on now Jimbo, cheer up."

"Do *not* call me that," he said as they approached a beautiful two-story home. Jimmy rang the doorbell.

The door opened and Norma Jones' raised eyebrow met Amy first then stared Jimmy up and down.

"How can I help you, Detective?"

"Good—" Jimmy checked his wrist, "— late morning Mrs. Jones. I'm Detective Wimblestyn and this here is—"

"Amy Devine. Seventeen years of age, granddaughter of Rezna Devine. Living at 267 Bleecker Lane, and an avid watcher of the graves. What's she—what are you both doing here? Also, it's *Ms.* Jones. I'm separated."

"Oh." Jimmy cleared his throat. "Well, Ms. Jones, I'm here because I had a few questions relating to the unfortunate crimes against your family, in relation to their home and such. Ms. Devine here is a key witness in a recent similar case. May we come in?"

Jimmy sat on the couch as Amy walked around the living room, studying the various ornaments that sat on the fireplace, end tables, and wall shelves.

Amy clutched her chest and her eyes lingered on a photograph of a young boy, sitting on the fireplace. She stole a glance at Jimmy. He returned a raised eyebrow.

"I suppose you're done snooping around, Devine?" Ms. Jones said, handing Jimmy a steaming cup.

"None for yourself?" Jimmy asked.

Ms. Jones waved a hand. "Nothing I make comes close to what my butler, Fegaro, whips up for me."

"I suppose this is okay though?" Jimmy chuckled, raising his cup, but cleared his throat as Ms. Jones' eyes narrowed on him. "Kidding. So the Bates house—"

"I'm still trying to understand the connection with Ms. Devine here in relation to my case?" Ms. Jones said, watching Amy move around the room.

"Well, Ms. Devine here recently came in contact with a suspect in another case that may relate to the Bates murders. You could say I'm multitasking today, seeing as how this case is of the utmost importance to me and I am personally dedicated to getting to the bottom of it."

Amy stood at Jimmy's side, nodding at what seemed to be a satisfied face on Ms. Jones.

Ms. Jones' niece entered the room with a blue ball in hand. The small silver-eyed girl looked at Amy sideways and smiled.

"I quite love that jacket you're wearing," the little girl said.

"Thank you," Amy replied.

"This is Detective Wimblestyn and Ms. Devine," Ms. Jones said.

"You can call me Amy. What's your name?"

"My name is Issa."

"Well, it's quite nice to meet you, Issa."

"Perhaps the children can run along and play while the adults engage in conversation," Ms. Jones said.

Amy grilled Ms. Jones and the woman gifted her with a small smile on the end of her mouth.

Jimmy put his hand on Amy's arm, laughing. "You know I could use a little harder drink. Amy, maybe you can see what Issa's been up to."

"Come on, Amy, I'll show you my room!" Issa ran up to Amy and dragged her off by the hand. Amy shot a look back at Jimmy before turning the corner.

"You know, Norma can be a bit of a bore at times, so don't you mind her," Issa said. She led Amy up the stairs and down a long, gold and white hallway full of elegance.

"Norma, eh?"

"She's my aunt, but only on paper. She surely doesn't act like one." Issa pushed her room door open and ushered Amy inside.

Amy did a small circle, taking in the many colors dominating the white room. The window was only recognizable because it was open. There were dozens of papers laying across the bed with even more markers spread across them. The room of the floor was spotless while everything else had gone through at least three wars with crayons.

A group of dolls sat in a ring under the window. In the center of them sat a single candle.

"Am I late for the ceremony?" Amy pointed at the circle of dolls.

"They're for good luck. Keep out the bad spirits." Issa sat on a white circular carpet in the middle of the floor and beckoned for Amy to join her. "So what is it you *do,* Ms. Devine?"

"You can call me Amy." Amy sat across from her as Issa began doodling on a blank sheet. "What do you mean by *do?*"

"Like for work and stuff. Are you a detective too?"

"No, I'm in Intermissionary school. I'm just helping the other detective figure some things out for his case."

"I see. I used to help my dad with things at work. He was a lab rat at the police department. When I turned eight this year, I was finally old enough to help him in his office for a bit. It was fun."

Amy watched the girl color a complex-looking web with big dots connecting the lines without lifting her hands or eyes off the paper once. Similar drawings in various colors hung along every wall of the room.

"What are you drawing there, Issa?"

"Oh, it's just something I dreamt about. My dad said it was my overly creative and beautiful mind. He told me that all the time. I miss dad." A tear fell onto the paper. Issa stopped coloring to wipe her face.

"I know. You miss your mom too, I bet."

"Oh yes, lots. I used to wake her up every morning by poking her with my crayon. I'd show her the new thing I drew. She loved that."

"Issa," Amy pulled the drawing out of her jacket and unfolded it, "do you remember this drawing?"

Issa's eyes widened and a big smile grew. "Oh yes, absolutely! I drew that the night before..." Issa's head went down and she went back to working on her drawing.

"You know Issa..." Amy shifted herself closer to Issa. "I lost my parents a long time ago before I was even old enough to understand what happened to them. If I had been old enough, and I had any information that could help them, I would absolutely use it to help find out exactly what happened to them."

Issa hunched her back as she dipped lower to her drawing, darkening some lines. Amy drew back a little and admired the walls of the room.

"I like to write lyrics. It comforts me."

"Oh!" Issa looked up at Amy, smiling. "Like music lyrics, do you mean? I love music."

"Yeah. It's one of my favorite things to do."

"Drawing is one of mine, in case you couldn't already tell."

The two shared a laugh. Amy moved closer to Issa.

"I would absolutely love to help the nice detective downstairs find out what happened to your parents. I just wish I could find something to help me."

Issa put her marker down and bolted up, past Amy. Amy bit her lip and put her head down. She had pushed too hard.

The door shut behind her and Amy looked over her shoulder. Issa ran back to her and sat crossed-legged in front of her, her hands shaking as the girl bore a hole into the door behind them.

"Are you alright Issa?"

Issa stared back into Amy's eyes. She shook her head. Amy moved closer and put a steady hand over the girl's shivering ones.

"What's wrong? You can tell me."

Issa sat quietly for what felt like hours to Amy before exhaling.

"I mentioned the bad spirits. Well, I think something's wrong with Aunt Norma."

"What do you mean?"

"She… acts strange… sometimes. It scares me."

"What strange things does she do, Issa?"

"Sometimes…" Issa shook her head. "It's like, something takes over her." Issa looked past Amy and stared at the door. "She's here."

Ms. Jones slammed the door open with one hand, her eyes on her niece. A startled Amy stood fast, dropping the drawing she held.

"You little witch," Ms. Jones said. "Where is it?!"

Jimmy ran up behind her, holding his hand out to Amy, whose eyes pierced into Ms. Jones.

"That's quite uncalled for," Amy said.

"Stay out!" Ms. Jones said, pointing at Amy. Her eyes returned to Issa and walked towards her. "I said where is it, Issa?! Dammit girl, tell me now!" Before Issa could answer, Ms. Jones turned to Jimmy.

"This girl has been chucking out my good bottles of liquor for weeks!" She turned back to Issa. "And I'm sick of it!"

"It's not me!" Issa said as she stood up, her nose flaring. "It's not me!"

Jimmy stepped in between the aunt and niece. "I'm sure there's a reasonable explanation for this Ms. Jones."

"She's a little thief! And I will not tolerate her behavior any longer!"

"It's not me! It's not me!"

"You said it isn't you." Amy knelt down to Issa. "Is someone—or something else doing it?"

Issa's eyes went wide. Her mouth opened.

"Get out." Ms. Jones' eyes darted between Jimmy and Amy as she pointed out the door. "Both of you, get out right this instant!"

"Now hold on Ms. Jones," Jimmy said, holding a hand up to Ms. Jones, "if Issa has something to say that'll be important to our investigation, then I'll need to hear it."

Amy could hug Jimmy but her hardened stare was too focused on Ms. Jones and the pure hatred she saw in the woman's face.

Issa looked from her aunt to Jimmy to Amy. Amy gave the girl a little nod. She could almost feel the nerves building up in the girl, but she could feel something else hiding somewhere in this house as well. And that thing even drowned out Jimmy's bustling aura.

"No." Issa looked back at Jimmy. "There's nothing I can say about that."

"Are you sure?" Jimmy asked.

Issa took a second then nodded.

"There you have it." Ms. Jones' nose went up to the ceiling. "Now get out with the lot of you."

As Jimmy drove away from the Jones' house, Amy stared out the window back at the house. She stared into Issa's window, hoping the girl would pop up and send her some last-minute signal. But it never came.

As they drove down the road, Jimmy's voice drove in and out of Amy's ears.

"She went to pour us a glass out of her good bottle, as she calls it, then went ballistic seeing that it was missing. It all happened so fast."

"We can't just leave the girl there, that woman is unstable!"

"She hasn't technically done anything wrong Amy, and we can't just pull the girl out of the house without reasonable doubt for her safety."

"Her barking alcoholic aunt isn't enough reason?"

"We need something concrete. *Concrete.* It just won't fly. I'm sorry."

"This is maddening," Amy said, rolling her eyes as she pushed herself deep into her seat. "She was about to tell me something. She said her aunt had been acting weird. She was going to tell me more, Jimmy."

"I hear you, I really do. We don't have a case yet. I did get some info though."

"What's that?"

"PC, uncover all the information you can on Thomas Jones of 386 Denver Road. Send all files to Home." Jimmy nodded at the screen on the dashboard as it lit up. "The estranged husband. They're currently separated. Seems they had a falling out the night after the murders. We were digging into it when she suggested opening a new bottle."

"So you think the uncle may play a part?"

"If I know anything about uncles, they always play a part."

Sometime later, Jimmy's car pulled up in front of Amy's home. Jimmy sighed and looked at Amy.

"Look, I'll see what I can dig up on the husband and let you know. I do appreciate your help here Amy, but we've still got to do this by the book or none of it matters, alright?"

Amy nodded. She turned her jacket collars up against her face and got out of the car.

"In the meantime, keep a low profile. And stay out of Norma Jones' sight. I'll see what I can do about that little glass project you gifted me as well. We got a deal?"

"Deal," Amy said. At least she wasn't being completely dismissed.

"Stay out of trouble!" Jimmy drove off.

Amy gave a small smile as she watched Jimmy's odd brown Maserati drive up the road and turn a corner, humored at how out of place it was compared to the parked cars it passed.

Maybe he's alright after all.

Maybe not.

Down the opposite end of the block, a car's engine roared up. The car and its blank license plate drove past Amy. Although Amy waited for it to follow Jimmy, it didn't, and she watched it until it disappeared in the distance. Amy peered up and down the block before hiding behind her jacket collars and running up her front steps.

Chapter Seven

Amy met up with Demora the next morning in front of Highbridge Intermissionary School. They gave each other small smiles before walking up the concrete steps. Archie flew off of Amy's shoulder when she reached the top and they bid each other farewell.

As they entered the school, the best friends did their best to avert their eyes from the gazing eyes around them.

"This couldn't be any worse," Demora leaned over and whispered to Amy.

"Agreed." Amy smiled. That was the first word, apart from texts, spoken to her since their encounter. She welcomed Demora's cheekiness and felt relieved it made its return. "Wish we could leave right now."

"You're the one who made us sign up for seven courses."

"Hey!" An Asian student with big round glasses jumped in front of them. "Hey Amy, it's Amy, right? Of course, it is," he said, wiping his glistening hands on his trousers.

"Hey, Hideko?" Amy replied. These were the first words they've ever exchanged and his excitement overwhelmed her.

"Is it true? You ran into a Peculiar?"

Behind him down the hall, a small group of students watched them. Amy rolled her eyes. "I can't comment on anything, it's an open case."

"But it's true? It is then, isn't it? Wow. Just wow. For my dissection, may I ask you—"

"Goodbye Hideko." Amy walked past him, with Demora close behind.

"Don't go." Hideko's raspy voice said behind them.

"What?" Amy and Demora said.

"Oh, don't go in there yet," he said, pointing to a classroom door behind him. "Gina is getting chewed out by Mr. Perry and it's a bit nasty if you ask me."

Demora turned to Amy. "The hell is Perry doing here? He teaches at Hemlith."

Amy explained the weird departure of Professor Watson right before the classroom door in front of them slammed open. Gina came dashing out, chucking her bag over her shoulder. She wiped tears from her face as she ran by Amy and down the hall.

Amy turned back to Mr. Perry, wiping his glasses with a cloth. He smiled and beckoned them inside.

"Ah come in, children. Come in."

Amy and Demora entered the class. As Amy headed to her seat, Demora faced Mr. Perry.

"What was that about?" Demora asked with her hand on her hip.

"Oh, that was just a bit of rough news for Ms. Gallagher. Little academic pow-wow."

"Gina's got the best grades in the class," Amy chimed in.

"Well, I—" Mr. Perry shrugged and chuckled. "I couldn't tell you otherwise. Sometimes we have outside influences, perhaps at home, that distract us from our objectives. Couldn't tell you otherwise." He pointed at Amy and winked, approaching her desk. "You, however, are sure to stay on track. You have a dazzling future ahead of you. If you really want it."

Perry tapped his glasses on Amy's desk before turning back to point them at Demora.

"It's really nice to see you back, Ms. Corbyn-McDonald."

After class, Demora walked out of the classroom, ahead of Amy.

"Ugh, that guy gives me the absolute creeps. Pervy vibes," Demora said. "It's a wonder why the three bumbling bitches weren't in class today. What are they up to?"

"Who cares?" Amy said.

"Hey, Amy!" A freckled-nosed girl ran up to Amy, an actugraphic camera floating beside her. "Hideko confirmed you saw a Peculiar! A real-life Peculiar! Can I run your story in the school's column?"

"No," Amy said, walking right past the girl.

"Can I at least get some quotes?" The freckled-nosed girl asked. "NoteBud, quote 'No', end quote, return, hyphen, Amy Devine. Sole survivor of a Peculiar attack."

"Give 'em a week, they'll back off," Demora said.

"You know damn well this town's too boring to let a bit of drama go free," Amy said. "Besides, that's easy for you to say. I don't see anyone pestering you."

"My proper parents threatened the Mayor, so he made sure the Dets kept me anonymous."

"Lucky you."

"It's not my fault they work for the County Committee."

They moved down the busy hall and turned a corner, coming nose to nose with the Lockheart Girls.

"Well…" Madeline moved ahead of her comrades and right up to Demora. "Look who dragged her ugly snout back to school."

"I'd be keen for another little vacay, you snotty nose bitch," Demora said, pressing her shoulder right into Madeline's.

"Ladies!" Headmistress Graves strolled up behind them all, her arms behind her back. "Ms. Corbyn-McDonald, I'd like to speak with you in my office. Now."

"I'll catch you in history, Ames," Demora said. She straightened up and followed Graves. "Yes, Headmistress."

Madeline got side by side with Amy. "Watch your back."

Kassandra and Tilly did an about-face in the opposite direction, while Madeline's eye lingered in Amy's before following suit.

Amy continued her walk alone, trying her best to ignore the stares she got, but without Demora there it just seemed harder. She sped up, but the sound of the ringing school siren took enough attention off of her.

"Good morning, students and faculty. I hope you are striving for your best in every class today. If we could have Malcoby Holders, Fenwick Dunly, and Earlena Edmunds come to the office of the Headmistress, please. Once again, Malcoby Holders, Fenwick Dunly, and Earlena Edmunds, please come to the Headmistress' office please. Thank you, students, and have a wonderful day."

Shortly after, Amy's head laid flat on her crossed arms as she stared at the chalked WORLD HISTORY on the board ahead, wondering why Demora wasn't at the empty desk beside her. The drawling voice of the four-foot blond Mr. Ribbers seemed to regurgitate the same sentence repeatedly.

"Ms. Devine?"

Amy picked her head up as it shook off the long note that her last name had just suffered through. "Yes, Mr. Ribbers?"

"Ms. Devine, perhaps you can tell us why it's important we go over the origin and structure of the World Committee as we near the end of the calendar year."

Kill me.

"They found the World Committee in 2051 after Callisto created the Doctrine of Peace Among Nations." Amy rolled her eyes as Mr. Ribbers put a finger up to silence her and pointed to another student.

"The people of the six regions," the chosen student recited, "The Americas, Africa, Australia, Europe, Asia, and Antarctica—each elected one Governor to represent them at the World Committee Table."

Mr. Ribbers put a finger up and pointed to yet another student.

"At the start of the new year," the student began, "the Committee overlooks each of their regions and discusses needs for change. All for the betterment of our community."

"Very good, Carlton! Now Ms, Devine, if you'll please come up and write that on the board so we can help you, and everyone else, remember!"

Amy's feet dragged across the tiled floor, the tips of her feet bumping along behind her with every step. She took the piece of chalk Mr. Ribbers offered her and wrote on the board.

"I was going to finish," she whispered.

Mr. Ribbers waved his hand towards the board, and Amy put the chalk to it. The snickers came in from behind her as she wrote, but they turned into groans as Mr. Ribbers instructed the class to recite the same message.

Amy shook her head as she checked her vibrating GCID.

Talk later. I left early. Sorry.

She's still avoiding me.

Amy threw her bag over her shoulder and ran down the school steps.

Wanting some alone time, Amy made her way towards the opposite direction of her way home. This section of town was always a peaceful distraction from the ramblings of Jadesfeld's townsfolk. Shops closed early, and no residences were around for a few blocks.

After her usual turns, Amy stopped at the corner of the street and glared as Madeline and Tilly walked her way.

Amy turned and walked down the parallel street, using her peripheral to see if she was being followed. She cut around the next corner—her stomach meeting Kassandra's fist. Amy buckled to her knees, her bag falling over next to her.

"Well well, seems we've found a stray in need of an adjustment, girls," Madeline said, stepping right in front of Amy.

"Little lonely straaaay." Tilly giggled and sang over and over. She squealed as Kassandra lifted Amy's head by her hair and Madeline moved down close to her.

"You know, Devine. You could make this a whole lot easier if you'd just come clean," Madeline said. "I mean, I'd hate to be picking on such a powerless normie."

"Normie, normie, hehehehe," Tilly squealed. "Too bad your little girlfriend isn't here to pick you up!"

"What was that Tilly?" Amy smiled. "I couldn't hear you with Mad Maddy's cunt on your tongue."

Tilly slapped her. Kassandra punched her. The blows kept coming as Amy tried to push them away, but felt only a fourth of her strength filling her arms and legs. Her aura was nowhere to be found, but it wasn't like she could have used it to help her anyway without being outed. The pain crescendoed throughout her limbs in increasing waves. It was more the sheer shock of trauma after her ordeal just two days prior. The audacity of Amy to put her body through more physical torment with little recovery. She'd almost thought herself stupid for ending up in this mess, but her mouth surely didn't do her any wonders.

"That's right, girls," Madeline said, looming over the trio, a wide smile on her face. "Let's make sure the trash remembers its place. Get her up. Grab that and let's gift-wrap her."

"Help me and stop your giggling," Kassandra snarled at Tilly, as Kassandra hugged the corner's light pole and uprooted it. Tilly rushed over and helped her bring it behind Amy. The pair held either end of it and pushed it around Amy's torso, with sparks and wires jumping out of it as the metal bent and cracked at the points of friction.

"You brainless, bumbling bitches are really after it this time. Following the orders of a mad dog who, by the way, is not getting her own hands dirty. A bit convenient, init? Let—Me—*Go*." Amy fought to free herself as the girls bent the pole around Amy's torso three times over, leaving her a stick inside a twisted metal pretzel. She coughed up some blood and spit it on the ground beside her.

"Oh, Devine," Madeline said, bending down beside her. "If this doesn't prove you're a normie, I don't know what will. You never fight back." Madeline kicked Amy square in the nose.

Amy fell back, the metal being the only cushion between her and the concrete. She rolled over on her side, now unable to see her abusers.

"Look at the little rolling rubbage!" Tilly jumped up and down, clapping. "Look at her go, look at her go! We should find a bin to dump her in!"

"That's not a bad idea, Tilly," Madeline said.

Well, I'm still conscious. Hm. Shouldn't push it but...

"Hey, Maddy…" Amy laughed, catching her breath. "You know, my grandmother hits harder than that. You may want to reconsider which one of us is the normie."

Unable to twist her head too far back, her peripheral caught Madeline's feet stomping towards her. Amy struggled in her binding and twisted her body to see Kassandra put an arm in front of Madeline.

"No. You can't." Kassandra said.

Madeline glared at her.

This was the first time Amy ever saw Madeline give one of her own squad members such a nasty look. Perhaps they weren't the perfect bunch they pretended to be after all. Or Madeline's just a power-hungry princess who hates to be challenged.

Madeline held her stare for a couple of uncomfortable seconds before stomping away, pursued by a scoffing Tilly.

Kassandra sighed, eyed Amy, and shook her head before taking off after the others.

Amy blew a lock of her hair out of her face. She rolled towards the nearest building and after a valiant struggle with it, used her butt to help herself sit upright against the wall.

In a shoe store window across the street, a man shut the blinds.

Amy scoffed.

Such a quiet, lovely block.

Chapter Eight

As the sky darkened, Amy and her metal-wrapped torso crept past the Murder House. She kept her eyes down, not wanting to relive her recent venture there.

Archie flew up to her and fluttered around her head. He clawed at her metallic prison from different angles.

"It's alright, Arch. I'm gaining some strength back," she groaned as she pushed her arms against the surrounding metal. It slipped down a little, freeing her steps.

Behind her, a group of policebots followed, rambling on.

"Ma'am, let us help you!"

"Who did this to you, ma'am?"

"Excuse me, you seem to be in a bind."

"Do you need assistance, ma'am?"

"Get bent," Amy said, hating the irony as she did. She stretched her arms, the metal creaking, and with a couple more grunts, she wiggled out of the binding light pole's clutches. She stepped over it and felt her already healing bruised face.

"Unbelievable."

"No littering. ma'am."

"I'm afraid I will have to write you up. For your record, this is Strike Four."

Amy raised her arm up, her GCID facing the bots. A green light scanned her arm.

"Would you like a receipt for your ticket, Ms. Devine?"

Amy kept walking, with Archie close behind.

One by one, lights along an empty wall blinked on.

Amy stood at the end of the long, dark hallway, which stretched far within the depths of the old chapel building.

"Is this the place?" Amy asked.

There was no response but her echoing voice. She towards the light at the end of the hall, the lights on the wall cutting off behind her as she passed them.

Amy froze in the doorway of a well-lit oval room, her eyes peeled on the altar ahead.

"Your training truly begins now," Rezna's voice echoed throughout the room, but she was nowhere to be seen.

Amy nodded. She moved around the water fountain embedded in the marble stone floor. The statue in the middle of the fountain was of a beautiful woman with a crescent-shaped emblem in her hands. The rest of the emblem was obscured with lengthy vines full of thorns.

Amy followed the statue's gaze, which was stuck on the stained glass windows to Amy's right-hand side. She rubbed her eyes, but the images in the stained glass windows were blurry.

"You let everything but the necessary distract you," Rezna's voice said. "Your cloudy vision will bring you one step closer to death."

Amy found herself right in front of a large emerald casket. Her mouth dropped as it opened up.

I can't move.

Inside the casket, a half skeletal faced man turned to Amy. He smiled.

"You bitch," the skeletal Mr. Conrad Bakers said. He jumped up, his hand gripping the back of Amy's head, shaking it. "You killed me!"

Amy's eyes shot open.

"Gma?" She sat up on her bed and looked around her messy room. "Arch?" Amy rubbed her arms, shivering as she searched under piles of clothes, behind drawers, and under her bed.

Amy rushed down the stairs, passing Archie's food tray

To her relief, Rezna had not returned yet. It would be quite the task to hide her depleted aura from the wise old woman.

Something smacked into the glass panels of the front door before falling out of sight.

A small figure reemerged and tapped against the glass.

Amy opened the door. "Where were you, Arch?"

Archie flew in as Amy shut the door behind him. He 'cooed' around Amy's head, holding something in between his left foot.

Amy held out her hand as she caught the small piece of glass Archie dropped for her. She lifted it high, confused as to what she was supposed to do with it.

The rectangular piece of glass had parallel black lines running on both sides of it. Its edges were dull, including its rounded corners.

"ZLynx, can I get a reading on this?" Amy held the piece of glass over her GCID.

An upside down pyramid of white light from the GCID's screen. Its rays illuminated the small rectangular glass.

"Drive contains a message," the GCID's A.I. voice said. "Would you like to view it?"

"Yes, please."

Thousands of ziccolights emerged around Amy. The ziccolights flew down next to her and formed a set of feet, followed by legs, torso, arms, and head.

The ziccolights shimmered. The human figure they formed stood obscured behind the light.

Seconds later, the form became clear. Jimmy. The actugraphic

Jimmy's white, ghostly figure smiled Amy.

"Hey Amy!" actugraphic Jimmy said. "I see this message has found you well. Just wanted to give you a little update on the case. Turns out Thomas and Norma Jones' thirteen year old son Jonathan disappeared about a year ago. No one in town heard or seen anything. Quite strange. The Jones' reached out to a private investigation agency but they also came up with zero leads."

Actugraphic Jimmy exhaled and took a seated position. Although here he sat on nothing but air, clearly Jimmy took a seat at this point where he was.

"My unit didn't formulate until three months after Jonathan Jones' disappearance. I didn't transfer over to Jadesfeld until a month after that. Had to fight tooth and nail to get the green light over here. I don't know what's going on, but it's clear to me that this town has been covering something. No idea what. Anyway, you take care now. We need a better communication system but I've got something in the works. Talk soon!"

Actugraphic Jimmy burst into ziccolights once more. The lights disappeared.

"What the hell is the Jones family hiding?" Amy said.

Sitting in World History, Amy cradled her head in her hands, rolling her eyes at Demora, who typed on a holographic keyboard.

Amy shook her head.

"Dammit!" Demora said, banging her fists on the table, causing students around her to jump. She snatched her earpiece off and bent it into a circle. "This connection is quite shit today, init?"

Demora reached down to lift the right pant leg of her bulky jeans, revealing a strap around her leg with various small instruments on it. She pulled a long tool with a tiny arrowhead off of it and worked it into her now circular earpiece.

"You know, I hear this shit-show is built on top of an old, collapsed radio center. Explains the rubbage connection." Demora banged her earpiece against her desk.

Amy took out and opened her textbook when Mr. Ribbers entered the classroom.

"You're quiet." Demora rapidly blinked at her. "And your book is… open. What's eating you, Devine?"

Amy turned pages as she remained silent.

Amy continued to give Demora a series of grunts and bare minimum acknowledgment throughout the day. She caught an ounce of peace finally as she sat alone in the cafeteria, eating a yogurt cup. A backpack dropped in front of her. Amy rolled her eyes.

"I thought we agreed to go out for lunch this week, Ms. Forgetful," Demora said as she sat across from her, throwing her arms up. "I was waiting outside for like ten minutes. Is your GCID getting interference again?"

Amy's GCID lit up.

"So it is on." Demora's head cocked to the side. "What gives?"

Amy glanced up, meeting eyes with the Lockheart Girls, who smiled and waved at her. Amy pulled her hand away from Demora's approaching grasp.

"Well," Demora said, pulling her hand back and taking a drink from Amy's water bottle. "Someone's burning up. Keep it together."

"What can I do for you, Demora?" Amy said.

"Why have you been acting so weird today?"

"I'm acting weird. A bit strange, init? You running off without a word, but I'm the weird one."

Across the room, Tilly reenacted Amy taking blows from the lot of them while Madeline just laughed.

Amy popped up and made her way out of the cafeteria with Demora in tow.

"What is going on?" Demora said.

"Those bitches got the best of me yesterday. I could've been home if I hadn't waited around for you," Amy said, leaving Demora paces behind.

"Wait, they what!?"

"You would think we're still in primary school. They're so lucky." Amy stormed into the restroom and threw her bag up onto the sink.

"Amy, slow down—"

"I just want to know what Graves told you that was so important that you had to run home."

"Oh that." Demora shrugged. "It was about the upcoming Animalia Gems matchup. Tilly is having some arm surgery two days before and they needed a Bolter. Since I had the best track records in our old school, the Headmistresses asked me to take over for her. I'd rather *die* than work alongside Mad Maddy, but it would be nice—" she stopped, looking down from Amy's glare. "That's beside the point Ames, there is something I wanted to talk—"

"I'm so happy for you," Amy said, digging through her bag for nothing at all. "Really. I hope you and your new besties put on a good show."

"Calm down, alright! It's not my fault the blundering bitches jumped you! I—"

She's right.

I don't care.

"Demora I just—You're impossible." Amy waved a hand under the faucet turning it on, then threw water on her face. "You borderline ignored me ever since *that day* in the forest, and now you ditch me and I get pulverized by Madeline and her goons. Now you're here twirling a fit over your new Bolter position—"

"Ames, calm down," Demora pointed at Amy's hands, which had a small line of aura growing around them.

"Stop telling me to calm down!" Amy whipped towards her.

Amy's aura spread throughout the bathroom. Her bag strap caught on her hand and flew across the tiled floor. The lights flickered and all of the faucets cut on. Amy stared at her glowing orange eyes in the mirror.

"Ok." Demora's hair flew past her ears before returning to her sides. She passed a hand through her hair's side part. "Definitely told you to calm down. Sorry," she added after seeing Amy's face. "Look, I wanted to talk about the other day. That whole thing threw us both for a loop."

"I'm sorry, Demora, I can't help when I fucking freeze up! You know I hate…"

"I know, I know. It's not that, Ames. It's…" Demora leaned against the sink and stared at the floor.

"I'm sorry Demora. That's all I can say." Amy threw her hands up, then leaned right beside her.

"It's not that Ames." Demora scratched the back of her left middle finger with her right index. "The other day, when that boy attacked us… His aura grew around me. Locked me good in a fucking bind. It was incredible. I was burning up, and he just kept squeezing. I started to fade."

Amy turned towards her, not believing what she was hearing. That level of aura control was something she and Demora could only achieve in small amounts, holding a book or another small object. To hold an entire person was unfathomable, at least to them. She was sure Gma had that level of power but never actually saw it for herself, so wasn't sure.

"Next thing I knew," Demora continued, "he let me go. I was on my ass, looked up, and there he was. Wrapped up like a fucking burrito. In your aura."

"Wait, what do you mean?"

"There you were. Standing there, completely out of it. It was like you were in a trance. But your aura was alive and well. It had him wrapped up like a fucking burrito and you weren't breaking a sweat."

Amy leaned back into the sink again, staring at the stall in front of her. What was she even hearing? Her shallow breaths escaped her after clutching her chest to make sure she was still breathing.

"It got worse. Your aura then grew around his neck. He was starving for air but your aura kept squeezing. He turned blue and I was screaming your name, screaming for you to stop, but you couldn't hear me. Until I slapped the *shit* out of you, then you finally dropped him. I picked up the log and smashed his noggin and he was out. That's when you woke up."

Amy couldn't look her in the eyes. Demora wasn't ignoring her, mad at her for her being a coward.

She was scared. Scared of me. Her best mate.

"I didn't know how to tell you. I didn't think…"

A bathroom stall slammed open. Gina's blank stare scanned the surrounding floor, clutching her handbag. She sped past the girls and left the restroom.

Demora charged towards the exit, but Amy held her back.

"Are you mad? She heard everything!" Demora said.

Amy's gaze bore a hole through the restroom's door.

Shit.

Chapter Nine

"It's called aura regression," Rezna said, as she dropped a cup of tea into Amy's hands.

Amy shifted in her seat at the kitchen table, looking down into the cup. Her GCID lit up, blinking 11:15 PM.

"As I've told you before," Rezna said, sitting across from her, "the half-age complex is a gift and a curse. Once we hit the age of twenty, the aging process pauses and does not start again until we reach the age of forty. We then age at the pace of half the age we actually are. However, approaching the age of twenty, we need to keep our minds and bodies in top form or else we're unable to control the birth of our aura inside." She sipped from her teacup while twirling her other hand in the air. Her green aura circled around her fist.

Archie's mouth opened wide as he watched it, his head circling to follow its pattern.

"Regression," Rezna continued, "happens when our bodies aren't able to properly hone our auras. The aura becomes dominant and acts of its own accord. This is mainly because of the owner not being insufficient in controlling their aura."

Rezna's aura exploded in several directions, filling the kitchen with its light before disappearing.

"To become one with your aura is the key to beating this. It just means you have to work harder." Rezna rose out of her seat. "Let's get started immediately to avoid any future episodes."

"Can we wait until after school tomorrow?" Amy asked. "I'm exhausted."

"You'll have more than enough time to rest. Come along now."

Rezna placed her shawl on her throne as Amy mooched paces behind her.

I think I'd rather be in captivity right about now.

It was a wonder why Detectives hadn't busted down her door yet. Based on the face Gina had, Amy was quite positive she and Demora were done for. The night was as quiet as usual, but the paranoia wouldn't settle.

Maybe Demora got to her after all.

Her mind replayed the half-hour she spent holding Demora back in the restroom, missing their next class, the stares they got from other girls coming in as they stood against the sink waiting for an army to come for them. But nothing came for the rest of the day. Everything had gone as usual.

"What are you waiting for?" Rezna asked. "Charge up your aura girl, why are you..."

Amy closed her eyes, thinking of that small hot spot that she felt in the pit of her stomach, trying to amplify it. All she felt, however, was a sharp pain in her lower abdomen. A breath on her neck caused her eyes to jerk open.

"What's happened to your aura?" Rezna was against her back, staring her down. She placed a hand on Amy's shoulder, but Amy slid out of her grasp.

"I overdid it with Demora. We were training really intensely and I sort of blew my fuse." She avoided Rezna's narrowing eyes. "I'm sorry, I didn't want to tell you because I thought it'd be back by now."

"We never deplete our aura! Never! You know the forces out there mean we must be strong at all times. What is the matter with you?"

"Nothing." Amy dropped her arms to her sides, fists shaking, bumping against her legs. "Nothing is the matter with me. I was training. You always say it's of the utmost importance. I just took it further than intended. Demo's a tough opponent. She keeps me on my toes, and my training with her strengthens me, but it also strengthens her. I had to keep up. It won't happen again. I just can't train with you right now. My aura needs to restore."

"Restore!" Rezna rushed towards Amy. She cut to the side of her and sat on her throne.

"The great Lady Callisto was a genius, yet when the world needed focus most, she gave up on her smaller ambitions. She dropped out of her second year of secondary school so that she could pursue something too many were scared to do. She spent years traveling the world, uncovering the secrets to what made us what we are today. The fear towards our kind reached dangerous levels, as the more evohumans that appeared across the world, the more we were hated. Revered for being nothing more than the next step in humanity's evolution."

"Quite the history lesson," Amy whispered.

"It took two wars," Rezna continued, "to reach an agreement that suited each side of this issue. Even then, even when we filled forty-eight percent of the population, we were still looked down on and discriminated against. The laws back then were abysmal towards the superhumans. Still, Callisto fought. She was at the front seat of every debate and at the forefront of every war."

Driving me mad...

"With her wit," Rezna went on, "she uncovered the secrets behind a new element that was the direct cause of our evolution. It was the greatest scientific breakthrough humanity had ever known. She did this for us while learning and building her own strength, as Callisto herself was an evohuman. She taught herself to hone her abilities, keeping it secret for decades, while still fighting both physically and mentally."

Amy held the bottom of her stomach, calming a sharp pain.

"She did not rest." Rezna remained still, looking off into a corner of the room. "Not until her people were safe. She established the World Committee, taking the very first seat because the people unanimously voted her in. She brought about the many changes we see in our social and political climates as they stand today. She took her last breath after years of peace in our world. Her soul refused to leave this Earth until it was sure we would be okay."

Always lecturing...

"There has not been a war since. Many people regard her as though she's some... God. I see her as one of us. The one who took a stand against unimaginable circumstances, and fought until justice saw its day."

And yet, here we are. Hiding in the shadows...

"I have been on this Earth for one hundred and forty-nine years, and in that time I've gone through an obscene amount of training practices. Sometimes the basics are all you need to bring you back to form. Pushups."

Amy sighed. She got down on her hands and knees.

"Two hundred," Rezna said.

"I am—" Amy's eyes went wide then narrowed. "—my own deterrent." She steadied herself up and completed a pushup. "I am my own deterrent," she repeated as she came back up. She repeated the phrase after every rep.

"And then," Amy said, facedown on the desk between her outstretched arms, "there were three hundred situps and an hour running in place."

"Glad to see old Rezna hasn't lost her tenacity," Demora said as she banged her earpiece against her desk. "I swear it's getting worse."

The classroom's back door slammed shut behind them.

Gina took her seat in the corner of the class. She stared out the window, her face resting on her palms.

Demora tapped Amy's arm over and over, harder each time. Amy slapped her hand away.

"I can see, Demora," Amy whispered, punching her arm.

"Good morning class!" Mr. Perry dropped his briefcase on his desk and wrote on the board. He rambled on but the words seemed lost to Amy.

Gina's eyes were low, her face devoid of anything as she stared down at Mr. Perry.

"BEE SWARM ALERT. BEE SWARM ALERT. BEE SWARM ALERT." The blaring siren made many students and Mr. Perry jump.

Metal sheets whirred up from the window slots and covered them whole, the room losing its natural light.

"ALL RESIDENTS MUST GET INSIDE A STRUCTURE. THIS IS NOT A TEST."

The students panicked. 'In the middle of the day?', 'how strange', and other sayings were building up. Demora gave Amy a look and shrugged.

"The perfect learning opportunity!" Mr. Perry slapped his hands together and reached under his desk. He pulled up a monitor on a hinge that sat on top of the desk and turned the screen to face the class. "Let's analyze the pattern and overall movement of the swarm, shall we?"

The screen came on and after what seemed like an eternity; the swarm raged past. Their thick hairy coats and hefty bodies buzzed by on-screen, some bumping into the camera. As their numbers increased, the camera bumps got worse.

"They're an aggressive bunch," Mr. Perry said, adjusting his tie. "You can see from their coats, these aren't actually your normal variant. They've traveled from far. Where? I haven't the slightest idea. If I had to take a guess, definitely closer to the southern hemisphere." He tapped his forearm and ziccolights formed an actugraphic keyboard that he typed into. "I hope all of our residents can find their way to safety…" His words trailed off as kept talking, lower with each word, as he rubbed his chin.

"They're beautiful." Gina giggled from the back of the room. She stared right at the metal-covered windows, wearing a wide, toothy grin. "Splendidly perfect."

Demora led Amy down the concrete steps of their school.

"I'm not so worried about Gina anymore, to be honest," Demora said. "What the hell was that? She wore that same dumb look on her face that she had yesterday in the restroom. That creepy blank stare, except this time she laughed. Mental."

"The way she was looking at Mr. Perry was so much different, though. It's a wonder, considering how she left his class the other day."

Archie flew up to Amy and tugged at her shoulder.

"Stupid bee swarm," Demora said, her eyes scanning the area. Ruined lunchtime. Want to grab a bite before practice?"

"Actually, Demora, I've got to go get Archie some supplies."

"You said you'd help me train for the matchup!"

"I know, but he's been a temperamental little thing lately. Think it's his food. I'll have to run some errands for him, maybe take him to the vet. Come on, Arch."

"Fine." Demora crossed her arms.

Amy followed Archie down the block. The little bat pulled at her hair.

"Alright, bugger off. We'll train tomorrow D! Text you later."

Several blocks later, Amy followed Archie through an empty cake shop. He led her to the back and through a side door. They continued down a weed-infested road, where Jimmy waited, leaning against his old brown four-wheeled Volkswagen.

"This thing gets older everytime I see it," Amy said, pointing at his car.

"Another strike, huh?" Jimmy said. "Littering, though? And why a freaking light pole?"

Amy explained what happened the other day with the Lockheart Girls, despite her embarrassment.

"What were you doing in that part of town, anyway?" Jimmy asked.

"I just wanted some ZenDrops. Normal ones. There's a little shop called—"

"Tasty's Mirage. They've got a warehouse right outside New Enfield, but you can definitely nab some of Zenith's lemon drops from there. You know, the non-medicinal sort."

"Maybe worth the trip. I try to get over to Tasty's but they sell out so fast. I'd kill for one. Anyway, Did not know the Lockhearts were tracking me."

Jimmy's jaw dropped, and he whipped off his thick, black shades. "*The* Lockheart Girls? They are—Sorry, that's quite unfortunate. But wow! *The* Lockheart Girls."

Amy rolled her eyes. "Keep your panties dry Jimmy."

Archie chucked a nut at Jimmy's head. He went to pull another off a nearby tree and threw it, but Jimmy dodged.

"Hey! What's his problem?"

"He's not quite fond of being your little messenger. Archie, don't pick with nature."

"I got the message." Jimmy twirled a small flute-like device in his hand. "This bat whistle comes in handy. It's been the best way of staying off the grid. Until now." Jimmy pulled something out of his breast pocket and handed it to Amy.

"How old is this thing?" Amy looked over the device, realizing it was a phone. She pressed the glass screen, and it lit up. "How do I get the keyboard out?"

"It's an Android G-XSR, 2041 model." Jimmy chuckled. The keyboard comes up on the screen only."

"Ugh, that's barbaric. Where'd you get it?" Amy said.

"Uncle Rogers has his connections. I've got a hold of some of them. Wasn't hard to snatch up a reconditioned model. That's the reason I called you here. To give you that and have a chat. Five more bodies were found. Two couples and a single parent."

"From my school. They called three kids away the other day. Must've been their parents."

"Yup. You don't know any of this information though. And also what I'm about to tell you. The Policebots have been decommissioned."

"What?"

"That metal piece your boy Arch found was a broken part of one of the p-bots. There hasn't been a single assault, much less murder, by a bot in over fifty years. Since that testing accident in 2129. The Mayor isn't taking any chances, so he had us shut the bots down until we solve the murder cases and prove the bots had nothing to do with it."

"We haven't been without them… ever."

"If word gets out that the policebots may somehow be malfunctioning and going rogue killing people, the entire system goes to shit. We'd be stripped of our authority. We apprehend. We don't kill. Wars used to be fought with guns. We incapacitate if absolutely necessary, but all suspects get their day in court. "

"Are pobos even capable of something like this?"

"Policebots are intentionally made devoid of any level of humanity, other than deliberately fun speech patterns and mannerisms. Just to make people not feel intimidated by the fact that they are machines. But, they *are* machines, and machines can be programmed. So even if someone was altering the machines to do some despicable, same result. The force would take the bill."

"That's quite the bill if it turns out the pobos are somehow involved in this madness."

"Detectives solve cases while the policebots police the people. Without the bots around, that means double-time for the rest of us." Jimmy pointed at the G-XSR. "That thing's connected to our Wi-Fi but communicates on a private network. We'll be able to talk without being tracked from now on."

Amy beamed. "Sick! Guess this means I'm an unofficial detective then? That's right, init?"

"Absolutely not."

Chapter Ten

"Although the last swarm was a week prior, the county has initiated a curfew of 9 pm. This comes after the deaths of three Jadesfeld residents and the disappearance of seven more..."

Amy swiped away the holographic news reporter. She waved her hand over the holographic book hovering in front of her as she crossed the street and the page turned.

"Bees first circulate the area of interest, triangulating three points of reference," Amy read. "A disturbance in their nest or—hey!"

Amy's body rocked to the side as someone shouldered past her.

The man's head spun towards her. His icy grey gaze ran down her forehead to the tip of her chin. His eyes narrowed, and even with his careful movements, his decaying grey flesh stretched down off his face, some of it falling off. Underneath the meat around his gritted teeth, his cheekbones peeked out. Every inch of his tattered clothing flapped in the light breeze. The stocky man pressed his bowler hat down onto his head, the bone from the top of his pinky pointing at Amy.

Amy stepped back and tripped, falling flat on her butt. She lost sight of the walking corpse for a split second before finding that he was now pale with ivory-colored flesh.

"Darn brats," he said, his deep indigo eyes burning into her before storming off.

Amy watched him disappear farther down the busy streets until he was out of sight. She jumped as her GCID's alarm blared awake and picked herself up.

Minutes later, Amy strolled across the glinting white floors and leaned up against the front desk of Lakewood Hill Medical Center, ten minutes late for her appointment. A bronze-colored receptionist whirred towards her. Its name tag said 'Lucy'. The metallic arms of Lucy pulled her along, twisting and winding through several corridors until they reached a silver door.

"Tardy Misses get the worst stitches, Ms. Devine," Lucy's monotone voice sang out. An emerald light beamed out of its oversized monocle and traveled up and down Amy's face. "Temperature ninety-eight degrees." Lucy's eye scanner beam hit the silver door. "Fifth floor."

The silver elevator door opened and Amy stepped inside as the doors shut behind her. A chime boomed inside.

"Welcome to Lakewood Hill Medical Center, where your health is important to us. We have medical staff available for you twenty-four hours a day, seven days a week. It's your health, your money, your life that is valued here."

Amy rolled her eyes and crossed her arms.

"Please note," the automated voice continued, "all subhumans please report to level eight for your safety and convenience. If you're here for Peculiar testing, level five is your destination. Thank you for choosing Lakewood Hill Medical Center."

Amy exited out the opening elevator doors. A flying ovular-shaped robot flew up to her and an emerald light beamed out from it and scanned her.

"Follow me," the robot said. It flew off to the right and Amy followed. They stropped in front of a door and it opened up. "Please wait inside, remove your shirt, and Dr. Vinity will be with you shortly."

Amy entered the room, and the door closed behind her. Amy stared into space for a moment before lifting her shirt over her head. The door opened. Amy turned around and threw her shirt up against her chest.

"Oh, don't mind me!" A male doctor with four white holographic clipboards chuckled as he adjusted his glasses. "Just waiting for Dr. Vinity." He walked over to the desk and checked inside some cabinets, speaking to the clipboards as notes appeared on them. He pulled out a bottle and leaned up against the desk, still dictating.

Amy did not move, looking from the doctor, then around the room, then back to the doctor. "Excuse me?"

The man continued dictating.

"Excuse me?" Amy said louder.

"Yes?" The doctor looked up at her, smiling.

"Do you mind waiting outside for Dr. Vinity?"

"Oh," a smile crept on one side of his mouth. "I'm a doctor, it's fine."

"I think I'd prefer otherwise." Amy held her arms tight to her chest as one corner of the man's smile grew small.

"Very well." His eyes looked her up and down before walking towards the door.

"A size too small there, init?"

The door shut. Amy sat still, staring into the floor, cradling her arms. The heat in her chest seemed to burn a hole straight through her. The hairs on her arms stood up straight as she clenched her fists. A drop of blood fell from her palm and onto her shoe. It felt like an eternity before the door would open again, and Amy's eyes bore a hole into the intruder. Her narrowed eyes softened and her fists relaxed as Dr. Vinity walked in, wearing an enormous smile.

"Amy! Long time! It takes a police order to get you in here, huh?"

Amy cracked a small smile. "Yeah, 'pose so."

"Well, don't be shy now; get that shirt down and let's see what's up."

The examination went on for about thirty minutes. Dr. Vinity continued her usual warm, carefree conversational routine, but Amy was less eager to chime in.

Did he really just say that?

Amy couldn't piece together her weird morning and was ready to leave the hospital as soon as possible. Until something resonated.

"Right, you're leaving Friday?" Amy said. "I didn't realize time went by so fast."

"Yeah, Friday's the big day. I'm a bit nervous, actually. Working directly on the team of the world's most renowned pain specialists. Very intimidating."

"That's true." Amy's eyes drove over Dr. Vinity's parted afro. "You worked hard for it, though, didn't you? You're going to make an impressive addition."

"Thanks, girl." Dr. Vinity smiled. "Noticed you checking out my puff, is it looking alright? Tried something new with all this hair."

"Quite the contrary. It's a madhouse."

"What, really?!"

"I'm just being a cheeky shit. Your hair looks amazing, as always. I'm jealous."

"'Preciate you girl. You know, my sisters in Georgia would have a field day with your locks. If you're ever in the States, look them up. Quite hard over there to not hear about the Vinity hairdressers."

"Noted." Amy gave a half-smile.

"What's wrong? You've given me only one clap-back in the thirty minutes we've spent together, so I know something's up."

Amy's skin crawled into herself as she wanted to avoid the subject at all costs, but she knew Dr. Vinity was too smart to be lied to. She told her about the weird encounter with the male doctor and explained how she could've just been hearing things.

"I'll talk to him. That sounds… yeah. I'm going to follow up with this. I pray there's been some misunderstanding, 'cuz that… Let me let you go. Lucy will have your paperwork for you upfront. You passed the exam. Stay 'outta girl okay?"

"Yeah. You bet."

"Talk later, Amy. See me before Friday!" Dr. Vinity placed a hand on Amy's shoulder, then power-walked out of the room.

Amy jumped off the examination table and grabbed her stomach as the pit of it dropped to the floor. Her stomach continued to drag its way behind her as she exited the exam room and walked the halls. She made her way into the elevator and held her ears, trying to block out the automated message.

As Amy made her way towards the front desk, she paused as a piano key rang out in the room next to her. She looked into the room's window of a huge playroom.

Inside was a huge playroom, where several small kids sat laughing and singing along to the tune being played by a teenage girl behind a piano in front of them.

Amy's eyes met Issa's, who sat amongst the crowd, smiling and waving at Amy. Issa beckoned for Amy to come inside.

Amy put her hand on the door, but a hand landed on her arm.

"I should have been clearer before." Norma Jones moved in close to her. "The next time you come around either my niece or myself, one of us will land themselves in one of these hospital beds."

Amy grilled the sour-faced woman and opened her mouth, but was interrupted by Issa opening the door.

"Amy, how delightful! Come inside and read the *Book of Clouds* with us!"

"Ms. Devine is in quite the hurry. She must be going now."

"No, she isn't," Issa said. "She didn't seem in a rush at all—"

"Girl, enough!" Norma pushed Issa back inside the room and shut the door, stepping in front of it.

With a final glare, Amy turned on her heel and marched away.

I'll find you out, you wicked witch.

Was it the smartest thing in the world to provoke a woman as rich as Norma Jones? Probably not. Amy's mind went to the dirt beneath her, thinking of the underground cities and the thugs that inhabited them. The 'landing back in the hospital' line ran like a broken record inside her head.

But that little girl needs me. She needs someone to reach out to her and pull her from that awful woman's clutches.

Amy kept seeing the smile on Issa's face and it reminded her of the way she looked at ZenDrops. A pure delight to be seen.

Her mind stayed on the matter as she stood inside a large sandy clearing, placing stones at specific points on a diamond-shaped line Demora had just finished drawing.

"I guess that'll have to do. Bit rubbish if you ask me though." Demora dropped her drawing instrument, a large stick, and crossed her arms.

"Hush up," Amy said. "Archie here will drop those water balloons every twenty seconds, hoping to land one on you. As per the rules of the game, that means you'll have to revert to the previous base. Now—"

Archie dropped a balloon onto Amy's head, and it burst, the water inside drenching her head to mid-chest. The little bat laid back, still floating in the air as he snickered, trying to cover his face with his wings.

"You did say 'now'!" Demora laughed.

Amy took a deep breath. "Just remember who feeds you," she said.

Archie stopped laughing.

Amy closed her eyes and let out a large breath of air. Her orange aura thinly outlined her entire body. Steam rose off of her as the wet patches on her shirt diminished until they were gone. She smiled as

Demora's jaw dropped.

"I demand to know how you've done that!" Demora circled Amy, her eyes darting over every inch of Amy.

"Gma's been working my ass off without telling me the new technique she's preparing me for. So I've been focusing my aura in smaller amounts. I was rubbing my hands together the other day on that particularly nasty chill. My aura felt like my aura was... reading me. It got warmer, as though responding to me being cold. The first time that's ever happened. I just kept focusing my energy on that feeling I had and eventually I was just able to do it without rubbing my hands together. Never mind that now, Demo—" She stopped Demora from rubbing her own hands together.

"Fine," Demora said. "But after practice, you must teach me!"

"I'll try my best," Amy smiled. "Now, tell me how this game works again."

"The game of Bolter, Boxer, Brains has a few rules." Demora marched around the makeshift diamond field they created. "The Bolter must run in pattern, landing on the bases in order." She stopped in the middle of one side of the diamond field between corners labeled 1 and 2, walked a straight line to the side between corners labeled 2 and 3, walked to the side between corners labeled 3 and 4, then walked over to the side between corners 4 and 1, before finally waking to the corner labeled 2 and stopping. "The Bolter then has to continue this pattern between sides in order to catch that base, and they keep going until they reach base one. One point is then awarded to that team."

"Right..." Amy rubbed her chin, nodding. "Right, I've got that part, I think. Confusing, but whatever. And the Boxer's gotta try and knock the Bolter off their path, in order to send them back to their previous captured base, right?"

"Right. And the Brains sits in the center, controlling their team's Boxer pods that are underneath the arena. Here, Archie is the

Brains—Don't you dare." Demora pointed a finger at Archie, who was aiming a water balloon overhead. The small bat retreated behind Amy. "The huge difference with Friday's game is that we're playing the Animalia Gems variant."

"Ugh, barbaric. It's no wonder why the Animalia Kingdom hates us."

"The arena uses robots, Devine. It's all a bit of entertainment."

"It's the symbolism that leaves me buggers. Believe it or not, I have done my research."

"You have fun with your symbols, but I'm here to win, so help me." Demora ran in pattern from base to base, leaving Archie dizzy from trying to follow her.

"This game is more than just running as fast as you can Demo, you won't get any awards for that. Conserve your stamina and think before trying to take a base."

"One point!" Demora found her way back to first base and started running the pattern again. A balloon fell way too late behind her as Archie chucked another. Demora dodged balloons Archie threw from all angles, making her way back to first base again. "Two points!"

"Your opponents will not make it as easy for you as Archie has—no offense, Arch—so you need to think strategically about your movements before making them. And stop using your aura, it won't help you."

"Three points!" Demora's aura smacked a balloon back at Archie, dousing him in water as he fell to the ground. Demora gained speed, cackling. "Four points!"

Archie shook off his wetness and charged towards her, dropping more balloons around her, but missing each shot.

Amy groaned. She waved her hand and her aura escaped it. It tripped Demora, landing her flat on her face. Archie's whole body shook with laughter.

"Hey what the hell, Devine? You just said no aura!"

"The Boxers have those bats, do they not? Maybe now you'll focus on strategy over speed."

"Fine," Demora scoffed. She angled herself on her knees and dashed forward. She ran in pattern until again, landing on first base. "Five—" Demora tripped, spun in the air, and landed on her ass. Her eyes glowed pink as she punched the ground and jumped up, with her fists engulfed in her pink fury. "I've had enough of that—"

"You're missing the point of the game," Amy said. She circled Demora as Demora circled in the opposite direction of her. "The meaning behind each role in the base game; what do you think they are about? Bolter, Boxer, Brains. Relate it to auraism."

"What are you on about?"

"*Think*. The three positions represent the three basic elements of aura manipulation. The spirit of the Bolter. The physicality of the Boxer. The mentality of the Brains. Although the world hasn't figured it out yet, you have that advantage. Also, you need to keep tabs on your speed. I'm not just gonna stand here and watch you run as fast as you can when it's of no use to you during the actual game."

Demora's aura subsided. "You win, coach. I'm your slave. Guide me."

Chapter Eleven

Amy hurried after a crowd trekking down a path through a wooded area. Her hand recoiled as she pricked her thumb on the tree bark she leaned against. She jumped back at the rustling bushes next to her.

The heads of a dozen moxpeckers popped out of the bushes.

Amy stuck her bleeding thumb in her mouth as the moxpeckers jumped towards her on their thin hind legs, squawking. At the very end of their squawks was a noise that sounded like two thin pieces of rope being rubbed together.

"Shoo!" Amy waved her other hand at them while guarding her bleeding thumb. "No, it's not for you."

In unison, the moxpeckers let out one final squawk before jumping back into the bushes.

Amy had been walking for another ten minutes before some sounds of life, besides the quiet conversations between her fellow walkers, came into earshot.

Up ahead, casting a shadow upon them all, stood an enormous emerald stadium, appropriately named Emerald Stadium. It sat at the exact midpoint between Jadesfeld and New Enfield. The founders of the neighboring habitats had come together to create a place where massive gaming events could take place, but that was decades ago when things were less hostile between the two communities. These days, there was very little that could bring the citizens of either town together.

The structure perfectly blended in with its surroundings within this forest. The only thing giving away the aesthetic of the scenery were the drones flying overhead, with beams of lights emanating from them that created a screen that a movie trailer played. Right above the stadium, several dozen Nightgators flew in organized circles. Their screeching roars punched through the air.

Amy held her palms over her ears and pressed forward. She made her way down to the front of Emerald Stadium, then through a scanner at the stadium's entrance. The message CLASS APPROVED - TICKET VALID displayed on top of the scanner. A security bot stuck out a flattened scanner arm, stopping Amy, and waved its scanner arm up and down her body.

The inside of the stadium was just as colossal as the outside. Vendors sold all sorts of propaganda throughout every corner of the lobby, calling out to the massive crowds that moved about the floor. Digital banners hung from the stadium ceiling:

The Bromley Bruisers vs The Lockheart Girls, Draco vs Tabitha, Match of the Year!

Amy passed through the refreshment area and considered grabbing a small bite, but the growing lines quickly changed her mind. She made her way up a glass staircase amongst an enormous crowd, all making their way up towards another mixed group of security bots and human guards.

"Sections A through M this way, N through Z that way please," one of the human guards said, pointing left and right.

Amy made her way to the left amongst a dozen others and through a set of double doors, where another guard stood waiting.

"Levels one and two this way, three and four that way," the guard directed them.

Amy followed a group of people to an elevator and stepped inside.

"Heading to level one," the robotic elevator voice rang out. The doors shut and the elevator moved up. "Level one."

The elevator opened up to a floor where some guards waited at the end of it and some people moved out. The doors closed, and the elevator continued upwards.

Amy got off on level four with her group and she made her way towards the next set of guards down the hall.

"Please make your way through either side, depending on your ticket label," a roboguard said. "Prime Box ticket holders, make your way to the right, and your seats are the very first set."

Amy went right and through another set of scanners before entering the stadium's gorgeous arena. The bottom floor of the arena was white with four large blood-red diamonds, one within another right in the center. There were red circles at various corners and smaller circles creating paths within the diamonds. In the center of it all was a glass spherical dome with two consoles sitting inside of it across from each other, along with seats behind each one. The seating area all around the arena had red seats with some smaller sections colored black.

Amy walked up to the frontmost black-colored section. She made her way inside the barely populated section, and walked into the first row, stopping right beside her seating neighbor.

"Hello, Tilly," Amy said, rolling her eyes at the unpleasant frowning face glaring back at her.

"Callisto's ghost must haunt me," Tilly said. She adjusted the arm sling holding her left arm tight to her body.

"Hey! Amy!" Jimmy's voice called from somewhere behind them. Jimmy walked over to the row and shook Amy's hand. He cleared his throat. "How are you, Ms. Devine? I see you've got Prime Box seats for today's game. I'm a few rows back."

"I'm only here for Demora. I'd rather be drained by Nightgators than sit here next to Terrible Tilly."

"Ah yeah, the promoters hired them to avoid a random bee swarm. Those bees will be sure to avert their path if they choose to fly by today. Tech guys also reinforced the stadium's defense shields just in case. I'd say we're pretty safe. Hey, isn't that—"

"General Aba of the Primary Guild of Animalia Defense," Amy finished.

Her eyes followed a bulky gorilla dressed in a uniform of green and gold with some red accents to it, with several metals decorating his chest and arms. He walked into a Prime Box directly across the stadium from them and was in the company of three other gorillas, two of them almost as big as he was, their sizes towering over the humans sitting in the rows behind them. The two wore beige uniforms with considerably fewer medals, but still an impressive number. The last gorilla donned a similar uniform to General Aba but had no medals. He was also a lot smaller compared to the others, and he smiled as he looked over the massive stadium, while the others looked like they were ready to kill.

"Hm. Didn't think he'd come all the way from Ethiopia for the games. Still baffled *that* guy needs guards," Jimmy said.

"It is rather interesting."

"GEMS ARE FILLED!" a random voice in the crowd yelled.

"WHEN BLOOD IS SPILLED!" Jimmy and a sizable amount of the crowd finished the declaration.

General Aba and his guards looked around the stadium, gritting their teeth. The smaller gorilla clapped and jumped in his seat. He stopped when General Aba gave him a look.

Amy rolled her eyes. "It's no wonder the Animalia Kingdom hates us."

Jimmy laughed nervously and pointed over at the smaller gorilla. "At least Aba's brother seems to be a fan."

"Here." Amy flicked her finger across her GCID, grabbed Jimmy's arm, and waved her GCID over his right forearm. "You take this seat. Seems you'll enjoy this more."

"Really?!" Jimmy looked like a kid who just won a lifetime supply of candy. "That's—wow thanks A—Ms. Devine! Thank you very much! Hey, I'm Detective Jimmy Wimblestyn." Jimmy extended his hand out to Tilly, who just rolled her eyes and popped her gum.

"It's starting," Tilly said.

"Catch ya later gents." Amy waved goodbye and made her way out of the row and up a couple of rows to the seat shown in her GCID.

Moments later, the lights throughout the arena dimmed. The diamonds on the arena floor lit up along with each of the circular bases. Each side of the arena's seating split apart and slid away from the arena floor. Above, the arena's ceiling broke into four and the Sun shined down inside. A stage lowered from one side of the ceiling and a man dressed in elaborate white robes that danced around every inch of his body stood on top of it, smiling at the crowd.

"Welcome!" The man on stage waved around to the audience. "Welcome citizens of Jadesfeld! Welcome citizens of New Enfield. Welcome esteemed guests of today's game of ANIMALIA GEMS! I'm your Gamemaster and host—Gerard Mikaal Montewell Miachelsteen!"

"That's a mouthful," Amy said.

"Shhh!" A bowl-cut-haired teen leaned towards Amy from the row behind her, his finger up to his lips.

"Sorry." Amy gave a small smile. She rolled her eyes as she turned back around.

"And now—" Gerard said, "—let's introduce our two teams! First up—hailing from the bright community of Bromley—I give you the Bromley Bruisers! The Brains—Brenton Keens! The Bolter—Mason Smith! And their Boxer—'Disaster' Daisy Davies!"

Three screens appeared in the air, each showing one player. Down in the arena, a door slid up, and out walked three players adorned in uniforms of green and silver. The two teen boys of the group bowed down and presented their third member to the audience. She was a girl much shorter than them, wearing ponytails with red, yellow, and silver bands on them. She swung a silver Boxer's bat with green balls on either end of it and screamed into the air as the crowd roared.

"Let's not forget the mascot of the Bruisers—controlled by Brenton Keens—Draco, the Draconic Equus!"

A yellow halo made of ziccolights formed around Brenton Keens' forehead, the source of light coming from his earbuds. Above, from outside, a massive mechanical being flapped its wings and collapsed them close to its body before diving nose-first towards the arena. The mechanical beast caught itself just before hitting the arena floor and spread its wings wide. As it moved, its metallic body parts creaked as they rubbed together. The horse-like body of the Draconic Equus had scales that opened and closed, as though breathing individually. The tongue of the beast slithered out and licked around its long snout as it opened up and roared, revealing razor-sharp teeth. Its lizard eyes narrowed as it watched every corner of the audience.

"And last but not least—" Gerard said, "—introducing your Jadesfeld hometown heroes! The undefeated—one and only—Lockheart Girls! Tilly Thomp— Oops, sorry, we have an update on players. Introducing their Bolter—Demora Corbyn-McDonald! The Boxer—Kassandra Owens! And the Brains—Madeline Watts!"

Three more screens appeared in the air alongside the first set, showing each of the Lockheart team. Across the arena floor, another door slid open, and out walked Madeline with Kassandra and Demora behind her. They wore uniforms of bright red and gold. Madeline swung a long red cape from off her shoulders and waved it into the air. Her earbuds formed a yellow halo around her head as she bowed and placed a finger to her lips. The stadium went almost silent, many members of the crowd placing their fingers to their lips as well.

Somewhere under the arena floor, the sound of dozens of moving parts clinked together and got closer and closer to the surface with every passing second. The innermost diamond on the arena floor dropped inwards as Madeline waved her cape in a circular motion and danced her way towards the opening in the floor. She dove inside the hole.

Complete silence. Amy shifted her body to get a better look down into the hole in the arena and was met with some annoyed stares. She slumped back into her seat.

A flush of silver jumped out of the hole in the arena floor and spun in the air, unraveling the long legs that concealed its body. It was a massive, robotic taracede with Madeline riding on top of it. The crowd went insane. The taracede landed back onto the re-covered floor and crawled around the Bromley Bruisers and their Draconic Equus.

"Their mascot, controlled by Madeline Watts—Tabitha The Terrible Taracede!" Gerard yelled.

The four eyes on either side of Tabitha the taracede's head spun in their sockets as they locked onto the Draco the Draconic Equus and Tabitha opened its small mouth as silver fluid drooled out of it.

Madeline, arms crossed, looked down at the Bromley Bruisers and smirked. Disaster Daisy stepped forward and raised her bat towards her. She made a cutthroat signal with it. The crowd somehow got even louder.

"I think we're in for one hell of a match!" Gerard yelled. He threw back his glorious blue hair and his rosy cheeks puffed up as he threw on an enormous smile. "Alright players, bump it up!"

The Bromley Bruisers and Lockheart Girls met face to face. Each bumped elbows with a player on the opposite team until they had all bumped every other player.

"Take your positions!" Gerard said.

The glass dome in the center of the field opened up and Madeline and Brenton Keens took a seat at either console, across from each other. They both started messing with the controls in front of them.

Kassandra and 'Disaster' Daisy took spots on top of circles on opposite sides of the field. Daisy swung her bat around. Kassandra snapped open her uniform and pulled a small pole out of her uniform's inner pocket. She tossed it up and caught it- the pole extended into a scarlet bat.

Demora and Mason Smith walked diagonally across from each other and took positions on two square blocks on the end of the outermost diamond on the field.

"Let's get our referee out here! He is the Head of the National Oversee of Gaming—hailing from Trinidad—Anthony Yorke!"

A buff man in an all-black uniform marched across the field, waving at the crowd. He reached the dome at the center and nodded at Madeline and Keens.

Madeline looked over at Kassandra and nodded, with Kassandra returning her nod. Madeline rolled her eyes over at Demora and said something. Demora rolled her eyes at her.

Given Demora's stance, Amy knew she was nervous. Amy could only hope that the other two wouldn't be trifling enough to sabotage her best friend over winning this game, but Amy had a feeling that wouldn't be the case. The way Madeline strutted across that field was as if she owned it.

Amy glanced down at Tilly, who leaned forward over the railing with her focus on the field below. This is where Mad Maddy and her Lockheart sisters truly thrived.

Referee Yorke lifted a gold baton into the air. A gold spark of light shot out of it and straight up towards the open sky, then exploded into many smaller sparks that flew across the stands.

"LET THE GAMES BEGIN!" Gerard screamed, and the crowd roared.

Madeline and Keens worked many dials on their respective consoles and touchscreens in front of them. Draco the Equus and Tabitha the taracede charged towards each other. Draco took a huge bite out of Tabitha's torso and tossed it to the arena floor. Some silver fluid leaked from the gash it left onto the arena floor. The red diamonds around the arena lit up. The silver fluid siphoned itself to the nearest diamond and got sucked underneath.

Three holographic gems appeared under the Bruiser team's player screens floating in the air, and the bottom of the leftmost one filled up a tiny portion at the bottom with a green bar.

A green light appeared on the square Mason Smith stood on top of. He rushed forward, straight towards the perpendicular side of the field, lighting that base as well. He continued towards the next perpendicular side's base, but stopped midway as one circle in the ground ahead of him opened up and Kassandra emerged from it, swinging her bat. Mason grimaced and ran back to the previous base he captured.

"Ooooo and Mason almost caught two bases, but Killer KO is not having it!" Gerard said. "We're off to a bloody start! Let's see how the Lockhearts fight back!"

Tabitha stretched all of its legs straight out and squeezed them tight to its body. The taracede spun on its back several times, completing an arch on the arena floor, nearly tripping Draco, but the Equus flew up just in time. Tabitha rolled over onto its stomach, its legs underneath, and jumped up straight into Draco. Tabitha turned over, its legs wrapping around Draco's torso, stabbing into it. Draco cried out, flapping its wings, trying to shake Tabitha off, as its silver fluid leaked onto the floor below and sucked into the ground.

Three more holographic gems appeared under the Lockheart team's player screens and a blue bar filled the first one up a little more than the previous team's gem had.

On the arena floor, Demora hesitated before running forward. She hit the starting base, then made a move for the perpendicular side's base, but a hole opened up right in front of her and Disaster Daisy emerged, striking Demora right in the stomach with her bat. Daisy celebrated the hit before being dropped back under the arena floor.

"There it is, folks! Both teams are in the game now!" Gerard said. "But the Lockheart's new Bolter is gonna need a little time adjusting to that hit! Back a base she goes!"

Demora got up from off her knees, rubbing her stomach. On her player screen, she grilled the camera as she retreated to the base she was last on.

"Just shake it off Demo, no sweat," Amy said.

"She better get her shit together!" Tilly yelled from the rows below.

Amy shot her a dirty look.

Don't make me break that other arm.

The game raged on, with the two massive mechanical beasts digging into each other. In the center dome, Madeline and Brenton worked tirelessly at their consoles, controlling their mascots and the movement of the Boxers underneath the arena. It was a grueling match. There were some tough hits taken by both sides, but Demora was on the receiving end of the brunt of the abuse. Both teams had filled up one and a half of their gems, and the physical wear-and-tear of the beasts on the field reflected that. Mason had gotten two full runs in-pattern around the arena, and Demora had gotten one. Each team's score was displayed under the player screens:

Bruisers-2, Lockhearts-1

Amy stirred in her seat, her face hiding between her fingers. She couldn't believe that Demora had kept her cool for this long, more than she had ever seen her friend do, but a boiling point was imminent.

Amy waited as long as she could for a timeout to be called, but her body's natural flow was calling for release into the nearest loo. She bolted up out of her seat and excused herself as she made her way out of her row, but paused.

Across the way, General Aba whispered something to one of his guards. The guard nodded and rose, beckoning the general's brother to join him.

Amy apologized to the lady who had told her to move and continued out of her row. She dropped to untie then slowly redo her sneaker laces, waiting for the general's guard and brother to head out their exit.

The general and brother went through their exit, and Amy dashed towards her exit as well.

Amy crept down the hall, waiting for the general's guard and brother to enter the next hall.

"Timeout!" Gerard's voice yelled from inside the arena. "First time out called by the Lockheart Girls! Game continues in five!"

"Shit," Amy said, as crowds quickly swarmed the halls.

Amy sprinted down the hall and past the elevator. Around the corner, the general's guard and brother made their way across the room and through the next hall. Amy followed, blending herself amongst the crowd, paces behind the gorilla pair.

The general's guard pointed towards the restroom and the general's brother went inside. The guard looked around before continuing to walk into the next hall.

Amy followed him, making herself smaller within the crowd, easily able to keep an eye on his massive figure, but he was moving a lot faster than Amy had expected. This was the first time she was in the same vicinity as the Great Apes, and their legend had remained true. They were much bigger than the humans but also much faster.

Amy cut around the corner that the general's guard had turned, but he was nowhere to be found. She checked a door off to her side and another ahead, but both were locked.

"Shit," Amy whispered. She headed back the way she came, remembering her bladder.

Once she finished up in the restroom, she came out and froze at the general's brother, who was hanging upside from the ceiling. He jumped down and ran up to Amy.

"Hi there friend!" he said. "Have you seen my guard, Mumba? We're missing the game!"

"I'm afraid I haven't, chap," Amy said. "You got any idea where he was headed?"

"He had to take care of some business. Busy, busy, busy. They're always busy, busy, busy. My brother and the royal guards." He walked up the wall, his webbed feet sticking to them, then hopped over onto the opposite wall and kept jumping back and forth between walls.

"You're an active young chap, aren't you? What's your name? Never thought I'd see an arachniape up close."

"My name is Bosti!" he said. He sat on the floor and picked at his feet, removing a string of webbing between them. "And I'm sixty-three years old! I practice martial arts! How old are you? What's an arachniape? Where's Mumba?"

"That's what you are, chap," Amy said, stepping closer to him. "I'm old enough. I didn't know your kind enjoyed these sorts of games."

"My brother hates them. He says they're nonsense. But I love it! It's so exciting!" Bosti fell onto his back and flipped into a handstand. "The big robot family members are so cool!"

"Family members?"

"Mhm. Big bro says we're all related. Everyone in the Animalia Kingdom. But not those pesky humans, no sir!"

"Nice. So what's your brother doing here if he hates us so much?"

"Big bro says we're here to meet the man who plays with insects. Then we're getting the hell out! That's what he says."

"Bosti!" The general's guard came thumping down the hall and pushed his way past Amy. "We don't fraternize with the savages. Let's return to our seats."

"Yeah, yeah! Let's go! Bye ugly human!" Bosti waved goodbye to Amy. He and Mumba left her behind.

Amy waited for them to disappear from view before making her way back as well. Upon reaching the hall before the arena, a loud crash came from inside, followed by screams.

Amy burst inside, and crowds rushed past her, pushing her from all angles. Down on the arena floor, the players, including Demora, ran off the field as large chunks of the ceiling and other metal parts laid across the floor.

Amy fought her way past the commotion in her seating area and froze. The large, movable stage that Gerard the host had stood on laid in pieces on her side of the arena. As she walked towards the wreckage, the blood and glimpses of the crushed bodies underneath were enough to kill her curiosity. It wasn't for another couple of seconds before a thought shot through her mind like a bullet through flesh.

Jimmy.

As though her prayers had been answered, Jimmy ran up beside her, grabbing her shoulder as he dropped the bucket of popcorn and soft drink in his hands.

"Amy! Are you alright?" Jimmy said.

"I'm good. What happened?"

A glint of light blinded Amy as fast as it left. In one corner of the ceiling above where the stage used to be connected, a figure stood covered in shadows. On this bright sunny day, there were shadows on this corner of the ceiling. The figure stepped back, and the darkness ate them.

"There's someone up there," Amy said. "Where the stage was. Someone's up there!"

Jimmy followed her finger and stared at the bright corner of the ceiling she pointed at.

"I don't see anyone."

"Someone was up there, Jimmy, I saw them!"

"I'll let the squad know. Come on, you don't need to see this."

Jimmy led her away through the chaos.

Sometime later, Amy stood crossed armed with some Detectives around her. She'd rather be anywhere, as she was getting rather annoyed with the probing questions about her whereabouts before the incident. Detective Burt made his way over to Amy.

"We meet again, Ms. Devine," Burt said, flashing his toothy smile. "Although I wish it was under better circumstances. Seems tragedy keeps drawing us together. "

"Has your squad found the culprit on the upper floor?" Amy asked.

"We looked into your report, but we found no one in the area. Mind telling me where you were a few minutes before the stage fell?"

"Like I told your boys over here, I went to the restroom and came right back."

"Just the restroom, Ms. Devine? Because after a check of the footage that wasn't erased, it seems you got a little lost on your way to the restroom."

"What erased footage?"

"Let's stay on topic. What were you doing before entering the restroom?"

Amy sighed. She wanted to avoid what she was about to say.

"Okay. I was heading to the restroom and I thought I saw someone headed towards a secure area. I just… wanted to see what they were up to, but I lost track of them."

"When you say *someone*, do you mean someone like the General's guard? He too lost his way on the way to the restroom." Burt pointed over at General Aba and his group. General Aba's solid black eyes bore right through Amy.

"Listen, I don't want to cause any unnecessary trouble."

"But you are saying the guard was making his way towards a secure area?"

"I can't say for sure. I lost track of him. It could have been anyone. Sorry."

That was it. Although she had indeed lost track of Aba's guard and the figure she saw at the roof of the arena was large, there was no way she was inciting a war between them and General Aba. Not without solid evidence.

"Whatever you're trying to get this adolescent cunt to mutter—" General Aba made his way over to them. "—just remember, mother nature has gifted us with superior listening skills compared to your pathetic species."

"*Cunt?*" Amy said, her eyes buried into General Aba.

"Now, now, General," Burt said, stepping in between them, giving his hearty chuckle. "No need for that language, as we mean no disrespect. We're simply trying to fit pieces into a puzzle that doesn't quite fit just yet. We've had a troubling amount of misfortunes lately and we're—"

"Your insignificant human troubles are of no concern to mine," Aba snarled. "We are here to witness how you continue to mock us in your games while taking a break from our tour of England."

"He's lying." Amy's eyes met General Aba's. "I ran into your brother in the restroom area and he told me you were here to meet the 'man who plays with the insects'. Care to tell us what that's about, General?"

General Aba's widened, veiny eyeballs bore right into Amy as he marched up to her. "My brother suffers from a rare condition that renders his brain as small as a Class One human infant on its worst day. This affliction came from an insect bite he received from a Northfaced Bunglebee when he was a child. We are here to visit the Insect Research pop-up on the edge of your shitty sister city so that we may hope to find an answer to what ails young Bosti."

Amy opened her mouth, but nothing came out. She didn't move until Detective Burt put a hand on her shoulder.

"There's an IRC pop-up on the edge of New Enfield," Burt said. "Our Governor ordered a renowned entomologist to come to help us figure out the cause of the frequent bee swarms." He turned back to Aba and pulled off his bowler hat. "I am terribly sorry to hear about your brother. We had no idea. Terribly, terribly—"

Detective Burt stepped back to avoid General Aba's massive right palm, which shot upward, facing him. He put back on his smile and pointed over at Aba's guard, Mumba.

"We just ask that your friend there remain in town until we're able to wrap things up in regards to today's unfortunate events."

"I've had enough of this meaningless banter," Aba said. "Once our private business has reached its conclusion, we will be leaving your less than desirable communities, regardless of the status of your human affairs. If you have any issues with that, you can take it up with the Ambassador of Animalia and Human Liaisons. In the meantime, we'll continue our business as stated without bother."

General Aba took a few steps but stopped, turning to face Amy. "Girl. Life is but a breeze. I'd suggest you mind your tongue or else it may choke you up."

General Aba marched past his crew, shooting a look at Bosti. Bosti's head went down and he followed his older brother. On the way out, Jimmy avoided a stiff shoulder from Aba as he walked in.

"Wimblestyn!" Burt said. "We'll need to get a request out to the Ambassador of A and H. Any other witnesses came forth?"

"Zero," Jimmy said. "What are the chances this is related to our current case? Why don't we just bring in a telepathist, read everyone's mind in town? Or a spiritualist even. Maybe find out if any of those who passed have seen anything—"

"You can try getting the Mayor to sign off on that," Burt said. "He wants this wrapped up clean without hysterics."

"Well, I think we're a bit past hysterics, Burt. Come on Ms. Devine, let's get you home."

"Are you her personal escort, Detective?" Burt asked.

"Given what she came across and the poking around the department has given her, I think she'd enjoy an easy ride home. Your call, Ms. Devine."

Amy nodded. She followed Jimmy towards the exit, taking a final glance back at Detective Burt.

Chapter Tweleve

"I am going to murder someone if I miss this film." Demora pulled the couch away from the center of the room. "There, how's that?"

"ZiccoLynx, start MovieRoom," Amy said.

The ZiccoLynx box chimed awake as a beam of white light formed a wall in front of it.

"Please reduce viewing size. Room dimensions are too small for safe viewing."

"Goddamn you to Hell!" Demora yelled as she punched the couch. "I refuse to watch the movie of the year on a small screen!" Her face lit up. "UnderCity Cinemas."

Amy groaned. "I really don't feel like traveling, Demo. And we've only got about forty-five minutes."

"Yes, so let's hurry then. I do not want to miss trailers either."

Archie fluttered up to Amy and flew around her head, but she waved him off.

"No, Archie. You get too cranky the morning after you stay up late, you know that."

Archie's ears and wings slouched.

"Ah, c'mon now, Ames!" Demora put her hands on her hips. "Don't be a party pooper. Let him tag along. He needs fresh air!"

"You don't have to deal with him in the morning, Demora. Why are we having this—"

"C'mon! Let him have some fun. He can stay over at my place if you're really concerned."

"And your folks would be cool with that?" The doubt was strong.

"I'll deal with them. Deal? We've gotta go. Deal?" Demora rubbed Archie's head as his dropping mouth quivered and his eyes grew big.

Amy and Demora strode down a long block, with Archie right behind them. The streets were dark except for some dim lamp posts on every corner.

"This is a waste of time," Amy said.

"You used to love going to UCC. Besides, this is necessary for this film!"

"You don't even know if this movie will be good!"

Demora gasped. "You take that back!"

Whispers.

Amy stopped. "Did you hear that?"

"Hear what?"

More whispers.

Demora stopped walking. "Okay, I heard that."

The two girls scanned the area. The streets were empty. Half of the lamp posts ahead buzzed off, then the other half dimmed to almost nothing. The trees blew in the wind, carrying the echoes of the whispers with them.

"It's probably just—"

Amy put her hand in front of Demora. "There. In that tree to the right." She nodded towards the tree in question, and Demora's eyes followed. Obscured in the shadow-covered leaves on the tree, a pair of eyes the color of a corn moon stared right back at them. A second pair appeared beside them. Several pairs followed right after on either side. The leaves on the branches shifted.

"Let's get the hell out of here." Demora pulled Amy's arm forward, with Archie close behind. The fluttering sound of dozens of wings not too far behind them.

The dim lamps went out behind them as the flying creatures passed. One pair of eyes caught up, just inches behind Amy. Amy groaned as she fell backward, grabbing her hair.

Demora punched the darkness-covered creature, causing it to drop the lock of Amy's hair it had a hold of. Demora helped Amy up, and they continued their escape.

"What's the password?!" Demora asked.

"Spanner in the works after Creaevix shit hit the fan, then took the piss after a bloody bender," Amy said.

"Bloody mouthful."

They cut into a corner, Archie stumbling into a wall before regaining his composure. Amy swiped him into the inside of her jacket, then dashed down the alley, catching up with Demora. Midway down the alley, Demora banged her hand on a section of the brick wall.

"Spanner in the works after Creaevix shit hit the fan, then took the piss after a bloody bender!" Demora said.

Amy and Demora looked at each other, sweat running down their faces. They turned at the sound of the fluttering wings, as the dozens of moon-colored eyes came around the corner and shot straight towards them. Both of the girls thrashed their hands against the wall.

"Spanner in the works after Creaevix shit hit the fan, then took the piss after a bloody bender!" both of the girls said, looking back and forth between the wall and the moonbats.

"Bloody hell!" Demora said.

Amy massaged her throat and stepped out in front of Demora, her eyes lighting up orange. She threw her hands out towards the oncoming swarm and her aura flushed in front of the swarm, its light revealing the large iron-colored bone exoskeleton of the moonbats.

The jaws of the moonbats dropped and blood-curling screeches escaped them.

Amy smashed her palms over her ears, yelling into the ground. Her eyes flickered like a flame being doused as she tried to catch her breath. She dropped to her knees, coughing up some blood as the last of the moonbats flew off into the night sky.

"I know, just get it out, Ames," Demora said, stooping down to her, grabbing her shoulders. "Just get it out." She held Amy's hair back as Amy emptied the contents of her stomach.

The brick wall pushed out and to the side, with a dingy man pushing it along. He looked down at the girls. "You girls hear something out there?"

Moments later, Mr. J led Amy and Demora down the dusty passageway.

"Don't you mind ol' Osmosis, he's a blundering idiot. Here—"

A disheveled woman standing along the wall passed him a small sack. He pulled the string around its opening and waved the sack back to Amy.

"Take one'a those and you'll feel back to jack in no time."

Amy reached into the sack and pulled out a sky blue bean-shaped candy. She brought it to her mouth, dodging Demora's hand swipe.

"You don't know what's in that," Demora said.

"I'm sure it's fine," Amy replied. She swallowed the piece of candy. A couple of seconds after a big gulp, her eyes went wide. She looked down at her feet to hide the flash of orange light that flashed across her irises.

"What the hell, are you alright?" Demora asked.

"I'm fine. Actually, I haven't felt this great in ages." Amy opened and closed her hands, flexed her arms, bent her legs, and twisted her torso, feeling like she had a new body. "What are those?"

"You ask too many questions, Devy. Best you not know. If the wrong lot got to ya, best you not able to tell them nothing."

"That's sketchy," Demora said.

"Sketchy keeps you alive in the Undercity. Teh. Moonbats in town. Deep shit isn't the word. Nasty buggers. Screech will turn your insides out. Here—"

He led them down a deep trench leading into another hall in the maze. He pointed forward towards four pieces of metal embedded into the dirt wall, floor, and sidewalls.

"Can't take any chances," Mr. J said. "With all these Peculiar attacks and people gone missing."

"All these Peculiar attacks?" Amy asked.

"Ah, suppose you wouldn't a'heard. They been keeping it hush-hush. They found two Peculiars, brother and sister, right outside New Enfield. Killed six tourists. But yer police and Mayor don't wanna talk o'bout it. Scamps."

Amy gave Demora a look before walking through the scanner. A beep followed a green light on the top of it. Demora walked in after her, garnering the same result.

"Be careful in Enfield center. Heard they're under different management. Still safe, but don't know the personality. Take these—" Mr. J handed each of the girls a paper ticket, then leaned in close. "If they get all in your shit, tell em I sent ya." He shooed them towards the exit ahead of them.

The girls made their way down a ladder and faced a set of tracks with a large brown train in the middle.

"That train is supposed to be silver," Demora said.

"Been some years since we took it," Amy replied as she pulled some black latex gloves out of her pocket and slipped them on.

The girls walked towards a group of four that stood in front of a light coming from an open train door. Amy pet Archie's peaking head that came out from her jacket and gently pushed him back inside.

One of the loiterers outside the train stepped up to Amy. His bison face's green eyes and long snout moved inches from Amy's face as his massive figure towered over her.

"You lost?" he asked.

"No, loser," Demora said, pulling Amy's arm and walking around him. "Give me a reason."

Moments later, Amy stared out the grimy window next to her on the moving train. Archie's snore snapped her out of it and she smiled as Archie rested on Demora's lap, being pet by Demora.

"What do you reckon he's up to?" Demora asked. She nodded over at a man with green and white scales all over his body, who took a seat near the end of the train's car.

"Don't be a twat, Demo," Amy said, slapping Demora's knee. "I can't imagine what it must feel like being judged for your appearance. Must be hard."

"I wasn't judging his appearance. It's more about what he's carrying." Demora tapped her hip.

Amy followed Demora's gesture to the reptilian man's hip. A sharp, shiny object stuck out of his pants.

"We should alert detectives," Amy said.

"Well, now who's being judgmental, Devine? Here it comes."

The storm door at the end of the car shot open as the train buckled. The reptilian man jumped out of his seat, pulling out the sharp object.

Amy rose, but Demora held her back.

The reptilian man opened his sharp object at the base, it becoming an accordion-like instrument with several buttons on it. He kept expanding and condensing the instrument's internal fans as delicate, string-piano tones came from it. He played a soft melody as fireflies rushed inside and circled his head.

"The fireflies are attracted to the massive amount of energy. They hover around the lights outside of every train car like ants to sugar.

The light powers their own, but it also burns them to death if they hang around long enough. The only other thing that'll distract them is music. That instrument he's playing is called an Acciano. I recognize them from the band performance that starts up every pro-Animalia Gems game. Never seen one up close, so he must be a bandmate or really lucky 'cuz those things are really expensive. Anyway, he's saving them. The fireflies."

Demora scratched Archie's head as the bat turned over onto his belly and let out a small 'cooo'.

"I respect him," Demora continued. "He's carrying one of the most expensive pieces of equipment just to do this, probably every night, I reckon. He has no choice but to take the Undercity's rails anyhow, because of how the surface dwellers view his kind.

"History tends to repeat itself," Amy said. "There used to be a time when you and I couldn't have even been friends." Amy placed her caramel-colored hands next to Demora's pale ivory ones. She looked back up at the man, who propped the door with his foot, joyfully playing the Acciano as hundreds of fireflies filled the surrounding area.

"The world still needs changing, even after all this time," Demora said.

The reptilian man flew onto the ground, his Acciano flying out of his hands. The bison-faced man stepped into the car and stomped on the reptilian man's stomach, then picked up the Acciano, smiling.

"Little fairy twat," the bison-faced man said, chuckling.

"Give that back," Demora said, walking towards him, clenching her fists.

"You gonna make us, kid?" He nodded behind Amy, and the other three members of his gang stepped in from the other car.

"We'll take that bat, too. Nice pounds for that shit," one of the gang members said. She shook her wild, puffed rainbow hair and several black spots on her face shifted, growing more on them.

Behind her, the remaining two gang members smiled simultaneously. The identical twins focused their one eye on Amy. Yellow drool crept down their open mouths as they scratched their blue skin feverishly.

"Let us have a look, girl," the identical twin thugs said.

Amy and Demora smiled.

"The great thing about being in the UnderCity..." Demora started.

"...is that no one will blink at a little extra strength," Amy finished. "I love a good spar."

Amy and Demora walk out the opening train doors, leaving behind the unconscious bodies of the gang inside the train car. The girls jogged down a long tunnel towards a door at the end.

"Z-Lynx, what time is it?" Demora said.

"It's 07:54 pm," a robotic voice chimed from out of her earpiece.

"We're going to miss the previews."

"Relax, Demo. We're right here."

The wall in front of them snapped open. Two women—sharing the same body—stood in their path. Their respective necks left an even creak in between their heads. The left woman's eyes narrowed on them while the right woman smiled.

"Tickets!" the head on the left said.

"Please?" the right head said.

The girls raised their tickets, which the women's left hand snatched from them.

"The premiere's about to begin," the lady's left head said.

"Right this way!" the right head said, beaming.

The women spun on their heels and dashed away. Amy and Demora jogged after them.

"Put some pep in your step! Bad enough you're this late to the showing," the left head said.

"Don't mind her, my sister's temperamental," the right head said. "Welcome to Undercity Center Cinemas. I'm Gilly!" She smiled back at the girls. "This here's my sister, Jenidine."

"Charmed," Jenidine said. "First time here, I reckon."

Demora frowned. "We've been here before—"

"We here at UCC have a strict showtime policy. All patrons are to be here at least fifteen minutes before showtime—"

"Oh, give um a rest, Jeni. I'm sure the train was late, as always. Let's give our guests a warm first impression."

"The impression is only as good as the audience allows," Jenidine said. "Will you stop? I control the left side!" Their left arm jerked away from their body.

"Did you not feel that itch?" Gilly said.

"Same shit you said with Michael."

"Do not bring up Michael! You said you'd be fine with me there!"

"I didn't say you could fu—never mind."

The hosts led them into an oval-shaped room with a higher ceiling than the last. Seven rows of seats faced a single ZiccoLynx box in the room's front. It was a lot bigger than the set in Amy's house.

"Where's Dante?" Amy asked.

"I believe he's taking a sick day," Gilly said.

"Sick week more like it." Jenidine pointed towards a room a few patrons moved into. "If you're grabbing snacks, I suggest you visit concessions now."

"I am feeling a bit famished," Amy said.

Demora's eyebrow raised. "I thought you said you weren't hungry?"

Amy shrugged.

After getting the largest available popcorn size and two drinks, they took seats in the third row. Amy stuffed her mouth with popcorn, as Archie reached out from inside her jacket and grabbed some as well.

Her eyes met with an Asian girl's, who had yellow-colored tips on her hair. Amy cleared her throat and smiled back at her.

"It's starting!" Demora shook her fists in the air.

A beam of white light shot out of the ZiccoLynx box and formed a large screen that stretched from floor to ceiling. Several images appeared on screen, with ziccolights forming them as they came. Although the light from these boxes usually gave her a headache, this time around, Amy felt fine.

"It's actually not as nauseating as it usually is," Demora said, reading Amy's mind. "But that's definitely not a Gen4 or even a Gen3 box. You can see the zlights forming the images!"

Amy and Demora walked down Amy's block as Archie flew around their heads, dodging Demora's swinging arms.

"And did you see the cinematography! Absolutely mad man, like how'd they do that?"

"With a camera, I'd reckon," Amy said.

"Wiseass. You seem awfully quiet. The movie wasn't that bad, was it?"

"Can I tell you something, Demo? And keep your cool, okay?"

"Sure."

She told Demora all about running into Jimmy at the campsite, how he saved her after the murder house, their partnership over the past few weeks, and how he *saved her* after the murder house. Demora didn't care.

"Have you lost your bloody mind?!" Demora stopped in front of Amy and pushed her shoulder back. "A bloody Detective! You've actually gone off the deep end and spoke to a bloody detective!"

"Demora, he's different, I swear it. He's with aura and he just wants to figure it all out." Amy sighed. "He just wants to understand. He's the first one to actually want to understand. This is a huge win for auraists!"

"Un-fucking-believable. You're going to get us all in trouble."

"Demo, he's not your typical detective. He's rather, I don't know—quite nice. He's got this uncle—"

"I don't care if he's got a fucking ickledragon! Are you mad?!"

"*No.*" Amy threw her hands up. "Listen, I'm going to be working with him to figure out what the hell is going on in this town. It's the closest thing I'll get to any genuine detective work."

"So now you want to be a detective?"

"Not exactly, but exploring the paranormal has always been the goal. That thing at the Murder House attacked us and it showed up again at the game. Murdered all of those people. And I want to track down the murderer before they strike again," Amy concluded.

"Chasing ghosts. Holy Callisto Ames, what are you thinking?"

"You and I both know what this could be, Demora."

"If it is a rogue auraist, then shouldn't you bring this to Rezna's attention?"

Amy stared past Demora's head. She hadn't thought about that, but couldn't figure out why. If indeed the murderer was a rogue auraist, then who better to confront it than the great Rezna Devine herself?

"No," Amy said. "I—I didn't pick up any aura from it. It just had an excess amount of energy. There's a considerable amount of things with energy in this world. It could be any creature or being, but I'm sure it's not an auraist."

"I don't know what you expect me to say, Ames, but I just don't want to see you get hurt. You're risking everything Rezna ever worked for in order to buddy up to some asshole in a uniform. I just—I can't do this right now."

A taxi pulled up and the Remsen bot inside waved at her.

"Pickup for Demora Corbyn-McDonald!" the Remsen bot said.

"Later." Demora got in the taxi. It sped off.

She'll come around.

Amy pulled her jacket collars up and ran past her gate and up the stairs. She swung her GCID in front of the small screen on her door, but nothing happened.

"Old shit."

The front door opened up before she could try again. Two detectives walked out and nodded their heads. Amy watched them get into their car. The car raised, hovering as a white beam of light grew underneath it. They sped away.

A few moments later, Amy sat at the kitchen table across from Rezna, steaming mugs of tea in their hands.

"There was a sting mark on every fucking corpse," Rezna said. "Every fucking corpse. Fucking bees. How the hell did I miss that?"

"It wasn't your fault Gma," Amy said.

"Child, you wouldn't understand. There is a specific routine I have every single time. Never fails. Never. Yet here we are."

Amy rarely saw Gma lose her cool to the point of cursing. She wanted to help. In these moments, she'd forget about the powerful woman that stood in front of her and felt herself revert to that little girl who just wanted to help her Gma feel good again.

"Do you think something… bigger is going on?"

"Bigger?" Rezna raised an eyebrow. "Speak clear, girl."

"With everything that's been happening in town." Amy traced the top of her mug with her fingertips. "The bee swarms. The murders. The missing people. Do you think it's all connected?"

"No." Rezna stared at Amy's face for more than a few uncomfortable seconds. "No, I don't think anything is connected to anything else. We let the uninitiated deal with the problems of common folk. We have our own fights to master."

"But…" Amy felt a vibration in her pocket. "Okay. I'm going to head off to bed." She rose from her seat and stooped down to kiss Rezna's forehead. "G'night."

"Night, dear."

Amy jogged up the stairs and pulled out her G-XSR.

Meet @ 8 AM. Riverside.

Chapter Thirteen

Jimmy, arms crossed, leaned against a small yet bulky white tank of a vehicle.

"Where's your car and what the bloody hell is this thing?" Amy's eyebrows raised as she walked around it.

"It's what they call a discreet messenger. I've got Skitinsky in there."

"What?!" Amy jumped back.

"Don't worry, he hasn't come back," Jimmy chuckled, tapping the tank's hood. "I'm going to truck him over to the Insect Research Center on the skirts of New Enfield for testing. You want to tag along?"

"Really? That'd be sick!" She looked back at the trunk. "Minus the corpse." Her expression died down. "Oh wait, I actually had something to do today."

Demora...

She had promised Demora they'd get some aura practice in, as well as practice for Demora's next Animalia Gems game.

"Don't sweat it. Hopefully won't have to make too many trips out there once we settle this beeswax debate. I know some detectives spoke with your grandmother last night."

Amy nodded. "There may be another missing person. Dante—shit, I don't know his last name."

"Dante Carmichael. Yeah, we've gotten some info on—how do you know that? Never mind, don't wanna know." Jimmy got into the driver's seat and started the vehicle. The muscular vehicle raised into the air as a white beam of light glowed underneath it. "Hate these things. Sometimes you just need to stick with the classics. But my old tires wouldn't make it on these roads."

"Wait," Amy said, opening the passenger side door and sitting inside. "I can get to it another time."

"Alrighty, let's roll."

As Jimmy pulled out onto the road, Amy grabbed her chest as a sharp pain invaded it.

"Are you alright?"

Amy looked into the rearview mirror. Although no one stared back at her, she could swear a pair of eyes was burying into her soul. Amy sat back in her seat and nodded to Jimmy. "Bit of heartburn."

Jimmy hit the gas and moved on as Amy kept her eyes on the rearview mirror.

Guilt is eating me.

Halfway through the hour, they pulled up at the drive-thru window of a russet-colored restaurant with a sign that read The Neighboring Shack. The out-of-place fast-food spot sat in the middle of a passage, surrounded by trees and dirt. At the window, a service bot in a brown and green uniform caught a falling piece of the building's ceiling that tumbled down in front of them.

A beautiful woman in an orange blazer walked up beside the bot and scratched the thick black hair that complimented either side of her face. A tag on her front read Manager.

"Hey Jimmy," the manager spoke through her sharp, bared teeth. "Sorry about that. Damn racist bandits again."

"Fazura! Didn't realize you were in town. It's, uh, great seeing you again." Jimmy massaged the back of his head. "I've talked to someone in Protection of Outliers. They've got a suspect in custody that has some information about these attacks. Think we'll get a big break soon, so stay strong "

Fazura smiled. "Thanks, Jim. Wish your sweetness could flush the Earth. Isn't he sweet?"

"Oh, the sweetest," Amy said, trying her best not to laugh.

"Don't mention it!" Jimmy's cheeks went red. He cleared his throat. "Oh! This is Amy, she's just—there was a relation—she had a related case and—"

"No worries, Jim. I know this underage girl isn't your girlfriend."

Amy turned her head opposite them and held her laughter in.

"Everyone knows about the Devine girl," Fazura said.

Amy's smile diminished.

"And frankly, she seems like a real charmer to me. It's really nice to meet you, sweety."

Amy smiled back. "Thanks. Call me Amy. Nice to meet you too, Fazura."

"Thought I mentioned my schedule last time," Fazura said. "Just had to stop by this branch but heading back up to Liverpool tomorrow. We should catch a drink tonight if you're free."

"Yeah!" Jimmy cleared his throat again. "I, yeah, I wish I could. This case is picking up steam. Sure you've heard about it all."

"Yeah, it's crazy. Well, let me know if you get some free time. You stay safe out there. I owe you a drink or two. Give me your arm."

Jimmy stuck his arm out towards Fazura and she outstretched her forearm, palm down, over his.

"ZLynx, send contact info," Fazura said.

The ZLynx chimed.

"Forgot last time. Catch you later. Bye, Amy." Fazura turned to the service bot. "Get Jim and Amy whatever they need, on my discount." She walked away.

"Bye!" Amy stabbed an elbow into Jimmy's side. "She's absolutely stunning. Catch you later, huh Jim?"

Jimmy fixed his tie and smiled at the service bot.

Amy and Jimmy walked the dirt pasture towards an out-of-place gray lump of a structure surrounded by nothing but trees. There were no visible windows, nor doors. Past the building, the edge of New Enfield city and its tall buildings and busy life went on without bother.

Jimmy swallowed the last bite of his home fries and flashed his badge at two yellow uniformed security bots, who approached him.

"Mm—Detective Jimmy Wimblestyn of the Jadesfeld Police Department. I have a package your team's expecting."

"Please allow us access to your vehicle, Detective," one bot said.

"You got it. Permission granted."

The eyes of the security bots turned green, and they made their way past Jimmy and over to the white tank. A green beam of light left one of their eyes and washed over the tank, with the trunk opening for them.

"They've got this. Let's get inside, shall we?" Amy said, pulling Jimmy's arm.

Amy and Jimmy walked up to the front of the unmarked gray building and stopped as a humming noise echoed from its walls. The front of the building separated, revealing a door behind the wall. The automatic door shifted into the inner walls.

Jimmy and Amy moved into the empty reception hall. Jimmy flashed his badge at four more security bots on either side of him and a metal door ahead slid into the inner wall.

Jimmy marched on with Amy in tow. Amy slowed down, taking in the dozens of glass panels in the walls surrounding them. Inside the compartments, various creatures of different colors, shapes, and sizes inhabited the walls—flying, running, eating, some even fighting each other. Amy stopped in front of a panel, behind which small dots floated in the air. A second later, smaller dots shot out from under the current ones. The uppermost layers of dots sucked up into a hole in the ceiling.

To Amy's right, white-faced monkey-like creatures crept out from caves, moving towards the glass. Their horizontal amphibian eyes moved up and down, staring at Amy. Their black, leathery skin raised and flickered as their backs hunched more. A green liquid shot from around their eyes onto the glass.

Amy jumped back as their fists banged against the glass.

"Amy, this way!"

Jimmy and Amy walked into a room where a man in a long white coat sat behind a desk, working on an old computer. A nameplate on the desk read Director of Operations, I.S. Lewkraith.

"Detective Jimmy Wimblestyn of the JFPD." Jimmy stuck his hand out.

"Yes," Lewkraith said, as he pointed over to a hand sanitizing unit on the wall. "I know who you are, detective."

Amy raised an eyebrow at the man as she followed Jimmy's lead and used the wall unit to sanitize her hands. They then took the two seats in front of the man's desk.

"So Lewkraith, that name originates on the Isle of—"

"Four weeks, detective," Lewkraith said, still looking at his computer screen. "I'll need one week to study the specimen and two to three weeks for complete lab results."

"All due respect, we've got open cases on our hands that require faster processing, Mr. Lewkraith—"

"Specialist Lewkraith, detective. I am under contract with various organizations, including government agencies, on several projects. Your small town's blips are closer to the bottom of my list."

Amy had enough. "A little respect goes a long way, *Specialist*. I also find it alarming that an illegal zoo is being operated in the middle of nowhere. Seems sketchy to me."

Lewkraith kept his eyes on his screen. "Zoos are, in fact, illegal. However, this center is far from a zoo and is government-funded. You can take up your concerns with the World Committee."

"A rescue center would yield the same results without the captivity. These poor beings are clearly under duress because of your *studies*."

"Detective, are we here to discuss politics or to solve a mystery?"

"We're all scrambling for answers here, Lewkraith," Jimmy said. "But I'll need a quicker response than two weeks. People are dying."

"People die every day and so do many other living organisms. That does not change a thing."

"Did you know," Amy said, "that only fifteen percent of all bee species land on their backs once they've fallen? Their weights automatically shift because of the amount of saliva secretion—"

"I can assure you I'm quite knowledgeable about everything there is to know about bees, Ms—who are you again? Doesn't matter, you're not telling me anything new—"

"Well, this species that's been swarming our small town rolls over onto their backs when they're dying. Meaning the distribution of saliva and beeswax is overwhelming them. The beeswax leaking underneath the one I saw when it fell—"

"Wait, leaking?" Lewkraith's eyes shot into Amy. "Did the beeswax harden? Did you get a look at this up close? What color?"

"It was orange with white jelly around it, and no, it didn't harden."

"That can't be." Lewkraith sat back in his chair. "That wasn't just beeswax. Possibly a sort of venom. Do you have the specimen?"

"Threw it out."

Lewkwraith groaned. "It's too far a travel for any species with that compound."

"Not at the speed they travel."

"Even with aggravated flight, it'd take at least three months to arrive, and they would just be passing through. They wouldn't linger this long."

"Unless…" Amy said, realizing. "Unless they were searching for something."

"Even so, there are a few species that dare challenge that, but still… How big was the stinger?"

"Maybe about 3 inches. Narrows it down to about twenty species."

"Not all bee stinger lengths are known. They're some of the most aggressive insects in the world. Getting near one long enough…"

"The amount of beeswax I saw narrows that down to at least the southern-east hemisphere. And the dead bee stuck to my window. Like, I really had to dig it off there."

"Hm." Lewkwraith typed like a madman into his computer. "One week, detective. Final offer."

"That works for me!" Jimmy said. "Thank you, Specialist—"

"Make sure to sanitize before leaving and touch nothing on the way out."

"Right." Jimmy got up and Amy followed him to sanitize, then to the door.

"Wait, what's your name, girl?" We could use an inquisitive mind like yours in my division."

"Amy Devine. And, no, thank you."

Back outside, Amy and Jimmy got into the white tank. Jimmy threw his hands up.

"That was mad! I have no idea about the science stuff you two were getting at, but I got the gist. Our first real lead. Definitely glad you could tag along."

Amy beamed. "Something tells me he'll have some answers for you before the week's up."

The side of Amy's head rested in her palm as Mrs. Colt explained various formulas on the chalkboard. Amy stared into her textbook. She rubbed her eyes with vigor.

Amy sat up straight in her seat as a burning sensation forced her to squeeze her chest. Her head spun around the classroom as a tingling sensation moved through her arms and down to her feet. She peered out at a bird on the windowsill across from her, flapping its wings. Every flap and maneuver slowed until it was nearly still. All other sounds muted around Amy.

Through the cracked door leading into the hallway, a piece of paper glided by the classroom.

"I need to be excused," Amy said, finding herself standing.

"You're excused, Devine," Mrs. Colt said without facing her. "Take the pass."

Amy walked into the hallway, a brown pass in hand. Down the empty hall, the gliding paper continued its free-flowing path.

Amy followed the gliding sheet, but hesitated as it turned a corner. After a breath, she took careful steps as she approached the corner.

She turned the corner. The paper was nowhere in sight.

Now I'm definitely going mad.

That thought washed away as she spotted something disappear into a room some doors down the hall. She walked forward with a sinking weight inside her chest that fell down to her legs, her knees buckling with every step. As she got closer to the room in question, a clinking sound grew in clarity, coming from one room ahead.

Amy's eyes squinted, then grew wide. A pool of red sat outside the room that she approached; the red stream disappearing underneath the cracked door.

Amy pushed open the door of the room, the trail of red continuing past the teacher's desk and off to the left inside the classroom. Amy swallowed and pressed on, stepping over the blood and passing by the teacher's desk. A squelching sound stabbed her immediate hearing environment coming from the back of the classroom.

Someone hunched down in between two desks, at the back of the room, mounting someone else. The mounter's arm pulled back a small knife, confirming the source of the squelching sound. Blood ran down the knife and down her arm as the girl stood up and shook her white hair, drops of blood shaking off of it.

Gina turned to face Amy, a pearly white smile adorning her bloody face. Underneath her was a man whose body quivered before taking his last breath. Amy had only seen him in the teacher's lounge a few times when she passed by, but knew he taught Astrohabitance. She wasn't even sure of the name of the man whose body now laid stiff just a few feet away from her.

What Amy was sure of was the way her lunch wanted to launch out of her stomach. An incredible amount of pressure pushed against the walls inside her head, and the headache grew worse by the second. She blinked down at the blood she tracked underneath her feet. It was amazing how much blood the human body held, and Amy could feel her own pulsing throughout her shaking body.

Amy jumped as her legs moved backward, seemingly on their own, and her right arm flailed to the side. Her own body reacted before her mind caught up. She knew better than to scream, even as Gina raised her knife and walked towards her. Amy could feel her aura building around her fingertips, but her eyes stayed on the dead man's feet, and her aura subsided. She had to find a way to fight. Maybe not in her way. A fistfight was nowhere near ideal, either. So instead she did what a normal person would do under the circumstances.

"Help." It was a whisper. Amy backed out of the classroom. "Help!" A little louder, but even the sound of her moving feet drowned it out. Her fists found the walls and banged against them to aid her voice. "Help!"

"Amy Devine." Gina strolled out of the room and continued stalking her. She licked some of the blood off of her hand. "I'm so happy we get to officially meet Amy. You have been quite the entertainment. There's something… different about you. The pieces have to be put together just a little more. More time."

"G—" Amy slipped on the blood she tracked and scampered back on her elbows. "Gina, I don't want to hurt you. Please. Help!" Her small voice echoed into the hall.

"You'll join us soon enough. It's only a matter of time. Time is all. Just time. And we'll be together forever, Amy. But for now… let me give you something to remember me by—" Gina launched herself forward, the knife coming down right between Amy's feet.

Amy kicked her arm away, and using the wall, got back on her feet.

Gina ran at her with the knife stabbing wildly in the air. She grabbed Amy's hair with her free hand and raised her knife.

Beige tentacles burst around Gina and wrapped themselves around her. The tentacles lifted Gina into the air as she bit into them and stabbed her knife, missing the tentacles by mere inches.

"This school's going to shit, I tell you!" Gina's knife sliced into one tentacle, drawing blood that squirted across the floor, walls, and onto her face. "Shit! Shit! Shit!" She laughed and shook her head as the tentacles tightened.

Pores opened up on each of the tentacles as a black gas expelled from them and into Gina's face.

Gina's body went limp. Her eyes stared at the floor in front of her.

Amy backed into the wall. Students and faculty crowded the hall from all directions. Sound once again found Amy's ears as screams from the crowd filled the hallway.

Amy's eyes followed the tentacles as they relaxed and placed Gina on the floor. The tentacles unwrapped themselves from around Gina, shrunk, and retreated into the fingertips of Mr. Perry's hands.

Mr. Perry adjusted his glasses, his widened eyes going between Amy and Gina. He cleared his throat and wrapped his bleeding finger into a handkerchief.

Chapter Fourteen

Amy followed four detectives, who escorted her down the halls and out of the building. Amy kept her head down, avoiding all eye contact as the voices of the students and teachers punctured her eardrums.

"She's the one."

"They're closing school, you know."

"That's so crazy."

"Gina did that? It was just her birthday…"

"Guess she got shit gifts."

Several police cruisers surrounded the front of the school. Police-bots held hands, forming a barrier running from the school's steps up to the cruisers.

Amy squinted at the intruding rays of the sun. She stepped into one of the police cruisers and the door shut behind her.

Amy stared at the long steel table she sat at in the JFPD interrogation room. She looked away as blue light violated her vision.

Across from her, Detective Burt wore his signature smile as he rearranged pieces on his crime scene hologram. He scratched his mustache.

"Run this by me again, Ms. Devine. You were heading to the ladies' room. The same ladies' room that is located on the opposite end of the route you took."

"I told you," Amy said, still avoiding the blue light of the hologram, "that particular loo floods because of a Dragonface pipefish infestation, so I took the safer option. You can check the school's records on that."

"And you had no prior relations with Gina Gallagher?"

Amy shook her head.

"I must admit. It's quite curious. You seem to be around a lot of misfortunes. The Baker's funeral of 2170. The well incident of 2175."

"What does that have to do with anything?" Amy's nose flared. "I don't appreciate you digging into my past."

"I'm a detective, it's my job. There's an air of uncertainty in our little town, and I've got to follow the traces as they come. And they seem to keep leading back to you."

The door burst open and Jimmy marched in.

"What the hell's going on, Burt? Why wasn't I informed that our witness arrived! We're partners now!"

"We had trouble reaching you, Wimblestyn, and the matter had to be recorded as soon as possible. The interview is good, so we're done here."

"Unacceptable Burt, unacceptable! Ms. Devine, grab your coat and let's go!" Jimmy fixed his tie and exhaled. "Please. I'm taking you home."

Amy grabbed her coat off her chair and made her way after Jimmy.

As he led her down the halls and out of the building, several detectives stopped what they were doing and watched her and Jimmy.

Minutes later, Jimmy drove his car with Amy beside him.

"Unbelievable. Did they say anything threatening to you?"

"No, it was fine, Jimmy. Really. Just a mess. A hot mess, all of it."

An alert flashed on the dashboard screen. Jimmy hit his earpiece. He swerved the steering wheel.

"Why are we turning?"

"Issa's in the hospital."

Amy and Jimmy jogged through the clean, white hallway. Ahead of them, a group of detectives surrounded Norma Jones. Jimmy motioned for Amy to 'stay here'.

Amy took a seat along the wall. She winced, groaning at the dried-up blood at the edges of her off-white sneakers. Down the hall, Jimmy and the other detectives moved away, isolating themselves in a private conversation. Ms. Jones had her head in her hands, sobbing.

Amy rubbed her stomach.

They don't know what you know.

I've got to try.

Amy got up and walked over to Ms. Jones, who wiped her face as she turned to face Amy.

"Oh, not now, girl," Ms. Jones said.

"What happened? What did you do to Issa?!"

"You know nothing!" Ms. Jones stumbled back, looking around and biting her nails, as though something had startled her.

"You hear them too. The voices. I hear them too." Amy could not believe that those words left her mouth, even more so in the company of a woman she despised.

"Wha—" Ms. Jones wiped the last of her tears away. "What are you talking about? Voices? You're crazy girl, stay away!"

Amy backed up, but stopped. The determination grew on her face and she moved towards Norma.

"Based on that look you have on your face, I'd say I'm onto something. I thought it was just me in my head, but it's not. I know you hear them."

"No! Stop it! STOP IT!" Issa's small voice screamed out.

Amy and Ms. Jones turned to the room behind them. Inside, medical staff fought to restrain Issa as she struggled to free herself.

"It's Cloudy's story! It's Cloudy's story!"

Tears ran down Ms. Jones's face as her jaw dropped.

"Who's Cloudy?" Amy asked.

Ms. Jones' eyes slowly turned to Amy. She looked over Amy's head.

"Nothing can help us."

"What's the meaning of this?!" A stocky man wearing a bowler hat approached them. Amy recognized his icy indigo gaze as he nearly knocked her over the other day. The man's scrunched-up face pointed a finger towards the detectives. "This is a family matter. There is no reason for the police to be involved!"

Jimmy walked up to meet him.

"Thomas Jones, I presume? Listen, I—"

"No, you listen here, detective! I don't know what you're playing at harassing my family—" Mr. Jones pointed at Amy "—and bringing this girl along with you. I want to know the meaning of this intrusion and I want to speak to your superior immediately."

"Mr. Jones, if you just give me a second to explain—"

"No, no, no. Forget that. I don't want to hear your excuses because there are none! My wife and niece are free from your reigns at this instant!"

"Hey Jim!" a detective called out to Jimmy. "The chief's on notice, doesn't sound too happy."

"Great," Jimmy said, letting out a breath of air. "Boys, take what you can from Mr. Jones. I'll be back in a sec." Jimmy guided Amy away from the barking Mr. Jones and down the hall.

Amy and Jimmy stepped into an elevator, and Jimmy hit the ground-level button.

"Something tells me his bite is worse than that awful bark," Jimmy said.

"What happened to Issa?"

"She broke her arm."

"What?!"

"Keep your voice down."

"Jimmy, Ms. Jones has something she's not saying. She's hiding something."

"Amy—"

"Her husband came barking like a madman before she could tell me what it was." Amy chased behind Jimmy as he led them towards the exit. "I'm sure of it! Something bigger is going on here. I think… this will sound crazy… I think—"

"What Amy? What do you think?"

They stepped outside. Amy waited until some doctors passed by, then dragged Jimmy towards the parking lot.

"Jimmy, I think someone's possessing the adults."

"Possession?"

"Yes! All the murders. Someone's either possessing the other adults to kill one another or maybe off-ing some and possessing others. Like, covering their tracks or something—"

"Amy, there hasn't been a single case of possession in over fifty years. And the only one possible of possession that strong is rotting in a cell half a world away."

"Gina just turned eighteen, and not long after she goes mad and offs someone? Quite out of the norm. She was possessed. You know it's not entirely out of the realm of possibilities and would explain why no one has been caught yet."

"There are a lot of possibilities, Amy. Thing about yours is that the only possession possible these days is the illegal kind, and the lifesnatchers wouldn't dare cross that boundary."

"Aura changes the course of everything you thought you knew, Jimmy." Amy dragged him away from a group of medical staff passing by. "With aura manipulation, an individual may be able to channel their energy into another. It hasn't been seen yet, but—"

"I'm not trying to say I understand this stuff yet, but it's a theory, Amy. A theory with zero evidence to back it up."

"You said you were open to possibilities."

"Open, yes. But not ready to toss my whole career away on a possibility. Forget that, toss my main mission away. Did you forget about that, Amy? What my mission is?"

"Of course not. If your uncle were here, he'd probably tell you to go with your gut."

"But he's not here and we just need to chill out right now, alright? I had a unit watching the Jones' house and Ms. Jones was sitting in the living room the entire time when Issa's screams were heard. Thomas Jones? He visited the night before and left thirty minutes later. No one else entered or left that home."

Amy stood, defeated. She shook her head.

"Issa said 'It's Cloudy's story' and Ms. Jones was about to tell me something before her husband—ex-husband—whatever, interrupted."

"Who's Cloudy?"

"I don't know."

"Amy…" Jimmy rubbed his head, smoothing his hair back. "We can't guess or assume what people are thinking. We just can't!"

"You've got to at least bring this up to your department, Jimmy! This is serious!"

"I know that it's serious, Amy."

"And it could be anyone!"

"Could be me." Jimmy wore a wide, devilish smile and narrow eyes. He licked his lips.

"What?" Amy uncrossed her arms and backed away.

"I said, I doubt it could be." Jimmy sighed, his face back to normal. "Look, lay low. I told you this before and now I need you to be even lower. Be invisible, completely and utterly invisible. Please! For both of our sakes."

Jimmy ran back inside. Amy stared at the spot he was at and took a deep breath.

He's affected too...

Her eyebrows raised.

Gma...

Amy turned a corner, her face lighting up, as Demora and Archie waited at the corner of her block.

"Demo." Amy hugged Demora. She petted Archie's head. "Good to see you, buddy, but get inside, it's getting late."

Archie flew onto her forehead and hugged it. He flew up the block and towards the front gates of home.

"How are you feeling?" Demora asked.

"Like a block of shit shit me out."

"Should have twisted Gina's little ass into a pretzel. Think she'll talk?"

"Honestly, she's not herself, Demora. Something's possessing her, something's possessing every adult in this town."

"What?" Demora scoffed. "Is that detective filling your head with this rubbish?"

Amy rolled her eyes and walked towards her home.

"Really not in the mood for a lecture."

Demora marched after her.

"Someone needs to be lecturing you since you seem to be making quite erratic decisions as of late, Devine." Demora stopped. "Or maybe I should just tell Rezna."

Amy stopped at her front gate. She cocked her head to the side, staring at her feet.

"It's a good thing I know you're too afraid of her boogeymen to ever step foot in this house again." Amy pulled open the gates, chucked her jacket collars up, and headed inside.

Moments later, Amy threw herself down into the kitchen seat and threw her head back. She jumped at the clink of a mug on the table.

Rezna stood beside her and crossed her arms.

"I came to the station to pick you up, but they said you already left with a detective. Where were you?"

"Gma, I've got to talk to you, something's happening—"

"Yes, we should talk. But after training. We've got to take advantage of your pent-up state."

"Not today, Gma, please. I'm exhausted."

"And those feelings of exhaustion are when your aura awakens best. Let's train."

"No." Amy's arm came down hard on the table, leaving a small dent in it. She exhaled. "I'm sorry. I'm just not up to it tonight. I've had a really long day."

"You think evil waits for your exhaustion to extinguish?"

"I think even evil takes a holiday, actually."

"Joking. Of course. It's always just one big joke for you. You have little time—"

"Time for what?! Time to be training for an unspecified amount of time, towards an unspecified reward that will 'greatly aid me in the battle of evil'?"

"You watch your tone with me."

Amy stared into the sink ahead. She had enough of everyone. Gma, Demora, even Jimmy for not hearing her out. Something was taking over the town's matured residents and aura training seemed last on the list at the moment. It was time.

"Gma, there is something taking over the town. Something controlling people—the adults—and I don't know how long until it consumes them all."

Rezna smiled.

"Silly girl, there's no such thing as possession anymore. You know that."

Amy's fingers trembled. The unfamiliar smile on her beloved Gma's face launched her insides into a pit of despair she had not felt prior. It was a similar smile that Jimmy wore earlier. The woman who raised her was no longer present.

Rezna's smile widened as she bent over the table, inches from Amy's face.

"You want to know so badly what you've been training for, do you?" Rezna banged her fists into the table, creating bigger dents than Amy did.

"Your aura. When you manipulate it, what happens?"

Amy's lips trembled as she avoided eye contact with this stranger.

"What happens when I manipulate my aura?" Rezna's head twisted to the side.

"Ha—" It barely came out. Amy's mouth opened and closed a few times.

"WHAT HAPPENS!?" Rezna banged into the table even harder, craters where her fists landed.

"I-I-d-d-d-don't know!" Amy jumped out of her skin. A tear sat right under her eye. She wanted to wipe it off but dared not move.

"Careful dear, use your inside voice, remember? Of course, you don't know. You are always wanting more without mastering the proper knowledge. We are as deaf as ignorance allows us to be."

Rezna's fingertips danced on the tabletop.

"Well, as you know, your eyes glow up so bright and your aura follows after. My eyes do not. Not very observant, are you?"

Amy took shallow breaths so as to not disturb the intruder. Her eyes did not leave the table as Rezna leaned in close to her ear.

"Well, what if I told you that you can train yourself to manipulate your aura, like me, without your eyes glowing? A new level of control, so focused that your aura's most obvious tell doesn't happen... What if I told you your aura's power would... be... amp-lified?"

Amy wanted to be anywhere else in the world right now. If she had known this was coming when she awoke, she would have stayed fast asleep.

"But of course, it's not that easy," Rezna continued. "In order to reach this level of aura mastery, you'll need a level of focus like never before. This base state you refuse to work at would need to be your main objective before taking on more powerful forms. And there are so many powerful forms you can only imagine."

Amy's eyes fell onto Rezna's fingers as they tapped rhythmically on the tabletop.

"But it's so much harder to accomplish without the necessary drive. And even more difficult when you need to do the work—tedious as it may feel—to unlock your true potential."

Rezna stood up straight and tapped her fingertips together.

"But the all-knowing Amy Devine can surely figure it out on her own, can't she? CAN'T SHE?!"

Amy hit her leg against the table leg.

"Good luck." Rezna whipped her cloak and stormed out of the kitchen.

Amy adjusted herself upright in her seat and cleared her throat.

Something's wrong with the adults in this town.

Chapter Fifteen

Face yourself.

Amy jolted upright in her bed, awaking Archie right next to her. She smiled at him.

Then frowned.

On her nightstand, a framed photo sat upright. In the photo, Rezna sat on a stone stairwell with a five-year-old Amy sitting in between her legs, smiling.

Amy set the photo facedown. A humming noise came from underneath her. She reached under her pillow and pulled out her G-SXR. The screen:

Authorities on their way. Talk later.

Amy crept out of her room door and leaned over the banister with Archie over her shoulder.

"Hey, good morning, Feebs," Amy said.

A brown aura floated in mid-air out in the hall. It paused.

"You alright? No obnoxious knocking today, huh?"

The brown aura, Feebs, darted away and down the stairs.

That was weird.

Multiple voices, radio sounds, and movement came from downstairs.

"They're pulling it out of the grave now," one voice said.

Amy moved down the upstairs hallway and stopped at the door at the end. She had never gone into Rezna's bedroom before and wasn't too keen on it now. But she'd have the safest vantage point from there.

Amy opened the creaky room door and stared at the window at the far end. She stepped in but looked back.

Archie stopped at the door, shivering, and flew back the way he came.

Amy didn't bother putting on any of the lights, as Rezna didn't have the coziest decor to help ease the situation. As she walked through the room, the various shadows and faces of barely lit figures along the walls seemed to move.

Several glints awoke in the dark corners of the room, as though watching Amy. A low growl filled the air.

"I'm not here for you," Amy said.

Amy reached the window and opened its blinds, as several hisses crescendoed.

"Shut it," Amy spat into the darkness behind her.

She peered down at the cemetery grounds below. A football team of detectives filled the green field with Rezna in the middle. They all surrounded a grave that had been dug up and some detectives were pulling a coffin out.

Amy held the G-SXR to her ear.

"I can't really talk right now, it's a madhouse," Jimmy's voice said through the phone.

"What the hell is going on? Why are they digging up a grave?"

"The beekeeper completed the testing. Didn't take long after all. The bee stinger left behind an alarming amount of propolis mixed with a special venom."

"Bee stingers don't leave behind anything other than venom, and only honey bees produce propolis."

"That's the thing, they left behind both. The bee you found on your window was one of the trackers in the group, that's why it had beeswax with it. Someone must've disturbed their home nest. Lewkraith says the swarm may be looking for misplaced beeswax. The propolis and venom mixture in Skitinsky wasn't fatal, but was enough to lower the vitals and cause paralysis. And there's only one bee type that can do that."

"Australian Buzzkills." Amy's hand shook as it held the cell phone. "They're the most proficient at adapting their compounds as they see fit. Can go undetectable."

"Right. Skitinsky died of a heart attack for sure," Jimmy continued, "but it's becoming more apparent that it may have been more than just the sting."

Amy put her free hand over her mouth.

Down in the cemetery, detectives unhooked the clamps around the coffin and shifted the top of the coffin off.

"We're pretty sure at this point all the supposed victims were still alive when we buried them. But without oxygen, they're sure to be gone by now. Except for the latest victim. They're digging her up to confirm."

Detectives laid the coffin cover on the ground. A woman laid shivering inside the coffin, her eyes staring into the sky.

"I've gotta go, Amy. The chief's got me on press duty. Remember, keep a low profile till further notice."

The woman's chest heaved up and down, gaining speed every second as her eyes grew red veins that flirted with her irises.

Her head jerked to the side.

Her wide, reddened eyes burned a hole straight through Amy.

Amy dropped the cell phone and tripped back, falling over. She grasped her throat, hyperventilating, as tears filled her eyes.

Amy rushed downstairs. She froze as Rezna approached the bottom of the stairwell, rubbing her head.

"Good morning darling," Rezna said. "Hope we didn't wake you. I was hoping this would all be over by then. Woke up with a bloody headache myself. Shit's all to pot. Are you alright, you look a bit pale?"

Amy gave her best smile.

"Brilliant! Just need to get some fresh air." Amy hustled past Rezna, grabbed her coat, chucked it over her head, and ran out the open front door.

Amy walked through the long, winding rows of Jadesfeld Library. The nauseating paths gave her a headache as she perused through the Occult section. She ran her fingers along the many book spines in a particular section and stopped on one. She pulled the book out. Its cover bore the title *Cryptics of the Hidden World.*

Amy sat hunched over at a small desk in the corner of the room, away from the other silent book heads, with stacks of books piled to her left and right. She skimmed through many pages of *Cryptics of the Hidden World*, finally stopping somewhere in the middle of the book.

The left page and right pages had intricate drawings with annotations all around.

"Rubbish," Amy said, louder than she anticipated.

"Shh," a few random voices came.

Amy flipped the page and scanned the block of texts.

"Hidden messages lay in illustrations that… these can only be forged by… and can only be seen by an eye touched by the grace of Callisto… This says nothing about possession—"

"SHH!"

Amy slammed the book shut and sat upright. She blew one of her free hairs out of her face.

Across the room, a man with a large stack of books under one arm walked out of an aisle and made his way towards a back door.

Professor Watson.

Amy got up and made her way towards him as he slipped through the back door. She picked up her pace and made her way to the door.

The door wouldn't budge. Amy pulled on the doorknob in frustration.

She made her way over to the librarian's desk.

"Excuse me, I was wondering where that door over there leads?"

The librarian stared at her. His dandelion-colored irises never left her face.

Amy stared back, waiting for some type of reply.

"HI KIDS!"

A screen had materialized above the children's section of the library. The TV host of The Basic Survival of Tomorrow's World came dancing and smiling from one corner of the screen.

Below the screen, a group of children sitting on a rug clapped for him.

"Dammit—hey!" The librarian was already around the counter and pointing at the kids. "Keep it *down*. ZLynx, power off TV!"

The screen broke apart into tiny lights, and they disappeared. The librarian made his way towards Amy.

"Third time today. Damn defective boxes."

"What's that show about?"

"Some kids show. Made to keep them busy so us grown folk can have some peace. Something to keep um busy." The librarian pointed at the back door. "Did you read the sign?"

Amy looked back at the door Professor Watson went through. Above it was a sign that Members Only.

"That wasn't there before," Amy said.

"Now you're calling me a liar. Time for break."

The librarian disappeared into a room behind his desk and shut the door.

Amy sighed. She went back to her original seat and waited.

Twenty minutes went by and Professor Watson still hadn't come out of the room.

Amy returned to the librarian's desk just as he returned from his break.

"How do you become a member?"

"Twenty-five UDs a month, charged yearly."

"Look, I'm just looking for someone who went in there. Just have to talk to them. Can I just—"

"There's no one in there right now."

"What do you mean? I just saw him go in a little while ago."

"And according to my cameras, there's no one in there at this moment. We have another exit in there. Your *friend* had to have left out that way."

A small actugraphic map floated in front of Amy as she strolled down a quiet block full of trees. This block had only a few houses, with plenty of space between them, and browning bushes filling the empty spaces.

Amy walked up to the front door of a small seaweed-colored two-story home. Dozens of ziccolights emitted in front of the front door.

"Please state your business," an A.I. voice chimed from the house.

"Professor Watson, it's me, uh, Amy. Amy Devine from Highbridge."

"Good morning, Ms. Devine," the A.I. voice answered. "Sorry to inform you that Professor Watson is away on vacation. We'll let him know that you stopped by."

"Great." Amy walked away from the house and stepped onto the curb.

A man ran towards Amy, hustling down the block. Behind him, another man she recognized ran after him.

"Help! He stole my wallet!"

I remember him. Gave Gma hell last year when his uncle died. So nasty to her. Serves him right.

We're better than this town.

Amy watched as the robber passed her by. Then his pursuer.

Amy walked in the opposite direction.

On her way home, a large group passed Amy.

"Yeah, I can't believe it!"

"It's wicked. I'm getting an autograph."

"Town square's gonna be packed, let's hurry!"

Amy raised an eyebrow. She went in their direction.

Enormous crowds filled a busy street, more crowds than normal for Jadesfeld, and it confused Amy as she meandered through them. A flyer flew into her face and she grabbed and unfolded it. A picture of Mr. Perry wearing what was sure to be his best suit was under the title: HEROIC TEACHER WITH C.O.H.I. ORIGINS TO BE AWARDED BRITISH MEDAL OF BRAVERY: CITIES OF JADESFELD & NEW ENFIELD UNITE FOR TREMENDOUS OCCASION

Amy entered an area where four roads crossed, leaving a big empty space in the middle. Jadesfeld Town Square. She moved through a crowd that surrounded a large center stage.

A large white screen floated above the stage, featuring a well-dressed man in a blue suit and impeccable gray hair. In front was a podium where Mr. Perry stood with many other well-dressed people. Next to him was a large plaque with a silver star on it. Amy stopped a few rows away from the stage.

A woman with red hair walked up behind the podium. Her hair turned blue, then green, then yellow. It kept changing many colors.

"And now citizens of Enfield and Jadesfeld, we give you the man of the hour—Maynard Perry!"

"Maynard?" Amy whispered. She grilled a woman next to her that shushed her.

Mr. Perry took over the podium.

"Thank you so much, Ms. McGreavy. I truly adore your eloquence.

And Mr. Mayor! Wish you were here, but I hope you're enjoying the vacation in St. Bart's!"

The man on screen raised a fancy glass of alcohol and tilted towards him.

"Shots on me, Perry."

Mr. Perry threw his arms towards the plaque.

"This is quite the honor, just an absolute honor. Now, let me just say that the unfortunate closing of Highbridge Intermissionary School is tragic beyond measure. Our young adults need the guidance intermissionary schooling requires in order to help them figure out what it is that they want to do to contribute to our world. I'm happy to announce that all professors have decided to continue remote learning to make sure that our students are not left stranded!"

The crowd erupted. Mr. Perry looked quite pleased. He pointed out a young student Amy recognized from Highbridge.

"Yes young mind, have at it."

"Mr. Perry, are the rumors true? Are you really related to Oliver Perry, one of the founding members of the Call of Hero Initiative of 2060?"

Mr. Perry chuckled. "Although there are many a Perry in the world, a very common name," he nodded at laughs from the gallery, "I am, in fact, the great-great-grandson of Oliver Perry. Couldn't you tell from the tentacles?" He wiggled his fingers as the crowd roared with excitement.

"Hey! That's the girl he saved!" Someone shouted from the crowd. Amy looked around as people gasped, some pointing at her.

"That's the Devine girl."

"Really?"

"Come on up here dear, let's hear from you," Ms. McGreavy said.

Amy groaned as she smiled, shaking her head. She gasped as some suits pushed her from behind, guiding her all the way through the crowd and onto the stage.

Ms. McGreavy squeezed Amy with a side hug and pulled her behind the podium. Mr. Perry beamed and squeezed her shoulder once Ms. McGreavy had let go.

"It was a tragic scenario for any person to walk into, but Ms. Devine here stood her ground like a real champion," Mr. Perry said. "Even so, the odds were stacked and I'm glad I was able to step in when I could."

"Tell us, love," a reporter said, pushing his way up to the foot of the stage as a mechanical bird-like device with a microphone for a head flew near her. "How scared were you?"

Amy let out a breath of air as the bird-mic flew around her head.

"I guess I was as scared as anyone would be in that sort of situation."

"Why were you targeted, you think?"

Her eyes fell on General Aba and his two guards towering over others in the crowd.

"I wouldn't say I was targeted," Amy said. "I just happened to be walking by."

"Were you that girl from that well incident six years prior?!" a random voice called from the crowd.

Amy peered out into the crowd, searching for the idiot that brought that up. Her fists clenched, angrier that her eyes watered despite her fighting against it.

So many faces. Faces of the uninitiated.

"Ms. Devine," the reporter cut in, "could you elaborate on the incident in question? Over in New Enfield, we've heard the rumors. Maybe you can perhaps—"

"Well now," Mr. Perry chuckled, "let's not bombard Ms. Devine with questions of the past. Let's stay on topic, shall we—"

"She's a fucking murderer!" another random voice yelled out from somewhere.

They don't respect you. They should be careful. It's the smallest things that make us mad.

Amy scanned the crowds with clenched teeth. "Get. Bent."

"Alright, let's go dear, that's quite enough." Mr. Perry pulled Amy off stage as detectives moved into the crowd. "Are you alright Amy?"

"Yeah." Amy's body shook in his grasp. "Thanks. Sorry."

"No, no, it's quite alright. That was extraordinarily uncalled for. Listen, I know the abrupt end of the school year will be taxing on your lot. Your interests in Animalia Criminology speak volumes in Mr. Watson's notes on you. I'd like to offer you private lessons as I'll be working overnight at Highbridge. Think it'll be good in addition to your continued remote studies."

"Thanks, but probably won't have—"

Within the crowd, a tall dark figure shuffled just out of view, disappearing within the depths of scattering citizens.

"Listen, think it over and get back to me," Mr. Perry continued. Or better yet, feel free to stop by. Any night you want."

"Amy Devine." Two detectives marched up to Amy. One of them flicked his GCID and held out his hand to Amy. "We have an order for your immediate house arrest."

"My what?"

"We'll explain on the way to your home. Please come with us."

One of the Detectives escorted her from behind while the other stayed in front of her, moving her swiftly through the crowds and towards a police cruiser.

"I am responsible for every account of death over the past month, and I regret nothing at all."

Chapter Sixteen

Amy sat, staring blankly in front of her. Her eyes glowed orange for a second before returning to normal.

Do you believe they'll care what you think? Your whys, hows, et cetera, et cetera. They don't give a shit about you.

"This town may deserve a lot of things. But justice is one of them," Amy said. "It's the smallest things that make us mad, right? Right?!" Amy stared at the empty spot next to her. She turned back up to face the TV screen in front of her, coming from her ZiccoLynx box.

On-screen, a press conference was being held outside the Jadesfeld police precinct. Several detectives, reporters, and other personnel moved about. The reporter from Mr. Perry's rally earlier was speaking.

Rezna walked into the living room.

"Did you say something, dear? Oh, it's starting." She sat down next to Amy, who moved an inch away from her.

On-screen, the reporter gestured to the precinct behind her.

"We now bring you live, inside the Jadesfeld Police Department, where the suspect has requested to make a confession, in return for giving Detectives more details on the murders."

Two Detectives stood behind Thomas Jones, who sat at an interrogation table, with cuffs on his wrists, connected by a solid beam of light emanating from either of them.

Mr. Jones smiled into the camera.

"I am responsible for every account of death over the past month, and I regret nothing at all. Justice. Justice was my clear and earned motivation, as justice against this town was a long time coming." He sniffled as he tapped his fingertips together. "A year ago, my son Jonathan Jones went missing under mysterious circumstances and this town barely gave an effort. No one's ever come forth with any information. All of you only choose to live in your dreadful, up-spirited lives as mine was ripped from me! Even my own sister-in-law's husband, who worked in the crime labs at this precinct, failed me. Therefore, Codwell Bates was the first victim. Then his wife Melanie."

Mr. Jones shifted in his seat and detectives moved towards him. He held his hands up and cleared his throat. "I methodically picked each and every victim, choosing the best time to slip into their homes and inject them with a strong enough dose of propolis mixed with venom that would paralyze them to the point of their heart stopping long enough to be buried. Living out the rest of their shitty lives below the ground. You'll note that there isn't any other way for me to have that classified information as it's unreleased to the public."

Mr. Jones's fist clenched.

"My next victim would have been Amy Devine. Detective Jimethy Wimblestyn kept bringing the girl around my family. Snooping. I feared they were getting too close. My wife had also seen me come with blood on my hands the other night, so I confessed in order to make sure she could not be held as an accessory. She had no knowledge of my great deeds."

Amy's eyes bore into the screen, ignoring her peripheral vision, as Rezna's head turned towards her.

"I have cooperated with the JFPD and have given the location of my latest victim," Mr. Jones continued, "which they can confirm was found buried alive earlier this morning. There are more details to be worked out, and I am ecstatic that I was given this opportunity to laugh in all of your faces." Mr. Jones smiled. "I take great pride in my work."

Tears filled his eyes. "I'd give anything to see my boy again. Jonathan Jones, if you're out there still, your family misses you and wants you home. No matter what. We want you home, JJ!" A stream ran in between the creeks of his eyes and down his face. "Let this be a lesson to this shit town. Enfield, you're next."

Moments later, Rezna spoke to detectives at the front door with Amy behind her. Amy hugged her arms, looking down at her feet.

"Those are all the details of your house arrest and instructions for your security brace." One of the detectives pointed down at Amy's ankle, which wore a device that emitted four solid white beams of light going around the bottom of her left leg.

"Thank you, detectives," Rezna said. She closed the door and walked past Amy. "I suspect you'll need some time to get your story straight, so I'll give it to you."

"We can train now, and I can explain everything after," Amy said.

Rezna turned to her. "Like I said last night, good luck." She disappeared through the basement door.

Amy walked up to the second floor as Archie flew up behind her. She walked into her room and slammed the door behind her. She pulled out G-XSR, dialed, and put it to her ear.

"C'mon, Jimmy, pick up. Shit." She hung up the phone.

Amy tapped into her GCID and a holographic screen came out of it, with Demora's face and the word Calling underneath. After a few minutes, the screen disappeared.

"Shit."

Her GCID lit up, and she tapped it as the screen reappeared with text on it.

At practice

Amy swiped the screen away and flung herself back against the headboard of her bed.

Archie tugged at her hair.

"Not now, Arch." She shooed him off. She rubbed her eyes, sucked her teeth, and beckoned Archie towards her after seeing his sad eyes. "I'm sorry. I didn't mean anything by it." She hugged him as he hugged her face. "I love you."

Hours later, the mood shined bright on Amy's awakening face. She lifted her head off the mattress and stopped. She smiled.

Archie's little snores escaped him as he laid knocked out on her back.

Amy pulled out her G-XSR and checked the messages. Her eyes widened as she rose to a sitting position, causing Archie to fly off of her and onto her pillow. Amy dialed and put the phone to her ear.

"So, Jemithy, huh?"

Silence.

Maybe I shouldn't joke.

"Jimmy, I—"

"I've been suspended until further notice. I know they've got you on house arrest. They're saying Jones must've had accomplices."

"I don't think he's fully responsible, Jimmy. Something had to be possessing him to—"

"Amy, just—" Jimmy sighed. "It's over. Well, mostly. He's cooperating with the force and I'm confident track down his accomplices. I have to believe in the force finding justice. I was wrong to drag you into this. I know the past few weeks have been rough for you, but you need to let this go. Sit out your house arrest and don't do anything."

"I just can't—"

"Amy, *please*. Your life is in danger. Do you understand that? There is no safe place except for your own home. They don't know that, but because of what you and your grandmother can do, I'm confident you'll be safe."

"Gma's being affected too, Jimmy."

"And your secret will be safe with me. If there's an emergency, reach out. But no more playing detective. It's over."

Click. Amy looked at the phone and tossed it to the floor. She ran her hands back through her hair, then held her head in them.

Archie hugged her knee with his wings.

Amy nodded and stuck out the leg that wore her security brace. Her eyes glowed orange. Her aura grew around her hand as she waved her hand over her ankle monitor, her aura's rays of light hitting the device. Its beams of light flickered a few times before shutting off. She pulled at the device's hinges and snapped it off. She bent over and placed the ankle monitor around the leg of her nightstand, and the beams of light formed around it.

"Guess it's all up to you and me now, Arch. This is not over."

Not by a long shot.

Indeed.

An orange beam of light soared down a quiet street, setting off the alarms of all nearby cars. Detective cruisers pulled up all up and down the street.

A couple of blocks away, two detectives sat idle in their cruiser. A cloaked figure ran past their car.

"The hell was that?" The male detective drew his gun.

"Let's check it out," his female partner said.

They exited the cruiser and scanned the scene. The male detective crept to the back of the cruiser and aimed his gun behind it. Nothing there.

A large thump came from behind him.

He turned around to his partner, who lay unconscious on the

ground.

"What the—" The detective's legs caved in and he fell to his knees. A shadow grabbed his head and thumped it into the side of the cruiser.

The cloaked figure ran to the front of the Murder House and in through the front door.

Inside the living room, the cloaked figure pulled off her hood. Amy. She caught her breath, groaned as she held her stomach, then wiped her glistening face.

"We're good, Arch."

Archie flew out of her cloak, dripping in oil. He groaned and ineffectively shook his wet wings.

"I know, Arch, but the oil kept those moonbats off our scent. Let's get you washed up so you can start sniffing around." She took off her cloak and threw it on the couch.

Sometime later, Amy walked out of the bathroom and removed her rubber gloves. Archie flew out past her and shook himself dry.

Amy laughed as she wiped herself clean from his dousing. She took out a pair of black gloves and pulled them on.

"C'mon. Can't take too long."

Archie let out a series of 'coos'.

"Here's what we'll do. You sniff around this bottom level. Check every crevice. Stay low so they don't see you flying through the spot. I'll be upstairs."

Archie 'cooed'.

Amy made her way up the stairs, wiping her gloved finger along the banister. Dust. She continued to the second floor. Nothing seemed out of place since she was last there, but it was hard to say given she'd only been here twice now.

Amy went straight into Issa's old room. Still spotless, with loads of Issa's belongings all over the floor. Amy ran her fingers along the top of the furniture. Spotless.

Doesn't make sense.

Amy searched inside every drawer, behind every dresser, and under the bed. She had no idea what she was looking for but she was sure this house had it. Somewhere.

Last time...

Amy shut the door, but a coat hook was the only thing adorning it. Amy sighed and opened the door back up, but froze in her spot.

On the hallway floor, a shadow stretched across from the left side of the hall. Amy took a step closer to the door frame. Her eyes glowed with their orange flare as her aura circled her right hand. She took a deep breath.

Amy whipped around the corner, ready to strike. Her aura's light illuminated the hall. No one was there. She peeked over the banister, looking down the stairs, then returning her focus to a door at the end of the hall.

Amy opened the door and peeked inside this second bathroom. Her hand found the switch on the wall and cut on the light. It was the most beautiful bathroom she had ever seen and bigger than the one on the first floor. The sink was bigger than any other she'd seen, and the tub could surely fit at least four people. The shower curtain was half-closed with a shadow behind it.

Amy crept up to it and yanked the curtain open.

No one was there.

"This place is driving me buggers."

Her peripherals glimpsed a shadow moving behind her and she twirled around. Archie flew onto the top of the sink, shaking his head at her.

"You nearly gave me a heart attack. Nothing, huh? Let's go check the master bedroom."

Amy walked back down the hall with Archie close behind. She opened the door to the master bedroom, but Archie tugged at her shirt.

"What's the matter?" Amy looked back towards the bathroom. Archie shook his head.

"You're going to give yourself a headache. What's the matter, Arch?" Archie let out a 'coo'.

"We'll be gone soon, let's just check this last spot."

They entered the room, with Archie hugging her shoulder. There was a large false wall that now covered the hole Amy had created weeks prior, with her aura sphere, and the wind blew behind it.

Amy shivered, rubbing her arms. She moved about the room, checking every inch just as thoroughly as she did Issa's. The search was faster since the two bedrooms seemed to have a similar layout.

Amy pushed the wardrobe to her right. Something thumped inside. She opened it and moved various dresses aside before pulling open the bottom drawers and digging through the bundles of elegant garments.

Archie flew into her and fluttered around her head.

"Arch, not now. There." Amy pulled the bottom drawers out of the wardrobe and laid them on the floor.

Nothing was in the hollow compartment where the drawers were.

Archie flew to the top of the wardrobe and sniffed around. His ears stuck up straight. He flew back down and pulled at Amy's hair.

"You are driving me buggers." Amy shot him a look as Archie scratched at the top of the wardrobe. She stood up and examined the wardrobe's chrome-colored centerpiece. It was a pot with a substance spilling over the sides. "What is it, Arch?"

Archie sniffed around the centerpiece and moved inside the wardrobe, sniffing around the roof of it. Amy put her hand on the roof and pushed.

"It's stuck." She kept pushing.

Archie flew past her head towards the door then flew back to her. He pulled at her hair.

"Archie, what the hell?" She pushed too hard. The entire top of the wardrobe snapped off and fell to the ground. "Shit, look what I've done now."

Archie flew down to the fallen wardrobe top and scratched at it. Amy stooped down and ran a finger over a crack along the center. It was a clean cut. Too clean to have been her fault. Amy dug the tips of her fingers into the crack and pulled it apart. A ZiccoLynx box fell out of it.

Amy lifted the box and examined it. She placed it on the bed and opened up a compartment in the back of it. "It's missing the power source." Amy's aura grew around her hand and she stuck it inside the compartment.

After a few seconds, the box powered on. It shot out a white beam of light across the room and grew into a screen on the wall.

"ZLynx, go back to security cam of October 1, 2180."

The screen grew digital cracks. A few minutes of nothing else passed.

"ZLynx, show me the last recording."

A recording of the very room Amy stood in came on screen, with an arguing couple in the middle. Their distorted faces and voices became clear after a few seconds, and Amy recognized them, as she had seen them all over the news. It was Melanie and Codwell Bates.

"We can't let anyone know about this," Codwell said on screen.

Melanie reached out and grabbed his arms. "She's—"

The recording cut off and the screen went white then multicolored, with several digital cracks filling it almost entirely. A black silhouette popped up behind the cracks.

"Do-do-do-do-do-dee-le-do-do-doooooooooooooo" The blaring audio from the box came out distorted and ended in a low hum, the last syllable continuing to play. Amy snatched her hand out of the box, causing it to power off. She held her ears and groaned, trying to shake the ringing sound in her ear.

Archie tugged at her shoulder.

"Kinda in a ringer here, Arch."

Rat-tat. Rat-ta-tat. Rat-tat. Rat-ta-tat.

The sound came from behind Amy.

Amy spun around and froze. Her mouth hung open as she stared out the door and down the hall. At the end of the hall, in front of the bathroom, a black silhouette stood in the shadows. With little light available, it was hard to make out much of whoever it was, but the hand of the figure tapped against the bathroom door behind it.

Amy did not move an inch.

Archie shivered into her arm, clutching it for dear life.

Amy felt her confidence gulp down her throat, but balled her fists.

"Who are you?" she said.

Rat-tat. Rat-ta-tat.

"Why are you following me?"

Rat-tat.

The figure stood still. For a moment, there was no movement between anyone. Even Archie stopped shivering and his wide eyes stayed glued to their unwelcome guest.

Amy swallowed. Breathing became difficult for her as her breaths seemed to forget their natural pattern.

The figure took a step. Amy jumped at the unexpected movement.

The figure took a step with its other foot. Then the next step.

It was at that step that Amy realized the figure had its back to her the entire time.

The figure moved slowly, as though carefully choosing its movements, with more of the figure revealed with every slight change. Its legs came first, followed by its swinging arm, with no other identifiable parts viewable as the darkness still engulfed it.

It kept walking back towards the master bedroom. Towards Amy.

Amy's eyes went orange as she grabbed Archie and put him inside her shirt.

Halfway down the hall, the figure slumped into the wall with an echoing bang, then continued its walk.

It skipped a step backward and kept its reverse walk going as smooth as it began.

Archie flew out of Amy's shirt and placed his feet on the door. He slammed it shut.

"Archie, what the hell are you doing?"

Archie shook his head feverishly.

Rat-tat. Rat-ta-tat. Rat-tat. Rat-ta-tat. Rat-tat. Rat-ta-tat.

The knocking now came from the other side of the bedroom door.

And it persisted repeatedly.

Amy and Archie watched the door as the tapping continued without end from the other side. Archie flew onto Amy's shoulder as she moved back, not taking her eyes off the door.

Rat-tat. Rat-ta-tat. Rat-tat. Rat-ta-tat. Rat-tat. Rat-tat. Rat-ta-tat. Rat-tat. Rat-ta-tat.

Silence.

The doorknob rotated from side to side.

The door inched open, then stopped.

A few seconds passed. The door continued opening, creaking along the way.

Amy's back bumped into the false wall. Nowhere left to go. Her fists balled up with her aura rotating around them. She bent her knees and gulped.

The moonlight from outside the window shined in between Amy and the figure, aiding Amy's aura in highlighting more of the figure. The figure's legs were gray, and it wore shorts or a dress, Amy couldn't tell. Its torso was still concealed in shadow and most of its face. Except for a single, white eye with black veins pulsing around the iris. It watched her.

"Change the world for the better." The figure's distorted voice croaked out, sounding like a dozen voices on a radio station with poor reception. "FACE YOURSELF!" The figure raised its gray arm.

A burst of black and white light left its palm and disbursed throughout the room. The impressive aura shot straight into Amy's chest, sending her flying through the false wall.

Amy flew into the cool night air and landed flat on her back with a thud outside the Murder House.

Amy groaned as police cruisers sounded off in the distance.

Through the reopened hole in the Murder House, the figure's pearly white smile looked down at her. The figure stepped back, disappearing into the darkness.

"Shit. Arch, let's—"

Dozens of moonbats flew out of nearby trees and fluttered about the entire area. They bombarded Amy, concealing her within their chaotic flight, as she tried desperately to get on her feet. She waved her hands, fighting back, but they overwhelmed her.

Amy's aura burst to life and swirled around her, killing the street-lights in the area and pushing the moonbats far away.

The blood-curdling screams from the moonbats pierced the night air.

As Amy's aura died out, police cruisers approached the street. Amy ran in the opposite direction as fast as she could, becoming a blur of orange light that disappeared into the night.

Chapter Seventeen

Do-dee-lee, do-dee-lee, do-dee-lee-doooo!

Amy wiped the crust from her baggy eyes. She groaned as she raised her head off of her computer desk and scratched her disheveled, golden-blond hair. It complimented the yellow, torn-up tank top she wore quite well.

Amy shook her arms out of the sleeves of a sweater and took in her room, wondering when the tornado had hit. She swept some clothes off her desk and pulled forward a stack of books that were against the wall.

Amy winced at the bright computer screen in front of her, with many tabs open in a web browser.

"ZLynx, PC brightness fifty percent."

As the screen dimmed, she placed a finger on it and flicked away many of the tabs, then leaned back in her chair.

"The seven stages of possession. First; cold drafts. Second; seeing things and hearing whispers. Third is—" She held her stomach and groaned. "Stomach pains. The fourth is an overwhelming chilly feeling that takes over the body, except for the chest, where the possession resides. The fifth… loss of personality traits and expressionless behavior. Guess we'll be there soon huh, Arch…"

Amy looked at her nightstand. On its edge sat a bundle of white socks stacked one on top of the other with toothpicks for ears. A tear ran down Amy's face.

"Six; extreme mood swings and violent behavior. Seven; extremely dilated pupils and discolored irises."

Three knocks at her bedroom door disrupted her study. Amy spun around in her chair.

"Come in."

Rezna peeked inside the room.

"I'm leaving now. Is there anything you need from me before I go?"

"Nope. All good here."

"I'll be back tomorrow morning. Stay out of trouble." Rezna lingered for a moment before closing the door behind her.

"Okay." Amy walked over to the full body mirror in the corner of her room. She tied up her pitch-black hair into a bun with her red headband. "Never let um see you sweat, kiddo." She flicked her GCID.

Moments later, Amy opened the front food to find Demora on the other side, her arms crossed.

"She's gone, right?"

"Yeah, come in."

Demora moved inside and looked around the hall and into the kitchen. "It's been ages since I've been inside."

"Thanks for coming."

"Well, I haven't got a load of time. Practice in an hour."

"How many more games are you playing for them?"

"Too many." Demora shrugged. "Poor bastards are just better with me. And Tilly's still recovering. Apparently, she took a really nasty fall. Healing has been slow as shit. Besides, I've got nothing better to do. Anyway, heard they rounded up the people working for Jones."

Amy nodded, looking down at her ankle monitor. It was quite typical for detectives to close up cases as quickly as they could, but even this seemed too fast. Not to mention part of her felt safer under house arrest.

"Now, what's so urgent?" Demora said.

"Archie's missing."

"What?"

Amy explained how she and Archie had investigated the Murder House days ago. She detailed her encounter with the shadow figure, which she was certain was the one responsible for possessing Jadesfeld's population. She told Demora how she thought Archie was in her shirt when the moonbats attacked, but when she got home, he was nowhere to be found. To make things worse, she expressed her surprise that she wasn't in jail yet because she left an old cloak of hers at the scene of the crime.

Demora sat on the stairs, leaning against the wall, shaking her head.

"What the hell Devine? What were you thinking? And poor Arch. I hope he's alright."

"Me too. That figure. It's powerful. Knocked the wind straight out of me."

"You've got to tell Rezna. She'll know what to do."

"She's under the influence, too. I saw it with my own two eyes. And she keeps disappearing, not saying where she's going." Amy paced in the hall. "I've got to stop this thing. It's taunting me, for some reason. But I've got to stop it."

"How?"

"There was a hidden ZLynx box in the Murder House. It had no power source and the serial number was scratched out."

"So..."

"Tonight. The telecommunication center just off the edge of town. It's where the boxes receive their signal. When I turned on the hidden box at the Murder Ho—the Bates' home, that person showed up. Maybe the Murder house is their base or something. I phoned it anonymously to the JPD but have heard nothing back yet. Issa's parents knew something, they were arguing. Maybe they were in on it. Maybe they were trying to stop it before it spread. I don't know—"

"You're taking the piss, yeah?"

"I am *not* taking the piss—"

"Alright, well then, slow down because you're spiraling."

"I'm not spiraling, Demo! I was attacked! I had to leg it 'round the neighborhood twice at my top speed just to knock out the security cams and outrun the pbots."

"I'm worried about you, Ames—"

"The boxes, Demora! The boxes!" Amy massaged her throat aggressively and took a deep breath. "They must be the key. Remember at UCC, their old gen boxes didn't give us such a headache? The possession is moving through the boxes. The murderer must be an auraist. I'm feeling it, I don't know how much time I have left." Amy got up and moved into the kitchen and then into the living room, as Demora slowly got up, watching her.

"What's happening?" Demora asked.

"I've already shut my ZLynx off and reinstalled the old one. Just making sure nothing's changed. I'll turn this off too." Amy yanked off her GCID and threw it under the kitchen table. "If I can get to the telecenter and destroy the main hub, then no more signal. No more possessions. No more murders."

"That's quite a plan you have there Devine, but what do you do when they just, I don't know, replace the hub eventually?"

"By then people will be back to normal and I can convince them otherwise somehow."

"Convince them? The same people who talk behind your back and run the shit over you every chance they get? Those are the people you're going to convince that…"

"That they're being possessed, yes." Amy scratched the back of her neck. "I'm running out of time, Demora. My birthday is next week."

"What does that have to—"

"I'll be an adult! Official adult and then I'll lose the whole bloody plot!"

"Ames." Demora hugged Amy. She pulled back and looked her in the eyes. "I love you, and I want you to really hear me when I say this. You need to—"

"I need your help. Tonight," Amy cut in.

"You're getting your brace off tomorrow and you want to break into the city's telecenter tonight? Maybe you've lost the plot already..."

"They're having me keep the brace on till further notice, actually. You're right about one thing. This town despises me."

"Those little shits! Of course, they want to keep you trapped inside. They always have! Well, even more reason for you not to go outside. Do you want to get thrown in the cooler? "

"No, of course not."

"Just give all this info to your little detective friend then."

"I can't, he's suspended."

"I'm sure it'll be alright, given this miraculous theory you have."

"Demora! *Please*! I need your help tonight. Don't be a selfish, sniveling twat."

Demora's narrowed eyes bore into Amy's eyes. She made her way towards the door.

"I'm not going to watch you destroy yourself. Some of us like to live in the real world instead of playing make-believe detective." Demora opened the door and marched out, slamming the door behind her.

Amy stared at the closed door.

Alone again, I see.

"No, I'm not," Amy said. "Leave me alone."

A security guard sat behind a series of monitors, sipping from a cup of coffee. The lights went off. Then the monitors.

"The fuck?" The guard hit a button on his front pocket. "Bots, can you do a perimeter check? Sure it's just another—" He looked up into one of the monitors and a pair of orange eyes stared back at him. The man's head slammed against the control board.

"Must find that control room," Amy said, walking past the unconscious guard. A hood covered most of her face, attached to a black bodysuit. "Stage five; loss of personality traits and expressionless behavior."

Moments later, Amy stared at the buttons inside an elevator as it carried her upwards.

"Elevator's still running. Separate power source."

The elevator doors opened and Amy stepped out, her eyes still glowing orange. She peeked her head out and looked left and right before exiting the elevator. It was dark, with the windows being the only source of light.

"Security breach. Security breach. Security breach." Two bots soared towards Amy.

Amy threw her hands out towards the bots, her aura shooting puncturing straight through their metallic bodies. They fell onto the floor and their eyes went dim.

Amy walked past them and checked the room they came out from. Nothing but lockers and a lunchroom. She walked back out and called for the elevator, but the button did not light up.

"That's annoying."

Amy's aura circled around her entire body and she raised herself a few inches into the air.

On the third floor, the ceiling caved in as Amy crashed down from the floor above. She ran at an incredible speed to get behind two bots that rushed her. Amy grabbed their heads and smashed them together repeatedly until they were as thin as oversized coins. She dropped them and smiled down at their metallic remains. She stepped over them and searched the three rooms the floor had to offer, still not finding what she needed.

The second and first floors went the same. More destroyed bots. More disappointment.

This is a waste of time.

Of course you'd think so.

You'll never find what you're looking for.

Shut. UP.

Amy called for the elevator and stepped inside once it arrived. She stared down at the buttons on the panel before smashing her fist into it and pulling it off. Inside the circuitry, a small glass surface was above the circuits for the buttons. Amy rubbed her finger over it.

"Access denied. Authorities will be alerted as main power is off," an automated voice said.

Amy smashed into the circuits repeatedly, then walked off the elevator. She stopped and turned back around. She knelt down and dug her fingers into the crevice between the elevator and the floor. With a couple of grunts, she lifted the elevator, its circuitry sparking, and tossed it up as hard as she could. Amy raised her aura-covered hand and shot a beam of light down the elevator shaft. A door laid in the depths below. Amy jumped down.

Amy landed on the bottom of the elevator shaft, right in front of the secret door. Above her head, the elevator came speeding back down towards her, sparks flying. Amy's aura outlined her entire body and she threw her hands above her head.

The elevator came crashing down on her.

Amy stood in the middle of the remains of the destroyed elevator. She waved her arms in front of her and shot a beam of aura. Her beam broke through the elevator and the secret door she had found. An alarm sounded off.

Amy stepped into the secret room, her steps clanking against the metallic floor. She walked towards a crater in the center of the room illuminated with white light.

Panels lit up red above glass compartments on either wall. The compartments opened up and security bots soared out of them, heading straight for Amy.

Amy ducked their mechanical arms, snatching and breaking a few of them off. She aimed her hand and her aura burst into two of the bots' chests, right as she grabbed the neck of another bot, crushed it, and tossed the bot into others.

Another round of bots came out, their arms splitting and morphing into shotgun-like devices. One barrel of their weapons zapped out a ring of white light that hit Amy square in the chest. The second barrel fired a stream of metal.

The metal broke apart into tiny pieces—shot right onto Amy's left leg—and reformed into a cuff that snapped around her leg. A string of blue electricity sparked around the diameter of the metal cuff.

Amy cried out, her arms not knowing whether to grab her leg or her throat first. She whipped off her hood as her orange eyes grew brighter, glaring at the bots circling her.

"Get bent, assholes." Amy's aura burst through the room, a wave of orange knocking down all the security bots. Teeth grinding, she dragged her ensnared leg as she walked towards the crater in the center of the room, approaching the edge.

Amy stood over the crater, studying the spherical device that sat in the middle of it, with a blinding white light inside of it. She lifted her hands, her aura coming to life once more, and aimed at the sphere.

Another cuff snapped around her right arm.

Amy grabbed her arm out of instinct but immediately pulled away, right as the cuff's blue current shocked her. She threw her free arm back, her aura escaping it and splitting a bot in two.

Another cuff caught around her free arm, shortly followed by yet another cuff around her right leg.

Amy fell over on her side, blue electricity riding around her limbs, writhing in pain near the edge of the crater. She crawled, placing her upper torso over the edge, her aura growing around her body.

The metal cuffs on her arms shattered into pieces.

Two more cuffs snapped around each arm to replace them.

Amy yelled into the ground, coughing up blood, as she tried to claw the cuffs off her arms, but only met further pain. Her body spasmed for seconds before she regained her composure.

"Shit!" She coughed up more blood, it spilling down the side of the crater. Her eyes fell on the blood for a few seconds.

Does it end here?

Not till I find you, you bastard.

Amy gritted her teeth and punched her knuckles into the ground, creating dents as she picked herself up.

A cuff snapped around her neck, and the blue electricity sparked around her head. Her entire body now encased in the blue rings of pain, Amy slumped onto the floor, her breaths growing rapidly as her body convulsed. Her right eye twitched.

For her peripherals, the security bots soared toward her flailing body.

No.

Amy slammed her fists into the metal floor again, lifting herself upright. She got up on one knee, and then the other, as the bots came inches from her. Amy got to both her feet, her aura growing once again. The blue electricity around her sparked in and out.

Amy's orange eyes grilled into them as the bots. She smiled.

The bots aimed their weapons at her.

A pink aura swept the bots into the walls on either side of the room.

Demora walked in, arms outstretched towards either wall, surveying the fallen bots. Her aura died out as her eyes lost their glow.

"Amy!" She ran up to Amy, but Amy held a hand out to stop her.

"I had that under control. What are you doing?"

"Really? We've gotta get out of here! Sirens on the way!"

Amy's eyes flashed between orange and her normal state repeatedly.

"I need to destroy it. I... need to destroy it."

"We have no time—"

"NO!" Amy's aura burst throughout the entire room.

Demora flew back and hit the floor, but she recovered quickly. Her eyes lit up as her aura circled around her. Her glare became a wide-eyed look as her jaw fell open.

Amy's eyes reverted to their normal state. Her sad brown irises staring blankly ahead.

But her aura raged like a burning torch as several shades of orange danced within it.

The fallen bots in the room melted into milky gray mush as the aura touched them.

Amy walked to the edge of the crater, looking down at the white spherical power source. She jumped up, levitating, her eyes focused on the sphere. Nose first, she dived into it.

A blinding light show of orange and white as broken metal parts flew everywhere. Sparks shot out, dancing around the room.

All sources of light died out. The room filled with darkness, with only a glint of Demora's pink aura still present.

That was the last thing Amy saw as her eyelids kissed.

Chapter Eighteen

"Do-dee-lee, do-dee-lee, do-dee-lee-doooo! Do-dee-lee, do-dee-lee, do-dee-lee-doooo! Le-Do-dee-lee, do-dee-lee, do-dee-lee-doooo! Do-dee-lee, do-dee-lee, do-dee-lee-doooo!"

Amy opened her eyes, throwing her arm in front of her as she adjusted to the single source of blinding light coming from somewhere in the room. A message scrolled by on the electronic band on her wrist: KEO: CONCUSSION.

Amy sat up in the hospital bed, eyes tracking the source of light. Every corner of the room hummed with a bright white light. A white screen spread across the wall to her left.

The man with the wooden smile was on screen, his green eyes unblinking, and a single bead of sweat running down the right side of his nose. His gaze and smile fixed on Amy.

"Hey there Amy! Boy, have we got a great promotion for you today!"

"The hell? ZLynx, shut off—"

"Don't touch that dial just yet!" The man leaned forward. His eyes rolled up until only the whites were showing. Black veins grew at the corners and a gray substance grew over the whites, passing through them like moving clouds. The man laughed. "Trust me, Amy, you're gonna want to hear this."

"ZLynx, shut off screen, now."

The screen went off. It came back on. The man was not smiling.

"I told you not to. It happens again and everyone you care about will suffer." His wooden smile returned. "Now then, here we go!"

The screen cut to the man dancing further away, wagging his finger. A woman soon joined him, followed by another man, and then another man. Soon the screen was full of men and women doing the exact same dance in different directions.

"You see, Amy," the man's voice continued, "it's come to my attention that you are quite the star. I knew you were special when we first met, but I had no idea… You've changed things. You. I almost had you."

The adults on-screen stopped dancing. One by one, their necks snapped in opposite directions, all except the original man. The others fall to the ground. The camera zooms right back to the wooden smile man's face, with his blank expression digging into Amy, and his teeth gritted together as though forcing himself into his signature smile. Tears ran down his cheeks.

"Your one-time, exclusive promotion!" The man's voice spoke through his grinding teeth. "You and me. Together. They won't be able to stop us. We can change the world, Amy. Time's ticking and you only have a few days to decide."

"Decide what?"

The man pulls out a gun and presses it to the side of his head.

"To decide if you're an agent of the future. Or a victim of the present." The man's head shook as he steadied the gun. His smile curled into a frown before regaining its composure, smiling wider than ever. "And that's the waaaaaaaay it goes!"

Amy's eyes shut as the gunshot goes off.

"What the fuck?" Demora's voice rang out.

Demora sat in a chair at Amy's side. She looked back and forth between Amy and the screen.

Laughter. Amy and Demora spun back around to the screen.

The man rose from the bottom of the screen, laughing, as blood gushed from his temple. His now off-centered, vacant grey eyes stared at nothing and his voice cracked, becoming more distorted with each sentence. "What's it gonna take to make you crack? What's it gonna take to make you crack? What's it gonna take to make you crack?"

The screen glitched several times, his face changing expressions rapidly.

Laughter. "We are one! The purple shall gov—"

Frowning. "These damn kids."

Crying. "Smoke 'em out. Smoke 'em out. Smoke 'em out."

Scowling. "Those damn kids."

Laughing. "Toss 'em in a lake."

"WHAT'S IT GONNA TAKE TO MAKE YOU CRACK?"

The screen broke into many tiny ziccolights that disappeared in seconds.

"What... What was that... the fuck," Demora said. She got up and ran her hand through her hair feverishly. "Amy, what the fuck was that?"

"Cloudy," Amy said. "It... speaks to me sometimes. I think it speaks to Issa too."

"Why just you two?"

Amy shrugged. She hadn't put the pieces together before, but there had to be some connection between herself and Issa. And they both had some connection to the murderer. The confirmation of her greatest fear was clear as it ever was.

"You were right. This has got to be an auraist," Demora said, as though reading her mind. "You've got to tell Rezna."

"She's been possessed, too. She keeps leaving town for *work*."

"You think she's being sent away on purpose?"

"She is the strongest threat."

"So we can't trust any adults in this town? What the hell are we going to do?"

"What floor are we on?"

"Third."

"We need to get to the second floor. I need your help getting into Issa's room."

Demora sighed. "Can't ignore shit now, can we?"

Sometime later, Amy and Demora stalked the dim halls of the hospital. They snuck past two nursebots and hid behind a corner.

Across the hall, Norma Jones exited Issa's hospital room. A nursebot approached her.

"I'll be returning in the morning," Ms. Jones said to the nursebot. "Don't allow any visitors inside."

"As you wish, Ms. Jones," the nursebot replied.

As Ms. Jones disappeared down the hall, the nursebot rolled over to a small desk across from Issa's room.

"Think you can distract that bot?" Amy said.

"I'll get her away and give her a little overcharge," Demora smirked. "You eat that candy bar. You need to regain your strength."

"I know, I know."

"Now."

Amy peeled back the wrapper of a chocolate bar and bit into it. "Happy?"

"Very. Now disappear."

Amy ran down the hall behind them and dipped behind the corner.

"Nurse! Nurse!" Demora called out. "Please, I need help now."

The nursebot left the desk and approached Demora. "What is your concern, ma'am?"

"I'm going to shit all over this floor if I can't find the restroom. I can't find it!"

"Please don't desecrate the floors. Come with me." The nursebot led Demora away down the adjacent hall.

Amy ran up to Issa's room and carefully opened the door before slipping inside. She shut the door behind her.

Issa slept on the bed, with an IV bag hooked to her right arm and a mechanical band around her head. Her face made several movements as though she was having a terrible nightmare.

Amy crept up to the bedside and shook Issa gently.

Issa's eyes opened. She smiled. "Amy! You came to see me. Two visitors in a day. Norma's going to have a cow."

"Let her," Amy smiled back. "Who was your other visitor?"

"Well, he wasn't really my visitor. He was talking with Norma in the hallway."

"What did he look like?"

"He was kinda old I guess. He had grey hair and round glasses."

Professor Watson?

"No idea what they were talking about, huh?" Amy asked.

Issa shook her head.

"That's okay. Well, I was hoping we could have a little chat if you're up to it. How are you doing?"

"Not well, actually. They're keeping me heavily sedated." Issa stared into the ceiling. "Let's skip the small talk, Amy. You're not just here to visit, are you?"

"You're right. Did your aunt hurt you, Issa?"

"I can't answer that." Issa kept her eyes on the ceiling.

"Okay. Who's Cloudy?"

"I can't say. I don't want you to get hurt."

"It's really important. I can help, I promise I can."

Issa shook her head again. "Can't say."

"Why?"

"I told you. I've got to protect you."

Amy looked down at the trembling girl's hand. She grabbed ahold of it. "That's very admirable, Issa. You know, a long time ago, when I was even younger than you are, I got hurt by people I thought I could trust. An older individual who should have known better. This person was angry at me for something that was out of my control. One day, I was waiting for my grandmother to come pick me up from my first day of school. She was just a bit late, unfortunately, due to her work. This woman, who was angry at me for something that happened to her son, came to the school and tried forcing me to come with her. She bruised my arm up pretty badly when I refused. My grandmother got there just in time and you can bet she did not hesitate to protect me. I missed my entire first year of school because she refused to leave my side. Ever since then, Gma's never left me alone for more than a day or two."

Amy stared into a corner of the room, wiping a tear from her eye.

"I'm thankful for her protection, but it did overwhelm me. I had fears of my own that I couldn't quite grow out of. It took me exploring with my best friend before I became comfortable seeing the outside world again. Now my Gma's in some trouble and I'd like to get her out of it. I'd like to get a lot of people out of whatever's coming. But I just need a little help, Issa. Please."

Issa's teary eyes looked into Amy's. "Why is the world so cruel to us?"

"It's not the world. Just a few bad apples. But we can't let that ruin us."

Issa nodded. "Go to my room at Norma's and get the drawing you brought back to me. It's a puzzle. I know you can solve it."

Amy combed the girl's hair back with her free hand.

"Thank you, Issa. I'll make this all right. I promise."

Issa smiled back. "Please be careful."

"I will." Amy got to her feet and made her way to the door. She turned back. "Issa, what did you mean by 'it's Cloudy's story'?"

Issa's eyes went wide, staring up at the ceiling and her body stiffened.

"You'll see."

Amy, wearing a hoodie and baggy clothes, jogged up to the front of Mr. Watson's home.

"Please state your business."

"Professor Watson, it's Amy Devine. From your Animalia Gems class."

The front door whirred open. Professor Watson appeared behind the door, a bit more disheveled than Amy was used to seeing him. He wore a baggy t-shirt and basketball shorts.

"Ms. Devine? Pardon my bewilderment. I thought you were on house arrest?"

"Let's just say I'm taking a break."

"Say no more." He gave a small smirk. "It is nice to see a friendly face. Please, come right in."

Amy walked into the box-littered hallway and followed Prof. Watson into the living room. The wooden walls held many photos on every side, most of which sat right over the room's entertainment center, creating some imbalance. Many water bottles dressed the floor, torn couch, and coffee stand. Various statues of creatures within their world stood around in various poses. Amy moved close to a bear-like one, with long backward curving horns and red eyes.

Prof. Watson returned from the kitchen and handed Amy a water bottle. He took a swig from his own, then guzzled down half of the bottle of water in one shot.

"Must stay hydrated," he said.

Amy nodded. Just as Prof. Watson turned to toss his bottle into the kitchen, Amy's free hand twitched, her aura escaping it, and hitting the ZiccoLynx box at the center of the entertainment stand.

The box lit up and chimed.

A naked existographic woman appeared on the couch, facing Amy and Prof. Watson. Her blue transparency morphed into brown flesh seconds later. Her pointy breasts dipped behind the couch as she eyed Prof. Watson.

"Daddy, are you ready to keep playing? I'm waiting for you." The existographic woman bit her lip and ran her hand over the top of the couch. She squeezed it.

"ZLynx, shut off, now!" Prof. Watson said.

"Daddy, I'm hor—"

"ZLynx, shut off now! Now!"

The existographic woman disappeared and the ZLynx box's light went out.

Amy and Prof. Watson stood in silence, not facing each other.

"I'm terribly sorry about that," Prof. Watson said. "I-I was just—"

"It's okay. Let's forget about it. Why'd you leave school?"

Prof. Watson made his way over to the couch and motioned for Amy to sit.

"I think I'll stand," Amy said, stepping over some books.

"Right." Prof. Watson took off his glasses and cleaned them with his shirt before putting them back on. He stared down into the cushions of the couch. "She was murdered. My wife. She was the third victim. That's why I left school."

"I'm sorry. I can't imagine…"

Prof. Watson raised a hand to her. "It's alright, Ms. Devine. Unlike some others in this town, I can tell you are being absolutely sincere. Thank you."

Amy nodded again, feeling a deep pit in her belly. Here she was, ready to confront her own teacher for his part in the town's mess. Although he wasn't an auraist, he had been the next most knowledgeable figure in their town after Gma. Yet here he was, just a man in deep mourning.

"Our children are staying with relatives down South. I'm staying in town until they find the murdering bastard."

"You don't believe Thomas Jones is responsible?"

"That blundering idiot couldn't look a numbat in the eye without wetting himself. Literally."

"What did you and his wife talk about at the hospital?"

"Quite the detective, Ms. Devine."

"I wasn't following you or anything. Well, except the other day. At the library. I was there and saw you go into that members-only section. Came here to find you after."

"Ah, yes. Had to do my own little research. Left to meet a colleague out of town that is more familiar with animal criminology in relation to insects. Been building my own wild theory about all of this."

"What's your theory?"

"It is just a theory." Prof. Watson walked over to his entertainment stand and stared at the photos surrounding it. "His sister-in-law, the deceased Melanie Bates—Callisto, bless her—has a brother who took over operations for the Alliance Against Animalia Crime down in Australia, their homeland. I follow the organization's work closely. The brother once brought his companion numbat with him to visit. Old Thomas nearly passed out. He's a squeamish shit. I brought my case to the JPD, and they basically pushed me right back out the door. They're very happy to make this a shut case, so long as they can get their bots clear and out and running again. They're just willing to sink their teeth into the first lead they get."

"But he confessed. He knew details about every murder."

"I never said he didn't hold some responsibility, but someone else did the dirty work. I don't believe the bees are just attacking people for no reason. They're smart but not vengeful. They understand that the lifespan of a human pales in comparison to their own. Especially the Australian Buzzkills. They're called Buzzkills because they don't attack despite their clearly dominant biology compared to other species of bee and insect alike."

Prof. Watson picked up a book from his entertainment and threw it onto a stack of other books on the ground. "There's a saying, Ms. Devine. 'We are all the heroes of our own stories.' Bless young Jonathan Jones' soul wherever he is. I don't know what they have over Thomas Jones and I'm not even sure what's going on just yet. And I don't care. Rest assured, I will not rest until I find out who took my wife from me."

Amy walked away from Prof. Watson's home. Her GCID lit up. A message from Gma saying that she'd be a bit late coming in.

"ZLynz, call Demora," Amy said.

Her GCID rang.

"Ames, how'd it go?" Demora's voice said.

"Watson's not it. It's someone else. I could use your help again. Tonight."

"Oh, boy."

Chapter Nineteen

"How late is late?" Demora's voice rang out in Amy's earpiece. "Late usually means after midnight, so we have some time before Gma's home." Amy checked her GCID screen: 09:54 PM.

"Alright Demo, let's cut the noise." Amy leaned behind a tree as her aura grew around her.

Street lights went dark with only a single source of light at a house somewhere near the end of the long block.

Amy ran up to the front door of Norma Jones' home. Her aura grew over her hand and illuminated the door. The door buzzed open, and she slipped inside.

"Remember when we used to break into Clark's General and nick some cream soda?" Demora said through Amy's earpiece.

"I'd give anything to go back to those simple break-ins."

"By the way, Ames, are we going to talk about last night?"

Amy slipped up the staircase. "What is there to talk about?"

"Oh, I don't know. How your aura nearly blew us all to smithereens. Something along those lines. Patch me in."

"ZLynx, render call actugram," Amy said.

Dozens of ziccolights came to life next to Amy. They formed the outline of a human body, seconds later becoming Demora.

Amy crept through the second floor as the actugraphic Demora floated inches off the floor behind her.

"Gma told me that we have access to higher levels of aura manipulation. She was training me to use my aura without my eye glow. I had no idea when it happened, but I could feel power like never before. It wasn't like feeling like you're inside a barrel of tar when we usually use our aura. I felt… free."

"It was mad. Also, absolutely sick. If old Rezna didn't hate me, I'd be trying to get in on that training."

They slipped into Issa's room and searched around.

"She doesn't hate you, Demora. She just got a little peeved you broke her favorite ornament. And her *pets* attacked in defense."

"Right."

"Where's Norma?"

"She's fine. Sitting outside Issa's room like a hawk. I wonder where she was earlier today…"

"Up to no good, I'm sure." Amy pulled a paper out of a drawer. She unfolded it, revealing Issa's drawing of her family home. "I've got it."

"Alright, now get the hell out of there."

"Just keep your eye on her, I'm gonna peek around a bit."

"Can I ask you something else?" Demora asked.

"Sure." Amy twisted the doorknob.

"Where were you the night the Bates couple were killed?"

Amy tugged at the door but it wouldn't budge. "The hell?"

"What's wrong?"

"The door won't open all of a sudden."

"Well, bust it down."

"I can't just bust it down, Demo." Amy's pocket vibrated. "Shit. She took it out and answered the G-XSR. "Jimmy?"

"Amy! Hey, long time, hope you're good. I've got great news for you— I finished the box! And get this, it's what you'd call an energy prison of sorts."

"What? Wonder what it was holding…"

"Who's Jimmy?" Demora asked.

"Demo, never mind."

"Who's Demo?" Jimmy asked.

Amy yanked at the door. "No one, look, Jimmy, I'm kind of in the middle of something, can I ring you later?"

"Is that the Detective? Ugh, barbaric."

"Uh, yeah sure Amy. I'll talk to you later."

Amy stuffed the G-XSR back in her pocket. "Not a word Demora."

"I've said my piece. Get a move on, Norma's acting strange. She just got off the phone."

"I… am… trying!" Amy yanked the door and it opened. She sighed and walked out.

Two massive gloved hands grabbed Amy's throat and threw her against the hallway wall, choking her. Amy struggled to get out from under the immense hands of the cloaked figure. A single grey eye peeked at her from under the wraps of the figure's hood.

"Let her go, you piece of shit!" actugram Demora said.

Amy's aura burst around her, knocking her and her assailant on opposite ends of the hall.

Amy held her throat and got back to her feet.

Actugraphic Demora phased in and out of existence.

"Amy—her way home—get out of there!"

The assailant marched right through actugram Demora, grabbed Amy from behind, raised her into the air, and smashed her into the ground.

Amy dodged a fist coming for her head and punched the assailant into the wall across the hall, sending them into the next room. She coughed as she grabbed her throat and rose.

A crash from the other room.

Amy kicked the door open to the room with her aura-covered hands at the ready.

There were several pieces of wood laying across the floor. In the ceiling, a hole to the outside, rain pouring in.

Amy looked down at her smashed GCID. "Lucky bloke."

Amy and Demora both sit crossed-legged, across from each other in Amy's living room.

"I think I'm the killer, Demo."

"You couldn't be. According to your logic, you can't be the killer because you aren't eighteen yet."

"That's true."

"You've been through so much. This town doesn't deserve you."

"Doing what's right has nothing to do with what we do or don't deserve. We're all the heroes of our own stories. Sometimes that blinds us."

"But Rezna," Demora said. "She disappears too much, Ames. I'm worried. She is a master of aura manipulation."

"She could never—"

"Kill?"

"Gma's too strong to fall victim to possession for long."

"Where were you the night the Bates couples were killed?"

"Why do you keep asking me that?"

"What if she's the one doing the possessing?"

"Wait, what?" Amy grilled Demora. "What is wrong with you? Gma would never do such a thing."

"Wasn't she the one that said 'We let the uninitiated deal with the problems of common folk'? Maybe she's had enough of the common folk."

Amy shook her head. "What, no. No, she isn't. Why do you keep saying that?"

"Because she's right." Rezna strode into the room and took a seat in between the two girls. She smiled at Amy. "I am a killer. I've told you in the past, my dear Amy. I've silenced many beasts."

Jimmy came and sat across from Rezna. "And I've got just the thing." He lifted his hands towards the sky and a shimmering glass box the size of his torso came hovering down into his hands.

"Jimmy, you fixed it. You really—"

Amy was alone in the pitch-black living room. A spotlight shined down on her.

"Amy, Amy, Amy." Demora, half of her face unfinished with zero features, stepped up from behind her, on Amy's left side. "Always so Devine."

"Silly girl." Rezna walked up on Amy's right side with half of her face unfinished. "You need to train until your heart bleeds out onto the floor beneath you."

"Do-dee-lee-do-dee-lee-do-dee-lee-dooo!"

Jimmy and his half unfinished face leaned in close to Amy's ear. "Friends are family that you can eat." Jimmy cackled.

All three of their heads slowly twist towards Amy like creaky handlebars.

"You're going to get us all killed!" Demora, Rezna, and Jimmy said in unison.

Toss 'em in a lake.

Pitch black. Amy's shallow breaths cut into the silence. The lights cut on.

Demora, Rezna, and Jimmy are in front of all the other people in town. All of their smiles stretched to the ends of their faces. The wide black-veined whites of their eyeballs filled with blood as they stared at Amy. Their heads shook from left to right as they laughed.

Amy's eyes opened. Her sweat pooled around the creases of her face. Her arms sat at her sides, the fingers twitching, but she couldn't move the rest of her body.

A single breath of air brushed against the side of her face, moving her hair off her cheek.

Amy's eyes flashed orange before turning normal again. She shot upright in bed.

She charged down the stairs and straight into the kitchen.

Rezna looked up at her from the kitchen table.

"Couldn't sleep either?" Rezna said.

Later, Amy and Rezna sat at the table, mugs in hand.

"I'm sorry, dear," Rezna said.

Sorry.

"Yes, I can apologize when I'm wrong. I push, and I push, and I push you to the bitter end. I only want to avoid what happened to your parents."

"What happened to them?"

Rezna shook her head, but Amy wasn't letting it go this time.

"I deserve to know."

"Your voice, dear." Rezna sipped from her mug. "They fought valiantly, you know. Against the forces that they were up against. They wanted nothing more than to protect you." Rezna sighed into the ceiling. "In our world, light reigns supreme. Even if the commoners don't realize it yet. But where there is light, there is shadow. Aura is both light and shadow combined. You cannot have one with the other. There are those who manipulate their aura to "shadow" others. That's where the Berserker reigned supreme."

Amy straightened up. She had never heard Rezna discuss the legendary Berserker Peculiar that took so many lives in the old days.

"Some were around when the Berserker wreaked havoc after the Second Great War. Others only believe it to be a myth. I was only a child at the time. It took a band of powerful individuals to come together to put the Berserker down, but after it was captured, many followed in its path, trying to emulate the power that it had. As more evohumans developed, some of us learned how to progress our abilities. Some progressed far more than others, in the same way, that the Berserker had. This led to secret organizations being created, and they named their members, Auraists, but the general public saw us as threats, seeing as they knew nothing about how we obtained this new level of power. Hence we became Peculiars and, as they do, they hunted us, fearing us like witches from the older days of Salem. We fought, of course, but our numbers were not great.

"As I grew older, I studied and learned as much as I could about our ancestors of aura manipulation. It took me years but I managed to track down a few auraists. Their numbers had grown. I gained their trust and they showed me how to unlock my own aura. I planned on showing what we can do to the world. That was a joke. The bloodshed between auraists and those who opposed them was far worse than any conflict since World War II. And it wasn't a singular war. It was decades of bloodshed. The more we evolved, the more they came for us. Babies were ripped from their mother's clutches at birth in order to test their energy level. If it even teased a certain limit. Just the idea that you may be more powerful than some Senator or Mayor would cause you to lose your life before you had the chance to protest."

"What does this have to do with my parents?" Amy gulped, not sure she wanted to know the answer now.

"When your mother was born, I knew she'd be a firecracker. Just like her mother was. And when she met your father, he only added to her spirit. I swear those two worked each other up. They were cursed. Your parents stood on the front lines many, many times. After all my battles, I grew scared for them. Afraid of losing the only family I had left. They had you a month before…"

"What…" Amy's eyes welled up. "You said they were cursed. What happened to them?"

"It's true, they were cursed. But that curse was sent by none other than Class Ones, who were afraid of what your parents were trying to accomplish in our world. It was a weapon… a weapon whose origin I still have not discovered. But it wiped them out along with many other auraists."

Tears ran down Amy's eyes. She almost regretted making Rezna finally tell her the truth.

"They died because I let my fears get the best of me. I was too busy safeguarding them from afar, that I wasn't there, at their side. I could have saved them. I knew how. It's my fault your parents are dead and I am ashamed every day for it."

"What…" Amy stared at her tear-soaked sleeves crossed in front of her on the table. She closed her agape mouth and cleared her throat. "What do you mean you knew how to save them?"

"Through my travels and studies learning more about aura, I found there are ways to trap a spirit using your own aura. However, this results in the corruption of your own aura, potentially losing it altogether. I knew this yet I backed out of the trip where they died, vouching to watch over you instead. Truth was, I was too scared about losing my aura if push came to shove."

"You've lied to me. All this time."

"There was no need to dredge up—"

Amy jumped out of her seat and banged her fists into the table. "How could you lie to me after all this time?"

"Mind your voice, dear."

"Bollocks with that!" Amy struggled to catch her breath as she ignored the lightheadedness that swam over her. "I trusted you!"

"As you should." Rezna pointed her long, boney finger at Amy. "It's why I push you to triumph over your fears. You can't overcome your fears if you keep running from them. I meant it when I said that you can't save everyone, but that doesn't mean you can run when the chips are down."

"Where have you been going?" Amy asked. "Every time you leave for *work*, where have you really been?"

There was a knock at the door.

Rezna stood, glaring Amy down for a few seconds before marching out of the kitchen.

Amy stood still, fists in craters on the table, arms shaking.

"What do you need me for?" Rezna's voice said.

Amy's eyes went wide. She ran out of the kitchen.

Not now. Not this way. Please don't take her. It was me.

She reached the hallway. Two detectives were just inside the door speaking with Rezna.

"You catch the news?" One of the detectives said. "They're going to need you in Enfield."

"ZLynx, broadcast latest news report, location focus, New Enfield," Rezna said.

A TV screen materialized in front of them all. On-screen, a reporter some distance away from a huge building that was on fire.

"Authorities are still searching for the suspect or suspects that set ablaze Oldman Primary Academy right behind me. There have been multiple casualties and we're still rounding out the numbers, but so far, the only casualties have been faculty members with many more inside…"

"Give me a moment to speak with my grandmother," Rezna said. She closed the door as the detectives bowed out. Rezna put a hand on Amy's shoulder.

"It's out in the open now. There have been murders also happening over in Enfield for a few weeks now. Their coroner was one of the first, so I've been having to run back and forth. I've been doing my own investigations.

"I'm not a child. You could have told me."

"We'll talk about it when I return. I promise."

Amy turned her back on Rezna to face the TV screen. The door shut behind her.

She's been playing me all along. She knew something bigger was happening, but she just wanted to leave me out of it. But she can't seem to solve this one either. Same way she couldn't save my family.

On the TV screen, behind the reporter, a woman and small boy held hands, with their backs to the camera. The woman was hysterical, wiping her tears as her arm holding the boy's hand shook.

The boy's head slowly turned towards the camera. He wore a big smile. His eyes rolled up until the whites showed, with black veins creeping onto them. His eyeballs grew grey cloudiness that drifted from every corner.

Three slow knocks hit the front door.

Amy faced the front door as the TV screen cut off.

Amy opened the front door.

"What are you doing here?"

Chapter Twenty

Issa stood outside, rain falling down on her.

"I didn't know where else to go."

Moments later, Issa sat on the bottom staircase, staring at the floor, with a towel wrapped around her. Amy leaned against the banister, giving the girl a weak smile. Half their faces in shadow in the dimly lit hall.

"What happened?"

"You were so nice to me in the hospital. I just thought it'd be okay to come here," Issa said, eyes still on the floor.

"Of course I don't mind. You have to tell me what happened, Issa. No more secrets."

Amy picked up Issa's chin, and the girl's drooping eyes looked into her own. She tried to move Issa's right hand, which was covering her left arm, but the girl's hand wouldn't budge.

"Can I see?" Amy asked, placing a hand over Issa's.

Issa's hand shook underneath Amy's. She moved her hand off of her arm. A large red scratch went down a quarter of the girl's arm.

Amy gritted her teeth. "She did this to you?"

The girl nodded.

"Bitch," Amy muttered.

The girl giggled.

"Forget I said that. Don't repeat that ever. What happened?"

"I was just…" The girl shrugged. "I was reading the Book of Clouds with my friends when she came in and said it was time to stop reading. Sure, I argued with her a bit, but she got louder. I got scared because she kept yelling and I told her she was scaring me. That's when she slapped me." She rubbed her left cheek.

Amy clenched her fists.

"I said 'Auntie, please stop yelling, you're scaring me and my face hurts' and she grabbed my arm. I tried pulling away, but she held on tighter."

"She won't get away with this. I promise you."

Issa smiled. "I knew you'd be there for me Amy. That's why I told her 'I'm going to tell Amy and she's going to make you go away. Forever.'"

Amy caressed the girl's hair. "She won't get away with this. I swear it, Issa."

Issa hugged her. "Thank you, Amy."

"Stay here. I'm going to make a call. Do you want some tea?"

Issa nodded. She sat back on the stairs.

Amy walked into the kitchen. She got a pot of water and placed it onto the flames of the stove burner. She pulled two mugs out of the cupboard and placed them on the counter near the sink.

"ZLynz, lights," Amy said. The lights came on. "Call the police, please."

"Connection unavailable."

Amy frowned. She walked out, smiled at Issa, and came into the living room. "ZLynx, call the police, please."

The ZLynx box chimed and flashed red. "Connection unavailable."

"I'll try again in a sec." Amy walked out. She passed Issa, who was playing with her shoelaces. Amy stepped into the kitchen and frowned at the mugs on the kitchen table. She picked the mugs up and moved them to the sink. She put tea bags in.

"Amy, did I tell you about the night my parents died?" Issa said.

Amy peeked out at Issa from the kitchen. "No, not really. Was there something else you wanted to mention?"

"The water will boil over, Ames."

"Right." Amy walked back to the stove. She paused.

Ames?

"I told you I poked mommy with my crayon every morning. To wake her up."

Amy poured the water. "Yeah, I remember that. What about it did you—shit!" Amy shook her hand, rubbing the red spot on her finger and stepping out of the small amount of hot water she spilled.

The mugs sat on the table.

"The hell? I just—" Amy picked up a mug. "Issa did you—"

Issa was gone. Amy moved into the hall. "Issa? Where'd you go?"

"I poked her really hard, Amy," Issa's voice said from somewhere in the house. "She was a sound sleeper, so she didn't even budge. Daddy wasn't so lucky. He felt every. Single. Inch."

"Wha—" Amy went up the stairs to the second floor. "Issa, where are you? You shouldn't be lurking around."

"Like you were?"

Amy entered her room. She got down on one knee and took a deep breath. She lowered her head, checking under the bed.

Nothing.

"This isn't funny, Issa." Amy left her room.

"This isn't funny, Issa," Issa's voice mocked.

"Come out, please." Amy checked the upstairs bathroom. She pulled the shower curtain aside. She turned to the mirror over the sink. "Issa, what's going on?"

"Where were you the night my parents were killed?" Issa's voice echoed.

The hallway lights flashed. Amy froze in place for a few seconds before reaching in front of Rezna's door. Her hand lingered over the doorknob.

Three slow knocks came from the front door downstairs.

"Issa, you better not be in there," Amy said, leaning against Rezna's door.

Downstairs, Amy opened the front door. Non was on the steps, but behind the gate stood three children, the hoods of their raincoats covering most of their faces.

"Can I help you?" Amy called out to them.

Amy frowned as they did not respond, not moving a single inch as though not hearing her.

Amy grabbed her raincoat off the hook. She stuck an arm inside.

Behind the gate, the kids were gone.

Amy stepped an inch outside the door, peeking up either end of the block, trying her best to keep her peripherals off the cemetery. She shut the door and hung her raincoat back up.

Keep it together, Devine.

She walked back upstairs and returned to the outside of Rezna's room.

A piece of paper slipped out from under the door. Amy picked it up and unfolded it. Issa's drawing.

"Issa!" Amy opened the door. "Get out of here." She stared into the darkness. She brought her hand up. The drawing was gone.

"Please Amy, find us—" Issa yelled.

"ZLynx, lights on," Amy said, pushing into the room.

Nothing happened. A pair of yellow eyes stared at her from within the darkness.

Amy nodded. "So I'm guessing no one else is in here then. Copy." She backed out of the room and closed the door.

A series of thumps came from the hallway.

Amy ran to the staircase. A glimpse of a young boy walked out and closed the front door.

Amy took a step down the stairs. A hand grabbed her foot and she tumbled down the staircase. She landed flat on her back at the bottom of the steps.

Footsteps stomped away on the second floor.

Amy got to her feet and rushed up the staircase. Her room door was a few inches open. Amy moved towards it and paused. Whispers came from inside.

Amy pushed open the door. On the bed, another Amy laid asleep wearing a black dress with her arms crossed over each other. A group of children stood on either side of the bed looking down at this doppelganger.

"You're not real." Amy walked into the room and put her hand on one of the children. The child's shoulder shook and Amy retracted her hand. The children took a long breath simultaneously. They walked away from the bed, out of the room, then down the stairs.

"No," Amy said, turning back to the bed.

Her doppelganger stood right next to her, facing her, head cranked to the side, wearing a wide smile on her face.

"You're not real," Amy said.

"You're not real," Amy's doppelganger said.

The doppelganger levitated a few inches off the ground, then sped out of the room.

Amy ran in the doorway.

"Hey!" The doppelganger was in the room again, right behind Amy. Her face rotted right before Amy's eyes, greying with pieces falling from it. "Face yourself." The figure lifted Amy by her shirt and tossed her into the wall over her bed.

Amy collapsed onto the mattress. She picked herself up, backing away on the mattress, but she was now alone. The wall behind her and the dent that her body caused just seconds ago was gone.

Amy ran down the stairs and turned at the creak of the floorboard.

The door to the basement was open.

Amy peeked down the darkness leading into the basement. "ZLynx, lights."

The lights leading down into the basement flickered on and off.

"Nope." Amy closed the door and turned around.

Amy froze in her spot, finding herself inside of a small room.

Nothing was inside this room except for Amy. The walls were barren, with no windows and no door.

Amy stepped around the room, her footsteps echoing, disturbing the silence.

She stopped moving.

A pair of tiny, white balls of light swirled a few inches apart from one another on one of the walls.

How long do we sit back and watch?

The pair of white lights faded away.

Amy turned.

Four white sheets surrounded her. Judging by their shape, Amy had a good idea of what, unfortunately, laid underneath them.

They destroy our world. Haven't you had enough?

Amy blinked.

The room had gotten smaller, its walls a few inches from her. The four hanging sheets were gone.

They'll use everything up until it all is gone.

Amy's shoulders could barely turn without touching one of the room's walls. The room had somehow gotten even smaller.

What will you do, Amy? What will you do?

Amy closed her eyes. She opened them again.

A swooshing noise came above her head.

Amy hesitated. She slowly moved her head up.

The four white sheets hung right over her head. They leaned down towards her.

The outlines of skeletal faces peered down at Amy from underneath the white sheets.

"WHAT WILL YOU DO?!" the ghastly figures yelled in unison.

A trickle of blood ran down between Amy's eyes.

Amy jumped out of her skin, slapping her face and shaking her body as though full of fleas.

She opened her eyes, now face to face with the rotting face of her doppelganger.

Who smiled at her.

Her doppelganger thrust her hands into Amy's chest, pushing her down the stairs.

Amy rolled down the spiral steps, thumping hard against its edges before grabbing ahold of one of the bars, stopping herself midway down.

The doppelganger stood upstairs in the doorway. It moved down towards Amy as the basement door slammed shut.

Amy pulled herself up and hustled down the rest of the stairs, running backward until her back hit the wall. Her eyes stayed on the staircase, barely able to make out anything but edges in the dimly lit room.

The doppelganger was nowhere in sight.

At one corner of the basement, a light shined on the floor.

The light came from the inside of the open morgue prep room.

Amy stepped into the prep room. The seven examination tables each had a cream sheet on top of them, blue lights humming from underneath each.

"Kids? If you're really here, this isn't funny. I… I don't know what has a hold of you, but you've got to fight it."

Amy walked to the furthest table to the left and pulled off the sheet.

The blue light inside was accompanied by nothing else.

She moved over to the next table and pulled off the sheet.

Nothing.

She pulled each sheet off, and thankfully, found nothing.

She reached the last table, took a deep breath, and yanked the sheet off.

Nothing.

"I'm not playing these games anymore." Amy turned to leave.

Seven children laid on the floor parallel to the tables.

"Shit!" Amy jumped back, scurrying away from them. She coughed a small amount of blood into her hand.

The children's feet pattered against the floor as they slid towards her, still on their backs.

Amy crawled further away from them, not taking her eyes off of them.

The children laughed, got up, and ran out of the room. Their footsteps clunked up the spiral staircase.

Amy returned upstairs, shutting the basement door and bolting its huge lock in place.

These poor children. Not them too. It can't be.

The front door was wide open.

Issa was at the front gate. She walked out, closing it behind her.

"Issa wait!" Amy called out.

Issa looked back at Amy. The girl's eyes gazed blankly at Amy, the grey cloudiness floated over her whites. "You can't help me!" She walked away from the house.

Sometime later, Amy followed several steps behind Issa as the downpour grew more violent by the minute. Amy closed her raincoat's hood tight around her head, took out her G-XSR phone, and dialed. Her face lit up as she heard the receiver pick up. Words left her mouth, but the words didn't make sense to her and she hung up almost immediately after.

He can't help you.

Maybe you're right. This is on me to figure out now.

She thought about calling out to Issa again, trying to reason with the girl, but she needed to see where she was leading her. Whoever was controlling the children could see into their eyes. Could counter her every move.

She didn't know where Issa was leading her, but it didn't matter. She will save this girl and stop this curse. At any cost.

Chapter Twenty-One

Amy had been following Issa for about a half-hour now. It gave her time to think. Too much time to think about the one question she wanted the answer to most.

Where was I on the night Issa's parents died?

Amy thought of the old detective movies she loved to watch. How the detective got thrown off the case and usually sidelined, only to make a magnificent comeback and save the day.

Stop living in a fantasy world, Devine.

Amy stopped as Issa giggled and turned a corner. Amy rushed after her, cutting the corner so fast that part of her shoulder clipped the building as she passed.

The Cartier Hotel. The sign's illumination caught Amy off guard even from across the street of the ten-story building. It was the biggest building Jadesfeld offered and sat just at the edge of the town. It attracted a lot of tourists looking for a quiet area to retreat to while they spent most of their time in the sister city of New Enfield. Police cruisers sat on the surrounding streets.

Issa peeked out from the front door. She put a finger to her lips before running inside.

Amy answered her ringing G-XSR. "Jimmy."

"Amy, where are you? I've been waiting for like 20 minutes."

"There's a lot of shit going on. Issa came to my house with some other children, I think… I'm at the Cartier. Wait, what do you mean waiting?"

"You told me to meet you here. I'm on the eighth floor where you said you were and there are detectives everywhere. What the hell is going on?"

"I… I never told you that. I hung up before you answered. I just got here." Amy dashed into the hotel. She moved past the vacant front clerk's desk and hit the elevator call button.

"Issa's possessed, Jimmy. I-I don't know if the other kids are involved or if they were even actually there. I-I-I can't trust my own fucking mind."

"Amy, I told you, there's no possession anymore. There's nothing—"

The call cut off.

"Shit." Amy stepped inside the elevator. As the doors were closing, a young boy she recognized from her school sat behind the front desk. He smiled at her as the doors shut.

I need to get Jimmy out of here.

The doors opened on the eighth floor to a busy scene. Detectives flooded the entire floor, moving about different rooms and interviewing people. A bulk of the Detectives stood outside a particular room down the hall.

A detective stepped in front of Amy as she exited the elevator.

"You can't be right here right now Miss. The floor's been evacuated."

"She's with me!" Jimmy called as he ran up to meet them. He pulled Amy down the hall. "I did some digging on my own and got a trace back to Room 827. The room is registered under the name Marvin Bates, Issa's uncle on her mother's side. The room's got a private elevator that's usually reserved by a passing celebrity who wants to be invisible. They had trouble propping the elevator and the room door open."

Jimmy led her towards the detectives loitering around Room 827.

A detective approached them, holding his hand out.

"The hell are you doing here, Wimblestyn, you're not supposed to be here."

"I think we have bigger issues on hand than my suspension. I outrank you, O'Connor."

"Not when you're out of duty. C'mon let's go, I'm doing you a favor." O'Connor grabbed Jimmy and Amy by their arms and shoved them towards the elevator.

A loud clunk from behind them caused them all to turn back around. The detectives had opened Room 827's door and one of them yelled "Holy shit".

Amy and Jimmy pushed past O'Connor and ran up to Room 827. The door's frame wore a mustard-colored substance.

"Beeswax," Amy said.

"I'm guessing the Australian kind," Jimmy said.

Amy nodded. "It's a powerful adhesive. Amongst its many other properties."

Stepping inside caused them to throw their arms over their noses. It was an absolute pigsty. Clothing littered every inch and there were food wrappers all about. The windows were coated with beeswax as well as several spots on the floor. Detectives inside the room already had trouble making their way through, with their shoes sticking to the floor with every step. Two of them stepped over to a large freezer that sat in one corner of the room.

Amy pulled Jimmy aside.

"Something's not right here. Issa is somewhere in the building and I never told you to meet me here." Amy leaned in closer to Jimmy. "And I'm sensing something in this room," she whispered.

Jimmy looked from Amy to the freezer. He pulled her out of the room and waved over a female detective.

"Villin, can you escort her out of the building please?"

"You got it, Jim—"

A gunshot went off. The middle of detective Villin's head wore a fresh bullet hole that blood poured out of. She fell into Jimmy's arms, and he laid her on the floor.

Down the hall near the elevator, detective O'Connor shakily held his gun towards Jimmy. Several detectives pulled their guns, aiming at him.

"I-I-I d-don't know why I did that. I-I—" O'Connor said.

"O'Connor…" Jimmy said, holding his arm out. "Put your weapon down and kick it towards me.

"H-h-he di-he made me—" O'Connor pointed past Amy.

Over Amy's shoulder near the other end of the hall, a small body disappeared around the corner.

"What are you talking about, O'Connor?" Jimmy said, looking to the end of the hall.

"All of you have to get out of here," Amy said. "It's coming."

All of the sounds around Amy ceased to exist. She dropped to her knees, clutching her hot chest, as it was getting tighter by the second. In front of her, detectives tackled O'Connor to the ground and restrained him. Jimmy pulled her up and led her past the commotion and towards the elevators. Amy grabbed her nose as blood trickled from it onto the ground.

The elevator doors opened.

"Whose kid is this?" A detective behind Jimmy said.

A small boy stood inside the elevator. He smiled at them. His head twisted to the side inch by inch, moving like the shortest hand on an analog clock. It stopped halfway to his shoulder and hung there, his smile widening even more.

"Going down sir?" the boy said, with the voice of an eighty-year-old man. The elevator doors snapped shut.

Amy and Jimmy stared at the closed elevator doors. Then each other.

"That was… not okay," Jimmy said.

"Hey, we got something here in the freezer!" A detective called from Room 827.

Amy and Jimmy ran back to the room. Three detectives stood around the now open freezer. Something stuck out from the edge of it.

Several pings came from around the hallway. Several white screens with a flashing red light materialized from the earpieces, badge holders, and wristbands of all the detectives.

"Several reports are coming in… missing kids around the town…" Jimmy's breathless voice let out.

Amy stared at the freezer as a detective turned his back to her, examining something inside of it. A gray finger pointed out from behind the detective.

"It's… it's a boy…" the detective said.

Amy stepped behind Jimmy, clawing into his arm.

"We've got a bunch of young blokes hiding here in the closet," a Detective said, standing in front of a huge walk-in closet.

Inside the closest, a group of children sat inside, clumped up together. Their breaths were slow. Their eyes stared up at Amy.

The hotel's speaker system pinged.

"Sun sun, go away. Clouds can now come out to play." Multiple children's voices sounded over the loudspeaker.

"Sun sun, go away. Clouds can now come out to play."

"Sun sun, go away. Clouds can now come out to play."

Over and over again, they sang the line.

The lights flickered a couple of times before going completely out. Screams were heard from inside the room.

The lights came back on. A detective was laid out on the floor with deep gashes in his throat and left cheek. A syringe was stuck into his chest.

A young boy stood next to him, holding another syringe. The other kids stepped out from the closest and joined behind him. Their faces were expressionless. Their eyes rolled back, filling with gray cloudiness.

Three of the kids ran to the windows and smashed their fists into them. Glass fell out around them.

Detectives moved in to restrain the children, ignoring their cries.

The dead boy in the freezer bolted upright. Amy could only see half of the boy's gray, decayed face because two detectives stood in front of him. His smile widened and grew past the edges of his face as he licked his razor-sharp teeth.

"They're coming," he growled.

The undead boy jumped forward onto the detective nearest to him and bit into his neck. The detective screamed as blood gushed as he tried to get the undead boy off of him. His partner yanked at the boy's arm.

The buzzing of a large swarm came from somewhere outside in the near distance. Being on the edge of town meant the green pastures where the swarms rested were, closer than ever. Close enough to be seconds from the hotel, finally being able to find the prize they had been searching for all along.

The children in the room ran out as the bee swarm infiltrated through the broken windows.

"Let's go!" Jimmy pulled Amy's arm as they escaped with the only other two living detectives. He shut the room door before pulling Amy down the hall, towards the elevator as more screams pierced the air behind them.

"Come on, come on..." Jimmy punched the elevator button over and over again but it didn't light up. "Stairs it is!"

Before running off, Amy caught a glimpse of the scene they were leaving behind. A detective fired his gun and an electric cuff ensnared one of the possessed kids, downing them. Some detectives laid unconscious, others wrestled to restrain the children, whose numbers had doubled.

Jimmy led them around a corner and pushed open the door leading to the stairwell. They ran down flights of stairs.

"What now?" Jimmy asked.

"We've got to find out where it is," Amy said.

"What?"

"Cloudy. It's the person possessing the kids."

"Cloudy?"

"They must be like me, an auraist, maybe one of the hidden ones Gma's always referred to. They're possessing the kids through the ZLynx connections. I thought it'd be over when I destroyed the town's main hub…"

"You, what?! That was you?!"

"I thought I could stop it. But somehow they're still reaching us… Jadesfeld and Enfield too. It's making me see things, do things now… the possession is almost full on. We've got to stop it before it spreads even further." Amy was out of breath as she hustled down each flight of stairs. She stopped, Jimmy, bumping into her.

At the bottom of the steps, a group of cloudy-eyed children looked up at them.

"Where are you going, Amy?" They said one right after the other.

"No." Jimmy pulled open a door labeled <u>4</u> and dragged Amy through it. "They're not gonna get to you. I won't let them," he said.

They darted down the hall. They stopped at an elevator and Jimmy stabbed the call button. It opened and they stepped inside. Jimmy pushed for the lobby.

Down the hall, a teenage girl ran straight at them. The smile frozen on her face was the last thing they saw before the elevator doors shut in front of her. Jimmy threw his back against the wall, letting out a deep breath.

"You alright?" Jimmy looked up.

"What if I'm not? I've already been compromised," Amy said, staring at the floor. "I'm slipping away every second. I can feel it, Jimmy. I can hear it laugh at me."

"Yeah, well it won't get you. I know it. Even if it kills me. At least we know why the bee swarms have been getting out of hand. It'll take weeks to get that situation under control. I've got to get down to the station asap. Are we going up?"

The elevator doors opened up to the seventh floor. Outside the elevator, the assailant who attacked Amy at the Jones' house stood, wrapped in a dark ruby oriental cloak. The assailant's chest heaved in and out, staring at Amy with its vibrant gray eye.

"No escape," he said.

His fist punched forward, catching Jimmy's hand, who jumped in front of Amy.

"Dammit!" Jimmy held his palm, gritting his teeth.

The assailant threw Jimmy aside and towered over him, raising his arms high and bringing them down.

Amy blocked his blow, protecting Jimmy, as the elevator doors closed. The elevator moved again.

Amy spun around hitting away another fist the assailant threw. She kicked his midsection and charged into him, throwing him up against the right side of the elevator, leaving a huge dent.

"I remember your voice," Amy said.

The assailant growled as he thumped his arm into Amy's back, again and again, trying to free himself from her grasp. He pushed his foot off against the wall and climbed up backward, freeing himself from Amy. His left fist slugged her in the face, knocking her over. The assailant continued walking up the wall, reaching the ceiling.

Jimmy dodged the assailant's first arm but was caught by the neck by the assailant's second arm.

The assailant pulled Jimmy up, his massive arm choking Jimmy.

The elevator stopped and the doors opened up to the fourth floor. The assailant tossed Jimmy out of the elevator, jumped down, and started after him.

Amy pulled the cloak of the assailant and jumped on his back, putting an arm around his neck. She forced him back inside as the elevator doors closed, pulling his hood off in the process.

The assailant, General Aba's young brother Bosti, swung his body into the wall, knocking Amy off. His cloudy eyes narrowed on her. He wildly swung his fists as Amy dodged each one, each missed blow denting the walls.

Amy's eyes grew orange. She groaned as she kicked his shin and threw an elbow straight up into his chin before plucking his eyes. Her aura grew around her. Her fingers continued digging into his eyes.

Bosti turned away from her screaming as he held his bleeding eyes. On his back, four extra arms tore through his cloak, coming out of two pink, fleshy holes on either side of his spine.

Bosti jumped up and his extra arms stuck onto the elevator ceiling as he roared down at Amy. He jumped down.

Amy's aura burst around the elevator, knocking Bosti against the opposite wall.

Bosti held his head, shook it, then charged towards her.

Amy's aura formed two hands that grabbed both of Bosti's and pinned him against the wall.

"Bosti, you have to wake up," Amy said.

"It hurts! It hurts!" Bosti screamed, holding his eye.

"I'm sorry, I didn't mean to—"

Bosti charged out of Amy's aura grasp and delivered a fist to her face, sending her flying into the cold metal wall.

Amy fell to her knees. Her peripheral caught Bosti raising his arms over his head and bringing them down behind her.

Amy's eyes burned bright orange before returning to their natural color. She spun around, caught Bosti's arms in one hand, and formed a ball of aura with her free hand.

Amy twisted her hand holding her aura ball to the side, then swung her aura ball forward, straight into Bosti's chest, knocking him up into the ceiling. Bosti landed with a thud on the ground.

The doors opened up to the first-floor lobby. Jimmy stood there, his gun and handcuffs at the ready.

"Cloudy..." Bosti said, his eyes barely open. "Cloudy makes everything better. No... no one makes fun of Bosti anymore..." His eyelids fluttered before closing, his head turning to the side.

Jimmy stooped down to check Bosti's pulse.

"He's fine. Just unconscious, for now," Amy said.

"How'd you know?" Jimmy asked.

"It takes a lot more force than what I used to put someone like him down for good."

Amy walked out of the elevator.

"Amy."

Issa sat leaning against the front entrance, hugging her knees.

"Issa!" Amy ran over and stooped down to check on the girl. "Are you alright? How are you feeling?"

"I can't fight it anymore." Issa's tear-soaked face looked away from Amy. "I'm sorry Amy, I really am. It's just too hard to fight."

"You've got to keep trying love, okay? I know it's hard, I know. But—"

Issa's eyes rolled back and the gray clouds took over. She smiled at Amy.

Amy grabbed her head as a sharp pain stabbed from all sides. A ringing sound filled her entire head.

You and I are the same, Amy. We have to follow Cloudy's guidance. We have to save the world. Dump the cop and let's get on with it.

"No! Issa please," Amy said.

Next to her, Jimmy's mouth moved, but no sound came out, as he shook her shoulders.

Have it your way. By the way, Gma's home.

Issa pushed Amy back and bolted out of the hotel, disappearing into the night.

Amy shook her head so fast that she toppled over into the nearby wall.

"Amy! Are you alright?! Amy!" Jimmy called out to her.

How did she...

Amy grabbed her chest. She knew if she told Jimmy what she had just heard he'd follow her.

"Yeah. Everything's fine. She just had a hold of me. Get to the station. I've got to run home and check on things."

Amy burst out of the front doors of The Cartier Hotel. There was no time to waste. Time was testing her and she would not fail. The world around her seemed to close in, leaving claustrophobic anxiety filling her lungs.

As she ran, her sweat built up, drying faster than it came. She ran faster than she had ever run before as her aura ignited around her. Orange light sparked off of her limbs creating a ball of light around her. She knew someone would see, but she didn't care. She was too fast for them to recognize her anyway. The orange ball of light that blazed across the town would be a talking point for weeks to come. She'd worry about that later.

Amy reached the corner of her block, slowing herself just a bit to still be a speck in the wind but lost her orange glow. She stopped outside her front gate and her heart sank into her gut. Her front door was ajar by an inch.

Amy stepped inside her home, loosening her tightened hood from around her head. The lights were already on in the hallway, the rest of the house coated in darkness.

"Gma? Are you back already?" Amy took off her raincoat and stepped forward. Her eyes widened down at the pair of shoes upright on the kitchen floor.

Amy's aura flared up all around her body. Tears rolled down her face. Her knees lost their strength. Her aura trickled around her body, a bonfire tickling the ceiling.

Rezna laid on the floor. Eyes staring into the ceiling. Mouth agape.

Amy took her eyes off her grandmother's face, but they fell on the large kitchen knife lying deep between Gma's breasts.

The woman who took care of the dead now rested amongst their ranks.

Chapter Twenty-Two

"To be a truly powerful auraist, you've got to keep your emotions in check at all times. Expression only goes as far as what you can show your aura is capable of," Rezna said as she paced back and forth in front of a kneeling ten-year-old Amy. She stopped to tower over the girl, her lip curled upwards, and left eyebrow raised.

Amy's eyes followed her grandmother's as she huffed and puffed, struggling to get back to her feet. She dusted off her skirt. Balled her fists.

"A disgrace to your heritage! Simply intolerable," Rezna continued. She walked over to the edge of a cliff. "I can only imagine what our enemies would do to us after witnessing such frailty. Have you nothing to say?"

Amy walked next to Rezna and peered over the edge of the cliff. A violent ravine crashed against the large boulders below. Amy wiped the tears from her face.

"He… he was dead. His insides were oozing onto my face, into my mouth—"

"Oh, boo-hoo." Rezna marched away from the child. "You think wars are won in fields of sugar under bright sunny days? You have to grind your feet into the filth and come out of the other side a victor. Or else you'll end up dead! Dead! Just like your parents!"

Tears rushed down Amy's face as her little body shook. Strands of her hair raised above her shoulders. Balls of orange light flashed in and out of existence around her fists as her chest heaved in and out. The sensation prickled her from every pore.

"I can do better, Gma. I promise I can—"

"Then do better," Rezna said as her legs slid apart from each other, her feet digging deep into the earth as dust clouds danced around her body. In the blink of an eye, she ran right up to Amy's side and threw a fist at the girl.

Her fist stopped inches from Amy's face.

Amy fell onto her knees, not taking her eyes off of the ground. She flinched hard as Rezna made a move by her, but her eyebrows scrunched together as Rezna took a seat. She followed Rezna's beckoning to sit alongside her, hanging her feet just off the cliff.

"When I was your age, I used to love going over to the countryside for a little family vacation. Mum and pop used to take me to this little cabin near the most beautiful stream of water. You see, before I was born, Mum was a scientist of evohumanology. She studied how we advanced over time. Our strength, agility, intelligence—she studied every single aspect. Father used to say she was a madwoman. They used to argue over the Peculiar Law. He hated Peculiars while my mother sought to understand them. When they had me, all of that changed. Everything was about me. Mother quit. She dropped everything so that she could be around me. Father was happy he had his two best girls."

Rezna smiled at the rising sun in the distance.

"When my aura started to awaken, things changed for them once again. While mother was fascinated with what I could do, father wasn't so happy. I got good, real good at controlling my aura at such a young age and I was sensing the energy from other things before I was even your age."

Rezna patted Amy's head.

"Did he eventually come around? Your father?" Amy asked.

"Mother kept testing me to see how I could progress. Father felt it could be dangerous and feared for me. Mother and I sort of bonded, becoming closer and closer, and father didn't seem to like that."

Rezna closed her eyes and placed her left hand over her right.

"They argued a lot over what to do with me. One Summer, we all needed a break, so mother suggested we go to our little cabin at the end of the world, where all of our problems ceased. One evening, we needed some solution for mother's work so father went to gather some punsimate berries off this high tree… but he lost his footing."

Rezna rubbed her left hand back and forth over her right one.

"I used my aura to catch him just in time, just before he hit the ground. He was livid. He said if I were to ever show a speck of my aura's light again, he'd drop me into Tha Natos Forest."

Amy's eyes went wide. Her hands shook on her little knees.

"I swore to your parents that I would protect you," Rezna said.

Amy nodded. She gave a little smile, feeling her grandmother's warm palm along the middle of her spine.

Rezna returned her smile.

Amy's small body pushed off over the edge of the cliff. She screamed as her body barreled down towards a family of boulders.

"Gmaaaaaa!" Amy's hands reached up towards Rezna.

Rezna rolled her eyes. Her green aura outlined her body as she shot a beam of her power down towards Amy.

Rezna stepped back as she brought her aura-enclosed hand up. She smiled.

Rising above the cliff, wrapped inside a revolving ball of Rezna's aura, Amy stood with her arms and legs outstretched to the edges of her own orange aura ball. The green and orange aura balls orbiting in opposite directions forging a brilliant light show.

CHAPTER TWENTY-TWO

Amy's glowing bright orange eyes dug deep into her grandmother's soul.

"Brilliant." Rezna beckoned Amy towards her with her free hand as she backed away from the cliff's edge.

Amy held her pose. Once over firm ground, the aura ball dispersed, with Amy landing on the ground still enclosed in her aura ball. Seconds later, her aura also dispersed, although her eyes still glowed.

"What?" Amy asked.

"Prepare for the next phase, my dear," Rezna said. "Let's begin the real work."

Amy reached her hands out towards the body before her, but they shook and fell to the floor. Her fists pounded the ground, leaving gashes in the wood. She wanted nothing more than to hold her grandmother in her arms, a final time, and kiss her forehead. Wish her goodbye before her aura trailed away

Amy's eyes grew.

Her aura. Is it still here? It couldn't have gotten far, could it?

Amy's torso swiveled left to right, searching for a glimpse of green light. She hoped, prayed it had only just happened. Hoping she could at least see her Gma's aura float away into its next journey. Curious if the stubborn old woman's aura would stick or float away.

Or would she return to her dying corpse as Mr. Bakers did?

Amy shook her head.

What's wrong with me? Hoping the murder's still fresh. What's WRONG with me?

Amy fell onto her arms, her tears soaking into the deep mahogany floor. She crawled forward, stopping at the body's feet, her own body shaking so violently she thought she might be having a seizure.

"Come… come back, Gma… please…"

Amy allowed a single finger to rest on one of Rezna's feet. It was as much as she could manage.

What's wrong with me? This isn't normal. This isn't right. It's not fair to her. I'm so weak. I've always been so weak.

Two boys lifted a ladder out of an old cobblestone well and dragged it onto the beautiful green pasture underneath them.

At the bottom of the well, eleven-year-old Amy picked up a large smiley face pin. She smiled, cheek to cheek, raising the pin towards the well's opening.

"Hey Noah, Felix, I found it, I found it!" Amy said. A pebble smacked her right on the nose. She dropped the pin and fell to her knees.

The two boys laughed as they pelted more pebbles down into the well.

"Come now, Amy," Felix said, leaning against the well's edge. "Can't you get up on your own?"

Amy threw her hands up trying to block the pebbles. "Cmon, let me up now. This isn't funny."

"Felix?! Felix?! Boy, where are you?!" Mrs. Temeltry's voice called from somewhere in the distance.

Felix jumped up just as Noah's elbow spun around, right into Felix's back. Felix screamed at the top of his lungs as he fell into the well, his body hitting not once, but twice, into the walls.

Amy jumped back as Felix's body smacked into the ground, neck first. Her mouth opened but her hands clasped her throat, a small shriek escaping.

Noah looked down at her, his lip trembling.

"Felix?! Where are you, boy?!" Mrs. Temeltry called again.

Noah ducked out of view but returned seconds later, lifting and pushing the well's wooden cover over the opening.

"Noah please," Amy pleaded. "Don't!" Amy grabbed her throat, clearing it. "Don't—" Amy whispered as the last bit of light left her face.

Sometime later, Amy sat against the wall with her head buried in her knees. She lifted her teary face and stared at the faint outline of Felix's head, the only part of him that wasn't hidden in the darkness.

His vacant eyes peered at her. The inside of his mouth grew bright red.

"No, no, no," Amy said as she thrashed her hands against the ground. She threw her head back against the wall and closed her eyes. "Be the aura. Be the aura. Be the aura." She lifted her palms towards her face. Specks of orange light flickered, then extinguished multiple times. A warm flush swam over her face and she opened her eyes.

A ball of red light, Felix's aura, floated out of the dead boy's mouth and traveled up the well. It levitated in the air, occasionally drifting from one side to the next.

Amy's hand slapped over her mouth as her head trembled behind her fingers, eyes never leaving the red aura ball.

The red aura floated back down towards Felix's corpse.

Amy stumbled to her feet, her entire body shaking. She kicked her feet into the ground, psyching herself up for the horror she knew was coming next. A stream rolled down the insides of her pant leg and onto the ground, creating a small pond beneath her.

"Please. Please work." Amy closed her eyes. Took a breath. "Please please please work." She balled her fists and her orange aura flickered around them like weary flames.

The red aura hovered outside the boy's mouth. Then drifted inside of it.

Amy stomped her feet on the ground, mumbling hysterically, begging for someone, something, anything to stop this from happening.

Her flickers of orange light solidified into raging orbs around her fists. She raised her arms and threw her aura balls up at the wooden covering.

Amy's aura balls tapped the wooden cover, moving it a pinch off to reveal a peep of moonlight that shined into her eyes. She snapped her distraught face back onto Felix.

Felix's mouth let out a breath of air. His shoulder shifted, pushing a bit more of his neck meat onto the ground.

Amy gasped and fell back into the wall, then onto her butt.

"Please don't wake up."

"Please don't wake up."

Amy slapped her mouth and shook her head. She crawled towards the body's midsection, making sure to keep her eyes on the wooden floor beneath her.

I want to see you again, Gma. But not like this. Not...

For a moment, Amy thought she saw Rezna's shoulder twitch against the floor.

Noah was just a boy. He was scared. He panicked. He couldn't have been able to deal with the corpse of his friend. Similar to how I can't deal with... But there is one way. If I can just...

Amy closed her eyes.

Many colors zoomed around her before turning black.

Amy felt her mind slip away as she fell, now laying in the pitch blackness that surrounded her.

Amy's aura circled the dark space.

She let out a single, long note of air. Her heartbeat slowed, pumping seconds later than normal.

As she opened her eyes, half of the kitchen was gone, replaced by black space, while the other half remained.

Not perfect. But the Realm of Lucidity nonetheless.

Amy's orange astral form looked back at her sleeping human form kneeling inches behind her in the darkness.

Astral Amy raised her translucent hands in front of her, taking in the half of the kitchen that remained. The half with Rezna's body.

Astral Amy closed her eyes and reached her arms towards Rezna's body. She picked up the woman's head and brought it close to her chest, cradling it.

I'm sorry that I'm not strong enough, Gma. I had so many things to say to you. I'll never get to. I'll train harder than ever. I'll make the effort. I won't run from my fears. I promise.

I'll remember that day.

Eleven-year-old Amy threw another aura ball up at the well. And another. And another.

The well's covering had been slipped a couple of more inches to the side, allowing more moonlight to bless the bottom.

Amy gasped as Felix's corpse twitched.

Felix's head slid forward, dragging some stones across the floor with it.

"What's going on?" Felix said. "Where… I fell." Felix's arms flopped around as he tried to steady them on the ground. "It was so painful. My neck hurts. My neck hurts!"

Amy dug her fingers into the well's brick wall, wincing at the impact. Her now bloody fingertips retracted, shaking off the pain as pieces of broken clay fell from beneath her fingernails. She dug back into the wall, clutching for a tighter grip before digging her other hand into the wall. She climbed a few paces, her right foot leaving the floor of the well, followed shortly by her left foot.

Her right foot missed its mark, and Amy tumbled onto the ground. She groaned and flipped onto her stomach.

"What…" Felix sobbed as the exposed bone of his right wrist pushed into the floor. He pushed himself up and maneuvered to a kneeling position. "What did you do?"

Felix crawled into the moonlight. His eyes had lost their original brown color, now filled with the grey tint that the dead carried. A speck of red color matching his aura grew in his pupil. His head hung forward, unbalanced on the hinge of whatever pieces of the neck that he had left.

"What did you do?!" Felix charged forward.

"No!" Amy caught Felix's exposed wrist bone and hand in her own. "Help!"

"What did you do to me?" Felix pushed Amy into the wall, denting it. He slammed her back into it again. "I don't wanna die!"

"Please! Stop! Felix, please!" Blood trickled out the sides of Amy's mouth as she fought against Felix's thrashing body.

Felix threw his full body into Amy's, his head flopping onto her left shoulder. He chomped down into her the top of her shoulder and stayed latched on despite her scream.

A crashing sound came from above. A cloaked figure soared down, landing behind Felix. The figure—Rezna—took off her hood and snatched Felix up and away from Amy. She tossed the boy into the opposite wall and rushed into him, her arm choking him against the cracking brick wall.

"Rezna, please don't hurt my baby!" A woman's voice called from above.

Amy fell onto her hands and knees, coughing up blood. Her eyes met Rezna's before darkness took over her sight.

Astral Amy pulled back the left shoulder of her shirt, uncovering the greyish bite mark embedded deep into her skin.

"Death will forever follow me. I won't run anymore. You always encouraged me. You and Mom."

Her time in the womb was fuzzy now, but Amy remembered the woman's voice she came to know as her mother. She'd sing to Amy every single day, and those moments were the loudest of her pre-life memories. Amy knew from the moment she heard her mother's voice that she wanted to be just like this remarkable woman.

Amy frowned down at Rezna's body. Rezna's face. Something was… off. Something about the wrinkles. The structure. For a split second, the face Amy stared at did not match the one that she had been looking at for her seventeen years of life.

"Something's not right."

A creak of the floorboard brought Amy back to reality.

Chapter Twenty-Three

Amy whipped around, spreading her aura across every inch of the room. All the lights came on.

"Who's there?"

No one answered back.

They're still here. What if it's a child?

The anger inside her at this moment was scary for her. She wanted someone to hurt the way she was hurting. She couldn't even pay attention to the immense stabbing in the depths of her own noggin, and the weightless depths of her stomach boiled with a temperature of over nine thousand degrees.

Amy searched the entire first and second floor, but found no one hiding. She walked to the basement door but found it still bolted.

"I'm going mad."

Amy pulled a paper out of her pocket and unfolded it. Issa's drawing.

"What were you trying to tell me, Issa?"

Amy's eyes traced every line of the drawing. The Bates family home was drawn prominently in the middle of the artwork, but there was another building behind it. She could swear it wasn't there before. The aura burning around her hands spread light down the lines of the entire drawing. Her aura subsided and the lines of the drawing moved around the paper, becoming blurrier by the second.

"Stop it, you shit," Amy said. Orange flashed within her eyes before disappearing, and her aura flickered around her body.

The lines on the busy drawing returned to where they belonged. The building behind the Bates home looked so familiar, but where had she seen it before?

Amy's eyes went wide.

It's... Highbridge. This must be where the Book of Clouds is kept. The old collapsed radio towers Demora mentioned—

Amy's racing thoughts came to a halt as she jumped out of her skin.

A moonbat bounced off the side of her front door's viewing glass. Its wide, bright orange eyes bore into hers before flying away into the night sky.

Amy wondered where Archie was. If he was alright. Hiding somewhere until the stiffness in the town's air calmed. He was great at sensing things and probably knew something has been off with her this entire time.

Or maybe he was dead. Dead just like...

Amy needed a friend right now. She wished Demora was here. She'd know what to say in a spunky, matter-of-fact way. Or even Jimmy, who she's come to gain a tremendous amount of trust in. She could use his off-beat humor and sensible words of hope right now. He'd tell her everything was going to be alright. Though she knew that would not be the case, Amy just wanted to hear the words.

Jimmy. Demora. Of course! She needed to contact them, but not for her own selfish needs. She needed them to help work out her plan now. This is what Rezna had been preparing her for all her life. It'd be a waste for her to drown in her own sorrows right now when the evil energies she had been training for were right before her. She'd have to fight her mind off, sure, but Amy wasn't about to let the most important woman in her life down.

Fuck that.

Amy's aura died out as she dialed into her G-XSR. She kept her mind focused, doing her best to keep out that disgusting intruder. Corrupter of children. Murderer. She shook her free hand, realizing it hadn't stopped shaking for the eternity she spent in this room tonight.

"Amy, what's going on?" Jimmy's voice said through the phone.

"Listen carefully, Jimmy. I need you to bring the glass box and head to where you and I first met. Go a bit East until you reach a small circular clearing. I promise I'll explain later."

"And this is… you. Speaking… right?"

Amy considered. She could feel the intruder, this "Cloudy", attempting to invade her mind throughout her call with Jimmy. She wouldn't allow it. Not after what they had done to Gma.

"Absolutely. I'll meet you there in thirty." Her mind raced as she tried to piece together all the events leading to this current moment in time. Whoever had invaded her home would have to be forgiven. It was as simple as that. There was no way she could hold them accountable for what happened, so it was best to use her energy to focus on stopping Cloudy at all costs.

She dialed into the G-XSR again.

The lights went out. A thump behind her caused Amy to turn around, facing the dark hallway. Facing the outline of someone lurking in the shadows.

Amy's aura ignited around her as she rose to her feet, arms outstretched, ready for combat. Her eye's color remained unchanged, grilling the shadowy figure. She didn't want to hurt them, but she damn sure wouldn't let them get away.

The shadow moved towards her in the darkness. A small light lit up on their leg.

"No," Amy said.

"It was always going to end this way, you know. You, at my will. Seeking answers in the darkness of my light." A pink aura formed around the shadowy figure's steady hand.

Amy quivered as she fell to her knees. Tears returned, betraying her as they fell onto the floor. She shook her head as she watched the culprit kneel in front of her.

"No. Not you… Not you," Amy whispered.

"Why not?" Demora's hand caressed Amy's cheek as her pink irises peeked behind the cloudiness of her eyes, moving over every inch of Amy's defeated face. "She's fighting, but soon I'll have a full hold over her. Over you."

"You have to wake up, Demo!" Amy grabbed Demora's shoulders and shook her. "Fight it. Fight it and help me beat it. It—"

"Helped me uncover my true self," Demora said. "Without Cloudy, the world will be lost. The children must prevail and rebuild. You'll see soon enough, Ames."

"Don't call me that! You're not her. You won't have her." Amy knocked away Demora's embrace and stood fast. Her aura grew around her and pushed Demora back onto her butt.

"Hm." Demora cracked her neck from side to side. "Been a few weeks since we've sparred, hasn't it Ames? Better push yourself or Gma's death would have been in vain." Demora's aura flashed and her body disappeared.

Amy steadied her breaths. She gasped as Demora's arms came from behind her, placing her in a chokehold.

Amy struggled against her grip, her feet flailing against the floor as Demora raised her up off the ground. Her eyes rolled back as she struggled to breathe.

"It's all you," Demora said, tightened her grip. "This is your doing, Amy. You could have saved her. You—"

Amy threw her weight down, her feet hitting the floor, and she launched herself backward into Demora, sending them both crashing into the front door.

Demora kept her grip around Amy's neck as their bodies rode the front door, rolling down the front steps and onto the concrete ground. She twisted Amy's head to the side.

"Be mindful of your surroundings, right Ames? Look. LOOK." Demora's fingers forced Amy's eyes open, forcing her to look at the graves along the right side of her home. "Face your fears and Cloudy will set you free. Cloudy can save us all!"

"Get the fuck off me!" Amy twisted her body and her elbow found its way into Demora's abdomen. Amy dashed back into the house, but Demora was right behind her.

Demora grabbed Amy's hair and pulled her backward, sending Amy's head through the frame of the doorway, taking a huge chunk of the door frame with it. Demora yanked Amy by the hair and threw her onto the staircase.

Amy turned over from her side and was met by Demora's fist straight into her jaw, sending Amy further up the stairs.

Demora stomped her way up to Amy, grabbed her leg, and dragged her back down the stairs.

Amy's head bounced along each stair. She grabbed hold of the rail and kicked Demora in the stomach, sending her flying into the coat rack. Amy climbed back up the stairs on her hands and knees.

Amy got to her feet, using the banister to help her walk onto the second floor. She lost her footing and landed straight on her back.

Demora's eyes peered out at her from behind the banister. She grabbed hold of Amy's leg.

"The time for running is over, Amy." She pulled Amy towards her and to the side, breaking each banister's leg before letting go.

Amy flew into the wall near her Rezna's room. She groaned, holding her leg as her blood dripped out of holes in her pants.

"The time is now for the takeover. Taking back our world." Demora picked Amy up by the neck and pushed her onto the wall. "They'll continue ruining our world. The children are the future."

"I don't want to hurt you Demo, please."

"Hurt me? Please. As if. You may have learned a trick or two but you'll—"

Amy's hand found the knob of Rezna's room door and opened it. Demora dropped her and backed away.

Inside the pitch-black room, a pair of yellow eyes within leered out at the girls before keeping its gaze on Demora.

"Y—" Demora continued walking backward, shaking. "No, stay back!"

"Demora, watch out!" Amy said, pulling Rezna's room door shut.

Demora stepped off the floor, the missing piece of the broken banister not there to stop her as she fell backward.

Amy leaped up and grabbed Demora's neck before it hit the wall adjacent to the staircase.

The girls fell down the stairs together, taking hard bumps before smacking back down onto the first floor.

Amy groggily lifted herself up on her hands and knees. She held her head and wiped away the spot of blood that dripped down past her eye. In her peripheral, Demora got to her feet.

"You want to keep going then?" Amy said.

Demora kicked Amy's midsection, propelling her up into the air, then brought her elbow into Amy's back, sending her crashing back onto the floor.

Amy spun off her stomach and swept her legs towards Demora, but Demora jumped over them and stepped onto Amy's back.

"Come on now, Ames. Is this the best you can offer?"

Demora picked Amy up by the back of her neck and ran her face along the wall, peeling the wooden surface as Amy reeled against the assault.

Amy pushed herself back, using what was left of the wall for support, and flung her body into Demora, crashing down into her on the staircase railing.

"Shit." Amy's hand shook over a large wooden splinter protruding out of her cheek and gritted her teeth at the other splinters in her left hand. She threw her arm back, attempting to wrap it around Demora's neck to restrain her, but Demora caught her hand.

"That's your blind spot," Demora said.

Demora pressed her hand onto the floor. Her aura escaped her palm and highlighted the floor, the light wave moving across, up the walls, and flushed over the ceiling as well. She closed her eyes.

The ZLynx box in the living room chimed awake. It illuminated white and shook in its spot. It exploded, with its parts flying everywhere.

The walls throughout the home grew bright with white light.

Amy shielded her burning eyes.

Demora kicked Amy into the wall, then charged forward and grabbed her up by the throat. She punched Amy in the face, forcing the protruding splinter deeper into her cheek.

Amy's arms crashed down onto the arm that choked her and she punched Demora's face. The two best friends exchanged blows, taking turns grabbing and tossing the other into the walls surrounding them.

"Your fists could never match mine," Demora said.

Demora's aura formed around her palm, forming an aura-hand as she aimed at the coat rack. Her aura-hand ripped the coat rack out of the wall and it flew at Amy.

Amy's aura-hand yanked a chair out of the kitchen and threw it into the coat rack just as it was about to hit her face, knocking it away. She clenched her fist tight to her body and dug her feet into the floor, cracking the wood beneath her.

"But my aura can always best yours," Amy said.

Demora screamed as she charged at her again.

Amy's aura shot out from each of her arms and legs like four tentacles and wrapped around Demora's limbs. Her aura forced Demora forward into what was left of the wooden bars of the staircase railing, her head cracking through one of them, now locking her in place.

Demora struggled to wiggle herself out as Amy walked up to her.

"Demora, I need you to wake up now. We have to stop this madness. I know how to stop it but I need your help."

"The only thing you're going to stop is the breaths of everyone you hold dear. Let me guide you along the right path." Demora screamed as she fought against her entrapment, the broken wood cutting into her shoulders. "Amy please stop, you're hurting me!"

Amy's aura dropped. "You're back! I'm so sorry Demo—"

Demora's arm swung a wooden bar, cracking it into the side of Amy's head.

Amy stumbled and fell over. She turned and crawled away, shaking her head as blood poured from a deep gash in it. She found herself on the kitchen floor, staring at the ceiling, but jumped aside, dodging as a pink aura-fist that smashed right where her head just was, leaving behind a small crater in between the feet of Rezna's corpse.

Amy shook her head as she crawled away from the body, but Demora grabbed her foot and jumped on top of her.

Demora flung a hand out, and her aura formed a hand that snatched a knife off the sink. She laughed as she brought the knife down, slicing into Amy's arms, leaving deep gashes on either side.

"No matter what I do, you always seem to be one step ahead, Ames. Always a pace ahead in aura manipulation. But St. Cloudy's showing me the way. Cloudy can show you too. You just have to stop fighting. Let us in. Just let us in."

Demora mushed the side of Amy's face into the floor, forcing her to face the corpse next to them. She slowly sliced into Amy's cheek.

"Or we can gash you the way we did her. Poetic, the two of you lying side by side to the very end." Demora leaned in close, cutting deeper into Amy's cheek. "Then force you to come back to your body and serve me."

Amy cried out as blood and tears ran down her face, onto the floor, with her head used to smear it around.

"Okay," Amy said.

Demora's face lit up.

Amy clenched her teeth.

"Brace yourself, Demo."

Amy's eyes flashed orange before retreating to normal, and her aura burst alive, shooting Demora straight up into the ceiling.

Amy kicked Demora's falling body into the hall.

Demora groaned as she raised her head off the ground.

Amy's orange aura-enclosed fist sent ripples through her cheeks as it knocked her straight in the face.

Chapter Twenty-Four

She was on edge. Killing someone can do that to a person. Amy could see it in her best friend's face as she led them a few paces ahead of Demora. From her peripheral vision, she searched Demora's face for any signs. It was still quite possible that Cloudy could take over again at any moment, and they both knew it. The feelings inside Amy right now were far from settled, but there was a clear goal in sight. She just needed to keep Demora on the same page.

"Jimmy finished that project we were working on. I think… I know it'll help us contain whoever Cloudy is."

"How do you define evil?" Demora asked.

Amy kept her face straight. She felt the immense pain in Demora's words. She knew how steadfast her best friend could be, so she picked her words carefully.

"This thing is evil. The way it corrupts, the way it pollutes the mind. It's responsible for everything that's happened. It will pay for its crimes."

"So will I," Demora said.

Amy stopped and faced Demora, who stood in place with her fists balled up. Tears ran down her face. Amy moved in close to her.

"You will not be blamed for anything that it made you do. We will get through this, Demo. It cannot win. But that starts with you. Cast out any guilt and place the blame where it lies. As I have done."

"When it comes down to the literal aspect of things, I am responsible, Amy. Me. You can't shed a blanket over that."

"And once we put away this evil, we will discuss and find the best way to power through this. To heal." Amy turned and continued walking. Demora's steps followed her.

"And we will never be the same," Demora said. "It's impossible. We don't come back from this. Like it or not, you can't escape that truth. Everything's changed. What I did to… her. Doesn't change."

Amy wiped away a tear. She wouldn't turn back around, but she wasn't sure if it was because she wanted to hug Demora or send her away if she was too weak to fight now. She also wasn't sure whether some of that darkness had polluted her own mind again, for she felt colder and more removed than usual. Right now, all they needed to be was their best. Amy wouldn't accept weakness because Rezna wouldn't accept weakness.

About half an hour later, Amy spotted pieces of Jimmy's brown Maserati parked behind a large bush near the small hill. Amy watched Demora for a reaction, but Demora had her eyes locked onto her own feet, not seeming to notice a thing in the world.

As they dipped under the growing twigs and bushes of the season, Demora's footsteps ceased. Amy spun around, dodging as Demora's aura shot right past her, knocking her over.

Demora snarled as she ran towards a groan heard close by.

"Demo, wait!" Amy stumbled to her feet and ran after her.

Amy caught up to Demora and knocked her arms down. They both stared down at Jimmy, who sat in the middle of the circular clearing, grabbing his throat, coughing and spitting everywhere. Amy helped him back on his feet.

"You brought *him* to *our* spot?" Demora scoffed and shook her head.

"We needed somewhere discreet. Somewhere out of range. The surrounding wildlife must interfere with Cloudy's influence somehow.

My head always feels clear here. The trees, the animals. There's too much energy to focus."

"Hey," Jimmy said, sticking an arm out to Demora. He leveraged himself against a tree. "The name's Jimmy. Nice to finally meet you, Demora."

Demora's eyes rolled back as she crossed her arms. "You really have a problem trusting people far too easily, Devine. For all we know, he could be the one wielding the curse. Things seemed to escalate once he came into the picture! And he's been getting awfully chummy with you."

"I can assure you I have nothing but Amy's best interests at heart."

"Oh, is that so, cop? I'm the one who's been protecting her and I am very good at finding bullshit in the pantry." Demora stepped up to Jimmy, her nostrils flaring.

"Ms. Corbyn-McDonald, I'm going to have to ask that you take a few steps back," Jimmy said, sticking out his chest, his eyes staring at Demora's aura engulfed fists.

"Demora, enough." Amy stepped between them. "He is here to help us. He's been helping me since this all began and I'd probably be in terrible shape right now if he wasn't around."

"More helpful than me, I suppose?"

"It's not a competition. And more helpful than you're being right now. Calm down."

"Don't tell me to calm down." Demora's aura pushed Amy and Jimmy back, but Amy's own aura burst to life and pushed Demora further back. Demora smiled. "No matter how hard I try, I'll never best you."

"There's more at stake than your ego at the moment. Will you please just—" A creaking of the surrounding twigs caused Amy, Demora, and Jimmy to turn around at the same time.

A small handgun from an older time period pointed right at Amy.

The wielder was none other than Madeline Watts. Tilly and Kassandra walked up on either side of her. They moved to either the left and right sides, the Lockheart Girls effectively surrounding Amy, Demora, and Jimmy.

"Madeline, wait," Amy said, putting her hands up.

"Don't you fucking move!" Madeline yelled. Her eyes shot between Amy and Demora as she slithered closer. "Here I was thinking you were just a fucking normie. Turns out you're both Peculiars! Dangerous cunts!" She turned to Jimmy. "What's going on here, detective? You're working with fucking Peculiars?!" Her eyes returned to Demora, who took a small step forward. "I SAID DON'T FUCKING MOVE!"

"Hey," Jimmy said, throwing his hands up. "It's alright. Madeline, is it? You saved me. I've been undercover tracking these two for some time now. They're going down, not to worry."

"You piece of actual garbage!" Demora said.

"Okay." Madeline nodded. "Okay. detective, well arrest them at once. I've got them in my sights. They won't threaten you any further."

"Alright, I will. Just put the gun down. It's alright." Jimmy moved sideways, making his way past Tilly, getting closer to Madeline.

"How'd you find us twat?" Demora asked.

Madeline's face scrunched up. "I don't answer to you, *Peculiar.*"

"It's very important that we all remain calm here. You know how dangerous Peculiars can be," Jimmy said.

Demora grilled him and shifted her feet.

"He's lying," Tilly said. "That copper, the one they said was running around with Devine. That's him! He's lying, Maddy, he's a liar!"

"I know. He's a fucking liar, too. Running a case, huh?" Madeline's eyes darted between Demora's scowl and Jimmy's wide eyes. "I've known something was up with Devine, especially when I saw that old phone she had. I just had to find out what. You see, my Dad keeps a lot of old heirlooms around, like this pistol. We've also got an old scanner that picks up on old cell tower connections. Wasn't getting a thing until tonight. Lucky stars. I and brought along daddy's birthday gift to me," She shook the gun at Amy. "You're with them."

"He's certainly not with me," Demora said. "This is a ripe disaster, isn't it Ames? This is why we don't bring strangers in the midst."

"Enough of your shit, Demo!" Amy said. She held her throat as she shot Demora a furious look. Even in disaster, she had to babysit these childish antics. Enough was enough.

"It's not my fault! I wouldn't have had to act if I hadn't felt his bustling aura racing around like a mad lad."

"QUIET!" Madeline aimed her gun at Jimmy. "ALL OF YOU! Take his gun!" She shouted and Tilly followed her order.

"Fuck this." Demora shot her hands forward, her aura shooting into Madeline and throwing her feet away onto the ground.

Tilly's hands shook as she aimed Jimmy's gun at Amy. She pulled the trigger.

Nothing.

Madeline sat up and aimed her old pistol at Amy.

"NO!" Jimmy jumped into her line of sight.

The pistol fired.

Jimmy crumpled to the ground.

Amy raised her arms and her aura knocked Tilly into a nearby tree.

Demora raised her arms again, but an unseen force threw her to the ground.

Amy looked puzzled at the gust of wind that brushed past them. The air became still again.

Kassandra moved towards Madeline and helped her up. She reached down for the gun at their feet, but Amy's aura knocked both girls several feet away.

Amy walked over and shot a hand out towards Tilly, her aura

trapping Tilly against the tree she was stirring from. "Demora, check on Jimmy."

Jimmy raised a hand as Demora helped him to his feet. Jimmy held onto his bleeding right arm. "Just an arm puncture. I'll take those." Jimmy pointed out the two guns on the ground.

Demora ran up to each and passed them to Jimmy. Jimmy waved his gun.

"Security feature. Can only be fired by my hands." He holstered his and unloaded Madeline's before stuffing it into the waist of his pants and the ammunition in his pockets.

"Fun's over," Jimmy said. "We're all going to head over to my car and sort this thing out. Amy let them up. ZLynz, secure GCID tech in the vicinity."

Five winding down chirps sang across the crisp breeze.

Amy's GCID screen showed SECURITY LOCK before the screen went blank.

Jimmy beckoned the Lockheart girls to go ahead of him. He took off behind them after giving Amy and Demora a knowing look. There would surely be some messy ends to clean up.

The group walked in silence. As they approached Jimmy's car, Jimmy cleared the bushes off of it and pushed it out from behind.

Demora slid past Madeline. "Bet you're not feeling so mighty now, Watts. Who's the *normie* now?"

Amy motioned Demora towards her. "One of them can manipulate aura. I'm sure of it. I couldn't see it. It hit you, Demo. And I could feel it."

"Stop knobdicking, I just tripped over something."

"No. My aura's been coursing through me like clockwork ever since the incident at the media hub. I can... feel things differently. Sense more. I know there was no flash of light. But one of them can manipulate aura."

Jimmy's Maserati was a speck driving through the densely fogged streets. Inside the vehicle, Amy sat in the passenger's seat with Demora in the back behind Jimmy, squished in next to the Lockheart Girls.

"Where are you taking us?" Madeline demanded.

"Listen, you girls can do whatever it is you want after the day wraps up, but there's some serious shit going on right now and we have to get it done," Jimmy said.

"My father and the Mayor are great friends." Madeline leaned forward. "When he gets wind of this, he's going to have your badge by the end of the day."

"That's all fine and dandy, Ms. Watts. We've got bigger things at stake at the moment."

"Looks like we're headed towards school," Kassandra said.

"Box is in the trunk Amy, but why are we heading to your school? What's the plan?"

"Whoever's wielding the cursed book, their base of operations is at Highbridge. Demo, remember you said there was some old—"

"Radio tower, under the school. That's more of a myth. I was joking, that's real?"

"It's got to be. We've got to find a way of trapping it inside the box."

"I don't think it's big enough for a person," Jimmy said.

"We just need to get the storybook, the Book of Clouds. I believe it's a cursed object. They're using it as a conduit to possess the children. The aura from the book is traveling through the old radio center and into every new ZLynx box in town."

"What are you freaks talking about? There are no possessions anymore," Madeline said.

"I wish that were true," Amy said, staring out the window.

"The new sets…" Jimmy said. "The Jones family spearheaded that operation. In their records, they donated a huge amount to the Creaevix Corporation. The creators of ZLynx."

"That's it then," Amy said. "That's why our shitty little town got all those new sets free. And then Endfield got theirs next."

"Bribery. Typical rich people shit," Demora said.

"I demand that you stop this weird little car. We are not going anywhere with you freaks!" Madeline said.

"We're a bit pressed for time and it's getting dark," Jimmy said. He shuffled under his dashboard. "Where's that—"

"Shit!" Demora let out.

"Jimmy..." Amy grabbed Jimmy's arm.

Jimmy hit the brakes and stared straight ahead. "Holy Callisto."

A couple of feet ahead of them stood about a dozen small children and teens. Their eyes glowed a hint of white that cut through the dense fog.

"Alright," Jimmy said. "We're okay."

"Just keep moving Jimmy. Get us out of here," Amy said. She rolled her side window down and stuck her hand out.

"What are you doing?" Jimmy said.

"Preparing."

Demora looked at Amy and nodded. She rolled down her side window before sticking her arm out as well.

The children didn't budge. Just watched them.

"I'm getting the hell out of here," Madeline said as she popped the door's lock and flung herself out onto the road, her cuffed hands pushing her up and off the pavement.

"No!" Amy flung open her door and moved in front of her. "Get back in the car now." Amy helped Madeline to her feet.

"Get off me! I will not tolerate being held hostage any longer." She pushed past Amy, who grabbed her arm, pulling her back.

"Do you ever stop being a selfish brat? There are things bigger than you or I in motion."

"These *things* don't concern me, *Peculiar*."

Amy wasn't backing down. She pushed Madeline into the side of the car and raised an aura-enclosed fist towards her. "I'm not going to ask you again."

Madeline shrunk.

Amy grabbed her arm and stuffed her back into the car, shutting the door behind her.

Amy's eyes went wide as she fell to the ground, grabbing the side of her head as a piercing feeling shot into it. She picked up a large stone with what she knew was her blood on it.

The children laughed and pointed at her. One of them pulled another large stone out of her pocket.

"I'm alright. I'm alright." Amy rose to her feet and scampered back into her seat.

The group of children walked fast towards the car.

A flash of pink light shot straight in front of them, knocking the children to either side, out of the car's path.

The engine roared to life as another stone came bursting through Madeline's window.

Children approached from the left and right sides of the car.

Mayhem. Stones and other unidentified objects smashed into the sides of the car as Jimmy drove forward.

Amy shook her head as the obnoxious ringing from ear to ear left her unable to comprehend most of the surrounding commotion. Her blurred vision caught glimpses of Jimmy's face and Demora's aura-hand outside the window, knocking back their assailants, who were now running at full speed, smashing their own bodies into the car.

Amy acted on autopilot, sticking her arm out her window. Her aura joined Demora's, knocking the children and pelted items away from the car as the car swerved violently back and forth.

Minutes later, the car turned onto a road, with no more attackers in its path. Amy laid back in her seat, her unmatched labored breaths sinking into her chest before popping out once more. She squeezed the sides of her head.

You're so easy when you sleep.

"I will stop you," Amy said. She turned to her broken side window and drifted off.

Why do you fight me, Amy? Look at the world around you...

Amy's eyes opened, staring out at the cloudy sky with the moon creeping into full view. The clouds formed the outline of a face, with the moon playing the part of an enormous eye.

"I will stop you," Amy said.

Using our outside voice now, are we?

A shrill laughed echoed throughout Amy's head.

You're going to get them killed, you know. Just like—

Amy jerked forward as the car came to a halt.

"Amy!" Demora screamed. "Are you okay?"

"Yeah." Amy sat up, still holding her head.

"We're here," Jimmy said.

The structure of Highbridge Intermissionary School cast shadows in the moonlight that made it seem like a different place. Amy didn't recognize it at all. Especially knowing what's inside. Waiting.

"Tilly, wake up. You damn rock head, get up!" Madison pushed herself into Tilly, but the girl was out cold. "Kassandra, you too?"

Kassandra and Tilly were slumped in their seats against each other. Neither moved a muscle.

Madeline kept shoving herself into them as the others watched.

"I suppose we head in now then, yeah?" Jimmy said.

Before Amy could answer, Tilly's cuffed hands wrapped around Jimmy's neck.

A cloudy-eyed Tilly smiled at Amy while adding more pressure to Jimmy's throat.

Madeline screamed as Kassandra kept head-butting Demora, who struggled to restrain her.

Amy grabbed Tilly's hands and snapped the cuffs apart. She punched her twice within a second and pushed her back into her seat, knocking her out.

Demora opened her door and fell out with Kassandra landing on top of her, still head-butting her.

Madeline threw her body out of the car, and onto the other two, only to be pushed off by Demora shortly after.

Kassandra rolled on her back and got to her feet first. Her cloudy eyes looked from Demora to Amy. She sprinted away.

"Shit." Amy got out of the car. "Shit, where is she going?"

Kassandra disappeared around the corner of the school.

"I don't know," Jimmy groaned as he got out of the car. "But we've gotta get a handle on this thing and fast."

"I'll go after that batshit one," Demora said. "Ames, you get inside and find that storybook. Hey, cop, you think you can handle these two?" She pointed over at a heaving Madeline sitting on the grass and the sleeping Tilly in the back seat of the car.

"I've got it," Jimmy said, nodding. "Got an extra pair of cuffs in the trunk. Take this—" Jimmy took out a stun gun and tossed it to Demora. "Stun her *only* if necessary. Lemme show you how to use—"

"Oh, I know how to use one," Demora said.

"Don't even wanna know how. Now, for that box—" Jimmy led Amy to his opening trunk. Inside was a large white sheet with something glowing underneath. Jimmy pulled it off, revealing a shimmering glass box that overtook most of the trunk. Every edge shined, competing with the strong moonlight.

"So this is it?" Amy said.

"Far out," Demora said, stepping on Jimmy's other side to look.

"It's a beauty," Jimmy said. "It's called a Kukamata Prism. Haven't seen a piece of tech like that since... ever. No idea how your grandmother got a hold of it. I'll have to ask her sometime."

Amy picked up the Kukamata Prism and awkwardly held onto the massive thing. It barely fit under her arm. She threw it back inside the trunk.

"This should have been a breeze to carry."

"As I said, it's impressive tech. The energy it's holding must be adding a ton more to it."

"Maybe you should leave that thing behind. I'll bring it in after I catch the other one," Demora said. "Just get that damn book."

"Yeah," Amy said, nodding. "No turning back now."

Chapter Twenty-Five

Amy didn't think the halls of her school could get any drearier, but this was a place where it seemed only the dead would reside.

Bad thought.

Amy rubbed the fingertips on both hands together as she paced down the quiet halls. Moving slowly, but with purpose. It still hadn't registered that this was the place where one of her worst nightmares had been cooking. Tormented for weeks, her mind invaded for probably longer, and all hope seemed to be lost. Even if they succeeded in capturing the culprit and their cursed storybook, everything that had been ripped from life these past weeks would not return. All those children who lost their parents would still be orphans. The kids themselves would surely need lots of therapy after all they've been forced to endure. Rezna still wouldn't be alive and Amy's best friend had been the one to…

Get it together, Devine. Find this damn book.

Amy lost her sense of awareness, surprised at how far she had traveled within the school. She found herself staring down a familiar hallway. A light was on at the end of the hall. As Amy moved closer, she realized which classroom the light came out from. Mr. Watson's classroom.

She crept closer to the door, just a few paces away now.

The door opened.

Amy froze.

Mr. Perry stepped out of the classroom, stretching his arms out wide as his yawn echoed through the halls. He beamed at Amy.

"Ms. Devine! How lovely to see you! Please," he beckoned her over. "Come in, come in!"

Amy entered the classroom as Mr. Perry shut the door behind her. He picked his glasses up from the desk and wiped the lenses with his shirt before putting them on.

"I see you've taken me up on my offer. So glad you came around. Is it alright if I just call you Amy? Keep it a little casual, if you will."

"Yeah…" Amy faked a smile.

Is it... Perry?

"That's alright, Mr. Perry. I'm actually not here for that, I…" She didn't know what to say. "Listen, it's not a good night for you to be here. I'm afraid—"

"Here, sit, sit." Mr. Perry motioned for her to sit on a desk in the front row. "You look distressed, please have a seat." His hand found her arm and helped move her to the desk.

Amy sat on the edge. "I can't right now, Mr. Perry. You need to get out of here. There's—"

A cloud of black smoke penetrated the air. Amy's vision went blurry. She shook her head, balancing herself upright on the desk.

"Amy, are you alright? Relax yourself. Here, I've got you." Mr. Perry caressed her shoulder and down her arm.

"Wha…" Amy blinked a couple of times. "What's happening?"

"You just need to relax, my sweet girl," Mr. Perry said.

Amy brushed his hands away and got up. "What the hell are you doing?" She stumbled back.

Mr. Perry grabbed her by the shoulders. "I've told you, you've got tremendous potential. And you now know I've got a bit of reach.

Perks of being who I am. I can help you get anything you want. You just need to cooperate."

He's a snake. Just another example of them polluting the world.

"You're making him do this, aren't you?" Amy said.

Mr. Perry frowned. "Who are you talking to? Poor girl, I knew you seemed a bit out of your mind. Let me help you."

I'd NEVER work with the likes of someone like him. No. This is out of my hands. Ask him about Gina.

Amy dodged Mr. Perry's hand. "What happened with Gina?"

Mr. Perry froze. "What do you mean? Nothing happened."

He's lying.

Amy straightened up, this time throwing his hands off of her. "What happened with Gina?"

Mr. Perry chuckled. "I don't know what you're talking about, Ms. Devine."

"Stop lying." Amy stepped close to Mr. Perry, her eyes filled with rage. "What happened with Gina?"

"I-I-I..." Mr. Perry adjusted his glasses. "L-Listen, whatever Ms. Gallagher told you clearly came from a young woman who is out of her mind."

"That day. When she came running out of your office crying. Why? What was the real reason?"

"I-I-I told you already. She has not been doing so well, so I offered some help." Mr. Perry straightened his back and pulled on his suit jacket's lapels. "She needed extra assistance with her studies but was too stubborn to accept help. Don't you make the same mistake, Ms. Devine."

More black smoke shot around Amy, dizzying her once more. Her head felt light before regaining a ton of weight as a voice echoed through her skull once more. She had trouble hearing what it was saying to her.

"Cloudy… stop it…" Amy said, whipping her arms through the black smoke.

That's not my doing.

"Amy." Mr. Perry's face softened back into a smile. "You need to rest. You seem a bit tired and disoriented, dear. I can help you." His fingers stretched out and expanded into his long flesh-colored tentacles, all of which circled Amy. The tentacles slithered against her skin, entangling themselves around her arms and legs.

Amy wanted to break free of his hold, but the air in her head felt so good. So light in comparison to the heavy burden she had been feeling for weeks now. The voice of the intruder that had been talking inside her head for all these weeks was now a faint whisper that seemed to come from miles away.

His abilities are fitting for his slimy ways. Fight him now. Protect the children.

"Wait…" Amy's body was closer to Mr. Perry's than it had been just seconds prior. She moved her face to the side, dodging his breaths, which now blew against her cheeks. "Stop it. Please. Let me go."

"Don't be a fool," Mr. Perry replied. "You're not going anywhere right now. Remember the celebrity status I've gained. I'd hate if something were to negatively impact your academic records…" His lips leaned forward, just missing Amy's face by an inch.

He's VILE!

"I said STOP." Amy pushed Mr. Perry away. Her hands squeezed into the tentacles trapping her arms, causing them to let her go.

The tentacles retreated a bit before circling Amy again.

"Don't do that again," Mr. Perry said. "Now, I'm being as nice as I can be, but you are making this harder on yourself." His tentacles moved around Amy's torso.

He's an abuser of children. The worst kind of human. He must be punished.

"Stop…" Amy's hands squeezed into two of the tentacles as more black smoke hit her face.

Small holes running down each of Mr. Perry's tentacles spewed more of the black smoke out.

"You're a strong one." Mr. Perry chuckled.

Amy's eyes rolled back to only show the whites.

"But I'm only here to help you, Amy."

He's why I am NECESSARY.

"Necessary," Amy said simultaneously. Her eyes came back into focus and she raised off the desk she leaned against. She took quick steps forward, backing down Mr. Perry. "You're a vile little shit, you know that?"

Three tentacles left Amy's torso and shot forward; one around her neck and the other two joining two wrapped around each of her legs.

"Amy, unhand me at once and calm down. I'm only trying to—"

"Help me?" Amy's head flew forward, smashing into Mr. Perry's nose. Her legs stretched apart and pulled him in closer. Her hand tightened around the tentacles they had ahold of and she tossed her hip into Perry's stomach.

Amy hip-tossed Mr. Perry over her shoulder and slammed him into the front row of desks, breaking a couple of them as metal and wood to spread everywhere.

Mr. Perry's tentacles shot up, swinging wildly around Amy.

But Amy was ready. She knocked each away and stomped down on Mr. Perry's groin.

"Fuck!" Mr. Perry yelled. He turned over on his stomach, panting. "A-Amy. Please."

"You." Amy stomped one foot on his back, holding him in place. "You're a pathetic excuse for a man and your time has ended." Her aura grew around her. She waved her hand, and the aura mimicked it, picking up a metal leg from one of the broken desks. A sharp piece of splintered wood hung on its end.

"Ms. Devine, wait. Amy—*please!*"

Amy raised the broken leg and stabbed it straight down.

The sharp end landed inches from the back of Mr. Perry's neck. A single drop of blood ran down the side of his neck.

"No," Amy said. Her aura died out and her eyes rolled back into place.

Why do you resist me, my child? This man does not deserve the breaths he so abundantly takes.

"If I go around killing the monsters, I'll become one as well," Amy said to the voice in her head. She stepped off of Mr. Perry's back and chucked her would-be murder weapon to the side.

"T-t-thank yo—" Mr. Perry started, but was silenced by Amy's swift fist to the back of his head.

Amy walked out of the classroom.

You'd see him walk, knowing what he's done? You don't want to punish him?

"I don't care what happens to him, but murder isn't a sound justice. I don't what he deserves. I just won't be the one to deliver it. Right now, I'm coming straight for you."

Now you've got my attention. Meet me where we first met.

Amy frowned. Her eyes widened as the realization washed over her. The look of determination returned to her face.

Moments later, Amy walked up the staircase, peering at the door that led to the third floor. She took a deep breath, exhaled, then pushed forward.

Opening the door, she stepped into the dark third-floor hallway. The lights awakened one by one, leading up to distant noises at the very end of the hall.

Amy paced forward but stopped at the sound of a child giggling. The hall was empty on both ends, but the source of the disembodied echoing giggle did not appear anywhere near her.

Piano keys struck the air.

Amy almost paused but pressed onward despite more youthful sounds of joy joining the first. The joyous sounds turned into bursts of harmonious laughter as she crept closer to the end of the hall.

Amy, Amy, Amy. This is so exciting.

Reaching the end, Amy took in her options, left and right, at the paths she had to choose from. To her left, she could barely make out the outline of the doors going down the corridor. To her right, another row of doors along the walls, ending with a set of double doors leading into a dimly lit auditorium. The piano melody came from within.

It took forever for us to reach this glorious night. Those damn policebots interfered with my reach. They had to go. Luckily, little Issa was able to assist... getting us what was needed to make sure those bots stayed out the way.

Amy walked in and a spotlight shot down on her, tracking her as she moved towards the stage.

"She's just a little girl," Amy said. "Let her go."

On stage, someone sat in the dark behind what Amy could tell was a piano. Three figures were to the left of the piano player, slightly moving.

The auditorium's lighting grew a little brighter. Several small figures sat in the seats throughout.

As she passed each row, the audience of dark figures turned to face Amy. Their cloudy eyes watched her every move she made.

The auditorium lights grew brighter. The audience was full of children of many ages, some Amy recognized from her town. Every member of the young audience wore wide smiles, some of them drooling from their mouths.

Children! Let's give a warm welcome to our guest of honor!

The audience clapped.

Amy reached the stage and climbed up the steps along the right side. A stage light cut on, revealing the figures on stage.

A bushy brown-haired teen behind the piano stopped hitting the keys. Her head cranked inch by inch until it faced Amy, fixing her own wide smile onto her. She continued playing the melody from before while twisting her head from side to side.

The other guests were the one and only Lockheart Girls. They were on their knees, Madeline in front of the other two, with a microphone in front of them. Tilly cried and Kassandra just watched the ground.

"You shit! You bloody Peculiar, I knew you were up to something!" Madeline said, thrusting her body towards Amy.

Don't mind them right now, Amy. Go on. Take center stage.

Amy walked up to the microphone, facing the crowd of smiling faces before her.

"You all can fight this," Amy said into the mic, reeling from the horrible feedback it gave. "Don't listen to that coward. Why don't you come out already?"

The audience members gasped.

"She has such a beautiful voice!"

'She's astounding, really!"

"Amazing! Amy's so amazing!"

I was hoping you'd sing a little song for us, Amy.

"Clear your minds!" Amy begged. "Fight back. You've done nothing wrong!" Amy massaged her throat as she coughed.

"Fucking shit! Let us GO!" Madeline yelled.

If you're not up for singing... Fine. You spend a lot of time thinking about these girls. This... unworthy one, especially. Pick up your mic.

Amy lifted the microphone out from the stand. As the end of the mic pulled out, a small tube fell to the floor. Amy picked it up and inspected the syringe, bringing it close to analyze the yellow substance inside.

Cleanse the unworthy.

"Cleanse the unworthy!" a child's voice yelled from the audience.

"Cleanse the unworthy!"

"Cleanse the unworthy!"

Several voices piped up to egg Amy on. Amy faced Madeline, who glared up at her.

"No," Amy said. She turned back to face the audience. "I won't do it."

Come, my children, let's sing a little song for Amy... to help her...

A small boy came up behind Tilly with a syringe in hand. "Grow up and die; a painful dread. That's something that my head has said." He held the syringe to Tilly's neck.

A little girl walked beside him behind Kassandra, also holding a syringe to her neck. "Grow up and die; a painful dread. That's something that my head has said."

"Bullocks," Madeline said.

The children in the audience stood up one by one. One voice followed by another until all of their voices sang in unison, now coordinated along with the piano melody.

"Grow up and die; a painful dread. That's something that my head has said. Grow up and die; a painful dread. That's something that my head has said. Grow up and die; a painful dread. That's something that my head has said. Grow up and die; a painful dread. That's something that my head has said."

"Please." Amy's hand holding the syringe shook, her eyes darting from Madeline to the children on stage, to the children in the audience. "Please, wake up!"

Shlonk! The sound filled Amy's eardrums as her peripherals caught the metal microphone stand swing away from the side of her head.

"ENOUGH!" Madeline swung the microphone stand back and forth at the two kids threatening Tilly and Kassandra, then at the others on stage, causing them all to back away. She picked up the syringe Amy dropped and waved both it and the mic stand. "Listen, you little shits! I've had ENOUGH OF THIS SHIT! You've been tormenting me all night with your *stupid* little nursery rhymes and annoying laughter. I've just knocked your leader on her pathetic ass! Now you all better let me and my girls out of here!"

In unison, the children throughout the auditorium stopped smiling. They moved out of their rows and towards the stage.

The piano player kept playing.

"Maddy… stop…" Amy's eyes fluttered as blood dripped from the side of her head down her nose.

"You shits!" Madeline banged the mic stand on the stage floor. "I promise I will knock you all square on your asses!"

"Maddy, please!" Tilly cried out.

Kassandra grabbed Tilly's arm and pulled her to the side, close to the piano.

The piano player's tune stabbed into keys, sharp thumps startling Kassandra and Tilly, who backed up further back on the stage.

"What do they want? What do you want?" Tilly whimpered.

Amy jumped up and grabbed both of Madeline's arms. "Stop, listen to me! This isn't the way. They don't know what they're doing!"

"Don't—tell me—shit!" Madeline said, trying to yank her arms out of Amy's grasp. Get—OFF!"

Amy's body didn't budge as Madeline struggled. She easily wrestled the pole out of Madeline's hand and dodged Madeline's hand, which struck forward with the syringe. Amy pushed her back.

Several children from the audience blocked off the exits to the left and right of the stage.

"Don't you fucking come near me again!" Madeline said, aiming the syringe at Amy. "Think you're *so special*. All of you little brats! Think your Class matters to me? Huh?! You're not stronger than me. You all don't know the meaning of strength because you were gift-wrapped it all at birth. All your strength, all your speed. You're NOTHING! I will END you if you come any nearer!"

Amy backed away from Madeline, towards Kassandra and Tilly.

"Just give me a chance, Madeline," Amy pleaded. "Let me speak to it." She held her bleeding head as she scanned all around the auditorium. "Where are you?! Come out now, I'm here! Show yourself dammit."

"This is all your fault!" Madeline moved closer to Amy, stabbing the air with the syringe. You lead us here! You and your little girlfriend and your Peculiar—"

Madeline's mouth went agape. She stumbled towards Amy, who caught her in her arms. Several syringes stuck out of her back. Madeline's throat croaked as she fell to her knees, then landed on her side. Her body convulsed, her mouth spitting up a mixture of blood and saliva, with her eyes rolling back. Her spasms slowed until her body stiffened, her head resting near Amy's foot.

The children around the room giggled.

Amy backed away from Madeline's corpse. It was the first time she had seen Madeline's face so peaceful. So silent. But it's far from how Amy ever would have wanted it to happen.

The air fell silent around Amy. Her head swiveled at the laughing children, who pointed down at Madeline's corpse, but their voices were absent. Behind her, tears ran down Kassandra's straight face as she shook a kneeling Tilly by the shoulders, yelling something.

Amy stared at Tilly's face. She knew that look. She had that same look on her face the day the corpse of Mr. Bakers fell on top of her. The same look when she saw Felix's body crumple to the ground, neck first.

Maybe... it is me... Me all along. The voice in my head... Am I the one controlling them all? Without knowing?

The crowd of children surrounded Amy, Tilly, and Kassandra.

Amy closed her eyes and focused. She couldn't ignore it. That single thought that worried her since she first entered the building.

It's just not—

A wave of heat filled Amy's chest. She clenched her fists as she turned around.

Kassandra's eyes glowed purple as her feet dug into the ground. A gust of wind circled her.

Kassandra grabbed Tilly by the waist and shot towards Amy—picked her up as well—and ran straight into the crowd of possessed children.

The gusts around Kassandra—her invisible aura—knocked the children aside.

Kassandra carried the other two girls off the stage and up the aisles of the auditorium, then out the doors.

Kassandra dropped them. She slammed the doors of the auditorium and put the microphone stand in between the doors.

Amy shook as she stared at Kassandra, who panted heavily while twisting the mic stand around the auditorium doors' handles.

"C'mon, help me keep her up!" Kassandra said, grabbing the unmoving Tilly's arm.

Amy grabbed Tilly's other arm and helped carry her down the hall, hampered by Tilly's feet dragging along the floor. They reached the corner, but Amy stopped.

"I can't leave yet. I have to stop this thing. You go on, get her out of here."

"Are you mad? How do you intend on doing that?"

They looked back at the banging behind the auditorium doors.

"It won't hold for long." Kassandra pointed towards a room down the opposite end of the hall. "In there."

Moments later, they burst into the empty storage room carrying Tilly and sat her against a locker.

Kassandra went into a corner of the room and scraped her fingernails against the wall. She peeled away part of the wall and pried her finder into the grooves of a false wall, before lifting it out and putting it to the side.

"How did you know this was here?" Amy asked.

"I've brought a few girls here before," Kassandra said.

They picked Tilly up, and the three of them entered the hole. Kassandra lifted the false wall and put it back in place, concealing them inside the wall's darkness.

A few clicks of a chain filled the space.

"Old shit. Never works when you need it," Kassandra's voice said.

Amy's aura came to life around her. She reached up and grabbed the old lightbulb in the low-hanging ceiling. The lightbulb powered on.

"Neat trick," Kassandra said.

"So you're an auraist as well?"

"A what?"

"You don't know... does anyone else know—"

"No, and I'd like to keep it that way."

"You've got an invisible aura. My Gma's told me some auraist do. But it's rare, only happens when you regress-"

"I don't give a shit and I don't know what you're talking about, Devine, so can you quit it!" Kassandra sighed, running her hand through her long black hair. "Fuck."

"Dead," Tilly whimpered from behind them. "She's dead."

Kassandra stooped down to Tilly. "It's gonna be alright Til. I'm gonna get us out of this, I promise."

"Dead," Tilly said. "D-dead."

"I'm... I'm sorry," Amy said.

"Right," Kassandra said. "We know you didn't give two shits about her, so don't stand there pretending to be upset about it."

"She tormented me." Amy grilled her, but her look softened after a breath. "Of course, I didn't particularly like Madeline, but that doesn't mean I wanted her dead. Not at all."

"She was a complex thing, you know. Madeline." Kassandra sat on the floor next to Tilly. "She'd do anything to hide it. Her Class One status. She never admitted it to us but I always knew. She was complicated. Angry. But mostly sad."

"No one would have judged her," Amy said. "I know there aren't many Class Ones in London, but no one would have judged her."

"You're naive. But Maddy was enough. She judged herself hard enough." Kassandra straightened the buns in Tilly's hair. "You may have seen her as a bully, but I saw someone who was hurting deep inside. Tilly looked up to her. Loved her tenacity and determination. Maddy couldn't see or wouldn't believe any of this because she hated herself so much. She hated being born different from everyone else, so she punished herself for it daily."

Amy sat down across from the other two.

"She only hated you because you never showed off your natural strength or ability, as most others do. She still remembered the time in secondary school when you dropped out of mechanics because you didn't want to lift the car models we worked on."

"I was afraid of my own strength," Amy said. "It was harder to control back then."

"She was convinced you were like her and wanted desperately to prove it. To prove there was someone else like her here around here. Maybe even gain something from it."

Tears rolled down Tilly's face as she shook uncontrollably. Her eyes darted around the room then back at the ground.

"So she trained hard," Kassandra continued. "Trying to build her strength and speed as much as she could. She studied hard from early on to try to get a head start over others her age, but she just couldn't compete with the rest of us. It was never enough.

"Tilly lost her mother and father when her father beat her to death. Her older sister and grandmother raised her. About a year after Tilly's family adopted me, we met Maddy and we fell in love with her courage. She had a strength neither of us had known for all our lives so far. She was ironclad from the inside out, or so it seemed. I think even Tilly suspected Maddy was Class One, but it didn't matter. Tilly gave Maddy someone to be a role model for and Maddy gave Tilly someone to look up to. I was more than happy to look after them both. We'd all been missing… something. Up until we met. Together we were powerful."

"I may not have agreed with her methods, but she won't die in vain. None of the victims will." Amy stood up. "Stay here with her."

Kassandra raised an eyebrow. "Where the hell are you going?"

"It wants me. It wants to isolate me. And I'm going to let it. It's okay. There's a plan in play." Amy stopped and turned to Tilly. "I know that exact feeling. Staring straight into the abyss. Drives you to question your own morality. I know what it likes to watch someone die right in front of you. The world stops when we find the center of fear."

Tilly's blank eyes looked up at her.

Kassandra stood up and shook her head. "I can't stop you. But I can help clear your path for whatever you've got planned. Tilly, you stay right—" Kassandra cried out as her eyes glowed purple. She held her head and dropped to her knees.

You're putting up quite the fight. But my patience is running thin.

"What are you doing to her?" Amy said.

She's the one fighting me. She's a tough one. Trying to stop me from seeing where you all are hiding. But if she won't tell...

Kassandra fell forward, holding her stomach. Tilly gasped as her eyes rolled back and the gray cloudiness took over them.

Kassandra's elbow swung back, knocking Tilly out. "It knows we're here. We've got to—" Her head went down.

"Kassandra?" Amy grabbed her shoulder. "Kass—"

Kassandra picked her head up, her cloudy eyes on Amy. She punched Amy through the wall behind her.

Amy landed on the floor of the hidden room. She turned over and got to her knees.

Behind her, the false wall in the previous room was ripped open.

The decaying freezer boy from The Cartier Hotel stepped through the hole.

Amy thought he had looked familiar before, but now, seeing him in the light, she knew who he was. His body was horribly decayed, but it was undeniably the boy from the photos in Norma's living room. Jonathan; the missing son of the Jones family.

You'll join us in life or death, Amy. The choice is yours.

Jonathan raised a jagged knife as he moved past Kassandra.

Amy laid eyes on an enormous iron door below a large vent in one corner of the new room she was in. She sped towards it, but the door wouldn't budge.

Amy jumped up and pulled the vent door off, chucked it aside. She jumped again, grabbing onto the vent's opening and pulling herself up, and crawling inside. The vent walls gave her about four inches of extra room on every side, yet still, she got caught between walls every few seconds. As she made her way through the vent with haste, it seemed to get smaller with each sweaty forearm hitting the cool metal.

Amy's right forearm slipped. She fell forward; her face smacking into the vent floor, right into the small puddle of a yellow substance. Beeswax.

Amy strained as she pulled her face out of the beeswax puddle, strands of the substance sticking to her cheeks. She pressed forward, slower, as the beeswax stretched from between the vent floor and her limbs, the sticky substance deterring her every move.

Thumps against the vent came from behind her. She paused and turned her head to see.

Jonathan Jones followed her, his crackling bones twisting and shoving their way through the vent. His knife-wielding hand dug the blade into the vent floor to aid in his progression.

"Join us in death. The choice is yours," Jonathan Jones said, his voice raspy and disjointed by his damaged vocal cords.

Amy continued her crawl, feeling like one of the walking dead herself as she neared the end of the vent.

Amy screamed. Her echos filled the enclosed space.

She looked back at Jonathan's jagged knife plunged halfway into the back of her left leg, inches from her ankle. She kicked her right leg back, hitting the right side of Jonathan's face, pushing back part of his decaying skull.

Amy punched the vent's exit door off and dragged her body out, falling, landing with a thud on the floor of a new room.

Thumps came from the open vent above.

Amy's aura grew around her hand and she shot it towards the fallen vent door. The aura mimicked her hand, picked up the vent, and held it in place over the vent.

Jonathan's falling-apart finger came through the vent door's horizontal openings. His middle finger's meat hung right off the bone, pointing down at Amy.

Amy relaxed her hand and sat up against the iron door as her aura hand kept the vent door in place. She ripped off part of her left sleeve. She reached down and used one hand to grab the handle of Jonathan's knife while the other hand held her left leg tight.

"Okay. Okay." Amy closed her eyes and took a breath.

Her aura expanded around her. She pulled the knife out, biting her lip.

The inside of her leg wound slowly reconstructed itself.

It's amazing what you can do...

Amy groaned as she grabbed her head, shot by the sharp pain in both temples.

Only now had she paid attention to the room she found herself in. It looked like it had not seen the light of day in quite some time. The cramped room was full of construction lights probably left ages ago, hanging along the walls, some dimly lit and flickering. Several broken-in lockers lined the walls with dripping beeswax escaping the bottom of them. Classroom desks, some overturned, sat in random spots throughout the room.

The conflicted feelings Amy felt inside seemed to mesh together, but she wasn't able to escape the tight feeling in her chest. She didn't know how, but she knew. She knew this was where knowledge was born. Where the new world would form.

I could still get out.

You're here. It's time.

Amy's thoughts washed away. Her drunken body swayed, reduced to this weightless, floating, thoughtless piece of nothing, as she walked towards the middle of the room.

What were feelings? What were memories?

A bright white light floated towards her. Two black holes spread within the light.

Amy ignored the sense of overwhelming dread that filled her heart and lungs as joy took over and replaced any doubts.

The time to rejoice had come.

She was finally home.

Chapter Twenty-Six

The white light in front of Amy formed a small astral body that floated in front of her. Its face had hollow black holes for eyes. Small white lights lit up in the center depths of its eyes. Cracks along the sockets dug deep into its silver face and stretched some inches across. Small, off-white cloudlike hair formed on top of its floating head.

Its face, forever frozen in its expression.

Amy couldn't peel her eyes off of the figure, even as she flinched, as the vent door fell to the floor.

Jonathan limped up, feet dragging beside Amy, with his left foot laid on its side, the ankle bones busting out of the flesh. His gray skin peeled all over and his arms hung at his sides. His face was devoid of emotion and his half bashed-in skull dropped, his eye and jaw on that side hanging lower than they should have.

Amy's eyes welled up. Her body shook, being so close to the undead boy.

It's okay, child. Look at me.

Amy's eyes found the astral form in front of her again. "You're… you're St. Cloudy."

I'm thrilled you could finally join us.

Amy couldn't keep herself from smiling. She was so excited she could finally be here. Why hadn't she come before?

Because this murderous, manipulative shit is killing everyone.

The shock hit Amy's face, as her thoughts betrayed her, saying such words about the sweet St. Cloudy, and shunned that part of her mind. Cloudy knew best, after all.

"I'm here..." Amy's eyes rolled over and gray clouds took them over. "... for you."

The spirit of Cloudy glided behind Jonathan's head and little silver hands held onto it.

Do you know why I'm here, Amy?

"To free us. The children." Amy knew it only wanted the best for her. Her head turned and the smile on her face expanded even wider, going from cheek to cheek.

Yes. My mission is to guide those whose imagination never died. It took a great deal to get you here, Amy. Those damn bots. The power hub. All these things kept interfering with our feed. Of course, you overcame it and found your way... to me.

Amy shook her head. "But people got hurt. You made all those poor people get buried alive. You hurt the children—"

No! Not to hurt the children. Never will I hurt the children, Amy. The children are the only way in which this world can see a brighter future.

Amy kept shaking her head. Next to her, Jonathan raised his reclaimed knife.

No. She'll understand.

Jonathan lowered his knife.

Amy unwillingly dropped to her knees and followed Cloudy as the astral form flew up in front of her head. Its small silver hands caressed her cheeks.

"I just... I just want to understand," Amy let out. She no longer felt the weight of the rest of her body. The only thing she felt was Cloudy's warm embrace on her cheeks.

A hot flash of light pierced her skull as Cloudy's face came closer to her. Amy's eyes glowed, becoming white, fiery orbs of light that matched Cloudy's.

Her identity became his. She no longer knew where she began and Cloudy ended.

Long ago, a man created me in order to console a child who had just lost everything. My creator was troubled but meant well. The only adult I encountered that tried to do some good and make sense of the world that had broken him into pieces.

Amy's mouth hung open as black and white smoke appeared out of thin air. The smoke swirled together, the white smoke creating images inside the larger black cloud. White smoky figures without features formed within.

Many, many years after his demise, a gracious lady adopted me. She created stories about me. Children all around the world loved me. She had given me a new life. A strong, new purpose.

The smoke formed several outlines of small children, cheering as a woman read a storybook to them.

This woman, however, couldn't escape her own demons and fell victim to the same disease that adults do. The disease of impurity. The imagination she once knew was foreign to her. She fell weak to her adult vices and her creativity ceased to exist.

The smoke formed the outline of a woman drinking from a bottle, then the shape changed to the woman ripping books apart and tossing a table on its side. The smoke changed shape again, this time showing the woman with a cloud around her. Her aura. A piece of her aura broke off and absorbed into a book.

This was when I realized how lost all adults were. As they grow older, their imagination leaves them, if they ever had it to begin with.

The white smoke formed into two separate armies of people with guns. They clashed while spilling black smoke representing blood.

Granted, there are some children who are already lost, like that impossibly insufferable Madeline. She just wasn't strong enough to join the fight with us, Amy. Her imagination had already far gone. It was too late. She allowed her suffering to overtake her.

The white smoke formed into the outline of the Lockheart Girls standing over a downed Amy.

Let's not forget you have experienced what it means to be at the mercy of adults.

The white smoke formed into several adults all pointing down at a young Amy, who sat hugging her knees way down inside a well.

But there's more truth to it. Something I've discovered that they've kept from you.

The white smoke formed into a woman mourning a young boy in a coffin. A clock appeared above the woman's head and its hands sped in the reverse direction. The images went back in time showing everything before the funeral, to the well, then all the way to the woman stooping down to her now-alive son.

You make sure you give that little bitch a good scare for ruining your uncle's funeral. Lure her down there.

Amy looked away from Cloudy. "No."

Yes. The fault of so many adults. The world revolves around them and them only. They allow their own insecurities to plague their surroundings. And it's not fair to you. To any of you. The children of tomorrow suffer because of the adults of today. And a rotten few spoil the bunch.

"I'm tired of your games," Amy said, her left eye reverting back to normal as the right one remained under Cloudy's influence. "No more of your lies."

Amy flinched as the iron door behind her burst open.

The possessed Kassandra and Tilly dragged a screaming woman into the room. They dropped her across from Amy.

"NO!" Mrs. Temeltry, the sister of Conrad Bakers, sat up and scurried away from Amy. "PLEASE! Wha—what's going on? Please let me go! PLEASE!"

"Tell… her… the truth," Jonathan said with a croak. His vocal cords sounded as though they had been put through a blender and stopped midway through. "Tell her what you did to her. All those years ago."

"I-I-I didn't do—"

"TELL HER!" came the voices of several children ringing out in unison.

Amy peered around the room. Several children of different ages stood along every corner of the room. Their scowls bore into Mrs. Temeltry.

"TELL HER THE TRUTH!"

"Okay, okay, just," Mrs. Temeltry said. "Just—I was going through a lot at the time. I was just angry! I didn't mean…"

A tear ran down Amy's cheek. "Is it true?"

"M-my son. Felix is *dead!*"

"Is it true?" Amy snarled. "Did you tell him to lure me down there?"

"It's complicated. It-it—"

"Don't lie to me!" Amy screamed. She grabbed her throat as she coughed up blood.

"Yes," Mrs. Temeltry whispered. "I told him to… You ruined my brother's funeral, his wishes! He never wanted to be discovered as one of those—Lifesnatchers. He needed that boy to feed from! To retain his strength…"

"Wait," Amy said. She shook her, not believing what she just heard. "He… you let Mr. Bakers take Noah… to use for feeding? You… Felix tried to tell me…"

Do you see now Amy? She was willing to sacrifice another's life—a child's life—for that selfish brother of hers. And had her son follow along with her antics. Are these the motives of an innocent woman?

"No," Amy said.

Jonathan jumped behind Mrs. Temeltry, grabbed her head, and

bit into her neck. The woman screamed, crumpling to her knees as Jonathan fed on her.

"NO." Amy jumped back, holding her mouth. "Why… No, no, that's not right—"

You said it yourself. She's guilty. Guilty of abusing the innocent.

Mrs. Temeltry's head fell at Amy's feet. Her eyes met Amy's before she was completely still.

"You can't just KILL everyone!" Amy said. "You can't place judgment like that, judgment on life. It-it's not right."

I had been sleeping for quite some time until Jonathan found my book in the same place that woman used to steal your innocence. The warmth of a child's touch woke me again.

The black smoke reemerged with white smoke inside, creating an outline of Jonathan lowering himself down into the well using a rope. He dug out part of the well's floor and picked up a storybook.

But the power my storybook possessed proved to be too much for the boy's body to muster. He died from the encounter. Who is responsible for the infliction of this pain? Jonathan or the woman who cursed me?

"This isn't right." Amy snorted, wiping tears from her face. "This isn't right. I will stop you."

You speak on such high ground. Yet, you weren't interested in the Jadesfeld cleansings until you were involved.

"I'm not allowing you to get into my head anymore."

You were ready to judge that man on the train. You watch as others get their possessions stolen. You trip your best friend over and over claiming to be helping her.

"What does this have to do with anything?" Amy stomped her foot on the floor, digging into it.

Everything. You put yourself up on a pedestal, claiming you deserve it because of this town's attitude toward you. When was the last time you humbled yourself? You think that you'd make a great detective and you think you know aura, but you haven't seen anything yet, have you? Your grandmother sure thinks so...

Amy stared down at her feet. Her clenched fists loosened.

You see, I don't manipulate minds with new thoughts. I just bring out what's already hidden deep within. You humans fear acting out your true desires. I'm just here to shed some light and help the children face their fears before facing a new day. Where we can rebuild the world. Just imagine the world in the eyes of our children. It would be paradise.

"But... Rezna," Amy offered. The name seemed so distant to her now, but it was all too familiar the same. She closed her mismatched eyes for a second, but they kept forcing themselves open again. Her body shook as though she had to free herself from invisible restraints.

Yes...

"It's not right. You can't take life as you please." Her eyes narrowed on the spirit of Cloudy. "You killed her."

Cloudy floated right up to Amy's face.

I just needed to give you a little nudge. She can be put aside. My special gift to you.

Three teens moved over to a locker with a large amount of beeswax dripping underneath it. They opened the locker, revealing a cocoon inside.

Rezna Devine. There she was. Laying asleep within a dirty mustard-colored cocoon, her flaring nostrils giving away her status. Except for her face, most of her body had been covered.

"I... I saw... how? I saw her..."

Did you though? Part of making you better, Amy, is showing you what I need you to see. It was the only way you'd focus on the objective. You would have involved her in our business and what you needed was to act on your own. To find your way. To me.

Amy fell back into a pit of blackness that surrounded her. She fell back into the kitchen at her home, with the corpse still laying on the floor. The face of the corpse—not Rezna—but Norma Jones, Issa's aunt.

"She never really hurt that girl. Did she?" Amy asked. "You tricked me. I only saw—"

What you needed to see. You needed guidance in order to find your way.

"How much of what I've been experiencing is true? Mr. Perry—"

Now that was a device all of its own. He is a sorry, despicable leech who preys on children for his own pleasure. The woman, Norma, was cruel in the way she treated little Issa. She hated being her adoptive mother. The resentment seethed from her bones.

Amy's mind flashed images of everything that happened over the past few weeks and felt like she had been a stranger in her own body. Everything she had been forced to see was some tormented version of the world she knew. All because of this... *thing.* This thing perverted her mind and now wanted her to help it fulfill some horrendous plan it had in store.

You fought so valiantly. Once I saw how powerful you were, I had to have you. SO I used your fears to weaken you.

Cloudy's hand smoothed Amy's hair down like a cat being coddled.

My reach has its limits, Amy. But with you, and all that power you possess, you could help me expand my reach quicker and more effectively than ever before. The children of the world are more capable than ever. The emancipated are doing great on their own. We can guide all the children around the world. Give the world to them. Stop wars. Create the blissful world we know can exist. You and I could do that together, Amy.

Gma's alive. There's so much death and destruction. All Cloudy wants is peace.

Professor Watson's voice penetrated her head.

'Desolation. I reside inside a farce. These shallow forms of comfort and stability consume me.'

Cloudy's voice took over.

All it takes is a spark to ignite hope across the world, Amy. And all it takes to save your grandmother is to let me guide you. But first, you must prove your dedication to the mission.

Demora, also possessed, dragged an unconscious Jimmy into the room by his collar. The other children and teens in the room laughed.

Demora dropped Jimmy right next to Mrs. Temeltry's corpse and stood beside her.

"Join us, Ames," Demora said. "The world belongs to the children. Stand at my side." She stepped back, lining up with some other children against the wall.

Children and teens packed the room. Some Amy recognized from Jadesfeld, the others must have come from New Enfield. They watched Cloudy with those wide, wooden smiles on their faces.

Amy watched as Jimmy stirred awake, then stared at Rezna, whose head moved and whose eyes shifted in their sockets.

I could still save her. I can still save them all. I just need to find it.

Cloudy's eyes grew brighter on Amy's face.

You're still not convinced? I can feel you locking me out. Don't you see this is the way? I will let your grandmother go. You just need to kill the impurity in the room.

Amy looked down at Jimmy again, who was being picked up by Jonathan and made to sit on his knees. Jimmy mouthed something, but Amy could only faintly hear his words.

This is the way...

The battle raging within Amy's mind pierced the sides of her head, as an eruption spilled from her earlobes. She pressed her fingers up to her ears and looked down at the small amount of blood on her fingertips. She needed to settle this debate or else her mind would explode and its fragments would scatter across the room.

This is the way...

Amy closed her eyes and sank back into the darkness. The blackness crawled onto her limbs like slime and covered her entire body, except for her head. Her floating head moved throughout the darkness.

This is how we win...

A burning, thumping sensation ripped through Amy's chest.

And then she felt it.

Cloudy's astral face floated directly in front of her own.

Amy's mouth hung loose again as she stared into Cloudy's eyes. She moved her head forward.

Their heads became one.

You're powerful, Amy. A lot more than you even realize. You can lead us. You will lead us. Tell me, Amy. What do you dream of? More than anything else in the world. What do you dream?

Amy's eyes wore silver lights as her hair grew white. She knew the answer. It required no further thought. She knew that despite all the other things in the world one could want, and of all the things that could bring one joy and absolute happiness, she knew there was one thing that would be exactly what she would need in order to prosper.

"My dream?" Amy asked.

Cloudy nodded.

"My dream. My dream is to sing."

Amy's white eyes burned throughout the room. The children's jaws dropped as Amy levitated into the air. Her clothes burned away, becoming a white, flowy dress. Behind her, silver arms outstretched from her back. She smiled down at the others in the room.

"I want to sing."

Yes...

"I want to one day sing in the face of death."

Jonathan glared at her.

"I want the courage to face my fears. The strength to follow through and to conquer all that ails me. But until then, I will have to deal with the likes of you."

Amy's feet landed back on the ground as her clothes returned as they were. Her knees shook as her legs held their balance.

"My grandmother has introduced me to the Realm of Lucidity. You think you had me locked in there, except you have no mastery of it. I haven't mastered it either, but I have a better level of understanding than you. I stayed in there long enough to distract you while I maneuvered myself right where I needed to be."

Amy smiled. She now stood at the opposite end of the room.

"You take advantage of the innocent and call yourself a savior. You're no savior. And you're definitely no saint. You're just an old, sad, washed-up, child's plaything."

The white globes that had filled her eyes diminished, and her irises regained their natural color. She cocked back and punched the wall beside her, ripping away pieces of the concrete.

No. We were one.

Jonathan ran towards Amy.

Amy's aura burst to life, picked Jonathan up, and threw him into the wall of children on one side. She continued pulling the wall apart, knowing she didn't have much time before someone tried to stop her again.

Amy's aura shot out instinctively around her body, knocking back a few kids who tried to run up behind her.

Demora jumped her from behind, stronger than the rest, and she and Amy fell forward into the hollow hole in the wall.

Amy picked her head off the floor as a source of light shined on her face.

Hidden deep within the wall feet away from her was a thick book. Cloudy's storybook. A black and white aura grew around it, circling it, as though it sensed had Amy's arrival.

Amy elbowed Demora in the face and pushed her back. She crawled towards Cloudy's storybook but stopped as a crunching sound came from the side of her. Her aura lit up and illuminated the source.

Also hidden in the walls, and all around her—skeletons. Their dirty, moist, withered bones sat comfortably within the walls on either side, a greenish liquid dripping off them.

All the air seemed to escape Amy's chest as a glob of wetness fell on her cheek.

Above her—more skeletons.

Staring back down at the ground beneath her, she saw a skeleton lodged in the dirt straight ahead between her and the *Book of Clouds*.

It's all in my head.

Amy blinked, and the skeletons were gone.

She gasped as something grabbed her foot.

Demora climbed on top of her and pounded fists up onto Amy's back repeatedly. She then climbed past Amy and reached out to Cloudy's storybook.

Amy's eyes went wide. She grabbed Demora's foot. "No! Don't touch it Demo!"

Demora kicked Amy in the face. She reached a hand out to grab the *Book of Clouds*.

Amy scraped the dirt underneath her. She grabbed Demora's foot.

Demora looked back and aimed her other foot.

"Here's your blind spot," Amy said. She tossed the dirt in her palm into Demora's face.

"Damn you!" Demora said as her foot missed Amy's face.

Amy dodged Demora's kicking foot and grabbed it, pulling both her legs towards her. She climbed onto Demora's back and put an arm around Demora's neck.

"That damn, cursed book will ravage your body. I can't let that happen, Demo!"

Amy flung her free right arm out towards the book, and her aura grew around her entire body. An aura ball grew around her outstretched hand.

Amy looked back as several teens pulled at her and Demora's feet. She turned back to the *Book of Clouds*.

The aura ball around her outstretched hand shot forward and circled around the book.

The black and white aura around the *Book of Clouds* shot out shards of itself, stabbing into the orange aura ball surrounding it.

The outside edge of the orange aura blackened. The blackness crept up the linking chain of energy, leading back to Amy's hand.

Balls of sweat fell down Amy's face as she waited. She pointed a finger out towards the creeping black energy.

Amy... your power is awe-inspiring. It isn't too late to join the cause.

How can an inanimate object have so much power?

There are many things you'll come to learn that will change everything you've ever known. You're losing a lot by going this route.

The blackened energy found its way to her middle fingertip. Amy's entire body convulsed.

Amy... reconsider your decision. Bond with me. This world has and always will thrive on conflict. You're a deterrent looking to upset that. You'll need me. You'll see. What I've chosen to do is the least traumatizing way for the children to do what's necessary... but next time there will be no time for second thoughts.

Amy's eyes grew orange, shining like blinding headlights in the dead of night, then went normal. She smiled.

There won't be a next time.

Amy curled her hand into a fist.

The link of aura split like a twig off of her right middle finger.

Amy cried out as the aura around her body flashed out of sight, leaving her hand last.

Blackened from the middle fingertip up to the second knuckle, smoke rose from her right hand.

Her orange aura ball swirled around the *Book of Clouds*, as the book's black and white aura stayed contained inside it.

Faint voices come from somewhere behind Amy.

Those voices turned into *piercing screams.*

Amy scurried back, pulling Demora along with her. Both girls climbed out of the hole in the wall, blocking their ears for dear life.

Behind them, the children's eyes had dimmed to their natural colors as the kids slammed their palms against the side of their own heads. They all cried out, some falling to the ground.

Amy knew why. The multiple stabbing pain that reached every side of her head did not let up. It was a pain she never felt before. As much as she wanted to, she held back her own urge to scream.

After a few more seconds, the screams stopped.

A hand grabbed Amy's foot.

Jonathan, his eyes now an empty, light gray, sobbed as he stared up at her.

"Tell my Mom and Dad I'm sorry. It wouldn't let me go." His fingernails scratched against the floor as more tears soaked the floor beneath him. "I tried to leave but it wouldn't let me." Jonathan reached into his pocket.

Amy recoiled, but eased her stance.

"Thank you for setting me free." Jonathan's mouth grew into a small smile.

He handed Amy a small smiley face pin. The same one she found in the well when she was younger.

"Please tell Mom and Dad that I love them." Jonathan's head collapsed onto the floor. He exhaled. A small blue aura ball soared out of his mouth. It continued floating up and away, right out of the door.

Amy's hand shook as she looked down at the pin.

Demora rushed up to her and the two girls grabbed each other in a tight embrace.

"I'm so sorry," Amy and Demora said simultaneously.

Amy let go, and they rushed over to the cocoon holding Rezna.

"Please wake up. Please," Amy said as she checked Rezna's pulse. "She's alive."

"Good," Demora said. She turned to Jimmy, watching as he checked on the others in the room. Demora leaned in close to Amy. "I'd hate him more than I currently do if it wasn't for him jumping in front of that bullet for you."

Amy smiled and hugged Demora tight again.

"We can wake her," Jimmy said, nodding at Rezna as he made his beside Amy. "I'm sure with her *ability*, she'll recover quicker than most. Are you girls alright?"

"I have a terrible headache," Demora said.

"That seems to be the case around the room," Jimmy said. "I've phoned for my unit, they'll be here soon." Jimmy made rounds around the room to check on everyone.

"Good." Amy looked over at the hole in the wall, where the imprisoned *Book of Clouds* laid within. "We need to get that in the glass box. No one can touch it. I can lift it with my aura."

"Right. Demora, can you run up with Sandra and bring the glass box out from my car. Here are the keys." Jimmy passed her his car keys and pointed over to the girl who was playing the piano earlier. "Kids, all of you, follow these two outside."

Moments later, now alone, Jimmy returned to Amy's side.

Amy sat at one of the desks, her orange irises with white pupils watching Rezna's face. "They'll discover me. Us. I failed Gma."

"No, they won't," Detective Burt walked into the hidden room. He circled away from Amy, not taking his eyes off her.

"Burt." Jimmy put a hand on Amy's shoulder, stopping her from getting up. "How'd you find us?"

"I've been tracking the girl here for quite some time. Especially after what Mr. Jones revealed when he admitted to the murders. I'm not going to arrest you." Detective Burt took a seat in one of the upright desks. "You see, I want to thank you for resolving this. I had been aware of, *Peculiar,* dangers popping up over the past couple of years. Several small incidents around the world. Reports of possession and other strange occurrences. I couldn't make any cases without evidence. But this—" he pointed over to the *Book of Clouds.* "This proves everything. Proves all I need."

Detective Burt got back to his feet. "I don't know how you've done it, controlling that energy inside. I've never seen a Peculiar do that before. As long as you can keep a handle on it, you're a free woman." He bent over to Amy. "But the moment you lose control, I'll be there." He got back up and put on his trademark goofy smile. "But you'll be alright, Ms. Devine. You won't be seeing me for quite some time. I'll explain everything to the higher authorities. Jimethy, I'll restore your badge. Don't you two worry. I'll take it from here."

"You're going to lie?" Amy asked. "Don't you think this town has had enough of that, Detective Burt?"

"I'm going to preserve your freedom as well as Detective Wimblestyn's and craft a narrative that will be best for everyone," Burt answered. "I'm going to take control of the situation as best I can. Live with it. I suggest you do the same, Ms. Devine." Burt pointed over to the storybook again. "I'm assuming you've got a plan for carrying that thing?"

"We'll handle it," Jimmy said.

Burt nodded. He pointed at Amy. "And keep her out of sight. Don't want anyone else seeing her like that."

Amy's eyes narrowed on Burt. She wiped a heap of sweat from her forehead.

"You're looking a little pale, Ms. Devine. You should go get yourself checked out." Detective Burt tipped his hat and walked out of the room.

"Can we trust him?" Amy asked.

"Well." Jimmy sighed and scratched his head. "If there's one thing I know about Burt—he only came here for a quiet run before shooting to a bigger promotion. With this situation wrapped up, he'll do what he can to keep things under wraps."

"Thank you, Jimmy. For everything…"

Amy passed out on the floor.

Chapter Twenty-Seven

The week that followed was anything less than unpleasant. There was a change in the air around the town of Jadesfeld. Despite the season, it was hotter than it should have been and the air felt heavy. This was surprising given that the population of her small-but-actually-medium-sized town had diminished quite a bit. Most of the children in town were gone.

Amy hadn't heard from Demora in days, but Demora made it clear that she'd be around for Amy's birthday. Amy tried to phone her but knew once Demora was in a mood, it took time for her to come around. And the burden of murder, even involuntarily, was an unforgettable act that would stay with her best friend for life. Amy thought of ways she could help, spending hours researching trauma close to what Demora had dealt with.

She asked Rezna numerous times to contact her parents, but they never picked up. Jimmy had at least connected Demora with a youth therapist. Although she fought the idea at first, Demora eventually came around. Amy only hoped that someone could get through to her.

Demora wasn't the only one who needed help beyond what loved ones could give. That had become the theme of the town. The school year had been suspended, with courses scheduled online for students to take if they were up to it. Everyone, for the first time in Amy's existence, seemed to struggle. No longer were the people of Jadesfeld strutting about like royalty. Solemn hellos and goodbyes became the norm.

Even as Halloween approached, the usual decorations only dressed a few buildings, Amy passed on her errands around town. Amy stayed in often, a small part of her fearing that she'd hear that small yet powerful voice in her head again. Chanting, mocking, goading. She played music loud in her bedroom with the door and windows shut. She didn't even go on her computer much, as she did not want to run into anything to do with the case.

On the bright side, there wasn't enough time in the day any longer for wandering eyes and spiteful messages to be sent her way by the townsfolk. Parents had to deal with the aftermath and their kids' trauma, as schools shut down in not only this town and New Endfield, but the neighboring communities saw it best to close their school doors as well. Every inch of those buildings was checked for secret rooms and such.

Of course, no town had it worse than old Jadesfeld. The bodies of those affected by Cloudy's rampage had all been checked over twice to ensure they were truly dead. Amy dreaded every moment, being that their home was the center of it all. She hated Rezna's profession for the next few weeks, but watched and felt sorry for how hard her Gma worked. The Gma she thought she had lost forever not so long ago.

Amy would wait till she came upstairs from work and hug her tight at random times. Their training sessions had temporarily ceased as Amy was told she had to regain her strength after her loss of aura. The separation took its toll and Amy had to hydrate more, eat more, anything that could help her wave off the migraines that came on strong at the most random of times. Her low energy meant she slept for most of the days since. She lost weight so rapidly that she had to spend the past few days trying to regain as much of it as she could.

Once she could muster the strength, Amy walked up to the Jones' family home, not sure exactly what to expect. Jimmy had arranged for her to come to see Issa and her new caretaker, but Amy couldn't fathom who it could be.

The front door opened and Amy's heart sank.

Norma Jones held the door open for her.

"Looks like you've seen a ghost. Nice seeing you too, Ms. Devine. Come in."

Amy sat across the table from Norma Jones. She tried not to stare, but the noticeable cracks near Norma's jawline made it all too apparent she was wearing a considerable amount of makeup.

"Yes, I know it's not the best job right now," Norma said, massaging her jaw and neck. "But it'll do for now. After I have passed… I woke up, but not in my body. More looking down at my body. There was some confusion. I spent a bit of time just watching my decaying body, but not comprehending what had happened. Or not wanting to. Eventually, I realized what had happened and made a decision. I returned to my body, not because I was… afraid of death. I came back for Issa."

"How did… how did you keep it quiet?"

"Your Detective friend." Norma took a sip from her teacup. "He's been very helpful in helping me work with the JPD to conceal my new status. For the first time, I feel out of place. It'd be quite the uproar if the people of Jadesfeld found out they had a lifesnatcher living amongst them."

"I'm sorry for that," Amy said. "I… I can't imagine what that must be like for you."

"Yes, you can. I've watched and listened to how the people of this shitty town speak about you. Appalling. We know I've played my part in that, being quite nasty as all shit to you. One must know when to swallow their pride. I'm sorry for that."

"It's okay."

"I came back to protect Issa. You see, my sister Melanie, Issa's mother, had been keeping my niece away from us for years and I never understood why. She refused to come to see us anymore. I even went over there one time to visit them and we got into a huge argument. That was the last time we spoke. I grew to hate her, as she seemed to hate me.

"It wasn't until later on after taking Issa in that I realized why. Why she stayed away from me all of those years. Why she kept Issa from me. One day, I saw Issa playing with some building blocks. She had her hands up, controlling this yellow—I guess you'd call it energy—around the blocks. Peculiar energy. And years prior, I always preached about how Peculiars should be maimed and tossed into a river. My ancestors lost so much in the war."

Norma pointed over at a photo of a young couple on the fireplace.

"My mother and father. They were killed by Peculiars many years ago when I was about your age, actually. Ever since I grew fearful of Peculiars while my sister tried to understand them. That was her nature. I was always the bitch."

Norma chuckled. "I had hatred, so much hatred for Peculiars. I was honestly so fearful of them. And yet here was my niece. Wielding this Peculiar energy like it was nothing. That changed everything. I understood why my sister kept her from me. She was scared. Scared my hatred would cause her to lose her daughter. I understand that now and I will do everything I can to protect her."

Norma's hands shook as she rubbed them together. "Issa has a gift. She saw everything that happened at Highbridge. She told me what you did."

"She... saw?" Amy said.

Norma nodded and wiped her wet eyes. Even under that thing's control, she was able to keep her consciousness, unlike the other children. Once that *thing* realized what she could do, it targeted her. Made her plant that policebot part in her old home, amongst other things. I knew this meant she was in more danger. If anyone found out, she'd be taken away in an instant. I would never do anything to hurt my niece. I know what it's like to lose a child and I wouldn't wish that on anyone."

She went to place a hand on Amy's left hand, but Amy instinctively recoiled.

"Sorry," Norma said. "I just—"

"It's okay. I… I'm just a bit afraid…"

"Of death. Issa told me. But she also told me how brave you were in securing that book and all its evil. That's commendable girl, don't you forget that."

Amy gave a slight smile. She couldn't believe the woman who seemed to hate her the most was now complimenting her, chatting without animosity. Although she was in the company of the undead, Amy felt a bit at ease for the first time ever.

"We buried him," Norma said. "Jonathan. I've heard rumors."

"Rumors?"

"I've heard rumors about the spirit. Same way as I came back. I couldn't see mine. Did you see his?"

Amy nodded. "I saw it. It was a bright blue ball of light that floated away. Finally free."

"Good. Good. Did he say anything to you before? Was he in any pain at the end?"

"No pain. He said that he loved you both very much. He wanted to say sorry for everything he did and he just wanted you both to know that he loves you very much."

"He-just-I-want-it wasn't his fault! Oh, Jon, it wasn't your fault!" Norma pounded her fists into her lap.

"Hey." Amy took a breath and grabbed the woman's hand tight. "There was no pain. He was brave at the end. You'd be proud. You and your husband."

"Thank you." Norma ate her tears, smiling as she looked down at Amy's hands. "Thank you for releasing him. Thank you for getting him out of the grip of that…that thing."

"Cloudy."

"Don't." Norma's head shook as she looked up at Amy, her eye twitching. "Don't say its name."

"But you must," Amy said looking down at her blackened right middle finger, the scar running down to the wrist on her right hand. "You must say its name or else it'll truly win. That thing was a disease. A cancer that we overcame. Your son knew this. That thing invaded his body, took his life, and continued to overstay its welcome. We don't say its name to cherish it or because we fear it. We say it to recognize the disease as it was and shun it for all that it's done. We don't fear, we grow. We thrive."

"We thrive." Norma wiped her tears away and nodded. "Thank you for saving her."

Issa walked into the room and jumped onto Amy, hugging her.

"What's all this racket, I was napping."

"Sorry to wake you grumpy," Amy said, laughing. "It's so good to see you."

"I can't believe you did it, Amy," Issa said. "You fought back and protected us all. You did what you said you would."

"Absolutely. So, Issa, I heard you're a bit like me."

Issa beamed. "I saw you do the same. I thought I was the only one."

"Not at all. You were able to see past Cloudy's hold over you. That's impressive. You must be very strong."

"I think so. I started being able to be aware of what was happening sometime after my parents passed away. It was hard. I got terrible headaches trying to fight past Cloudy's visions. But meeting you and then seeing what you did at the school was amazing. I want to grow as strong as you one day."

"You already are."

"Can I see?" Norma said. "I… I just want to see it for myself."

Amy nodded and cleared her throat. She raised her left hand and a white aura grew around it. She twirled her hand as the white ball of light spun around it, rotating quicker with each turn.

"It's called an aura. Those of us able to manipulate it are called Auraists."

"It was orange before, wasn't it?" Issa asked.

"My aura's changed a bit after what happened."

"Will it be orange again?"

"I don't know. Now let's see yours."

Issa's eyes glowed yellow as a yellow aura grew around her body. She mimicked Amy's hand movements and an aura ball formed. She frowned as the ball's rotation was a lot slower than Amy's.

"You know, you're a fast learner. You're going to be really great at it someday."

"I will! Will you still come and visit me? Teach me a bit?" She turned to Norma. "Please, Aunt Norma?"

Norma smiled and brushed the young girl's hair back. "If she's got the time, she's more than welcome here anytime."

"Of course," Amy said. "Got to keep you from getting into trouble as well, don't I?"

"Most definitely." Issa grinned cheek to cheek.

Amy pinched one of those cheeks.

When the thirty-first of October came, Amy spent most of her day looking outside her window, happy to see all the Halloween decorations, despite there being not many kids around going door to door. The ones that remained in town sought out treats, as their parents wore smiles for the first time in a couple of days. Amy was surprised but delighted to see kids even stop at her door, as Rezna who was nicer than usual, giving them candies of all sorts.

It occurred to Amy that she wasn't the only one who noticed Rezna's hard work, as parents gave her Gma cards and shook her hand before leading their kids down the block. It had been a long time since anyone showed up at their door on Halloween, or any other time for that matter, besides when it was for business. The business of the dead.

Amy smiled. The magic of Halloween had done it again. What she always loved the most was how it brought people around the world together. Still, Cloudy's presence seemed to linger. The pots of beeswax found at the hotel had been moved, but the smell was still heavy in the air. This was just another reason for the annual parade running from Jadesfeld to New Endfield to be canceled because of the migrating bee swarms still in the area. It'd be another week or two before things would get back to normal. Maybe a month. But Amy wasn't about to let that completely ruin her holiday.

As she looked out her room's window, she smiled, seeing Jimmy's Maserati pull up at her front gates. Amy threw a t-shirt over her tank top and ran out of her room. She ran down the stairs and unfastened the locks on her brand new front door.

She ran past the gates and into Demora's open arms.

"It's so good to see you," Amy said.

"Sorry I've been so distant," Demora said.

"Don't mention it. I'm just glad you're here now."

"Love the little twists you've got going."

Amy grabbed the two box braids she had on either side of her face and shrugged. "Gma said my mum used to wear her hair braided. Just thought I'd see how it might look."

"Well, I think it would look wicked."

Amy and Demora do their special fist bump.

"H-hey! Fist-bump, very retro. How about sis-bump?" Jimmy said. "You know, I'm something of a classic man myself." Jimmy adjusted his tie and threw his fist towards them.

Demora bore holes into him. "Why is he alive and when can I end him?"

Amy laughed. "I'll meet you inside, Demo."

"See ya, Jimbo." Demora made her way into the house.

"What do I have to do to win her over?" Jimmy said.

"You don't," Amy said. She walked over to Jimmy's car and peeked inside, staring at the piles of boxes it held. "What's with all the junk?" Amy asked.

"Let's just say the Creaevix Corp isn't too happy about having to recall all of their ZLynx equipment, so they've delayed their pickup in this town. I've been rounding up the remaining few to prep for them."

Amy jumped onto the trunk of his car. "Sucks you get the clean-up job."

"Could be worse." Jimmy handed her a box of lemon ZenDrops.

"You remembered," Amy said, beaming. She opened it and popped one into her mouth.

"Horrible for your teeth, but I'll let your grandmother worry about that. How is she, by the way?" Jimmy lit a glass cigar with an old-fashioned lighter.

"She's doing really well. Really well." Amy caught a whiff of his smoke and looked taken aback. "Is that…"

"It's medicinal, helps my nerves."

"Didn't know you smoked the good stuff. Could have probably gotten it for you cheaper with my connect."

"Really? Never mind, I don't want to know."

"Suit yourself." Amy gave a small smile and looked off in the distance.

"What's new?"

"Not to bring the mood down, but I thought you should know before news breaks. Thomas Jones hung himself early this morning. He, uh, was set to be tried for his involvement, but he left a note behind. Losing his son was too much to bear. Stopped by Mrs. Jones' place to tell her before I picked Demora up."

Amy looked down, tracing the lines of her scarred right hand.

"How's, uh, how's the hand holding up? Aura came back yet?"

"Doesn't exactly work like that, unfortunately. I may be able to get it back someday if I train hard enough."

Amy knew that was a lie. There had been no known case according to Rezna of a Peculiar or Auraist regaining the color and strength of their aura after splitting it. But she'd rather keep lying to herself and to Jimmy right now than face the facts.

"Well, here's some good news. They finished moving the last of the kids into the Cox Institute for Mental Restoration. Sandra has sort of taken up a motherly role to the younger kids. Helping them through their pain while fighting her own."

"Story of the season." Amy tried to squeeze her blackened hand into a fist but winced about halfway through. "I can swear I still hear its voice sometimes, you know. When I sleep. When I'm awake. It's like it's always watching still." Amy crossed her arms. "Psychotic thing is, sometimes I wonder if Cloudy was right. All we humans do is destroy everything we touch. How long before we do ourselves in for good?"

"We do a lot of creation too," Jimmy said. "A lot of good. We let that thing win and I can promise the world won't be any better off. We can all do better though, that's for sure."

"Thanks." Amy nodded. "I needed to be reined in from my thoughts."

"Well, I'm here if that becomes a problem. With my overly optimistic self. Hey, can I ask—when we first met. You didn't take me out then and there. You spent years not trusting anyone with who you are. You could have, I don't know—"

"All in on the deep end," Amy said. It's something Gma has told me before. When you're out on the deep end, a point of no return, you can either be dictated by it or you can go all in, being quick thinking and directing the narrative yourself."

Amy pointed at Jimmy's holstered weapon. "You could have restrained me. I sensed when you activated it. But then you cut it off. You chose to listen. So did I. The world could use more of that."

"Glad I listened. Here's something else for ya. There were some reports of a green flash of light carrying people out of that burning building over in Endfield last week." Jimmy smiled and nodded towards Amy's home. "I'm glad you all are around."

Amy smiled. "She'd never take the credit. We're not really watching the news these days."

"I get it. You'll be happy to know the Insect Research Center was broken into and trashed. All the specimens were let free. The damage was catastrophic."

"They weren't specimens. They were living creatures like you or me. Not going to lie, I'm not exactly rooting for you detectives to catch whoever is responsible."

"Burt has a really good idea who's responsible, but he's definitely not going to step into that murky business. Especially after letting General Aba's brother walk quietly. Worked out a deal with the Office of Human and Animalia Affairs. This town and the next would be in an uproar if they knew about Bosti's involvement in everything."

"I hope Bosti gets the therapy he needs. He was a victim, too. We've all lost something."

"Oh, that reminds me—" Jimmy jumped up and opened one of his back doors. He rummaged around the boxes until he grabbed something covered with a sweater.

"Happy Birthday!" Jimmy pulled the sweater off the cage to reveal

Archie hanging upside down with his eyes closed. The little white bat yawned and opened his eyes before jumping off the wooden stick inside and cooing while flying around the cage. Jimmy opened the cage and the bat flew out and jumped onto Amy's head.

"Archie!" Amy said as she rubbed the bat's back. "Oh, I missed you too, buddy." She beamed at Jimmy. "How the hell did you find him?"

"This little guy had some guardians. They were cleaning out the old Bates home and in the basement, they found a bunch of moonbats. Within them was a little white speck. We were able to fish them out and got Archie to come to me. Looks like they were protecting him."

"Remarkable. I'm just glad to have him back home."

A fluttering came from some trees across the street. They all turned to see dozens of large orange eyes staring at them. The eyes leaned forward as the rustling of the trees became louder.

Archie flew up into the air and waved his wings in a circular motion while rhythmically 'cooing'. The tree rustling stopped. The wide eyes of the concealed moonbats retreated deeper into the leaves, disappearing altogether.

"I think he told them we're alright," Amy said.

"That's the most amazing thing about the Animalia Kingdom. They take care of each other and seem to have it figured out better than us. We humans can learn a thing or two from them."

"Agreed. That was insightful. I was kinda hoping you'd end that with a bad joke."

Jimmy chuckled in adjusted his tie. "Well, you know, they say reading is fundamental. This time, it was not."

Amy shook her head. "That was bad, Jimmy, even for you. You're an absolute shitshow."

Jimmy stretched his arms out. "Welp, I've got some runs to do. Thank you for saving my butt more than a couple of times. Great work on the case. You know, you might just make an outstanding detective after all. Still can't join the team though."

"Well, who says I wanted to join your funky little team, anyway? I think I solved this case just fine on my own." Amy crossed her arms.

They laughed. Amy turned and walked inside her gate, but stopped. Her peripherals caught the outlines of headstones in the cemetery on either side of her home. She thought she could hear Cloudy's laughter ringing through her head.

"Hey Devine," Jimmy called out. He tossed his sweater to her.

Amy caught it and raised it overhead. She lowered it. Threw it back to Jimmy.

"Keep it." Amy turned to face her front door again, took a deep breath, and walked forward, then up the stairs. "Gma always says 'we conquer our fears by living them.'"

Inside, Amy walked over to the kitchen table where Demora and Rezna stood waiting for her.

"We're ready for you darling," Rezna said. "Happy Birthday."

"Happy Birthday Ames!" Demora hugged Amy and pulled her in the middle of her and Rezna.

Amy marveled over her red velvet, sprinkle-covered cake and smiled. She closed her eyes. Then blew out the '1' and '8' numbered candles atop the cake.

It was at that moment that Amy looked down at her charred hand and wondered how many more candles she would get to blow out in her lifetime. How many more moments she would get surrounded by the people she loved the most. Death had always been quite the overstayed guest in her life, so naturally, her mind would go there.

Although she hadn't finished reading the book she was assigned weeks prior, three lines stuck in her mind.

'Desolation. I reside inside a farce. These shallow forms of comfort and stability consume me.'

Death was the end of something, but also a beginning. And when the odds once again came to suffocate her to the point of extinction, at least she knew that the one thing that would remain honest with her was death.

Until next time on PCSD.

About the Author

"You're Only As Good As Your Last Stand"
  — W.K. Phoenix

Hailing from the depths of NYC, W.K. Phoenix has lived a life full of intrigue. The horrific and supernatural have always fallen onto his radar, leading him to record these instances of inspiration. Although ignoring the writing craft for some time, inevitably, the stories and characters that roamed in his mind would spill out into reality. Now the Phoenix universe is here to stay...

Please take the time to leave a review after reading! Thank you!

You can connect with me on:
- https://linktr.ee/Wbjr
- https://twitter.com/wkPhoenixLegacy
- https://www.facebook.com/wkPhoenixLegacy
- https://www.instagram.com/wkphoenix
- https://www.amazon.com/author/wkphoenix
- https://www.goodreads.com/user/show/135840077-w-k-phoenix

Also by W.K. Phoenix

PCSD Book 2

What are you devoted to?